P9-DMJ-408

Praise for the novels of #1 *New York Times* bestselling author Debbie Macomber

"Macomber is a skilled storyteller."

—*Publishers Weekly*

Debbie Macomber "demonstrates her impressive skills with characterization and her flair for humor."

—*RT Book Reviews*

"Whether [Debbie Macomber] is writing lighthearted romps or more serious relationship books, her novels are always engaging stories that accurately capture the foibles of real-life men and women with warmth and humor."

—*Milwaukee Journal Sentinel*

"Debbie Macomber tells women's stories in a way no one else does."

—*BookPage*

"Macomber…is no stranger to the *New York Times* bestseller list. She knows how to please her audience."

—*Oregon Statesman Journal*

Praise for the novels of *New York Times* bestselling author RaeAnne Thayne

"Thayne's second Hope's Crossing contemporary is sweet without being cloying… Plenty of tenderness and Colorado sunshine flavor this pleasant escape."

—*Publishers Weekly* on *Woodrose Mountain*

"Readers will love this novel for the cast of characters and its endearing plotline…a thoroughly enjoyable read."

—*RT BookReviews* on *Woodrose Mountain*

"Thayne, once again, delivers a heartfelt story of a caring community and a caring romance between adults who have triumphed over tragedies."

—*Booklist* on *Woodrose Mountain*

DEBBIE MACOMBER

RAEANNE THAYNE

Country Bride

MIRA

ISBN-13: 978-0-7783-1868-2

Country Bride

Copyright © 2016 by Harlequin Books S.A.

The publisher acknowledges the copyright holders
of the individual works as follows:

Country Bride
Copyright © 1990 by Debbie Macomber

Woodrose Mountain
Copyright © 2012 by RaeAnne Thayne

Recycling programs
for this product may
not exist in your area.

CONTENTS

COUNTRY BRIDE

One

"I now pronounce you husband and wife."

A burst of organ music crescendoed through the largest church in Nightingale, Oregon, as a murmur of shared happiness rose from the congregation.

Standing at the altar, Clay Franklin claimed his right to kiss Rorie Campbell Franklin, his bride.

Kate Logan did her best to look delighted for her friends, even though she felt as if a giant fist had been slammed into her stomach. Tears gathered in her eyes and she lowered her gaze, unable to watch as the man she'd loved for most of her life wrapped his arm around his new bride's waist.

Clay should be marrying me, Kate cried silently. *I should be the one he's looking at so tenderly. Me!* During the past few weeks, Kate had repeatedly reassured herself that she'd done the right thing in stepping aside to bring Clay and Rorie together. But that fact didn't lessen her pain now. Kate loved Clay, and that wasn't going to change. He was her best friend and confidant, her compass, her North Star. And now Clay was married to another woman—someone he loved far more than he could ever care for Kate.

A clean white handkerchief was thrust into her hand by Luke Rivers, her father's foreman. Kate knew he'd been waiting for this moment, convinced she'd dissolve into a puddle of tears.

She declined the use of his handkerchief by gently shaking her head.

"I'm here," he whispered in her ear.

"So is half of Nightingale," she returned wryly. Luke seemed determined to rescue her from this pain—as if that was possible. All she wanted was to survive this day with her dignity intact, and his open sympathy threatened the composure she'd painfully mustered.

"You're doing fine."

"Luke," she muttered, "stop making a fuss over me. Please." She'd managed to get through the ceremony without breaking down. The last thing she needed now was to have Luke calling attention to her.

It was ironic that Kate had been the one responsible for bringing Clay and Rorie together. She should be feeling noble and jubilant and honorable. But the only emotion she felt was a deep, abiding sense of loss.

Rorie and Clay walked down the center aisle, and from somewhere deep inside her, Kate found the strength to raise her head and smile blindly in their direction. Luke's hands gripped her shoulders as though to lend her strength. His concern should have been a comfort, but it wasn't.

"I'll walk you to the reception hall," Luke said, slipping his arm through hers.

"I'm perfectly capable of making it there on my own," she snapped, not wanting his pity. She would've argued more, but since they were sitting near the front of the church, they were among the first to be ushered out. Holding her head high, Kate walked past her friends and neighbors, doing her best to appear cheerful and serene.

At least she *looked* her best; Kate had made certain of that. She'd curled her thick blond hair until it lightly brushed her shoulders. The style emphasized her blue eyes and sculpted cheekbones. She'd shopped long and hard for the perfect dress and had found one that enhanced her slender waist and outlined her trim figure. The minute she'd tried on the soft blue silk and viewed herself in the mirror, Kate had known this was the dress. Although the lines were simple, the look was both classic and sophisticated, a look she'd never bothered to cultivate before. Too often in the past, she'd been mistaken for a teenager, mostly, she supposed, because she dressed the part. But she was a woman now and she had the broken heart to prove it.

Kate paused in the church vestibule, waiting for her father. Devin was sitting with Dorothea Murphy, his widow friend. Her father's interest in the older woman was something of a mystery to Kate. Tall and plump and outspoken, she was completely unlike Kate's late mother, who'd been delicate and reserved. Kate sometimes wondered what it was about Dorothea that attracted her father. They'd been seeing a lot of each other in recent weeks, but the possibility of their contemplating marriage filled Kate with a sudden, overwhelming sense of alarm. Kate pushed the thought from her mind. Losing Clay was all she could deal with right now.

"Are you all right, Princess?" Devin asked when he joined her.

"I wish everyone would stop worrying about me. I'm fine." It wasn't the truth, but Kate was well aware that she had to put on a breezy, unconcerned front. At least for the next few hours.

Her father patted her hand. "I know how hard this is for you. Do you want to go to the reception or would you prefer to head home?" His eyes were warm and sympathetic, and Kate felt a rush of love for him. A part of her longed to slip away unnoticed, but she couldn't and she knew it.

"Kate's already agreed to accompany me," Luke inserted, daring her to contradict him.

Indignation rose inside her. Instead of helping, Luke was making everything worse. The pain of watching Clay pledge his life to another woman was difficult enough, without Luke's unsought demands.

"I'm glad to hear that," Devin Logan said, clearly relieved. He smiled as he slipped his arm around Dorothea's waist. "Mrs. Murphy invited me to sit with her and, frankly, I was looking forward to doing that." He released Kate's hand, kissed her on the cheek, then strolled nonchalantly away.

"Shall we?" Grinning, Luke reached for Kate's limp hand and tucked it into the crook of his arm. As if they'd been a couple for years, he casually led her out of the church.

The early evening air was crisp and clear. Autumn had crested on an October tide of bronze and gold leaves, huge pumpkins and early twilights. Normally, this time of year invigorated Kate. If she hadn't been fortifying herself against Clay's wedding, she could have appreciated the season more.

The walk across the parking lot to the reception hall was a short one. Kate didn't say another word to Luke, mentally preparing herself for the coming encounter with Clay and his bride. With each step her heart grew heavier. Rorie had asked her to be a bridesmaid, and although Kate was honored by the request, she'd declined. Rorie understood and hadn't pressured her. Despite the fact that they both loved the same man, Rorie and Kate had become close. Their friendship made everything more difficult for Kate, yet somehow easier, too.

By the time they arrived at the old brick building, Kate's

pulse was so loud it echoed like a drum in her ear. Just outside the double doors leading into the hall, she stopped abruptly.

"I can't go in there," she told Luke. Panic had worked its way into her voice, which was low and trembling. "I can't face them and pretend... I just can't do it."

"Yes, you can."

"How could you possibly know what I can and can't do?" she demanded, wanting to bury her face in her hands and weep. These past few hours had taken their toll and she couldn't keep up the charade much longer. Luke gazed down on her and for the briefest of moments his eyes registered sympathy and regret.

"You can go in there and you will," he repeated.

Kate saw determination in his serious dark eyes and swallowed an angry retort, knowing he was right.

At six feet, Luke towered over her, and the hard set of his mouth did more than hint at determination and a will of iron. "If you don't attend the reception, everyone in Nightingale will talk. Is that what you want?"

"Yes," she cried, then lowered her head, battling down wave after wave of depression and self-pity. "No," she said reluctantly, loath to agree with him.

"I'm here for you, Kate. Lean on me for once in your life, and let me help you through the next few hours."

"I'm doing fine. I—"

He wouldn't allow her to finish. "Quit fighting me. I'm your friend, remember?"

His words, hushed and tender, brought a burning to her eyes. Her fingers tightened around his arm and she nodded, calling upon a reserve of strength she didn't know she possessed. "Just don't be so bossy with me. Please. I can bear almost anything but that." She'd made it through the wedding ceremony on her own. Now she needed someone at her side to help her appear strong and steady, in control of her emotions, when she felt as though the entire universe was pitching and heaving.

"Anything you say, Princess."

Although she'd objected earlier, she felt comforted by his strong arm against her. She heard his voice, as if from a distance, too preoccupied with her own pain to respond to his concern. But his presence restored her determination to acquit herself well during the long evening ahead.

"Only Daddy calls me Princess," she said distractedly.

"You mind?"

"I don't know... I suppose it's all right."

"Good." His fingers intertwined with hers as he guided her into the brightly decorated reception hall.

The next half hour was a blur. Drawing upon Luke's silent strength, Kate managed to make it through the reception line without a problem. Still, her knees felt shaky by the time she reached Clay, who kissed her cheek and thanked her for being so wonderful. Kate certainly didn't *feel* wonderful—even particularly admirable—but she smiled. And she was sincere when she offered Clay and Rorie her very best wishes.

Somehow Luke must have known how frail she felt because he took her hand and led her to one of the round lace-covered tables. His fingers were cool and callused, while Kate's were damp with her stubborn resolve to hide her pain.

Wordlessly, she sat beside Luke until the cake had been cut and the first piece ceremonially fed to the bride and groom. The scene before her flickered like an old silent movie. Kate held herself still, trying not to feel anything, but not succeeding.

"Would you like me to get you something to eat?" Luke asked, when a line formed to gather refreshments.

She stared at him, hardly able to comprehend his words. Then she blinked and her eyes traveled across the hall to the three-tiered heart-shaped wedding cake. "No," she said automatically.

"When was the last time you ate?"

Kate didn't remember. She shrugged. "Breakfast, I guess." As she spoke she realized that wasn't true. Dinner the night before was the last time she'd eaten. No wonder she felt so shaky and light-headed.

"I'm getting you some wedding cake," Luke announced grimly.

"Don't. I'm—I'm not hungry."

He was doing it again! Taking over, making decisions on her behalf because he felt sorry for her. She would have argued with him, but he was already walking away, blithely unaware of her frustration.

Kate watched him, suddenly seeing him with fresh eyes. Luke Rivers had lived and worked on the Circle L for a decade, but Kate knew next to nothing about his past. His official title was foreman, but he was much more than that. He'd initiated several successful cattle-breeding programs and been involved in a profit-sharing venture with her father almost from the first. Devin had often remarked that Luke was certainly capable of maintaining his own spread. But year after year, he stayed on at the Circle L. This realization—that she knew so little of his past and even less about his thoughts and plans—shocked Kate. He'd always been just plain Luke. And he'd always been around—or so it seemed.

She had to admit that Luke puzzled her. He was handsome enough, but he rarely dated any woman for long, although plenty of Nightingale's finest had made their interest obvious. He was a "catch" who refused to play ball. He could be as tough as leather and mean as a saddle sore when the mood struck him, but it seldom did. Tall, lean and rugged adequately described him on the surface. It was what lay below that piqued her interest now.

Kate's musings about Luke were interrupted by the man himself as he pulled out the chair beside her and sat down. He pushed a delicate china plate filled with cheese and mixed nuts in her direction.

"I thought you were bringing me cake." His own plate was loaded with a huge piece, in addition to a few nuts and pastel mints.

"I brought you some protein instead. Sugar's not a good idea on an empty stomach."

"I don't believe you," she muttered, her sarcasm fuelled by his arrogance. "First you insist on bringing me cake, and then just when I'm looking forward to it, you decide I shouldn't be eating sweets."

Luke ignored her, slicing into his cake. "Just a minute ago, you said it would be a waste of time for me to bring you anything. Fact is, you downright refused to eat."

"That…was before."

He smiled, and that knowing cocky smile of his infuriated her.

"You'll feel sick if you eat sugar," he announced in an authoritative voice.

So much for helping her through the evening! All he seemed to want to do was quarrel. "Apparently you know how my stomach's going to react to various food groups. You amaze me, Luke Rivers. I had no idea you knew so much about my body's metabolism."

"You'd be shocked if I told you all the things I know about you and your body, Princess."

Kate stood abruptly. "I don't think it's a good idea for you to call me that. I'm not your 'Princess.' I'm a woman, not a little girl."

"Honey, you don't need to tell me that. I already know. Now sit down." His tone was brusque, and his smile humorless.

"I'll stand if I choose."

"Fine then. Look like a fool, if that's what you want."

No sooner had the words left his lips than she lowered herself back into the chair. The fight had gone out of her as quickly as it had come. Absently she scooped up a handful of nuts and chewed them vigorously, taking her frustration out on them.

Luke pushed his plate aside and took her hand, squeezing it gently. "I'm your friend. I've always been your friend and I'll continue to be your friend as long as I live. Don't ever doubt that."

Kate's eyes filled and her throat tightened painfully. "I know. It's just that this is so much more…exhausting than I thought it would be."

Voices drew Kate's eyes to the front of the room, where Clay and Rorie were toasting each other with glasses of sparkling champagne. Soon flutes were being delivered around the room. Kate took one, holding the stem with both hands as if the champagne would lend her strength.

When the newlyweds were toasted, she took a sip. It bubbled and fizzed inside her mouth, then slid easily down her throat.

The soft strains of a violin drifted around the hall, and, mesmerized, Kate watched as Clay claimed his bride and led her onto the dance floor. Just watching the couple, so much in love, with eyes only for each other, heaped an extra burden of pain on Kate's shoulders. She looked away and, when she did, her gaze met Luke's. She tried to smile, to convince him she wasn't feeling a thing, but her effort failed dismally. Ready tears brimmed at the corners of her eyes and she bent her head, not wanting anyone to notice them, least of all Luke. He'd been wonderful; he'd been terrible. Kate couldn't decide which.

Soon others joined Clay and Rorie. First the matron of honor and then the bridesmaids and groomsmen, each couple swirling around the polished floor with practiced ease.

Luke got to his feet, walked to Kate's side and offered her his hand. His eyes held hers, silently demanding that she dance with him. Kate longed to tell him no, but she didn't have the energy to argue. It was simpler to give in than try to explain why she couldn't.

Together they approached the outskirts of the dance floor and Luke skillfully turned her into his arms.

"Everything's going to be all right," he whispered as his hand slid around her waist.

Kate managed a nod, grateful for his concern. She needed Luke this evening more than she'd realized. One thing was clear; she'd never make it through the remainder of the night without him.

During the past few years, Luke had danced with Kate any number of times. She'd never given it a second thought. Now they danced to one song and then another, but when she slipped into his embrace a third time, and his fingers spread across the small of her back, a shiver of unexpected awareness skidded up her spine. Kate paused, confused. Her steps faltered and in what seemed like an attempt to help her, Luke pulled her closer. Soon their bodies were so close together Kate could hear the steady beat of Luke's heart against her own. The quickening rate of his pulse told her he was experiencing the same rush of excitement she was.

Kate felt so light-headed she was almost giddy. Luke's arms were warm and secure, a solid foundation to hold on to when her world had been abruptly kicked off its axis. It might have been selfish, but Kate needed that warmth, that security. Smiling up at him, she closed her eyes and surrendered to the warm sensations carried on the soft, lilting music.

"Kate, there's something I need to tell you about the Circle L—"

She pressed her fingers against his lips, afraid that words would ruin this feeling. Arms twined around his neck, she grazed his jaw with the side of her face, reveling in the feel of him. Male and strong. Lean and hard.

"All right," he whispered, "we'll talk about it later."

They continued dancing and Luke rubbed his face against her hair, mussing it slightly, but Kate didn't mind.

Like a contented cat, she purred softly, the low sound coming from deep in her throat. The music ended all too quickly and with heavy reluctance, she dropped her arms and backed up one small step. Silently they stood an inch or so apart until the music resumed, when they reached for each other once again.

But this time Kate decided to figure out what was happening between them. Knowing how much she loved Clay, Luke was trying to help her through the evening. Yes, that was it. And doing a fine job, too. She felt…marvelous. It didn't make sense to her that she should experience this strong, unexpectedly sensual attraction to Luke, but at the moment she didn't care. He was concerned and gentle and she needed him.

They remained as they were, not speaking, savoring these warm sensations, until Kate lost count of the number of times they'd danced.

When the band took a ten-minute break, Luke released her with an unwillingness that made her heart soar. As though he couldn't bear to be separated from her, he took her hand, lacing her fingers with his.

He was leading her back to their table when they were

interrupted by Beth Hammond, a pert blonde, who'd hurried toward them. "Hello, Luke," she said, ignoring Kate.

"Beth." He bowed his head politely, but it was evident that he didn't appreciate the intrusion.

The other woman placed a proprietary hand on his arm. "You promised me a dance, remember?"

Kate's eyes swivelled from Beth, who was pouting prettily, to Luke, who looked testy and impatient.

"If you'll excuse me a minute, I'm going to get a drink," Kate said. Her throat was parched and she didn't want to be left standing alone when the music started and Beth walked off with Luke.

The fruit punch was cold and refreshing, but she still felt warm. Kate decided to walk outside and let the cool night air clear her mind. Try though she might, she didn't really understand what was happening between her and Luke. It probably had to do with the confused state of her emotions, she decided. She'd think about it later.

The stars glittered like frost diamonds against a velvety black sky. Kate stood in the crisp evening air with her arms around her waist, gazing up at the heavens. She didn't hear Luke until he stepped behind her and lightly rested his hands on her shoulders. "I couldn't find you," he said in a voice that was softly accusing.

Kate didn't want to discuss Beth Hammond. For as long as she could remember, the other woman had been going out of her way to attract him.

"It's beautiful out, isn't it?" she asked instead. Instinctively she nestled closer to Luke, reclining against the lean strength of his body, seeking his warmth.

"Beautiful," he repeated, running his hands down her arms.

How content she felt with Luke, how comfortable—the way she imagined people felt when they'd been married for twenty years. But along with this familiar sense of ease, she experienced a prickle of anticipation. Her feelings were contradicting themselves. Secure and steady, and at the same time this growing sense of giddy excitement. It must be that glass of champagne.

The band started playing again and the music wafted outside. Gently Luke turned her to face him, slipping his hands around her as if to dance. Her arms reached for his neck, resuming their earlier position.

"We should talk," he whispered close to her ear.

"No," she murmured with a sigh. It seemed the most natural thing in the world to stand on the tips of her toes and brush her moist lips over his. Then she realized what she'd done. Her eyes widened and she abruptly stepped back, her heart hammering inside her chest.

Neither spoke. In the light that spilled from the hall, they stared at each other. Kate didn't know what her eyes told Luke, but his own were clouded with uncertainty. Kate half expected him to chastise her, or to tease her for behaving like such a flirt. Instead he reached for her once more, his eyes challenging her to stop him.

She couldn't.

The warmth of his mouth on hers produced a small sigh of welcome as her eyes slid languidly shut; she felt transported into a dreamworld, one she'd never visited before. This couldn't actually be happening, she told herself, and yet it felt so real. So right.

Luke's kiss was surprisingly tender, unlike anything she'd expected. "My darling Kate," he breathed against her hair, "I've dreamed of this so often."

"You have?" To her own ears, her voice sounded far, far away. Her head was swimming. If this was a dream, then she didn't want it to end. Sighing, she smiled beguilingly up at him.

"You little tease," he said, and laughed softly. He rained light kisses on her forehead, the corners of her eyes and her cheek, until she interrupted his meandering lips, seeking his mouth with her own.

He seemed to want the kiss as much as she did, but apparently saw no need to rush the experience, as if he feared hurrying would spoil it. Kate's mouth parted, inviting a deeper union. His willing compliance was so effective it buckled her knees.

"Kate?" Still holding her, he drew back, tilting his head to study her. Boldly she met his look, her eyes dancing with mischief. If he'd been kissing her out of pity, she was past caring.

A long moment passed before a slow, thoughtful smile played across his lips. "I think I'd better get you inside."

"No," she said, surprised at how vehement she felt about returning to the reception hall and the newlyweds. "I don't want to go back there."

"But—"

"Stay with me here. Dance with me. Hold me." He'd said he wanted to take care of her. Well, she was giving him the opportunity. She leaned into him and sighed, savoring his strength and support. This was Luke. Luke Rivers. Her trusted friend. Surely he understood; surely he'd help her through this most difficult night of her life. "I want you with me." She couldn't explain what was happening any more than she could deny it.

"You don't know what you're asking me." He stared down at her, searching her features for a long, breathless moment. Then the cool tips of his fingers brushed her face, moving along her cheekbones, stroking her skin as if he expected her to vanish.

Kate caught his hand with her own and gazed into his

dark eyes. They glittered like freshly polished onyx, full of light and a deep inner fire.

"I want you to kiss me. You taste so good." She moistened her lips and leaned closer to him, so close that she could feel the imprint of his buttons against her body. So close that the beat of his heart merged with her own. Excitement shivered through her in tremors so intense they frightened her. But not enough to make her pull away.

Her words spurred Luke into action, and when he kissed her their lips met with hungry insistence. Sensation erupted between them until Kate was weak and dizzy, clinging to him for support, her fingers bunching the material of his jacket. When he lifted his head, ending the kiss, Kate felt nearly faint from the rush of blood to her pounding temples.

There was a look of shock on Luke's face. His eyes questioned her, but Kate's thoughts were as scattered as autumn leaves tossed by the wind.

"How much champagne have you had?" he asked softly.

"One glass," she answered with a sigh, resting her forehead against his heaving chest. Luke hadn't said taking care of her would be this wonderful. Had she known, she wouldn't have resented it quite so much earlier.

Luke expelled a harsh breath. "You've had more than one glass. I doubt you even know who I am."

"Of course I do!" she flared. "You're Luke. Now don't be ridiculous. Only..."

"Only what?"

"Only you never kissed me before. At least not like that. Why didn't you tell me you were so good at this?" Finding herself exceptionally witty, she began to laugh.

"I'm taking you home," Luke said firmly, grabbing her elbow with such force that she was half lifted from the walkway.

"Luke," she cried. "I don't want to go back yet."

His grip relaxed immediately. "Kate Logan, you're drunk! Except you don't have the sense to know it."

"I most certainly am not!" She waved her index finger at him like a schoolmarm. "I'll have you know that it takes a lot more than one glass of champagne to do me in."

Luke obviously wasn't willing to argue the point. His hand cradling her elbow, he led her toward the parking lot.

"I want to stay," she protested.

He didn't answer. Then it dawned on her that perhaps she'd misread Luke. Maybe he was trying to get rid of her so he could return to Beth.

"Luke?"

"Kate, please, don't argue with me."

"Are you in love with Beth?"

"No." His answer was clipped and impatient.

"Thank heaven." Her hand fluttered over her heart. "I don't think I could bear it if you were."

Luke stopped abruptly and Kate realized they were standing in front of his truck. He opened the passenger door for her, but she had no intention of climbing in. At least not yet. She wanted to spend more time with Luke, their arms wrapped around each other the way they'd been before. The pain that had battered her heart for weeks had vanished the instant she stepped into his arms.

"Kiss me again, okay?"

"Kate, no."

"Please?"

"Kate, you're drunk."

"And I tell you I'm not." The one glass of champagne had been just enough to make her a little…reckless. It felt so good to surrender to these new emotions—to lean on Luke. From the moment they'd arrived at the wedding, he'd been telling her how much she needed him. Maybe he was right. There'd been so much upheaval in her life, and Luke was here, warm and kind and solid.

"I'm going to drive you home," he insisted. From the sound of his voice, Kate could tell he was growing frustrated.

The house would be dark and cold. How Kate feared being alone, and with Clay out of her life, there was only her father. And Luke. If Devin did decide to marry Mrs. Murphy, he might sell the ranch and then Luke would be gone, too. Alarmed at the thought, she placed her hands on his shoulders, her gaze holding his.

"Kate?" Luke coaxed.

"All right, I'll go back to the house, but on one condition."

"Kate, come on, be reasonable."

"I want you to do something for me. You keep telling me you're my friend and how much you want to help...."

"Just get inside the truck, would you, before someone comes along and finds us arguing?"

"I need your promise first."

Luke ignored her. "You've got a reputation to uphold. You can't let people in Nightingale see you tipsy. The school board will hear about this and that'll be the end of your career."

Kate smiled, shaking her head, then impulsively leaned forward and kissed him again. Being with Luke took the hurt away, and she refused to suffer that kind of pain ever again. "Will you please do what I want?"

"All right," he muttered, clearly exasperated. "What is it?"

"Oh, thank you," she murmured, and sighed expressively. This was going to shock him, but no more than it had already shocked her. She didn't know where the idea had come from, but it seemed suddenly, inarguably right.

Kate smiled at him, her heart shining through her eyes. "It's simple really. All I want you to do is marry me."

Two

Early the following day, Devin Logan walked hesitantly into the kitchen where Kate sat drinking her first cup of coffee. She smiled a greeting. "Morning, Dad."

"Morning, Princess." He circled the table twice before he sat down.

Kate watched him curiously, then rose to pour him a cup of coffee and bring it to the table. It was a habit she'd begun after her mother's death several years earlier.

"Did you and Mrs. Murphy have a good time last night?" Kate asked, before her father could comment on the rumors that were sure to be circulating about her and Luke Rivers. She hadn't seen Luke yet, but she would soon enough, and she was mentally bracing herself for the confrontation. What a fool she'd made of herself. She cringed at the thought of her marriage proposal and didn't doubt for a second that Luke was going to take a great deal of delight in tormenting her about it. She suspected it would be a long while before he let her live this one down.

"Looks like rain," Devin mumbled.

Kate grinned good-naturedly, wondering at her father's strange mood. "I asked you about last night, not about the weather."

Devin's eyes flared briefly with some unnamed emotion, which he quickly disguised. His gaze fell to the steaming mug cupped in his hands.

"Dad? Did you and Mrs. Murphy enjoy yourselves?"

"Why, sure, we had a grand time," he said with forced enthusiasm.

Kate waited for him to elaborate. Instead he reached for the sugar bowl and resolutely added three heaping teaspoons to his mug. He stirred it so briskly the coffee threatened to slosh over the edge. All the while, he stared blankly into space.

Kate didn't know what to make of Devin's unusual behavior. "Dad," she said, trying again, "is there something on your mind?"

His eyes darted about the room, reluctantly settling on Kate. "What makes you ask that?"

"You just added sugar to your coffee. You've been drinking it sugarless for forty years."

He glared down at the mug, surprise written on his tanned face. "I did?"

"I saw you myself."

"I did," he repeated firmly, as if that was what he'd intended all along. "I, ah, seem to have developed a sweet tooth lately."

It was becoming apparent to Kate that her father's experience at Clay and Rorie's wedding reception must have rivaled her own. "Instead of beating around the bush all morning, why don't you just tell me what's on your mind?"

Once more, her father lowered his eyes, then nodded and swallowed tightly. "Dorothea and I had...a long talk last night," he began haltingly. "It all started innocently enough. Then again, I'm sure the wedding and all the good feelings floating around Clay and Rorie probably had a lot to do with it." He paused to take a sip of his coffee, grimacing at its sweetness. "The best I can figure, we started talking seriously after Nellie Jackson came by and told Dorothea and me that we made a handsome couple. At least that's what I remember."

"It's true," Kate said kindly. Personally she would have preferred her father to see someone who resembled her mother a bit more, but Mrs. Murphy was a pleasant, gentle woman and Kate was fond of her.

Her father smiled fleetingly. "Then the champagne was passed around and Dorothea and I helped ourselves." He paused, glancing at Kate as if that explained everything.

"Yes," Kate said, hiding a smile, "go on."

Slowly Devin straightened, and his eyes, forthright and unwavering, held hers. "You know I loved your mother. When Nora died, there was a time I wondered if I could go on living without her, but I have, and so have you."

"Of course you have, Dad." Suddenly it dawned on Kate exactly where this conversation was leading. It shouldn't have surprised her, and yet… Kate's heart was beginning to hammer uncomfortably. Her father didn't need to say another word; she knew what was coming as surely as if he'd already spoken the words aloud. He was going to marry Dorothea Murphy.

"Your mother's been gone nearly five years now and, well, a man gets lonely," her father continued. "I've been thinking about doing some traveling and, frankly, I don't want to do it alone."

"You should've said something earlier, Dad," Kate interjected. "I'd have loved traveling with you. Still would. That's one of the nice things about being a teacher," she rambled on. "My summers are free. And with Luke watching the ranch, you wouldn't have any worries about what's happening at home and—"

"Princess." His spoon made an irritating clicking sound

against the sides of the ceramic mug, but he didn't seem to notice. "I asked Dorothea to marry me last night and she's graciously consented."

After only a moment's hesitation, Kate found the strength to smile and murmur, "Why, Dad, that's fantastic."

"I realize it's going to be hard on you, Princess—so soon after Clay's wedding and all. I want you to know I have no intention of abandoning you—you'll always be my little girl."

"Of course you aren't abandoning me." Tears edged their way into the corners of Kate's eyes and a cold numbness moved out from her heart and spread through her body. "I'm happy for you. Really happy." She meant it, too, but she couldn't help feeling a sense of impending loss. All the emotional certainties seemed to be disappearing from her life.

Her father gently squeezed her hand. "There are going to be some other changes, as well, I'm afraid. I'm selling the ranch."

Kate gasped before she could stop herself. He'd just confirmed all her fears. She'd lost Clay to another woman; now she was about to lose her father, and her home, too. Then another thought crystallized in her mind, a thought that had been half formed the night before. If the ranch was sold, Luke would be gone, too.

Clay. Her father. The Circle L. Luke. Everyone and everything she loved, gone in a matter of hours. It was almost more than she could absorb. Pressing her hand over her mouth, she blinked back the tears.

"Now I don't want you to concern yourself," her father hurried to add. "You'll always have a home with me. Dorothea and I talked it over and we both want you to feel free to live with us in town as long as you like. You'll always be my Princess, and Dorothea understands that."

"Dad," Kate muttered, laughing and crying at the same time. "That's ridiculous. I'm twenty-four years old and perfectly capable of living on my own."

"Of course you are, but—"

She stopped him by raising her hand. "There's no need to discuss it further. You and Dorothea Murphy are going to be married, and… I couldn't be happier for you. Don't you worry about me. I'll find a place of my own in town and make arrangements to move as soon as I can."

Her father sighed, clearly relieved by her easy acceptance of his plans. "Well, Princess," he said with a grin, "I can't tell you how pleased I am. Frankly, I was worried you'd be upset."

"Oh, Dad…"

Still grinning broadly, Devin stroked the side of his jaw. "Dorothea isn't a bit like your mother—I don't know if you're aware of that or not. Fact is, the only reason I asked her out that first time was so she'd invite me over for some of her peach cobbler. Then before I knew it, I was making excuses to get into town and it wasn't because of her cobbler, either."

Kate made an appropriate reply, although a minute later she wasn't sure what she'd said. Soon afterward, her father kissed her cheek and then left the house, telling her he'd be back later that afternoon.

She poured herself a second cup of coffee and leaned against the kitchen counter, trying to digest everything that was happening to her well-organized life. She felt as though her whole world had been uprooted and flung about—as though a hurricane had landed in Nightingale.

Wandering aimlessly from room to room, she paused in front of the bookcase, where a photograph of her mother stood. Tears blurred her eyes as she picked it up and clutched it to her chest. Wave upon wave of emotion swept through her, followed by a flood of hot tears.

She relived the overwhelming grief she'd felt at her mother's death, and she was furious with her father for letting another woman take Nora's place in his life. At the same time, she couldn't begrudge him his new happiness.

Mrs. Murphy wasn't the type of woman Kate would have chosen for her father, but then she wasn't doing the choosing. Suddenly resolute, Kate dragged in a deep breath, exhaling the fear and uncertainty and inhaling acceptance of this sudden change in both their lives.

The back door opened and instinctively Kate closed her eyes, mentally composing herself. It could only be Luke, and he was the last person she wanted to see right now.

"Kate?"

With trembling hands, she replaced the faded photograph and wiped the tears from her face. "Good morning, Luke," she said as she entered the kitchen.

Luke had walked over to the cupboard and taken down a mug. "Your father just told me the news about him and Mrs. Murphy," he said carefully. "Are you going to be all right?"

"Of course. It's wonderful for Dad, isn't it?"

"For your father yes, but it must be a shock to you so soon…"

"After Clay and Rorie," she finished for him. Reaching for the coffeepot, she poured his cup and refilled her own. "I'm going to be just fine," she repeated, but Kate didn't know whether she was telling him this for his benefit or her own. "Naturally, the fact that Dad's marrying Dorothea means a few changes in all our lives, but I'll adjust."

"I haven't seen your father this happy in years."

Kate did her best to smile through the pain. "Yes, I

know." To her horror tears formed again, and she lowered her eyes and blinked wildly in an effort to hide them.

"Kate?"

She whirled around and set her coffee aside, then started wiping invisible crumbs from the perfectly clean kitchen counter.

Luke's hands settled on her shoulders, and before she knew what was happening, Kate had turned and buried her face against his clean-smelling denim shirt. A single sob shook her shoulders and she gave a quivering sigh, embarrassed to be breaking down in front of him like this.

"Go on, baby," he whispered gently, his hands rubbing her back, "let it out."

She felt like such a weakling to be needing Luke so much, but he was so strong and steady, and Kate felt as helpless as a rowboat tossed in an angry sea. "Did...did you know Dad might sell the ranch?" she asked Luke.

"Yes." His voice was tight. "When did he tell you?"

"This morning, after he said he was marrying Mrs. Murphy."

"You don't have to worry about it."

"But I do," she said, sobbing brokenly. She felt Luke's chin caress the crown of her head and she snuggled into his warm, safe embrace. Luke was her most trusted friend. He'd seen her through the most difficult day of her life.

The thought of Clay and Rorie's wedding flashed into her mind, and with it came the burning memory of her marriage proposal to Luke. She stiffened in his arms, mortified at the blatant way she'd used him, the way she'd practically begged him to take care of her—to marry her. Breaking free of his arms, she straightened and offered him a watery smile.

"What would I do without you, Luke Rivers?"

"You won't ever need to find out." He slid his arms

around her waist and gently kissed the tip of her nose. His smile was tender. "There must've been something in the air last night. First us, and now your father and Mrs. Murphy."

"About us," she began carefully. She drew in a steadying breath, but her eyes avoided Luke's. "I hope you realize that when I asked you to marry me I…didn't actually mean it."

He went very still and for a long moment he said nothing. "I took you seriously, Kate."

Kate freed herself from his arms and reached for her coffee, gripping the mug tightly. "I'd had too much champagne."

"According to you, it was only one glass."

"Yes, but I drank it on an empty stomach, and with all the difficult emotions the wedding brought out, I… I simply wasn't myself."

Luke frowned. "Oh?"

"No, I wasn't," she said, feigning a light laugh. "The way we were dancing and the way I clung to you, and… and kissed you. That's nothing like me. I'm not going to hold you to that promise, Luke."

As if he found it difficult to remain standing, Luke turned a chair around and straddled it with familiar ease. Kate claimed the chair opposite him, grateful to sit down. Her nerves were stretched to the breaking point. Luke draped his forearms over the back of his chair, cupping the hot mug with both hands, and studied Kate with an intensity that made her blush.

"Listen," Kate said hesitantly, "you were the perfect gentleman and I want you to know how much I appreciate everything you did. But… I didn't mean half of what I said."

The sun-marked crow's feet at the corners of his eyes

fanned out as Luke smiled slowly, confidently. "Now that raises some interesting questions."

"I don't understand." Surely Luke knew what she was talking about, yet he seemed to enjoy watching her make an even bigger fool of herself by forcing her to explain.

"Well," he said in an easy drawl, "if you only meant half of what you said, then it leads me to wonder what you did mean and what you didn't."

"I can't remember *everything* I said," she murmured, her cheeks hot enough to pop a batch of corn. "But I do know I'd greatly appreciate it if you'd forget the part about marrying me."

"I don't want to forget it."

"Luke, please," she cried, squeezing her eyes shut. "This is embarrassing me. Could you please drop it?"

Luke rubbed his jaw thoughtfully. "I don't think I can."

So Luke was going to demand his pound of flesh. Kate supposed she shouldn't be surprised. She had, after all, brought this on herself. "You were so kind to me at the reception... After the wedding ceremony you kept saying you wanted to help me and, Luke, you did, you honestly did. I don't think I could've made it through Clay's wedding without you, but..."

"You want to forget the kissing, too?"

"Yes, please." She nodded emphatically.

He frowned. "That's not what you said last night. In fact, you seemed a little stunned at how pleasant it was. As I recall you told me—and I quote—'why didn't you tell me you were so good at this?'"

"I said that?" Kate muttered, already knowing it was true.

"I'm afraid so."

She covered her face with both hands as the hot color mounted in her cheeks.

"And you made me promise to marry you."

She bit down hard on her lower lip. "Anyone else in the world would have mercifully forgotten I said that."

With a certain degree of ceremony, Luke set his hat farther back on his head and folded his arms. His face was a study in concentration. "I have no intention of forgetting it. I'm a man of my word and I never break my promises."

Kate groaned. In light of her father's news this morning, she'd hoped Luke might be a bit more understanding. "It's obvious you're deriving pleasure from this," she muttered angrily, then pressed her lips together to keep from saying more.

"No, not exactly. When would you like to have the wedding? And while we're at it, you might as well learn now that—"

"You can't be serious!" she interrupted, incredulous that he'd suggest they set a date. If this was a joke, he was carrying it too far.

"I'm dead serious. You asked me to marry you, I agreed, and anything less would be a breach of good faith."

"Then I... I absolve you from your promise." She waved her hands as if she was granting some kind of formal dispensation.

He stroked the side of his face, his forehead creased in a contemplative frown. "My word is my word and I stand firm on it."

"I didn't understand what I was saying—well, I did. Sort of. But you know as well as I do that the...heat of the moment was doing most of the talking."

Luke's frown deepened. "I suppose everybody in town will assume you're marrying me on the rebound. Either that, or I'll be the one they gossip about. That doesn't trouble me much, but I don't like the thought of folks saying anything about you."

"Will you stop?" she cried. "I have no intention of marrying anyone! Ever!" She was finished with love, finished with romance. Thirty years from now she'd be living alone with a few cats and her knitting needles.

"That wasn't what you said last night."

"Would you quit saying that? I wasn't myself, for heaven's sake!"

"Well, our getting married sounded like a hell of a good idea to me. Now, I know you've gone through a hard time, but our marriage will end all that."

Kate brushed a shaking hand across her eyes, hoping this was just part of a nightmare and she'd soon wake up. Unfortunately when she lowered her hand, Luke was still sitting there, as arrogant as could be. "I can't believe we're having this discussion. It's totally unreasonable, and if you're trying to improve my mood, you've failed."

"I'm serious, Kate. I told you that."

Keeping her head down, she spoke quickly, urgently. "It's really wonderful of you to even consider going through with the marriage, but it isn't necessary, Luke. More than anyone, you should know that I can't marry you. Not when I love Clay Franklin."

"Hogwash."

Kate's head jerked up. "I beg your pardon?"

"You're in love with me. You just don't know it yet."

It took Kate only half a second to respond. "Of all the egotistical, vain, high-handed…" She paused to suck in a breath. If Luke's intent was to shock her, he'd succeeded. She bolted to her feet and flailed the air with both hands. Unable to stand still, she started pacing the kitchen. "I don't understand you. I've tried, honestly I've tried. One moment you're the Rock of Gibraltar, steady and secure and everything I need, my best friend, and the next moment you're saying the most ridiculous things to me. It never used to be like this! Why have you changed?"

"Is it really that bad?" he cajoled softly, ignoring her question.

"I don't know what happened to you—to us—at the wedding reception, but like you said, something must've been in the air. Let's blame it on the champagne and drop it before one of us gets hurt."

"If you gave the idea of our getting married some serious thought, it might grow on you," he suggested next.

Then he got to his feet and moved purposefully toward her, his mouth twisted in a cocky grin. "Maybe this will help you decide what's best."

"I—"

He laid a finger across her mouth. "It seems to me you've forgotten it's not ladylike to be quite so stubborn." With that, he slipped his arm around her waist and pulled her gently against him.

Knowing what he intended, Kate opened her mouth to protest, but he fastened his lips over hers, sealing off the words, and to her chagrin, soon erasing them altogether. Her fingers gripped the collar of his blue button-snap shirt and against every dictate of her will her mouth parted, welcoming his touch.

When he released her, it was a minor miracle that she didn't collapse on the floor. He paused and a wide grin split his face.

"Yup," he said, looking pleased, "you love me all right."

Three

Kate had never felt more grateful for a Monday morning than she did the following day. At least when she was at school, she had the perfect excuse to avoid another confrontation with Luke. He seemed to believe he was somehow responsible for her and to take that responsibility quite seriously. She had absolutely no intention of holding him to his promise and couldn't understand why he was being so stubborn. To suggest she was in love with him simply because she'd proposed marriage and responded ardently to his kisses revealed how truly irrational Luke Rivers had become.

Kate paused and let that thought run through her mind a second time, then laughed aloud. No wonder Luke insisted on marrying her. Kate had to admit she could see why he might have the wrong impression. Still, she wished she could think of some way to set him straight.

Luke was right about a few things, though. She *did* love him—but not in the way he implied. She felt for him as a sister did toward a special older brother. As a woman did toward a confidant and companion of many years' standing. The feelings she'd experienced when he kissed her were something of a mystery, but could easily be attributed to the heightened emotions following Clay's wedding. There'd been so many changes in Kate's life during the past few months that she barely understood herself anymore.

She could never love Luke the way she'd loved Clay. For as long as Kate could remember, she'd pictured herself as Clay's wife. Joining her life with any other man's seemed not only wrong but completely foreign.

"Good morning, Miss Logan," seven-year-old Taylor Morgenroth said as he walked casually into the classroom. "I saw you at Mr. Franklin's wedding on Saturday."

"You did?" It shouldn't surprise her, since nearly every family in town had been represented at the wedding. Probably more of her students had seen her there.

"You were with Mr. Rivers, weren't you? My mom kept asking my dad who you were dancing with. That was Mr. Rivers, wasn't it?"

"Yes." Kate had to bite her tongue to keep from explaining that she hadn't actually been "with" Luke. He wasn't her official date, although they'd attended the wedding together. But explaining something like that to a second-grader would only confuse the child.

"My dad made me dance with my older sister. It was yucky."

Kate managed some remark about how much of a gentleman Taylor had been, but she doubted that he wanted to hear it.

Before long, the students of Nightingale Elementary were filing into the classroom and rushing toward their desks. From that point on, Kate didn't have time to think about Luke or Saturday night or anything else except her lesson plans for the day.

At noon she took her packed lunch to the staff room. Several of the other teachers were already seated at the circular tables.

"Kate!" Sally Daley, the sixth-grade teacher, waved her hand to gain Kate's attention. She smiled, patting the empty chair beside her.

Reluctantly Kate joined the older woman, sending an apologetic look to her friend Linda Hutton, the third-grade teacher, with whom she usually had lunch. Sally had the reputation of being a busybody, but Kate couldn't think of a way to elude her without being rude.

"We were just talking about you," Sally said warmly, "and we thought it would be nice if you'd sit with us today."

"I'll be happy to," Kate said, feeling a twinge of guilt at the lie. She opened her brown bag, taking out a container of peach-flavored yogurt and two rye crisps.

"Clay's wedding was really lovely, wasn't it?" Sally asked without preamble. "And now I understand your father and Dorothea Murphy are going to be tying the knot?" Her questioning tone indicated she wasn't certain of her facts.

"That's right," Kate said cheerfully.

"Kind of a surprise, wasn't it?"

"Kind of," was all Kate would admit, although she realized she should've known her father was falling in love with Mrs. Murphy. They'd been spending more and more time together since early summer. If Kate hadn't been so blinded by what was happening between her and Clay, she would've noticed how serious her father had become about Dorothea long before now.

"It's going to be difficult for you, isn't it, dear?" Sally asked sympathetically. "Everyone knows how close you and your father have been since Nora died."

"I'm very pleased my father's planning to remarry." And Kate was. The initial shock had worn off; she felt genuinely and completely happy that her father had found someone to love. He'd never complained, but Kate knew he'd been lonely during the past few years.

"Still, it must be a blow," Sally pressed, "especially coming on the heels of Clay and Rorie getting married. It seems your whole life's been turned upside down, doesn't it?"

Kate nodded, keeping her eyes focused on her sparse meal.

"Speaking of Clay and Rorie, their wedding *was* lovely," Susan Weaver, the kindergarten teacher, put in.

"I thought so, too," Kate said, smiling through the pain. "Rorie will be a perfect wife for him." The words nearly stuck in her throat, although she was fully aware of their truth. Rorie was an ideal complement to Clay. From the moment she'd stepped into their lives, she'd obviously belonged with him.

"The new Mrs. Franklin is certainly an ambitious soul. Why, the library hasn't been the same since she took over. There are education programs going on every other week. Displays. Lectures. I tell you, nothing but good has happened since she moved to Nightingale."

"I couldn't agree with you more."

Sally nodded. "You've taken this…disappointment over Clay rather well," she murmured with cloying sympathy. "And now your father remarrying so soon afterward…" She gently patted Kate's hand. "If there's anything I can do for you, Kate, anything at all, during this difficult time, I want you to call me. I know I speak for each and every staff member when I say that. Your father must see what a wonderful daughter you've been, and I'm sorry all of this is being added to your burden just now. But if it's ever more than you can bear, your friends at Nightingale Elementary will be honored to stand by your side. All you have to do is call." The other women nodded.

If Sally was expecting a lengthy response, Kate couldn't manage it. "Thank you. That's…really good to know," she said in a faltering voice. To hear Sally tell it, Kate was close to a nervous breakdown.

"We're prepared to help as you pick up the shattered pieces of your life. And furthermore, I think Luke Rivers is a fine man."

"Luke Rivers?" Kate repeated, nearly choking on her bite of rye crisp. A huge lump formed in her throat at Sally's implication.

"Why, yes." Sally smiled serenely. "Everyone in Nightingale saw how the two of you were gazing into each other's eyes at the dance. It was the most romantic thing I've seen in years."

"Dance?"

"At the wedding-reception dance," Sally elaborated. "From what I understand, Beth Hammond's been so depressed she hasn't left her house since that night."

"Whatever for?"

Sally laughed lightly. "Surely there's no reason to be so reticent—you're among friends. Everyone knows how she's had her eye on Luke for years."

Susan nodded vigorously. "Apparently they dated a few times a year ago, but Luke's kept her dangling ever since."

"I don't have a clue what you mean," Kate said faintly, her heart beating hard enough to pound its way out of her chest. She'd hoped that with her father's engagement, the rumors about her and Luke would naturally fade away. So much for wishful thinking.

Sally exchanged a meaningful look with the other teachers. "Well, I thought that, you know…that you and Luke Rivers were involved."

"Luke and me?" Kate gave a short, almost hysterical laugh. "Nothing could be further from the truth. Luke's a dear friend, and we've known each other for years, but we're not romantically involved. There's nothing going on between us. Absolutely nothing." She spoke more vehemently than necessary, feeling pleased that for once Sally couldn't get a single word in.

After a moment, she made a show of looking at her watch. "Excuse me, ladies, but I've got to get back to my classroom."

As she left the faculty lounge, she heard the whispers start. Groaning inwardly, Kate marched down the hall and into her own room. Sitting at her desk, she snapped the cracker in half and examined it closely before tossing it in the garbage.

"Don't you know it's wrong to waste food?" Linda Hutton said, leaning against the doorjamb, arms folded.

"I wished I'd never talked to that woman," Kate muttered, feeling foolish for allowing herself to be manipulated into conversation with a known busybody.

"Well, then," Linda said, with a grin, "why did you?"

"If I knew the answer to that, I'd be enjoying my lunch instead of worrying about the tales Sally's going to spread about me…and Luke Rivers."

Linda walked into the room.

"The least you could've done was rescue me," Kate complained.

"Hey, I leave that kind of work to the fire department." Linda planted her hands on the edge of Kate's desk. "Besides, I was curious myself."

"Curious about what? Luke and me? All we did was dance a couple of times. I…was feeling warm and went outside for a little bit. Luke met me there and after a few minutes, he…drove me home. What's the big deal, anyway?"

"A couple of dances… I see," Linda said, her words slow and thoughtful.

"I'd be interested in knowing exactly *what* you see. Everyone keeps making an issue of the dancing. Taylor came into class this morning and the first thing he said was that he'd seen me at the wedding. He didn't talk about running into me at the grocery store earlier that day."

"Did you have your arms wrapped around a man there, too?"

"Don't be silly!"

"I wasn't. Honestly, Kate, nearly everyone in Nightingale saw the way you and Luke were dancing. You acted as though there wasn't anyone else at the reception. Needless to say, rumors were floating in every direction. Everyone was watching the two of you, and neither you or Luke even noticed. Or cared. I heard the pastor mumble something about maybe performing another wedding soon, and he wasn't referring to your father and Dorothea Murphy— which is another matter entirely." Linda paused to suck in a deep breath. "Are you sure you're going to be able to handle this on top of—"

"Clay and Rorie? Yes," Kate answered her own question emphatically. "Oh, I had a few bad moments when Dad first told me, but I got over it." The comfort she'd found in Luke's arms had helped her more than she cared to admit. He seemed to be making a habit of helping her through difficult moments.

Linda eyed her sceptically. "There's been so much upheaval in your life these past few weeks. You know, sometimes people go into shock for weeks after a major change in their lives."

"Linda," Kate cried, "everyone keeps looking at me as though they expect me to have a nervous breakdown. What is it with you people?"

"It isn't us, Katie girl, it's you."

Kate pushed her hair off her forehead and kept her hand there. "What do I have to do to convince you that I'm fine? I'm happy for Clay and Rorie. I consider myself resilient and emotionally strong, but this makes me wonder why you and Sally and the others don't."

"I don't think anyone's waiting for you to fall apart," Linda countered. "We all have your best interests at heart. In fact, with one obvious exception, everyone's really pleased you have Luke."

"But I don't *have* him. Luke isn't a possession, he's a man. We're friends. You know that." Kate expected Linda, of all her friends and colleagues, to recognize the truth when she heard it. Instead she'd made it sound as though Kate's dancing with Luke and then letting him take her home meant instant wedding bells.

Linda shook her head. "To be honest, Kate, you're doing a whole lot of denying and I don't understand why. It seems to me that the person you're really trying to convince is yourself."

By the time Kate arrived home that evening, she was in a fine temper. Her father had already left for a meeting at the Eagles Lodge. He'd taped a note to the refrigerator door telling her not to worry about fixing him any dinner because he planned to stop at Dorothea's later for a bite to eat.

Kate read his scrawled note, pulled it off the fridge and crumpled it with both hands. She was angry and impatient for no reason she could identify.

Heating a bowl of soup, Kate stood by the stove stirring it briskly when Luke let himself in the back door. After her encounter with Sally and Linda, Luke was the last person she wanted to see. Nevertheless, her eyes flew anxiously to his.

"Evening, Kate."

"Hi."

He hung his hat on the peg next to the door, then walked to the kitchen counter and examined the empty soup can. "I hope you're going to eat more than this."

"Luke," she said, slowly expelling her breath, "I had a terrible day and I'm rotten company."

"What happened?"

Kate didn't want to talk about it. Dredging up her lunch-hour conversation with Sally Daley would only refuel her unhappiness.

"Kate?" Luke coaxed.

She shrugged. "The other teachers heard about Dad and Dorothea and seemed to think the shock would do me in, if you know what I mean."

"I think I do." As he was speaking, he took two bowls out of the cupboard and set them on the table.

Kate stirred the soup energetically, not looking at him, almost afraid of his reaction. "In addition, people are talking about us."

When she glanced in his direction, Luke nodded, his eyes twinkling. "I thought they might be."

"I don't like it!" she burst out. The least Luke could do was show the proper amount of concern. "Sally Daley told me how pleased she was with the way I'd rebounded from a broken heart." She paused, waiting for his response. When he didn't give one, she added, "Sally seems to think you and I are perfect together."

Luke grinned. "And that upset you?"

"Yes!" she cried.

"Sally didn't mean anything. She's got a big heart."

"And an even bigger mouth," Kate retorted. "We're in trouble here, Luke Rivers, and I need to know how we're going to get out of it."

"The answer to that is simple. We should get married and put an end to all the speculation."

Kate's shoulders sagged in defeat. "Luke, please, I'm not in the mood for your teasing tonight. We have to get serious about…"

Her voice dwindled away as Luke, standing behind her, placed his hands on her shoulders and nuzzled her neck. "I'm willing."

His touch had a curious effect on Kate's senses, which sprang to sudden life. It took every ounce of fortitude she possessed to resist melting into his arms and accepting his comfort. But that was how they'd got into this mess in the first place.

"The gossips are having a field day and I hate it."

Luke drew her away from the stove and turned her toward him. He searched her face, but his own revealed not a hint of annoyance or distress. "I don't mind if folks talk. It's only natural, don't you think?"

"How can you *say* that?"

"Kate, you're making this out to be some kind of disaster."

"But don't you see? It is! There are people out there who actually believe we're falling in love."

"You do love me. I told you that earlier. Remember?"

"Oh, Luke," she cried, so disheartened she wanted to weep. "I know what you're trying to do and I appreciate it with all my heart, but it isn't necessary. It really isn't."

Luke looked baffled. "I don't understand."

"You've been so sweet." She laid her hand against his clean-shaven cheek. "Any other man would've laughed in my face when I made him promise to marry me, but you agreed and now, out of consideration for *my* pride, *my* feelings, you claim you're going through with it."

"Kate," he said, guiding her to the table and gently

pressing her into a chair. "Sit down. I have something important to tell you—something I've been trying to tell you since the night of the wedding."

"What is it?" she asked, once she was seated.

Luke paced the floor directly in front of her chair. "I should've told you much sooner, but with everything else that's going on in your life, finding the right time has been difficult." He paused and frowned at her as though he was having trouble choosing his words.

"Yes?" she coaxed.

"I'm buying the Circle L."

The kitchen started to sway. Kate reached out and gripped the edge of the table. She'd hoped it would be months, at least, before a buyer was found. And it had never occurred to her that Luke might be that buyer. "I see," she said, smiling through her shock. "I… I'd have thought Dad would've said something himself."

"I asked him not to."

Her troubled gaze clashed with Luke's. Despite her shock she felt curious. How could Luke afford to buy a ranch, especially one as large as this? She knew he'd been raised by an uncle, who had died years before. Had there been an inheritance? "Luke," she ventured shyly, "I know it's none of my business, but…"

"How did I come by the money?" he finished for her. "You have every right to ask. I inherited it from my uncle Dan—I've told you about him. He owned a couple of businesses in Wyoming, where I grew up. There was also a small sum left to me by my grandfather. I invested everything, together with most of what Devin's paid me over the years, and I've got enough now to buy the ranch outright—which'll leave your dad and Dorothea in good financial shape for their retirement. I'll be able to expand the operation, too."

Kate nodded absently. She hadn't known much about Luke's background, apart from the fact that he had very little family, that he'd lost his parents at an early age. She supposed those losses were the reason he'd been so sympathetic, such a comfort to her and Devin, at the time of Nora's death.

It still seemed too much to take in. Her home—it was going to belong to Luke. He'd move his things from the small foreman's house, though she knew he hadn't accumulated many possessions. But it meant that soon she'd be sorting through and packing up the memories of a lifetime.... She bit her lip.

He knelt in front of her, grasping her fingers with his warm, hard hands. "I realize you've been through a lot of emotional upheaval lately, but this should help."

"Help!" she wailed. "How could it possibly—?"

"There's no reason for you to be uprooted now."

For a stunned second she didn't react. "I don't have the slightest idea what you're talking about."

"Once we're married, we'll live right here."

"Married!" she almost shouted. "I'm beginning to hate the sound of that word."

"You'd better get used to it, because the way I figure, we're going to be husband and wife before Christmas. We'll let Devin and Dorothea take their vows first—I don't want to steal their thunder—and then we'll wait a couple of weeks and have the Reverend Wilkins marry us."

"Luke, this is all very sweet of you, but *it isn't necessary.*" Kate was convinced that this sudden desire to make her his wife was founded in sympathy. He felt sorry for her because of all the unexpected jolts that had hit her recently. Including this latest one.

"I can't understand why you're arguing with me."

Her hand caressed his jaw. How square and strong it

was, and the eyes that gazed at her had never seemed darker or more magnetic. She smiled sadly. "Don't you think it's a little…odd to be discussing marriage when you've never once said you love me?"

"I love you."

It should have been a solemn moment, but Kate couldn't help laughing. "Oh, Luke, that was terrible."

"I'm serious. I love you and you love me."

"Of course we love each other, but what we feel is what *friends* feel. The kind of love brothers and sisters share."

Fire leaped into his eyes, unlike anything she'd seen in him before. With any other man, she would have been frightened—but this was Luke….

"Instead of looking at me as if you're tempted to turn me over your knee, you should be grateful I'm not holding you to your word."

"Kate," he said loudly, "we're getting married." He spoke as though he was daring her to disagree with him.

She lowered her head and brushed his lips with her own. "No, we're not. I'll always be grateful to have a friend as good as you, Luke Rivers. Every woman deserves someone just as kind and thoughtful, but we'd be making the biggest mistake of our lives if we went through with this marriage."

"I don't think that's true."

"I'm sane and rational, and I'm not going to disintegrate under the emotional stress of Clay's wedding or my father's remarriage, or the sale of the ranch. Life goes on—I learned that after my mother died. It sounds so clichéd, but it's the truth. I learned to deal with losing her and I'll do the same with everything else."

"Kate, you don't get it. I *want* to marry you."

"Oh, Luke, it's so nice of you. But you don't love me. Not the way you should. Someday, you'll make some lucky woman a fantastic husband." Kate had grown accustomed to his comfortable presence. But while she felt at ease with him, she experienced none of the thrill, the urgent excitement, that being in love entailed. Well, of course, there was her reaction to Luke's kisses—but that was an aberration, she told herself.

With Clay, the intensity of emotion had wrapped itself around her so securely that she'd been sure it would last a lifetime. Kate hadn't fooled herself into believing Clay felt as strongly for her. He'd been fond of her, and Kate had been willing to settle for that. But it hadn't been enough for him. And she wasn't allowing Luke to settle for second-best, either.

"People are going to talk, so we both have to do our best to put an end to the rumors."

"I don't intend to do any such thing," Luke said, his jaw rigid. His eyes narrowed. "Kate, darling, a marriage between us is inevitable. The sooner you accept that, the better it'll be for everyone involved."

Four

"The way I figure it," Kate said, munching on a carrot stick, "I'm only going to convince Luke I don't intend to marry him by dating someone else."

Linda looked as if she were about to swallow her apple whole. The two were seated in the school lunchroom on Friday afternoon, reviewing plans for the Thanksgiving play their two classes would present the following month.

"Dating someone else?" Linda echoed, still wearing a stunned expression. "A few days ago you said you were finished with love and completely opposed to the idea of men and marriage."

"I'm not expecting to fall in love again," Kate explained impatiently. "That would be ridiculous."

"You talk about being ridiculous?" Linda asked, setting down her half-eaten apple. "We were discussing Pilgrim costumes and suddenly you decide you want to start dating. I take it you're not referring to Miles Standish?"

"Of course not."

"That's what I thought."

Kate supposed she wasn't making a lot of sense to her friend. Luke and the issue of marriage had been on her mind all week, but she'd carefully avoided any mention

of the subject. Until now. The rumors regarding her and
Luke continued to burn like a forest fire through Nightingale, aided, Kate was sure, by the silly grin Luke wore
around town, and the fact that he was buying her father's
ranch. True, he hadn't pressured her into setting a wedding
date again, but the thought was there, waiting to ambush
her every time they were in the same room. She used to
be able to laugh and joke with Luke, but lately, the minute they were together, Kate found herself raising protective barriers.

"All right, you've piqued my curiosity," Linda said, her
eyes flashing with humor. "Tell me about this sudden interest in the opposite sex."

"I want to stop the rumors, naturally." And convince
Luke that her marriage proposal had been rooted in self-
pity. He'd been so strong and she'd felt so fragile....

Linda pushed aside the pages of the Thanksgiving project notes. "Have you picked anyone in particular?"

"No," Kate murmured, frowning. "I've been out of cir-
culation for so long, I'm not sure who's available."

"No one," Linda told her in a despondent voice. "And
I should know. If you want the truth, I think Nightingale
would make an excellent locale for a convent. Have you
ever considered the religious life?"

Kate ignored that. "Didn't I hear Sally Daley mention
something about a new guy who recently moved to town?
She seemed to think he was single."

"Eric Wilson. Attorney, mid-thirties, divorced, with a
small mole on his left shoulder."

Kate was astonished. "Good heavens, how did Sally
know all that?"

Linda shook her head. "I don't even want to guess."

"Eric Wilson." Kate repeated it slowly, letting each
syllable roll off her tongue. She decided the name had a

friendly feel, though it didn't really tell her anything about the man himself.

"Have you met him?" Kate asked her friend.

"No, but you're welcome to him, if you want. My track record with divorced men isn't exactly great. The only reason Sally said anything to me was that she assumed you and Luke would be married before the holidays were over." Linda grimaced. "She thought I'd need her help in finding a date for the wedding."

A sense of panic momentarily overtook Kate. This wedding nonsense was completely out of hand, which meant she had to come up with another man *now*.

"There's always Andy Barrett," she murmured. Andy worked at the pharmacy and was single. True, he wasn't exactly a heartthrob, but he was a decent-enough sort.

Linda immediately rejected that possibility. "No one in town would believe you'd choose Andy over Luke." A smile played across her mouth, as if she found the idea of Kate and Andy together somehow comical. "Andy's sweet, don't get me wrong," Linda amended, "but Luke's a real man."

"I'll think of someone," Kate murmured, her determination fierce.

Linda started to gather her Thanksgiving notes. "If you're serious about this, then you may have no choice but to import a man from Portland."

"You're kidding, I hope," Kate groaned.

"Nope. I'm dead serious," Linda said, shoving everything into her briefcase.

Her friend's words echoed depressingly through Kate's mind as she pushed her cart to the frozen-food section of the grocery store later that afternoon. She peered at the TV dinners, trying to choose something for dinner. Her father had dined with Dorothea every night since they'd become engaged, and the wedding was planned for early December.

"The beef burgundy is good," a resonant male voice said from behind her.

Kate turned to face a tall, friendly-looking man with flashing blue eyes and a lazy smile.

"Eric Wilson," he introduced himself, holding out his hand.

"Kate Logan," she said, her heart racing as they exchanged handshakes. It was all Kate could do not to tell him she'd been talking about him only minutes before and that she'd learned he was possibly the only single prospect in town—other than Luke, of course. How bizarre that they should run into each other almost immediately afterward. Perhaps not! Perhaps it was fate.

"The Salisbury steak isn't half-bad, either." As if to prove his point, he deposited both the beef burgundy and the Salisbury steak frozen dinners in his cart.

"You sound as though you know."

"I've discovered frozen entrées are less trouble than a wife."

He frowned as he spoke, so she guessed that his divorce had been unpleasant. Sally would be able to provide the details, and Kate made a mental note to ask her. She'd do it blatantly, of course, since Sally would spread Kate's interest in the transplanted lawyer all over the county.

"You're new in town, aren't you? An attorney?"

Eric nodded. "At your service."

Kate was thinking fast. It'd been a long time since she'd flirted with a man—if you didn't count the way she'd behaved at the wedding. "Does that mean I can sue you if the beef burgundy isn't to my liking?"

Country Bride

He grinned at that, and although her comment hadn't been especially witty, she felt encouraged by his smile.

"You might have trouble getting the judge to listen to your suit, though," he told her.

"Judge Webster is my uncle," she said, laughing.

"And I suppose you're his favorite niece."

"Naturally."

"In that case, might I suggest we avoid the possibility of a lawsuit and I buy you dinner?"

That was so easy Kate couldn't believe it. She'd been out of the dating game years, and she'd been sure it would take a while to get the hang of it again. "I'd be delighted."

It wasn't until Kate was home, high on her success, that she realized Eric, as a new man in town, was probably starved for companionship. That made her pride sag just a little, but she wasn't about to complain. Within hours of declaring that she wanted to start dating, she'd met a man. An attractive, pleasant man, too. It didn't matter that he'd asked her out because he was lonely or that he was obviously still embittered by his divorce. A date was a date.

Kate showered and changed into a mid-calf burgundy wool skirt and a rose-colored silk blouse. She was putting the last coat of polish on her nails when her father strolled into the kitchen. Even from her position at the far side of the room, Kate caught a strong whiff of his spicy after-shave. She smiled.

"You look nice, Dad."

"Thanks," he said, tugging on the lapels of his tweed jacket, then brushing the sleeves.

"Do you want me to wait up for you?"

A flush worked its way up Devin's neck. "Of course not."

Kate loved teasing him, and as their eyes met, they both started to laugh.

"You're looking awfully pretty yourself," Devin commented. "Are you and Luke going out?"

"Eric Wilson is taking me to dinner."

Devin regarded her quizzically. "Who? You're kidding, aren't you?"

"No." She gave him a warning frown. "Eric's new here. We met in the frozen-food section at the grocery store this afternoon and he asked me to dinner."

"And you accepted?" His eyes were wide with astonishment.

"Of course. It beats sitting around here and watching reruns on television."

"But...but what about Luke?"

"What about him?"

"I thought... I'd hoped after Clay's wedding that the two of you might—"

"Dad, Luke's a dear friend, but we're not in love with each other."

For a moment Devin looked as if he wanted to argue, but apparently decided against it. "He's a good man, Princess."

"Trust me, I know that. If it wasn't for Luke, I wouldn't have survived the last couple of months."

"Folks in town have the impression that you two might be falling in love, and I can't say I blame them after watching you at the wedding."

Kate focused her attention on polishing her nails, knowing that an identical shade of red had crept into her cheeks.

"Luke and I are friends, Dad, nothing more," she repeated.

"I don't mind letting you know, Kate, that I think very highly of Luke. If I were to handpick a husband for you, it would be him."

"I...think Luke's wonderful, too," she said, her words faltering.

"Now that he's buying the ranch, well, it seems natural that the two of you—"

"Dad, please," she whispered. "I'm not in love with Luke, and he doesn't love me."

"That's a real pity," came Devin's softly drawled response. He reached for his hat, then paused by the door. "I don't suppose Luke knows you're going out tonight, does he?"

"There isn't any reason to tell him." She tried to act nonchalant. But she desperately wanted to avoid another showdown with Luke. Pleadingly, she raised her eyes to her father. "You aren't going to tell him, are you?"

"I won't lie to him."

"Oh, I wouldn't expect you to do that," Kate murmured. She blew at the dark-red polish on her nails, trying to dry them quickly. With luck, Eric would arrive soon and she could make her escape before she encountered Luke.

Kate should have known that was asking too much. She was standing at the kitchen window beside the oak table, waiting for Eric's headlights to come down the long drive, when Luke walked into the house.

Kate groaned inwardly, but said nothing. Her fingers tightened on the curtain as she changed her silent entreaty. Now she prayed that Eric would be late.

"You've got your coat on," Luke observed as he poured a mug of coffee.

"I'll be leaving in a couple of minutes," she said, hoping she didn't sound as tense as she felt. Then, a little guiltily, she added, "I baked some oatmeal cookies yesterday. The cookie jar's full, so help yourself."

He did exactly that, then sat down at the table. "If I didn't know better, I'd think you were waiting for someone."

"I am."

"Who?"

"A...friend." Her back was to him, but Kate could feel the tension between them.

"Are you upset about something?"

"No. Should I be?" she asked in an offhand manner.

"You've been avoiding me all week," he said.

He was sitting almost directly behind her and Kate felt his presence acutely. Her knees were shaking, her breath coming in short, uneven gulps. She felt light-headed. It had to be nerves. If Luke discovered she was going to dinner with Eric, there could be trouble. Yes, she told herself, that explained the strange physical reaction she was experiencing.

"Kate, love—"

"Please," she implored, "don't call me that." She released the curtain and turned to face him. "I made a mistake, and considering the circumstances, it was understandable. Please, Luke, can't you drop this whole marriage business? Please?"

His look of shocked surprise didn't do anything to settle her nerves. A strained moment passed before Luke relaxed, chuckling. "I've broken stallions who've given me less trouble than you."

"I'm no stallion."

Luke chuckled again, and before she could move, his arms reached out and circled her waist to pull her onto his lap.

Kate was so astonished that for a crazy moment she didn't react at all. "Let me go," she said stiffly, holding her chin at a regal angle.

He ignored her demand and lightly ran the tips of his fingers along the side of her jaw, stroking downward to cup her chin. "I've missed you this week, Princess."

A trail of warmth followed his cool fingers, and a foreign sensation nibbled at her stomach. Kate didn't know what was wrong with her—and she didn't *want* to know.

"I've decided to give you a chance to think everything through before we contact Pastor Wilkins—"

"Before we what?" she flared.

"Before we're married," he explained patiently, his voice much too low and seductive to suit her. "But every time we're together, you run away like a frightened kitten."

"Did you stop to think there might be a perfectly logical reason for that?" She'd told him repeatedly that she wasn't going to marry him, but it didn't seem to make any differences. "I'm sorry, I truly am, but I just don't see you that way."

"Oh?"

He raised his hand and threaded his fingers through her hair. She tried to pull away, to thwart him, with no effect.

"That's not the feeling I get when I kiss you."

She braced her hands against his shoulders. "I apologize if I've given you the wrong impression," she said, her voice feeble.

He cocked his eyebrows at her statement, and his lips quivered with the effort to suppress a smile. That infuriated Kate, but she held on to her temper, knowing an argument would be pointless.

"It seems to me," he continued, "that we need some time alone to explore what's happening between us."

Alarm rose in Kate's throat as she struggled to hide her response to him. The last thing she wanted was "time alone" with Luke.

"I'm afraid that's impossible tonight," she said hastily.

"Why's that?"

He was so close that his breath fanned her flushed face. It was all Kate could do to keep from closing her eyes and surrendering to the sensations that encircled her, like lazy curls of smoke from a campfire.

His mouth found her neck and he placed a series of kisses there, each one a small dart of pleasure that robbed her of clear thought. For a wild moment, she couldn't catch her breath. His hands were in her hair, and his mouth was working its magic....

"No," she breathed, her voice low and trembling. Any resistance she'd managed to rally had vanished.

"Yes, my darlin', Kate?"

He sought her mouth then, and excitement erupted inside her. She clung to him, arms around his neck as his lips returned again and again to taste and tantalize her.

When he buried his face in the hollow of her throat, Kate moaned softly. She felt nearly faint from the rush of pleasure.

"Call Linda and cancel whatever plans you've made," he whispered.

Kate froze. "I can't."

"Yes, you can. I'll talk to her, if you want."

"I'm not going out with Linda."

"Then call whoever it is and cancel."

"No..."

A flash of headlights through the kitchen window announced Eric's arrival. With a burst of frantic energy, Kate leaped off Luke's lap, feeling disoriented and bewildered. She rubbed her hands over her face, realizing she'd probably smudged her makeup, but that didn't concern her as much as the unreserved way she'd submitted to Luke's touch. He'd kissed her before and it had been wonderful—more than wonderful. But in those brief moments when he'd held her, at the wedding and then again the next day, she hadn't experienced this burning *need*. It terrified her.

"Kate?"

She looked at Luke without really seeing him. "I've got to go," she insisted.

"There's a man here."

Kate opened the door for Eric. "Hi," she greeted him, doing her best to appear cheerful and animated, but suspecting that she looked and sounded as though she was coming down with a bad case of flu. "I see you found the place without a problem."

"Actually, I had one hell of a time," he said, glancing at his watch. "Didn't you notice I'm fifteen minutes late?"

Well, no, she hadn't. Not really.

"Kate, who is this man?" Luke demanded in a steely voice.

"Eric Wilson, this is Luke Rivers. Luke is buying the Circle L," she said breathlessly.

The two men exchanged the briefest of handshakes.

Kate didn't dare look in Luke's direction. She didn't need to; she could feel the resentment and annoyance that emanated from him like waves of heat. "Well, I suppose we should be on our way," Kate said to Eric, throwing him a tight, nervous smile.

"Yes, I suppose we should." Eric's gaze traveled from Kate to Luke, then back again. He seemed equally eager to escape.

"I'll say good-night, Luke," she said pointedly, her hand on the back door.

He didn't respond, which was just as well.

Once they were outside, Eric opened his car door for her. "You said Luke is buying the ranch?"

"Yes," she answered brightly.

"And nothing else?" he pressed, frowning. "The look he was giving me seemed to say you came with the property."

"That's not true." Even if Luke chose to believe otherwise. After tonight, she couldn't deny that they shared a strong physical attraction, but that was nothing on which to base a life together. She didn't *love* Luke; how could she, when she was still in love with Clay? She'd been crazy about Clay Franklin most of her life, and feelings that intense didn't change overnight simply because he'd married another woman.

When Clay and Rorie had announced their engagement, Kate had known with desolate certainty that she'd never love again. If she couldn't have Clay, then she would live the remainder of her life alone, treasuring the time they'd had together.

"You're absolutely certain Rivers has no claim on you?"

"None," Kate assured him.

"That's funny," Eric said with a humorless chuckle. "From the way he glared at me, I feel lucky to have walked away with my head still attached."

Kate forced a laugh. "I'm sure you're mistaken."

Eric didn't comment further, but she could tell he didn't believe her.

After their shaky beginning, dinner turned out to be a pleasant affair. Eric took Kate to the Red Bull, the one fancy restaurant in Nightingale, a steak house that specialized in thick T-bones and fat baked potatoes. A country-and-western band played local favorites in the lounge, which was a popular Friday-night attraction. The music drifted into the dining-room, creating a festive atmosphere.

Eric studied the menu, then requested a bottle of wine with their meal.

When the waitress had taken their order, he placed his elbows on the table and smiled at Kate. "Your eyes are lovely," he said, his voice a little too enthusiastic.

Despite herself, Kate blushed. "Thank you."

"They're the same color as my ex-wife's." He said this in bitter tones, as if he wished Kate's were any color

other than blue. "I'm sorry," he added, looking chagrined.
"I've got to stop thinking about Lonni. It's over. Finished.
Kaput."

"I take it you didn't want the divorce."

"Do you mind if we don't talk about it?"

Kate felt foolish for bringing up the subject, especially
since it was obviously so painful for him. "I'm sorry, that
was thoughtless. You're trying to let go of the past."

The bottle of wine arrived and when Eric had sampled
and approved it the waitress filled their glasses.

"Actually you remind me of Lonni," he said, after taking a sip of the chardonnay. "We met when we were both
in college."

Kate looked down at her wineglass, twirling the delicate
stem between her fingers. Eric was so clearly in love with
his ex-wife that she wondered what had torn them apart.

"You were asking about the divorce?" He replenished
his wine with a lavish hand.

"If it's too difficult, you don't need to talk about it."

"I don't think either Lonni or I ever intended to let it go
this far," he said, and Kate was sure he hadn't even heard
her. "I certainly didn't, but before I knew what was happening, the whole thing blew up in my face. There wasn't
another man—I would've staked my life on that."

Their dinner salads were served and, picking up her
fork, Kate asked, "What brought you to Nightingale?"

Eric drank his wine as if he were gulping cool water
on a summer afternoon. "Lonni, of course."

"I beg your pardon?"

"Lonni. I decided I needed to make a clean break. Get
a fresh start and all that."

"I see."

"You have to understand that when Lonni first suggested we should separate, I thought it was the right thing

to do. We hadn't been getting along and, frankly, if she wanted out of the relationship, I wasn't going to stand in her way. It's best to discover these things before you have children, don't you agree?"

"Oh, yes." Kate nibbled at her salad, wondering what she could say that would help or comfort Eric.

An hour and another bottle of wine later, Kate realized he'd drunk the better part of both bottles and was in no condition to drive home. Now she had to tactfully make *him* realize that.

"Do you dance?" she asked, as he paid the dinner bill.

He frowned slightly. "This country-and-western stuff doesn't usually appeal to me, but I'm willing to give it a whirl, if you are."

Kate assumed all the wine he'd been drinking had quelled his reservations. When the band began a lively melody, Eric led Kate onto the crowded dance floor.

Kate was breathless by the time the song ended. To her relief, the next number was a much slower one. She recognized her mistake the minute Eric locked her in his embrace. His hands fastened at the small of her back, forcing her close. She tried to put some space between them, but Eric didn't seem to notice her efforts. His eyes were shut as he swayed to the leisurely beat. Kate wasn't fooled; her newfound friend was pretending he had Lonni in his arms. It was a good thing her ego wasn't riding on this date.

"I need a little more room," she whispered.

He loosened his grip for a moment, but as the song continued, his hold gradually tightened again. Kate edged her forearms up and braced them on his chest, easing herself back an inch or two.

"Excuse me, please." A harsh male voice that was all too familiar came from behind Eric. Kate wished she could crawl into a hole and die the instant she heard it.

"I'm cutting in," Luke informed the other man, who turned his head and looked at the intruder incredulously.

Without a word of protest Eric dropped his arms and took a step in retreat. Neither man bothered to ask Kate what *she* wanted. She was about to complain when Luke reached for her hand and with a natural flair swept her into his arms. The immediate sense of welcome she experienced made her want to weep with frustration.

"Why did you cut in like that?" she demanded. She felt disheartened and irritable. Everything she'd worked for this evening was about to be undone.

"Did you mean for that city slicker to hold you so close?"

"How Eric holds me isn't any of your business."

"I'm making it my business."

His face was contorted with anger. His arms were so tight that Kate couldn't have escaped him if she'd tried. Judging by the looks they were receiving from the couples around them, they were quickly becoming the main attraction.

The instant the music ended, Kate abruptly left Luke's arms and returned to Eric. Her date stood in the corner of the room, nursing a shot glass filled with amber liquid. Kate groaned and hid her displeasure. Eric had already had enough wine without adding hard liquor.

"I thought you said there was nothing between you and Luke Rivers," he muttered, when she joined him.

"There isn't. We're just good friends."

"That's not the impression I'm getting."

Kate didn't know how to respond. "I apologize for the interruption. Do you want to dance?"

"Not if it's going to cost me my neck."

"It isn't," she promised.

Another lively song erupted from the band. Eric took her hand and she smiled encouragingly up at him. As they headed for the dance floor, Kate tried to ignore Luke's chilly glare.

Midway through the song, Eric stopped dancing. "I'm not very good at this fancy footwork," he declared. With that, he pulled her into his arms, tucking her securely against him.

"This is much better," he whispered, his mouth close to her ear. Once more his hold tightened.

"Eric, please. I'm having trouble breathing," Kate told him in a strangled voice.

"Oh, sorry." He relaxed his grip. "Lonni and I used to dance like this all the time."

Kate had guessed as much. It was on the tip of her tongue to remind him that she wasn't his ex-wife, but she doubted it would make any difference. Eric had spent much of the evening pretending she was.

At the moment, however, her date and his ex-wife were the least of Kate's problems. Tiny pinpricks moved up and down her spine, telling her that Luke was still glaring at her from the other side of the room. She did her best to act as though he wasn't there.

She smiled up at Eric, she laughed, she talked, but with each breath she drew she could feel Luke's eyes on her, scrutinizing every move she made.

When the music stopped, Eric returned to their table and his drink, swallowing the remainder of it in one gulp. The music started again and he pulled Kate toward him.

"I think I'll sit this one out." She hoped that would appease Luke, who looked as if he were about to rip Eric in two.

Her gaze fell to her lap and she folded her hands, concentrating on not letting him know how much a single glance from him affected her.

"How much have you had to drink, Wilson?"

While her eyes were lowered, Luke had come over to their table. His voice was controlled but unmistakably furious.

"I can't say that's any of your concern, Rivers." For his part, Eric seemed nervous. He leaned back in his chair, balancing on two legs, and raised his empty shot glass.

"I don't agree," Luke countered, moving closer. "From what I can see, you've had plenty. I'm taking Kate home with me."

"Luke," she protested, "please don't do this."

"Your date's in no condition to drive."

It was all Kate could do not to stand up and defend Eric. Unfortunately Luke was right. She'd known it even before they'd finished dinner, but she wanted to handle things her own way.

"I can hold my liquor as well as the next man," Eric said, daring to wave his glass under Luke's nose. It was apparent to everyone that his courage had been fortified by whiskey. Few men would have taunted Luke in his present mood.

Luke turned to Kate. "You've got better sense than this, Kate."

Kate did. But she had no intention of telling him so. "I think Eric knows his own limit," she returned.

"Then you plan to ride home with him?"

"I'm not sure yet." She wouldn't, but she wasn't about to give Luke an armful of ammunition to use against her.

Luke scowled at her with such fury it was difficult for Kate to swallow normally.

Slowly he turned to Eric. "If you value your teeth, I suggest you stay exactly where you are. Bob," Luke called to the sheriff's deputy across the room, "would you see that this newcomer gets home without a problem?"

"Sure thing, Luke."

"Kate," he said, addressing her next, "you're coming with me."

"I most certainly am not."

Luke didn't leave her any option. He leaned forward and pulled her upright, as if she weighed no more than a bag of popcorn.

She struggled briefly but knew it was useless. "Luke, don't do this. Please, don't do this," she pleaded through clenched teeth, humiliated to the very roots of her hair.

"Either you come with me willingly or I carry you out of here." Luke's composure didn't falter. When she resisted, he swept his arms behind her legs and lifted her from the floor.

"Luke," Kate cried, "put me down this instant. I *demand* that you put me down."

He completely ignored her threat as he strode toward the door, his gaze focused impassively ahead of them. The waitress who'd served her dinner came running up to hand Kate her coat and bag. Her eyes were flashing with humor.

"Stick by your man, honey," she advised. "That city slicker can't hold a candle to Luke Rivers."

"Luke's the man for you," someone else shouted.

"When you gonna tie the knot?"

Two men were holding open the lounge door for them. The last thing Kate heard as Luke carried her into the cold night air was a robust round of applause from inside the lounge.

Five

"I have never been so embarrassed in my life," Kate stormed as Luke parked his pickup outside the house. "How could you *do* that to me? How could you?"

During the entire ride home, Luke hadn't spoken a word, nor had he even glanced at her. He'd held himself stiff, staring straight ahead. For all his concern about her riding with Eric, he drove as if the very devil were on their tail. Only when they entered the long, winding drive that led to the house had he reduced his speed.

"I'll never forgive you for this," she told him, grabbing the door handle and vaulting out of the truck. She couldn't get away from him fast enough. By morning every tongue in Nightingale would be wagging, telling how Luke Rivers had hauled Kate Logan out of the Red Bull.

To her dismay Luke followed her into the house.

"I couldn't care less if you forgive me or not," he said darkly.

"The women were laughing and the men snickering.... I won't be able to show my face in this town again."

"As far as I'm concerned, the problem is one of your own making."

"That's not true!" She'd had no way of knowing that

Eric was going to start downing wine like soda pop. And she did *not* need a lecture from Luke Rivers. All she wanted him to do was leave, so she could lick her wounds in private and figure out how long it would be before she dared go out in public again.

Luke started pacing the kitchen floor. Each step was measured and precise. Clipped, like his voice.

"Please go," she beseeched wearily.

"I'm not leaving until I get some answers from you."

Gathering what remained of her dignity, which at this point wasn't much, Kate sank onto a chair. She wouldn't argue with Luke. Every time she tried, she came out the loser. Better to get this over with now rather than wait for morning. She sighed deeply.

"Who the hell is Eric Wilson and why were you having dinner with him?" Luke's heavy boots clicked against the kitchen floor as he paced.

Instead of answering, Kate asked, "What's happened to us?" She gazed sorrowfully up at Luke. "Do you remember how much fun we used to have together? Tonight wasn't fun, Luke. Just a few weeks ago I could laugh with you and cry with you. You were my friend and I was yours. Suddenly nothing's the same, and I don't understand why." Her voice quavered slightly. She fought an overwhelming desire to hide her face in her hands and weep.

She didn't win. Tears of pride and anguish spilled on to her cheeks. She brought her hands up, trying to hide her distress.

Luke knelt in front of her and pried her hands away. His fingers tenderly caressed her face. "Everything has changed, hasn't it, Princess?"

She sucked in a shaky breath and nodded.

"You're confused, aren't you?" His hands cradled her face and he eased forward to press his warm mouth over hers. Even as she kissed him back, her confusion grew. He'd been so angry with her, more furious than she'd ever seen him. Yet, when he kissed her, he was achingly gentle.

Luke seemed to believe that her ready response to his kiss would answer the questions that haunted her. Instead it raised *more* questions, more qualms.

"Do you understand now?" he asked, his voice a husky murmur, his eyes closed.

How Kate wished she did. She shook her head, bewildered and still uncertain.

Luke stroked her lips with his index finger. His most innocent touches brought her nerves to life with a prickling, wary excitement. Refusing to think about her own impulse, she held his hand to her mouth and brushed her lips across his callused fingertips.

"Oh, love," he moaned, and bent forward, caressing her mouth with his once more. "We've got to put an end to this madness before I go insane."

"How?" she gasped, as she braced her hands against his broad chest. He felt so good, hard muscle and warm flesh, and so strong, as if nothing could stand in his way once he determined a course. Not heaven. Not hell. And not anything in between.

"How?" He repeated her question, then chuckled, the sound rumbling from deep within his chest. "We'll have to do what you suggested."

"What I suggested?"

His mouth continued to tease hers with a series of small, nibbling kisses that seemed to pluck at her soul. "There's only one way to cure what's between us, Kate."

"One way," she echoed weakly.

"You'll have to marry me. There's no help for it and, considering how I feel right now, the sooner the better."

Kate felt as if he'd dumped a bucket of ice water over

her head. "Marry you," she shrieked, pushing him away so quickly that he nearly toppled backward. "Your answer to all this confusion is for us to get married?"

"Kate, don't be unreasonable. We're perfect for each other. You need me now more than at any time in your life and I'm here for you."

"Luke, please—"

"No." He stopped her with a look. "You're about to lose everything in life that you thought was secure—your father and your home. I don't have any intention of taking over Devin's role, but the way I figure it, I'd make you a decent husband."

"What about *love?*" Kate cried.

Luke sighed in frustration. "We've gone over that ten times. You already love me—"

"Like a brother."

"Princess, sisters don't kiss their brothers the way you just kissed me."

He apparently believed that was argument enough. Not knowing how else to respond, she shook her head. "I love Clay! You keep ignoring that or insisting I don't—but I do. I have for as long as I can remember. I can't marry you. I won't!"

"For heaven's sake, forget Clay."

"It's not so easy!" she shouted.

"It would be if you'd try a little harder," Luke muttered, obviously losing patience. "I'm asking you to marry me, Kate Logan, and a smart woman like you should know a good offer when she hears one."

So much for love. So much for romance. Luke wasn't even listening to her, and Kate doubted he'd understood a single thing she'd said. "This conversation isn't getting us anywhere."

"Kate—"

"I think you should leave."

"Kate," he said, firmly gripping her shoulders, "how long is it going to take you to realize that I love you and you love me?"

"Love you? How can you say that? Until a few weeks ago I was engaged to marry Clay Franklin!" Angrily she pushed away his hands and sprang to her feet.

"Yes. And all that time you were going to marry the wrong man."

Luke didn't seem to find that statement the least bit odd, as if women regularly chose to marry one man when they were really in love with another. Kate shook her head, releasing a harsh breath.

"It's the truth," he said calmly.

She glared at him. Reasoning with Luke was a waste of time. He repeated the same nonsensical statements over and over, as if his few words were explanation enough.

"I'm going to bed," she said, turning abruptly away from him. "You can do as you like."

A moment of stunned silence followed her words before he chuckled softly, seductively. "I'm sure you don't mean that the way it sounds."

As Kate expected, the small community buzzed with the news of her fiasco with Eric Wilson. Neighbor delighted in telling neighbor how Luke Rivers had swooped her into his arms and how the entire Friday-night crowd at the Red Bull had cheered as he'd carried her off the dance floor.

Kate needed every ounce of courage she possessed just to walk down Main Street. Her smile felt stiff and false and she was convinced she had the beginnings of an ulcer.

To worsen matters, all the townsfolk seemed to believe it was their place to offer her free advice.

"You stick with Luke Rivers. He's a far better man than that city slicker," the butcher told her Saturday afternoon.

Blushing heatedly, she ordered a pork roast and left as soon as she'd paid.

"I understand you and Luke Rivers caused quite a ruckus the other night at the steak house," the church secretary said Sunday morning after the service. "I heard about the romantic way Luke carried you outside."

Kate hadn't found being carried off the least bit romantic but she smiled kindly, made no comment and returned home without a word.

"What's this I hear about you and Luke Rivers?" The moment Kate entered her classroom Monday morning, Sally Daley appeared.

"Whatever you heard, I'm sure it was vastly exaggerated," Kate said hurriedly.

"That could be," Sally admitted with a delicate laugh. "You certainly know how to keep this town talking. First Clay's wedding reception, and now this. By the way, Clay and Rorie are back from Hawaii, and I heard they both have marvelous tans."

"That often happens in Hawaii," Kate said, sarcastically, barely holding on to her composure.

No sooner had Sally left than Linda showed up. "Is it true?" she demanded, her eyes as round as quarters.

Kate shrugged. "Probably."

"Oh, good grief, the whole thing about squelching rumors backfired, didn't it?"

Miserably Kate nodded. She was afraid she'd dissolve in a puddle of tears the next time someone mentioned Luke's name. "After what happened to me Friday night, well... I just don't think it's possible to feel any more humiliated."

"I thought you said you hadn't met Eric," Linda said, clearly puzzled.

"I hadn't when you and I talked. Eric and I ran into each other at the grocery not ten minutes after you mentioned his name."

Linda slumped against the side of Kate's desk. "I try for months to meet a new man and nothing happens. It doesn't make sense. A few minutes after you decide to look, one pops up in front of you like a bird in a turkey shoot!"

"Beginner's luck." Except that Friday night could in no way be classified as lucky.

"Oh, Kate, you've really done it now."

"I know," she whispered in a tone of defeat.

Kate's day ended much as it had begun, which meant that by four o'clock she had a headache to rival all headaches. After school, she stopped at the pharmacy and bought a bottle of double-strength aspirin and some antacid tablets.

When she left the pharmacy, she headed for the library, wondering if Rorie would be back at work so soon after her honeymoon. Her friend's smiling face greeted Kate the instant she walked through the doors.

"Kate, it's so good to see you."

"Hi, Rorie." Kate still felt a little awkward with Clay's bride. She suffered no regrets about bringing them together, though it had been the most painful decision of her life.

"Sally Daley's right," Kate said with a light laugh as she kissed Rorie's cheek. "You're so tanned. You look wonderful."

Rorie accepted the praise with a smile that shone from her dark brown eyes. "To be honest, I never thought I'd get Clay to laze away seven whole days on the beach, but he did. Oh, Kate, we had the most wonderful time."

"I'm glad." And she was. Rorie radiated happiness, and the glow of it warmed Kate's numb heart.

"I was just about to go on my coffee break. Have you got time to join me?" Rorie invited, glancing at her watch.

"I'd love to." Kate crossed her fingers. She hoped Rorie hadn't heard any of the gossip—no doubt colorfully embroidered by now—about what had happened Friday night. At the moment, Kate needed a friend, a good friend, someone she could trust to be objective.

While Rorie arranged to leave the library in the hands of a volunteer assistant, Kate walked over to Nellie's Café, across the street from the pharmacy. She'd already ordered their coffee when Rorie slipped into the red upholstered booth across from her.

"What's this I've been hearing all day about you and Luke? Honestly, Kate, you know how to live dangerously, don't you? And now Luke's buying the Circle L and your father's marrying Mrs. Murphy. We were only gone seven days, but I swear it felt like a year with everything Mary had to tell us once we got home."

Kate tried to maintain a stoic expression, although the acid in her stomach seemed to be burning a hole straight through her. There were no secrets in this town.

"To tell you the truth, Luke and I haven't been getting along very well lately," she admitted, keeping her eyes lowered so as not to meet her friend's questioning gaze.

Rorie took a tentative sip of coffee. "Do you want to talk about it?"

Kate nodded. She felt embarrassingly close to tears and paid careful attention to the silverware, repositioning the fork and the spoon several times.

"Luke was so good to me after you and Clay became engaged. He couldn't have been a better friend. Then… after the wedding I was feeling lost and alone. Luke had been dancing with me and I felt so…secure in his arms, and I'm afraid I suggested something foolish.... And now Luke keeps reminding me of it."

"That doesn't sound like Luke." Rorie frowned in puzzlement. "Nor does suggesting 'something foolish' sound like you."

"I had a glass of champagne on an empty stomach," Kate offered as an excuse.

"What about Luke?"

"I don't know, but I swear, he's become so unreasonable about everything, and he keeps saying the most ridiculous things."

"Give me an example," Rorie said.

Kate shrugged. "He claims I love him."

Her remark was followed by a short silence. "What *do* you feel for Luke?" Rorie asked.

"I care about him, but not in the way he assumes." Her finger idly circled the rim of the coffee cup while she composed her thoughts. "What irritates me most is that Luke discounts everything I felt for Clay, as if my love for him was nothing more than wasted emotion." Kate felt awkward explaining this to her ex-fiancé's wife, but Rorie was the one person who'd understand.

"And now that Clay's married to me," Rorie said, "Luke seems to think some lightbulb has snapped on inside your brain."

"Exactly."

"He thinks you should have no hesitation about throwing yourself into *his* loving arms?"

"Yes!" Rorie explained it far better than Kate had. "He keeps insisting I need him and that if I thought about it I'd realize I do love him. If it was only Luke I could probably deal with it, but everyone in town, including my own father, thinks I should marry him, too."

"That's when you agreed to have dinner with that new attorney. What's his name again?"

"Eric Wilson. Yes, that was exactly the reason I went out with him. Rorie, I tell you I was desperate. Every time I turned around, Luke was there wearing this smug, knowing look and casually announcing that we'd be married before Christmas. He makes the whole thing sound like it's a foregone conclusion and if I resist him I'd be…going against nature or something." She paused and waved her hand dramatically.

Rorie laughed. "Is he really doing that?"

Kate nodded grimly. "Actually there's more." She felt she had to tell Rorie everything. "To be fair, you should know I have no one to blame but myself. Luke may be doing all this talking about us getting married. But I was the one who…suggested it."

"How? When? Oh. The 'something foolish' you mentioned."

Shredding the paper napkin into tiny strips, Kate nodded again, flinching at the memory. "Honestly, Rorie, I didn't mean it. We were standing in the moonlight at your wedding dance and everything was so serene and beautiful. The words just slipped out of my mouth before I stopped to think what I was saying."

"The incident with the attorney didn't help."

Kate sighed. "And now that Dad's marrying Mrs. Murphy and Luke's bought the ranch, everything's getting worse."

"Luke can be a bit overpowering at times, can't he?"

Kate rolled her eyes in agreement. "But you know, what bothers me even more than Luke's cavalier attitude is the way everyone else seems to be siding with him."

"You mean about marrying Luke?"

"Yes." Kate gave another forlorn sigh. "Look at my

dad—he's the perfect example. And everyone in town seems to think that if I'm foolish enough to let another good man slip through my fingers, I'll end up thirty and a spinster for sure."

"That's crazy!"

Coming from San Francisco, Rorie couldn't understand how differently people in this small Oregon community viewed life, Kate mused. A woman already thirty years old and unmarried was likely to stay that way—at least in Nightingale. "You haven't lived here long enough to know how folks in this town think."

"Kate, you're over twenty-one. No one can force you to marry Luke. Remember that."

Kate rested her elbows on the table and cradled her coffee cup in both hands. "I feel like I'm caught in a current that's flowing too fast for me. I'm afraid to stand up for fear I'll lose my footing but I can't just allow it to carry me where it will, either."

"No, you can't," Rorie said and her mouth tightened.

"Luke—and practically everyone else—apparently sees me as a poor, spineless soul who can't possibly decide what's best for her own life."

"That's not true at all," Rorie declared. "And don't let anyone tell you you're weak! If that was the case, you would have married Clay yourself, instead of working so hard to make sure we found each other."

Kate dismissed that with a shake of her head. "I did the only thing I could."

"But not everyone would've been so unselfish. Clay and I owe our happiness to you." She clasped Kate's hands with her own. "I wish I knew how to help you. All I can tell you is to listen to your own heart."

"Oh, Rorie, I feel so much better talking to you." She knew her friend was right. She'd faltered for a step or two, but considering everything that had happened in the past little while, that was understandable. Luke might believe she needed him, but she didn't, not really. In the weeks to come, she'd have the opportunity to prove it.

"Before I forget," Rorie said, her voice eager, "Clay and I want to invite you over for dinner one night soon. As I said, we feel deeply indebted to you and want to thank you for what you did."

"Dinner," Kate repeated, suddenly dismayed. She'd need time to prepare herself before facing Clay again. Here she was reassuring herself in one breath and then doubting herself in the next.

"Would next Tuesday be all right?" Rorie pressed.

"But you've hardly had time to settle in with Clay," Kate said, turning her attention back to her friend. "How about giving it another week or two?"

"Are you worried that I'm going to serve my special seafood fettuccine?" Rorie asked with a laugh. When she'd first been stranded in Nightingale, Rorie had cooked it for Clay and his younger brother, Skip, one night. But, unfortunately, because both men did strenuous physical jobs, they were far more interested in a hearty meat-and-potatoes meal at the end of the day. Neither of them had considered seafood in a cream sauce with fancy noodles a very satisfactory repast, though Clay had politely tried to hide his disappointment. Skip hadn't.

Kate smiled at the memory of that night and slowly shook her head. "You serve whatever you want. I'm much easier to please than Skip."

"Actually Mary will probably do the cooking. She's been the Franklins' housekeeper for so many years that I don't dare invade her kitchen just yet. After the fettuccine disaster, she doesn't trust me around her stove any more than Skip does."

They both laughed, and to Kate, it felt good to forget her troubles, even for a few minutes.

"I should get back to the library," Rorie said reluctantly.

"I need to head home myself." Kate left some change on the table and slid out of the booth. Impulsively she hugged Rorie, grateful for the time they'd spent together and for the other woman's support. "I'm glad you're my friend," she whispered, feeling a little self-conscious.

"I am, too," Rorie said, and hugged her back.

By the time Kate pulled into the Circle L driveway, she was filled with bold resolution. She hurried inside just long enough to set a roast in the oven and change her clothes. Then she went into the yard, intent on confronting Luke. She wanted to get this over with—as soon as possible.

As luck would have it, Luke wasn't in any of the places she normally found him. Bill Schmidt, a longtime ranch hand, was working in the barn by himself.

"Bill, have you seen Luke?" she asked.

Bill straightened and set his hat farther back on his head. "Can't say I have. At least, not in the past couple of hours. Said he was going out to look for strays. I imagine he'll be back pretty soon now."

"I see." Kate gnawed her lower lip, wondering what she should do. Without pausing to question the wisdom of her decision, she reached for a bridle.

"Bill, would you get Nonstop for me?" Nonstop was the fastest horse in their stable. Kate was in the mood for some exercise; if she didn't find Luke, that was fine, too. She could use a good hard ride to vent some of the frustration that had been binding her all week.

"Sure, Miz Logan." Bill left his task and headed for the corral, returning a few minutes later with Nonstop. "Luke seemed to be in the mood to do some riding himself this afternoon," he commented as he helped her cinch the saddle. "Must be the weather."

"Must be," Kate agreed.

Minutes later Nonstop was cantering out of the yard. Kate hadn't ridden in weeks and she was surprised to realize just how long it had been. When she was engaged to Clay, she'd spent many a summer afternoon in the saddle, many a Saturday or Sunday riding by his side. That had ended about the same time as their wedding plans. She felt a stinging sense of loss but managed to dispel it with the memory of her talk with Rorie.

Bill pointed out the general direction Luke had taken, and Kate followed that course at a gallop. She found it wonderfully invigorating to be in the saddle again.

The afternoon remained mild, but the breeze carried the distinctive scent of autumn. These past few days had been Indian summer, with rare clement temperatures. Within the hour, the sun would set, bathing the rolling green hills in a golden haze.

"Kate." Her name floated on a whisper of wind.

Pulling back on the reins, Kate halted the mare and turned in the saddle to discover Luke trotting toward her. She raised her hand and waved. Much of her irritation had dissipated, replaced by a newly awakened sense of well-being. No longer did Kate feel her life was roaring out of control; she was in charge, and it exhilarated her.

Luke dismounted as soon as he reached her. "Is everything all right?"

"Of course," she said with a slight laugh. "I hope I didn't frighten you."

"No. I rode into the yard not more than fifteen minutes after you left, according to Bill. I was afraid I wasn't going to catch you. You were riding like a demon."

"I...had some thinking to do."

"Bill said you were looking for me."

"Yes," she agreed. "I wanted to talk to you." There was no better time than the present. And no better place. They were at the top of a grassy hill that looked out over a lush green valley. Several head of cattle dotted the pasture spread out below them, grazing in the last of the afternoon sun.

Luke lifted his hands to her waist, helping her out of the saddle. His eyes held hers as he lowered her to the ground. Once again, she was aware that his touch had a curious effect on her, but she stringently ignored it.

Still, Kate's knees felt a little shaky and she was more breathless than she should've been after her ride. She watched Luke loop the reins over the horses' heads to dangle on the ground. Both Nonstop and Silver Shadow, Luke's gelding, were content to graze leisurely.

"It's nice out this afternoon, isn't it?" she said, then sank down on the grass and drew up her legs.

Luke sat down beside her, gazing out over the valley. "It's a rare day. I don't expect many more like it."

"Rorie and Clay are back from Hawaii."

Luke had removed his leather work gloves to brush a stray curl from her temple, then stopped abruptly and withdrew his hand. "I take it you saw Rorie?"

She nodded, adding, "We had coffee at Nellie's."

"You're not upset?"

"Not at all."

"I thought you looked more at peace with yourself." He leaned back and rested his weight on the palms of his hands. His long legs were stretched in front of him, crossed at the ankles. "Did you finally recognize that you never did love Clay? That you're in love with me?"

"No," she said vehemently, amazed he could anger her so quickly.

Luke turned away. "I thought… I'd hoped you were willing to discuss a wedding date," he said stiffly.

"Oh, Luke," she whispered and closed her eyes. He was so worried for her, so concerned, and she didn't know how to reassure him.

"Luke," she said softly, "we've been having the same discussion all week, and it's got to come to an end." Luke faced her and their eyes met with an impact that shocked her. "Luke, I think you're a wonderful man—I have for years and years," she continued. "But I don't love you, at least not the way you deserve to be loved."

Luke's eyebrows soared, then his brow furrowed. He seemed about to argue, but Kate stopped him before he had the chance.

"I refuse to be coerced into a wedding simply because *you* feel it's the best thing for me—because you feel I need looking after. Frankly, I don't believe marriage is a good idea for us—at least not to each other."

"Kate, love—"

Lowering her lashes in an effort to disguise her frustration, Kate reminded him for what seemed the thousandth time, "I am not your 'love.'"

His eyes became sharper, more intent. "Then explain," he said slowly, "why it feels so right when I hold you? How do you answer that?"

She avoided his gaze, her eyes focusing a fraction below his. "I can't explain it any more than I can deny it." She'd admit that much. "I do enjoy it when you kiss me, though I don't know why, especially since I'm still in love with Clay. My guess is that we've lived all these years in close proximity and we're such good friends that it was a natural, comforting, thing to do. But I don't think it should continue."

His nostrils flared briefly, and she could tell he was angered by her words.

"I'm begging you, Luke, pleading with you, if you—"

"Kate, would you listen to me for once?"

"No," she said, holding her ground. "I'm asking for only one thing from you. I want you to drop this incessant pressure to marry you."

"But—"

"Give me your word, Luke."

His entire expression changed, and just looking at him told Kate how difficult he was finding this. "All right," he said heavily. "You have my word. I won't mention it again."

Kate sighed shakily and all her muscles seemed to go limp. "Thank you," she whispered. "That's all I want."

Luke lunged to his feet and reached for Silver Shadow's reins. He eased himself back into the saddle, then paused to look down at her, his face dark and brooding. "What about what *I* want, Kate? Did you stop to consider that?"

Six

Kate felt good. The lethargy and depression she'd been feeling since Clay's wedding had started to dissipate. She'd completely adjusted to the idea of her father's impending marriage. And even the sale of the Circle L—to Luke of all people—no longer seemed so devastating. Clearing the air between them had helped, too.

"Evening, Nellie," Kate called as she entered the small, homey café. She'd arrived home from school to discover a message from her father suggesting she meet him for dinner at Nellie's at six sharp.

"Howdy, Kate," Nellie called from behind the counter.

Kate assumed her father would be bringing Dorothea so they could discuss last-minute plans for their wedding, which was scheduled for Friday evening at the parsonage. Minnie Wilkins, Pastor Wilkins's wife, and Dorothea were close friends. Kate would be standing up for Dorothea and Luke for her father in the small, private ceremony.

Carrying a water glass in one hand, a coffeepot in the other and a menu tucked under her arm, Nellie followed Kate to the booth. "I'm expecting my dad and Dorothea Murphy to join me," Kate explained.

"Sure thing," Nellie said. "The special tonight is Yankee

pot roast, and when your daddy gets here, you tell him I pulled a rhubarb pie out of the oven no more than fifteen minutes ago."

"I'll tell him."

"Nellie, I could use a refill on my coffee," Fred Garner said. Sitting at the table closest to the window, he nodded politely in Kate's direction. "Good to see you, Kate."

"You, too, Fred." She smiled at the owner of Garner Feed and Supply and the two ranchers who were dining with him. Glancing at her watch, Kate realized her father was a few minutes late, which wasn't like him.

To pass the time she began reading the menu; she was halfway through when the door opened. Smiling automatically, she looked up and saw Luke striding toward her. He slid into the booth across from her.

"Where's your dad?"

"I don't know. He asked me to meet him here for dinner."

"I got the same message."

"I think it has something to do with the wedding."

"No," Luke muttered, frowning. "I've got some bank forms he needs to sign."

Nellie brought another glass of water, then poured coffee for both of them.

"Evening, Nellie."

"Luke Rivers, I don't see near enough of you," the older woman said coyly, giving him a bold wink as she sauntered away with a swish of her hips.

Astonished that Nellie would flirt so openly with Luke, Kate took a sip of her coffee and nearly scalded her tongue. Why, Nellie had a good fifteen years on Luke!

"Does she do that often?" Kate asked, in a disapproving whisper.

"You jealous?"

"Of course not. It's just that I've never known Nellie to flirt quite so blatantly."

"She's allowed." Luke gazed down at his menu and to all appearances, was soon deep in concentration.

Kate managed to squelch the argument before it reached her lips. There wasn't a single, solitary reason for her to care if a thousand women threw themselves at Luke Rivers. She had no claim on him, and wanted none.

The restaurant telephone pealed, but with four plates balanced on her arms, Nellie let it ring until someone in the kitchen answered it.

A minute later, she approached their table. "That was Devin on the phone. He says he's going to be late and you two should go ahead and order." She pulled a notepad from the pocket of her pink uniform. "Eat hearty since it's on his tab," she said, chuckling amiably.

"The roast-beef sandwich sounds good to me," Kate said. "With a small salad."

"I'll have chicken-fried steak, just so I can taste those biscuits of yours," Luke told the café owner, handing her the menu. "I'll start with a salad, though."

"I got rhubarb pie hot from the oven."

"Give me a piece of that, too," Luke said, grinning up at Nellie.

"Kate?"

"Sure," she said, forcing a smile. "Why not?"

Once Nellie had left, an awkwardness fell between Kate and Luke. To Kate it felt as though they'd become strangers, standing on uncertain ground.

Luke ventured into conversation first. "So how's school?"

"Fine."

"That's good."

She laughed nervously. "I've started washing down

cupboards at the house, clearing out things. I've got two piles. What Dad's going to take with him and what I'll need when I move."

Instead of pleasing Luke, her announcement had the opposite effect. "You're welcome to live on the ranch as long as you want," he said, his dark eyes narrowing. "There's no need to move."

"I know that, but the Circle L belongs to you—or it will soon."

"It's your home."

"It won't be much longer," she felt obliged to remind him. "I'm hoping to find a place in town. In fact, I'm looking forward to the move. You know what the roads are like in the winter. I should have done this years ago."

"You wouldn't have to move if you weren't so damn stubborn," Luke muttered from between clenched teeth. "I swear, Kate, you exasperate me. The last thing I want to do is take your home away from you."

"I know that." She hadn't considered relocating to town earlier for a number of reasons, foremost being that her father had needed her. But he didn't anymore, and it was time to exhibit some independence.

Nellie brought their tossed green dinner salads, lingering at the table to flirt with Luke again. He waited until she'd left before he leaned forward, speaking to Kate in a low, urgent voice. His eyes were filled with regret. "Kate, please stay on at the ranch. Let me at least do this much for you."

She thanked him for his concern with a warm smile, but couldn't resist adding, "People will talk." After all, Luke had pointed that very fact out to her when she'd made her foolish proposal. The night of Clay's wedding...

"Let them talk."

"I'm a schoolteacher, remember?" she whispered. She

felt genuinely grateful for his friendship and wanted to assure him that all this worry on her behalf was unnecessary, that she was fully capable of living on her own.

Their dinner arrived before they'd even finished the salads. Another silence fell over them as they ate. Several possible subjects of conversation fluttered in and out of Kate's mind as the meal progressed. Her fear was that Luke would divert the discussion back to the ranch no matter what she said, so she remained silent.

A sudden commotion came from the pavement outside the café.

"It's Harry Ackerman again," Fred Garner shouted to Nellie, who was busy in the kitchen. "You want me to call the sheriff?"

"No, let him sing," Nellie shouted back. "He isn't hurting anyone."

Harry Ackerman was the town drunk. Back in his and Nellie's high-school days, they'd dated seriously, but then Harry went into the military and returned to Nightingale more interested in the bottle than a wife and family. Within six months, Nellie had married a mechanic who'd drifted into town. Problem was, when he drifted out again, he didn't take Nellie or their two children with him. But Nellie hadn't seemed to miss him much, and had supported her family by opening the café, which did a healthy business from the first.

Fifteen years had passed, and Harry was still courting Nellie. Every time he came into town, he took it upon himself to sing love songs from the pavement outside the café. He seemed to believe that would be enough of an inducement for her to forget the past and finally marry him.

"Actually his singing voice isn't that bad," Kate murmured to Luke.

Luke chuckled. "I've heard better."

Fred Garner stood up and strolled toward the cash register. He nodded in Luke's direction and touched the rim of his hat in greeting. "I've been hearing things about the two of you," Fred said, grinning broadly.

Kate concentrated on her sandwich, refusing to look up from her plate.

Luke made some vague reply that had to do with the ranch and not Kate, and she was grateful.

"Be seeing you," Fred said as he headed toward the door. As he opened it, Harry's latest love ballad, sung off-key, could be heard with ear-piercing clarity.

Fred left and soon Harry Ackerman came inside. He stared longingly at Nellie, placed his hand over his heart and started singing again at the top of his lungs.

"You get out of my restaurant," Nellie cried, reaching for the broom. "I don't want you in here bothering my customers." She wielded the broom like a shotgun, and before she could say another word Harry stumbled outside. He pressed his forlorn face to the glass, content to wait until his one true love returned to his waiting arms.

"Sorry, folks," Nellie muttered, replacing the broom.

"No problem," Luke answered, and she threw him a grateful smile, then hurried over to refill their coffee cups.

The disturbance died down when Harry wandered down the street to find a more appreciative audience. Luke sighed as he stirred his coffee. "I don't think your father has any intention of showing up tonight," he began. "In fact—"

"That's ridiculous," Kate said, cutting him off. "Dad wouldn't do that."

"He's trying to tell you something," Luke insisted.

"I can't imagine what." She could, but decided to pretend otherwise.

For a long moment, Luke said nothing. "You're smart enough to figure it out, Kate." He finished off the last bite of his pie and pushed the plate aside. "I've got some things to attend to, so I'd best be leaving." The corners of his eyes crinkled with amusement as he glanced out the café window. "Who knows, you might be singing me love songs in a couple of years if you don't come to your senses soon."

Kate ignored the comment. "My father will be here any minute."

"No, Princess," Luke said, and the smile left his eyes. He leaned across the table to brush his hand gently against her cheek. "But his message is coming across loud and clear."

Kate stayed at the café another half-hour after Luke had gone and it took her that long to admit he was right. Her father *had* been giving her a message, this one no more subtle than the rest. Expelling her breath in disgust, Kate dredged up a smile and said goodbye to Nellie.

Kate didn't see Luke again until Friday evening, when they met at the Wilkins home for her father's wedding. Kate arrived with Devin, and Luke followed a few minutes later. Kate was busy arranging freshly baked cookies on a tray for the small reception to be held after the ceremony, when Luke walked into the dining room. Dorothea was with Minnie Wilkins in the back bedroom, and her father and Pastor Wilkins were talking in the office.

"Hello, Kate," Luke said from behind her.

"Hi," she responded, turning to give him a polite smile. Her breath caught in her throat at the elegant yet virile sight he made. He was dressed in a dark, three-piece suit that did nothing to disguise his strong, well-formed body, and his light blue silk tie enhanced the richness of his tan. Kate suspected that Luke was basking in the wonder she was unable to conceal, and yet she couldn't stop staring at him. Her heart skipped a beat, then leaped wildly as his penetrating brown eyes looked straight into hers. She felt the tears well up, knowing that only Luke truly understood how difficult this evening was for her.

Many of her emotions tonight were identical to the ones she'd experienced at Clay and Rorie's wedding. All day, she'd worried her stomach into a knot of apprehension. The acceptance and strength of purpose she'd so recently been feeling had fled. Tonight, she was reminded again that everything she loved, everything familiar, had been taken from her life. First the man she'd planned to marry, now her father, and soon, so very soon, her childhood home. It was too much change, too quickly.

Just as she had at Clay's wedding, Kate forced herself to show pleasure, to behave appropriately. She *was* happy for her father and Dorothea—just as she'd been for Clay and Rorie. But why did everyone else's happiness need to cost Kate so much?

Luke must have read the distress in her eyes, because he hurried to her side. "Everything's going to be all right," he told her quietly. He'd said the same thing at Clay's wedding.

"Of course it is," she agreed, braving a smile. She turned back to the flowers, although her fingers were trembling. "I couldn't have chosen a better wife for Dad myself. Dorothea's wonderful."

Luke's hands rested on her shoulders and began to caress them gently. "So are you, Princess."

It demanded every ounce of fortitude Kate possessed not to whirl around and bury her face in Luke's chest, to absorb his strength. But this was exactly how she'd lost control before; she had to remember that.

A sound came from behind them, and Luke released her with a reluctance that echoed her own. She needed Luke now, just as she'd needed him a few weeks before. But this time, she was determined to be stronger.

The ceremony itself was brief. Kate felt almost wooden as she stood next to the woman her father had chosen to replace her mother. Memories of the lovely, soft-spoken Nora, and of their happy, close-knit family, almost overwhelmed Kate. Twice she felt tears threaten, but managed to hold them back. Both times she found Luke's eyes on her, his gaze warm with empathy.

When Pastor Wilkins closed his Bible and announced that Devin and Dorothea were now husband and wife, Devin took his bride in his arms and kissed her. Minnie Wilkins dabbed at her eyes with a lace hankie.

"You look so lovely," the woman murmured, hugging her friend.

Soon they were all hugging each other. When Kate's arms slipped around Luke it felt…comfortable. In fact, it felt *too* comfortable, too familiar, and that frightened her. She stiffened and let her arms drop. Luke would have none of that, however. Locking his hands on her upper arms, he drew her back to him.

"What I wouldn't give for a full moon and some champagne," he whispered in her ear.

Kate could have done without his teasing, but she refused to satisfy him with a response.

The small reception began immediately afterward, and Kate was busy for the next hour, dishing up pieces of wedding cake, passing trays of sugar cookies and pouring coffee.

Her father came to see her in the kitchen, his eyes bright with happiness. "You're going to be fine, aren't you, Princess?"

"You know I am," she said, flashing him a brilliant smile.

"Dorothea and I will be leaving soon." He placed his arm around her shoulders and hugged her. "Don't forget I love you. You'll always be my little girl."

"You'll always be my hero."

Devin chuckled. "I think Luke would like to fill that position and I'd be pleased if he did. He's a good man, sweetheart. You could do a lot worse."

"Dad," she groaned, closing her eyes. "Luke is wonderful, and I understand your concern. You'd like all the loose ends neatly tied up before you leave for your honeymoon, but I'm just not ready for a commitment."

"You'd make a lovely country bride, Princess. I want you to be happy, that's all."

"I will be," she said, standing on the tips of her toes to kiss his cheek.

By the time Devin and Dorothea were ready to leave, more than twenty close friends had gathered at the parsonage. They crowded onto the porch to send the newly-weds off with a flourish of kisses and enthusiastic waves. Almost everyone returned to the warmth of the house but Kate lingered, not wanting to go back inside when tears were blurring her eyes.

Luke joined her, standing silently at her side until she'd composed herself.

"Your father asked me to see you home."

Kate nodded and swallowed a near-hysterical laugh. Despite their conversation Devin was still attempting to throw her together with Luke.

"You mean you aren't going to argue with me?" Luke asked with exaggerated surprise.

"Would it do any good?"

"No," he said and chuckled lightly. Then, suddenly, his strong arms encircled her stiff body. "It's been a long time since you let me kiss you," he said, his warm breath moving closer and closer to her mouth.

Kate stared at his chest, refusing to raise her eyes to his. Gathering her resolve, she snapped her head up to demand he release her. But Luke smothered her words with his mouth. Her hands tightened into fists as soon as the initial shock had subsided and she fully intended to push him away. But once his mouth had settled over hers, he gentled the kiss, and her resolve all but disappeared.

Again and again his mouth sought hers. Luke's sweet, soft kisses seemed to erase all the pain from her heart. Only a moment before, she'd been intent on escaping. Now she clung to him, tilting her face toward him, seeking more. He deepened his kiss, sending jolts of excitement through her.

When he stopped abruptly, Kate moaned her dissatisfaction.

"Kate…" he warned.

"Hmm… Luke, don't stop."

"I'm afraid we've attracted an audience," he returned mildly.

Sucking in her breath, Kate dropped her arms and whirled around so fast she would have stumbled if Luke's arms hadn't caught her. Eyes wide, she stared into the faces of the twenty or so guests who'd stepped outside, preparing to leave.

"I thought Taylor Morgenroth should play the Indian chief," Kate was saying to Linda when Sally Daley walked into the faculty lounge Monday afternoon. The two were discussing the final plans for their Thanksgiving play.

"Taylor's the perfect choice," Linda agreed.

"I see you girls are busy," Sally commented. "This

play is such an ambitious project. You two are to be commended."

"Thanks." Linda answered for them both, trying to ignore the other woman as much as possible.

"Wasn't that Rorie Franklin I saw you with the other day, Kate, dear?"

"Yes. We had coffee at Nellie's." She resumed her discussion with Linda, not wanting to be rude to Sally, but at the same time, hoping to dissuade her from further conversation.

But Sally refused to be thwarted. She settled in the chair opposite Kate and said in confidential tones, "You're completely over Clay Franklin now, aren't you, dear?"

Kate shared an exasperated look with Linda and nearly laughed out loud when the third-grade teacher playfully rolled her eyes toward the ceiling. To hear Sally talk, anybody would think Kate had recently recovered from a bad case of the flu.

"Sally!" Kate exclaimed when she realized how avidly the other woman was waiting for her reply. "How am I supposed to answer that?" She covered her heart dramatically with one hand and assumed a look meant to portray misery and anguish. "Do you want me to tell you that my pride's been shattered and I'll never love again?"

Sally shook her head. "I wouldn't believe it, anyway."

"Then why ask?" Linda prompted.

"Well, because we all love Kate. She's such a dear, and she's been through so much lately."

"Thank you," Kate said graciously, then returned her attention to the Thanksgiving project.

"Most of the fuss about you and Eric Wilson and Luke Rivers has died down now," Sally assured her, as if this should lessen the embarrassment of that Friday night.

"I take it you haven't talked to Eric lately?" Linda asked,

surprising Kate with her sudden interest. There'd been plenty of opportunity to inquire about him, but Linda hadn't done so until now.

"Talked to him?" Kate echoed with a short, derisive laugh. "I don't even shop at the Safeway store for fear of running into him again."

"I don't think you need to worry," Sally said blandly. "From what I hear, he's avoiding you, too."

Linda snickered softly. "No doubt. I'm sure Luke Rivers put quite a scare into him."

"How do you mean?" Kate demanded, already angry with Luke.

"You don't know?" Sally asked, her eyes sparkling with excitement.

"Know what?" Kate swung her gaze first to Linda, then to Sally. "Did Luke threaten him?" If he had, he was going to hear about it from her.

"I haven't got the foggiest idea what Sally's talking about," Linda said quickly.

"I didn't hear anything specific," Sally confirmed sheepishly. "I thought maybe you..." The older teacher's expression suggested that she hoped Kate would fill in the succulent details herself. "My dear, surely you understand that everyone in town is speculating about you and Luke," she continued.

"Rumors have been floating around since Clay's wedding," Linda added.

"But Sally just finished telling me those were dying down," Kate snapped, irritated with the entire discussion.

"The rumors aren't about you and that Wilson fellow," Sally rushed to explain. "As far as your one date with him is concerned, it's history. He's too smart to cross Luke."

"I'm sure he is," Kate said, anxious to quell the woman's gossip. "Aren't we about finished here, Linda?" she asked pointedly.

"Ah...yes."

"Now folks are talking about seeing you and Luke together at Nellie's last week, just before your father's wedding, and there've been a few rumors flying about the two of you at Pastor Wilkins's, too."

As fast as her hands would co-operate, Kate gathered up their materials. Sally seemed to accept that she was about to lose her audience. If she'd come to pump Kate for information she'd just have to realize Kate wasn't talking. Standing, Sally gave a deep sigh, clearly disappointed. She collected her purse and headed out the door, pausing to look back. "Frankly, I think Fred Garner's carrying this thing about you and Luke a bit too far. I consider what he's doing in poor taste." With that, she left the room.

"Fred Garner?" Linda echoed after a stunned second. "What's that old coot doing now?"

"Fred Garner owns the feed store," Kate said in a puzzled voice.

"Yes, but what's he got to do with anything?"

"Beats me." Still, Kate couldn't help wondering. Fred had seen them at the restaurant, and he'd been at the reception for her father and Dorothea. Although she hadn't seen him on the porch when a number of guests had found her in Luke's arms, she had very little doubt that he was there.

When Kate drove home an hour later, Luke was working in the yard. She climbed out of the car, took two steps toward him and halted abruptly. The lump in her throat was so large she could hardly swallow, let alone speak.

The trembling had started the minute she left Garner Feed and Supply. She'd dropped in at the store following Sally's remark, and from then on everything had grown progressively worse. The way she felt right now, she could slam her bag over Luke's head, or do something equally violent, and feel completely justified.

"Kate?" he asked, looking concerned. "What's wrong?"

She knew her emotions were written on her face. She'd never been more scandalized in her life, which was saying a great deal, considering the fiasco with Eric Wilson.

In fact, the blow her dignity had been dealt by Luke Rivers during that incident paled in comparison with this latest outrage. There was only one thing for her to do. She'd have to move away from Nightingale.

"This is all your doing, isn't it?" she demanded in a shaking voice. She held her head high, although it was a struggle to preserve her composure. Her pride was all she had left, and that was crumbling at her feet.

Luke advanced several steps toward her. "What are you talking about?"

She ground her fist into her hip. "I just got back from the feed store. Does that tell you anything?"

"No."

"I'll bet."

He frowned. "Kate, I swear to you, I don't know what you're talking about."

She made a doubting noise that came out sounding and feeling like a sob. Yet he appeared so bewildered. She didn't know how any man could cause her such life-shattering embarrassment and maintain that look of faithful integrity.

The tears wouldn't be restrained any longer, and they fell from her eyes, running down her face. They felt cool against her flushed cheeks.

"Kate? What's wrong?"

Kate turned and walked rapidly away from Luke rather than allow him to witness her loss of control. She hurried into the house and slumped in a chair, hiding her face in her hands as she battled the terrible urge to weep hysterically. The painful sensation in the pit of her stomach grew more intense every time she took a breath.

The door opened and she said, "Go away."

"Kate?"

"Haven't...you...done...enough?" Each word rolled from her tongue on the end of a hiccuping sob.

He knelt in front of her and wrapped his arms around her, holding her close, but she pushed him away, refusing the comfort he offered.

Kate's shoulders still heaved. With an exasperated sigh, Luke got up. He stood back on his boot heels and buried his hands in his pockets. "All right, tell me about it."

"Pastor...Wilkins...bet...twenty...dollars...on...December," she told him between sobs. Her fingers curled into fists. "Even...Clay...put in a...wager."

Seeing his name on that huge blackboard had hurt more than anything.

"Kate, I swear to you I don't know what you're talking about."

Furiously she wiped the tears from her face and tried to marshal her self-control enough to speak clearly. "The... feed store," she managed.

"What about the feed store?"

"They're taking bets—it's a regular lottery," she cried, all the more furious with him because he was making her spell out this latest humiliation.

"Bets on what?" Luke's frown was growing darker, and Kate could tell that he was dangerously close to losing his patience.

"On *us!*" she wailed, as if that much, at least, should be obvious.

"For what?"

"When we're going to be married!" she shouted. "What

else? Half the town's gambling on the date of our wedding."

Luke moaned, closing his eyes, as if he couldn't quite believe what she was telling him.

"You honestly didn't know?"

"Of course not." He was beginning to look perturbed as only Luke could. His dark eyes took on a cold glare that would intimidate the strongest of men. "How'd you find out?"

"Sally Daley said something about it after school, and then in the school car park one of the mothers told me March is a lovely time of year for a wedding. March sixteenth, she said. Then…then I made the mistake of stopping in at the feed store on my way home to…to check out what was going on."

Luke nodded, but Kate had the impression he was only half listening to her.

"As far as I'm concerned, there's just one thing for me to do," she said, gaining strength from her decision. "I'll offer my resignation to the school board tomorrow morning and leave the district this weekend."

Luke sent her a quick, angry look. "That won't be necessary. I'll take care of this my own way."

Seven

At one time Kate spent as many hours at Elk Run, the Franklin stud farm, as she did at the Circle L. But when she arrived Tuesday night for dinner, Elk Run no longer felt familiar. It seemed like years instead of weeks since her last visit. Kate's enthusiasm for this dinner with Clay and Rorie had never been high, but now she felt decidedly uncomfortable.

"Kate, welcome." Rorie flew out the door the minute Kate pulled into the driveway. She stepped from the car into Rorie's hug.

Clay Franklin followed his wife and briefly held Kate close, smiling down on her the same way he always had from the time she was thirteen. Back then, she'd worshipped him from afar, and she'd worshipped him more with each passing year. Kate paused, waiting for the surge of regret and pain she'd been expecting; to her astonishment, it didn't come.

"We're so glad you could make it," Rorie said as she opened the door.

Recognising Kate, Clay's old dog, Blue, ambled over for his usual pat. Kate was more than happy to comply and bent down to scratch his ears.

Mary, the Franklins' housekeeper, bustled about the kitchen, dressed in her bib apron, hair twisted into thick braids and piled on top of her head. Kate could scarcely remember a time she hadn't seen Mary in an apron. The scent of freshly baked pie permeated the room, mingling with the hearty aroma of roast beef and simmering vegetables.

"I hope that's one of your award-winning pies I'm smelling, Mary," Kate said. "I've had my heart set on a piece all day."

"Oh, get away with you," Mary returned gruffly, but the happy light that sparked from her eyes told Kate how gratified the housekeeper was by her request.

"When are you going to give me your recipe?" Kate asked, although she didn't know whom she'd be baking pies for now that her father had remarried. "No one can bake an apple pie like yours."

"Mary won't share her secret with me, either," Rorie said, giving a soft laugh. "I don't think she's willing to trust a city slicker yet."

"I never wrote down any recipe," Mary grumbled, casting Rorie a stern look. "I just make my pies the same way my mother did."

"I wish I could bake like Mary does," Rorie said, slipping her arm around her husband's waist. They exchanged a meaningful glance. Clay's smile showed he couldn't care less whether or not she could bake a pie.

Once more Kate braced herself for the pain of seeing them together, gentle and loving, but to her surprise she didn't feel so much as a pinprick of distress. She relaxed, wondering at what was happening—or rather, wasn't—and why.

"Where's Skip?" she asked suddenly. She missed Clay's

younger brother almost as much as she did Clay. They'd been friends for years.

"Football practice," Clay explained. "He's quarterback this year and proud as a peacock. He'll be home later."

"About the time Mary serves her pie," Rorie whispered to Kate. Skip's appetite for sweets was legendary.

The small party headed into the homey living room. The piano stood against one wall, and Kate noted the music on the stand. She'd always been the one who'd played that piano, but it was Rorie who played for Clay now. There'd been a time when Kate and Clay had sung together, their voices blending in a melodious harmony. But Clay sang with Rorie now.

Kate expected the knowledge to claw at her insides, and she did feel a small twinge of regret—but that was all.

"Skip's hoping to catch you later," Rorie said.

"As I recall, you played quarterback your senior year of high school," Kate reminded Clay as she claimed the overstuffed chair. "That was the first year the Nightingale team made it to the state finals."

Rorie smiled delightedly at her husband. "You never told me that."

"There wasn't much to tell," Clay said with a short laugh. "We were eliminated in the first round." He sat beside Rorie and draped his arm around her shoulders, as if he had to keep touching her to believe she was here at his side.

Mary carried in a tray of wineglasses and an unopened bottle of a locally produced sparkling white. "I take it Devin and Dorothea arrived safely in California?" she asked as she uncorked the wine.

"Yes, Dad phoned when they arrived at Dorothea's daughter's house."

"We didn't get a chance to say more than a few words to

you at the reception," Rorie apologized. "You were so busy pouring coffee, there wasn't much opportunity to chat."

"I know. It was good of you and Clay to come."

"We wouldn't have missed it for the world," Clay said.

"I wanted to tell you how nice your father and Dorothea looked together. And for that matter, you and Luke, too," Rorie added.

"Thank you," Kate said simply, wondering if her friends had heard about the incident on the Wilkins's front porch. It still embarrassed Kate to think of all her father's friends seeing her and Luke together…like that. "So much has happened in the last month," she said, trying to change the subject before either of them mentioned her father's wedding again. "Who'd ever have believed Luke would end up buying the ranch?"

"It must've come as a shock to you," Clay said evenly, "but I've been after him for years to get his own spread."

"What are your plans now that the Circle L's been sold?" Rorie asked.

"I'm looking for a place in town," she said, and sipped her wine.

"From what Luke told me, he'd rather you continued living on the ranch," Clay said, studying her as though he knew something she didn't.

"I know," Kate admitted. "It's very generous of him, but I'd prefer to get an apartment of my own."

"Good luck finding one," Clay murmured.

They were both aware that a decent apartment might be difficult to locate. Nightingale was a place of family dwellings, not singles' apartments.

They chatted easily as they waited for Mary to announce dinner. Every now and then, Kate saw Clay glance over at Rorie. His look was tender and warm and filled with the deep joy that came from loving completely and knowing that love was returned.

When Rorie Campbell had arrived in their midst, Kate had seen almost immediately that Clay was attracted to her. That was understandable, after all, since Rorie was a beautiful woman. In the beginning, Kate had done everything she could to combat her jealousy. Rorie had been due to leave Elk Run in a few days and once she was gone, Kate had told herself, their lives and feelings would return to normal.

Eventually Rorie did go back to San Francisco, but Clay couldn't forget her. Kate had done her best to pretend; she'd even talked Clay into setting a wedding date, pressuring him in a not-so-subtle way to marry her quickly. They'd been talking about it for years, and Kate wanted the deed done before Rorie realized what she'd given up. Their getting married seemed the perfect solution. Then, if Rorie did come to Nightingale again, it would be too late.

Kate's strategy had been a desperate one, planned by a desperate woman. And as often happened in such cases, her scheme backfired.

Kate didn't think she'd ever forget the day Clay told her he wanted to break their engagement. The words had scarred her soul like lye on tender skin. He'd come to the ranch, and from the minute he'd asked to talk to her, Kate had known something was terribly wrong. She'd tried to ease the tension with talk of bridesmaids' dresses and floral arrangements, but Clay had stopped her.

He'd sat with his hands folded, his eyes regarding her sadly. "I wouldn't hurt you for anything," he'd said, and his words rang with truth and regret.

"Clay, you could never hurt me." Which was a lie, because he was already inflicting pain.

He'd told her then, simply and directly, that it would be

wrong for them to marry. Not once did he mention Rorie's name. He didn't need to. Kate had known for weeks that Clay was in love with the other woman. But she'd chosen instead to involve her heart in a painful game of pretend.

Instead of accepting the truth when Clay had come to her with his decision, she'd insisted he was mistaken, that they *were* right for each other and had been all their lives. The memory humbled her now. She'd tried to convince him that all they needed was a little more time. By the next week, or maybe the next month, Clay would understand that he'd made a mistake and he'd want to go through with the wedding. She could afford to be patient because she loved him so much. Kindly, and as gently as possible, Clay had told her time wouldn't alter the way he felt. Then he'd left, although she'd pleaded with him to stay.

In the week that followed, Kate had felt as though she was walking around in a fog. She laughed, she smiled, she slept, she ate. The school year hadn't started yet, so there was little else to occupy her mind. The days bled into each other, one indistinguishable from the next.

Soon after he'd broken their engagement, Clay headed for San Francisco, purportedly to attend a horse show. In her heart, she'd expected Clay to return with Rorie at his side. As hard as it had been, she'd tried to accept the fact Clay loved Rorie and nothing was ever going to change that.

To everyone's surprise, Clay came home alone, and there was no mention of Rorie. Kate didn't know what had happened between them. Hope stirred in her heart, and she'd briefly entertained thoughts of Clay resuming their engagement, the two of them marrying and settling down together, the way she'd always dreamed.

Instead she stood helplessly by as Clay threw himself into his work, making unreasonable demands on himself and his men. At first she believed the situation would change. She began stopping off at Elk Run, trying to be the friend she knew Clay needed. But Clay didn't want her. He didn't want anyone.

Except Rorie.

Only then did Kate recognize that it was in her power to help this man she loved. She talked over her idea with Luke, even before she approached her father. Luke, and Luke alone, had seemed to understand and appreciate her sacrifice. When she couldn't hold back the tears any longer, it had been Luke who'd held her in his arms and who'd beamed with pride over the unselfishness of what she'd done.

As she sat, listening to the predinner conversation, even contributing now and then, she reminded herself that Luke had been the one who'd made it possible to survive that difficult time.

Luke.

Losing Clay had threatened to destroy her, mentally and physically. But Luke hadn't allowed that to happen. It was then he'd started bullying her, she realized. She'd thought of him as a tyrant, with his unreasonable demands and his gentle harassments. Kate had been so furious with him for assuming command of her life that she'd overlooked the obvious. Only now could she understand and appreciate his strategy. Gradually, the fire had returned to her eyes and her life, although it had been fuelled by indignation. Nevertheless it was there, and Luke had been the person responsible.

She'd been furious with him when she should've been grateful. Luke had never stopped being her friend—the best friend she'd ever had. She'd leaned heavily on him in the days and weeks before Clay married Rorie, though she'd never understood how much he'd done for her, how much he cared.

The wineglasses were replenished and Kate proposed a toast. "To your happiness," she said sincerely. It pained her to remember that Clay and Rorie had nearly lost each other. Because of her...

Nightingale had needed a librarian, and with her father's help, Kate had convinced the town council to offer the job to Rorie Campbell. When she'd turned them down, Kate herself had called Rorie, and together they'd wept over the phone and later in each other's arms.

So Rorie had returned to Nightingale, and she and Clay had been married. In October. The same month Kate had planned for her own wedding to Clay.

Kate's thoughts were pulled back to the present when Clay said, "Rorie has a piece of good news." He cast a proud look at his wife.

"What's that?" Kate asked.

Rorie blushed becomingly. "Clay shouldn't have said anything. It's not certain yet."

"Rorie," Kate said, studying her carefully, "are you pregnant? Congratulations!"

"No, no." Rorie rushed to correct that impression. "Good grief, we've been married less than a month."

"It's about Rorie's book," Clay explained.

Vaguely Kate recalled that Rorie wrote children's books. In fact, she'd been on her way to a writers' conference when the car she was driving broke down on the road not far from Elk Run.

"Has one of your stories been accepted for publication?" Kate asked eagerly.

"Not exactly," Rorie said.

"An editor from New York phoned and asked for a few revisions, but she sounded enthusiastic about the book and there was talk of a contract once the revisions are done," Clay said. His fingers were twined with his wife's and he looked as excited as if he'd created the story himself.

"Oh, Rorie, that's wonderful." Kate felt pleased and proud for her friend. "What's the book about?"

"Well, the story involves Star Bright and the night we delivered Nightsong, and it's told from the foal's point of view," Rorie said.

"I know I'm her husband," Clay broke in, "but I read it, and I don't mind telling you, the book's gripping. Any editor worth her salt would snap it up in a minute."

"Oh, Clay, honestly!"

"When will you know if it's sold?" Kate asked. "I don't think Nightingale's ever had an author living here before. Dad could convince the town council to commission a sign. You might even become a tourist attraction. Who knows where this could go?"

They all laughed, but Rorie cautioned, "It could be months before I hear, so don't go having your father commission any signs."

"You should've seen her after she got the call," Clay said, his eyes twinkling with merriment. "I didn't know what to think. Rorie came running out of the house and started shrieking and jumping up and down."

"So I was a little excited."

Playfully Clay rolled his eyes. "A little! That's got to be the understatement of the year."

"I'd behave the same way," Kate said. "And you seem pretty thrilled about all this yourself, Clay Franklin."

Clay admitted it, and then the discussion turned to the awards Clay had accumulated in several national horse shows in the past year.

A few minutes later, Mary announced that dinner was

ready and they moved into the dining room. The meal was lively, and conversation flowed easily around the table.

Kate had been dreading this dinner from the moment Rorie had issued the invitation. Now she was pleasantly surprised by how enjoyable the evening had become. She'd been convinced that seeing Clay and Rorie's happiness would deepen her own pain. It hadn't happened. She'd expected to spend this evening nursing her wounds behind a brave front. Instead she felt giddy with a sense of release.

She *had* loved Clay, loved him with a youthful innocence. But she didn't feel the same way toward him now. Clay belonged to Rorie and Rorie to him. The tender relationship Kate had once shared with him was part of the past. He would always be a special person in her life, but those old feelings, that adulation she'd felt for him, were relegated to her adolescent fantasies.

Kate Logan was a woman now.

She wasn't sure exactly when the transformation had taken place, but it had. She'd struggled with it, fought the metamorphosis, because change, as always, was both painful and difficult. Kate realized for the first time that all the pain, all the uncertainty, had not been for nothing.

"Kate?" Luke called, as he let himself into the kitchen. "You around?"

"Here." She was at the back of the house, packing away the library of books her father kept in his den. Every night she did a little more to get the main house ready for Luke to move in and her to move out.

She straightened and tucked in a few wisps of hair that had escaped the red bandanna. She wore blue jeans and an old gray sweatshirt and no doubt looked terrible. Despite that, she was pleased to see Luke, eager to talk to him. She was wiping her dusty palms on her jeans when he walked in.

"What are you doing?" He stood just inside the door, a frown creasing his forehead.

"What does it look like?" she said. "I'm packing."

He hesitated, then said, "I told you, I want you to live here, at least to the end of the school year. I thought you understood that."

"I do, Luke. It's just that this place is yours now—or will be soon, and there's no reason for me to stay on." For one despairing moment, she was swept away on a crashing wave of disbelief and misery at everything she'd lost in so short a time. She could barely walk through her home and not feel an aching throb at the prospect of leaving it behind. But the sale of the ranch was part of the new reality she was learning to face.

"Of course there's a reason for you to stay here," Luke insisted, his voice sharp with impatience. "It's where you belong—where I want you. Isn't that reason enough?"

Kate forced a laugh. "Come on, Luke, there's no excuse for me to continue living here. You don't need a housekeeper, or a cook or anything else. You're completely self-sufficient. And I could do without all the gossip my living here would start in town." She paused a moment, then added gently, "I really *can* manage on my own, you know. I'm a big girl, Luke, and I don't need anyone to take care of me."

He wanted to argue with her; Kate could sense it with every breath he drew. But when he spoke next, his remarks had nothing to do with her moving.

"I suppose I should tell you about the feed store," he said. His voice was controlled, though Kate heard a hint of anger in his words. He'd been just as incensed as she was over the incident. Once she'd come to grips with her own outrage, she'd seen how furious Luke was.

"No…well, yes, I guess I am curious to hear how you handled that. Would you like some coffee?"

"Please."

Kate led the way into the kitchen and filled two ceramic mugs. After giving Luke his, she walked into the living room and sat on the sofa. Relaxing, she slipped off her shoes and tucked her feet underneath her. It felt good to sit here with Luke—almost like old times. So often over the years, they'd sat and talked like this. Friends. Confidants. Companions. She cradled the mug in both hands, letting the warmth seep up her arms.

"I had dinner with Clay and Rorie last night," she said, wanting to share with Luke what she'd discovered.

"Yes, I heard. Listen, you can close the door on the situation with Fred Garner. You don't need to worry about it anymore."

Kate lowered her eyes. "Thanks," she murmured. There was so much she wanted to tell Luke. "I had a great time at Elk Run last night, although I honestly didn't expect to."

"I can personally guarantee the matter with Garner is over. If it isn't a dead issue, it soon will be."

Kate would rather not talk about the wedding lottery. The subject had become an embarrassing memory—a very embarrassing one—but as Luke said, it was finished. There were other, more important issues to discuss.

"All day I'd worried about that dinner," she said, starting over. "I wondered how I'd ever be able to sit at a table with Clay, knowing he was married to Rorie. But I did. Oh, Luke, I can't tell you how happy they are. Deep down, I knew they would be, and I had to brace myself for that, expecting to find it unbearably painful. But something incredible happened. During the evening, I learned a valuable lesson about—"

"Good." Luke's response was clipped, detached.

Kate hesitated. From the moment he'd walked into her father's office, she'd felt something was wrong, but she hadn't been able to put her finger on it. "Luke, what is it?"

"Nothing. I'd prefer not talking about Clay and Rorie, all right?"

"I...suppose so," she said, feeling hurt. After an awkward moment, she attempted conversation once more. "You'll never guess who I got a letter from today." If Luke didn't want to talk about Clay and Rorie, then she'd try another topic that was sure to pique his interest. "Eric Wilson. Remember him?"

A slight smile touched Luke's mouth. "I'm not likely to forget him. What'd he have to say?"

"He's moved back to Portland and is talking to his ex-wife. Apparently she's been just as miserable as he has since their divorce. It looks as if they might get back together."

"That's good news."

"He asked me to give you his regards, and sends his thanks." Kate paused. "But he didn't say what I was supposed to thank you for?" She made the statement a question, hoping Luke would supply an answer.

"We talked."

"Oh."

"I told him he was wasting his time on you because you're in love with me."

Kate was outraged. "Luke, you didn't! Please tell me you're joking."

He smiled briefly, then his eyes took on the distant look he'd been wearing a moment earlier. Kate couldn't ignore it any longer. "Luke, please, tell me what's bothering you."

"What makes you think anything is?"

"You don't seem yourself tonight." Something in his voice puzzled her. A reserved quality. It was as if he was distancing himself from her and that was baffling. After Clay's wedding, Luke had actually insisted they get married, and now he was treating her like some casual acquaintance.

Kate took another sip of coffee while she collected her thoughts. Luke was sitting as far away from her as he could. His shoulders were stiff and his dark eyes a shade more intense than usual. Gone was the laughing devilry she adored.

"I'll be out of town for a few days next week," he said abruptly. "I'm hoping to pick up a few pieces of new equipment from a wholesaler in New Mexico."

"When will the bank close the deal on the ranch?"

Luke paused and his eyes pinned hers. "Your father and I signed all the papers the day before he married Dorothea Murphy."

Kate felt like bolting from her chair, the shock was so great. "Why didn't you tell me?" she demanded, her heart racing. "Why didn't my father? I shouldn't even be here now. This is your home. Yours. Bought and paid for and—"

"Kate." He set his mug aside and wearily rubbed the back of his neck. "You're welcome to stay as long as you need. If you insist on leaving, that's fine, too, but there's no rush."

She brought her hands to her cheeks, which were feverishly hot one minute, numb and cold the next. "I'll be out as…as soon as I can find someplace to move."

"Kate, for heaven's sake, why do you persist in being so stubborn?"

She shook her head, hardly understanding it herself. All she knew was that this house, which had been a part of her from the time she was born, no longer belonged to her family. Despite everything Luke said, she couldn't stay on at the Circle L, and she had nowhere else to go.

Eight

Kate had just finished correcting a pile of math papers when her friend Linda Hutton entered her classroom. Linda's third-grade class had been on a field trip and the two friends had missed talking at lunchtime.

"Hi," Kate said, smiling up at her. "How'd the tour of the jail and fire station go?"

Linda pulled up a child-size chair and sank down on it, then started massaging her temples with her fingertips. "Don't ask. By noon I was ready to lock up the entire third-grade class and lose the key."

"It certainly was quiet around school."

Linda gave a soft snicker. "Listen, I didn't come in here to learn what a peaceful day *you* had. The only reason I'm not home in bed curled up with aspirin and a hot-water bottle is so I can tell you I was at Garner Feed and Supply yesterday afternoon."

"Oh?"

"Yes, and you aren't going to like what happened. While I was there, Mr. Garner asked me if I wanted to place a wager on the Rivers-Logan wedding."

Kate's heart stopped cold. "He didn't!"

"I'm afraid so."

"But Luke told me he'd taken care of the problem. He said it was a dead issue and I shouldn't worry about it anymore." It wasn't like Luke to make careless promises.

"I wish I didn't have to tell you this," Linda said, with a sympathetic sigh.

"But Luke told me he'd personally talked to Fred Garner."

"He did. Mr. Garner made a point of telling me that, too," Linda confirmed. "He claimed Luke was hotter than a Mexican chili pepper. Said Luke came into his place, ranted and raved and threatened him within an inch of his life. But, Kate, the whole time old Garner was talking to me, he wore a grin so wide I could've driven a Jeep through it."

Kate sagged against the back of her chair.

"Then Garner told me that the harder a man fights marriage, the faster he falls. Apparently he's taking bets from as far away as Riversdale and south."

Kate pressed a hand over her eyes. "What am I going to do now?"

Linda shook her head. "I don't know. At least Garner's taken it off the blackboard, but when I said something about that, he told me he had to, since half the county wants in on the action. It seems the betting outgrew his blackboard space."

"If nothing else, it proves how desperate this community is for entertainment," Kate muttered. "If the good people of Nightingale have nothing better to do than waste their time and money on something as silly as this, then it's a sad commentary on our lives here."

Kate's friend cleared her throat and looked suspiciously guilty.

Kate hesitated, studying Linda. No, she told herself.

Not Linda. Her closest childhood friend wouldn't place a wager. Her expression confirmed that she would.

"You chose a date yourself, didn't you?" Kate demanded.

Linda's gaze darted all over the room, avoiding Kate's completely.

"You did, didn't you?" Kate exclaimed.

Linda's fingers were curling and uncurling in her lap. "You're my oldest, dearest friend. How could I ever do anything like that?" she wailed.

"I don't know, Linda. You tell me."

"All right, all right," Linda confessed. "I did put a wager on June. The first part of summer is such a lovely time of year for a wedding...."

"I can't believe I'm hearing this." Kate had the sinking suspicion that her father had probably gotten in on the action, too, before he left on his honeymoon.

"I had no intention of betting," Linda hurried to explain. "In fact I never would have, but the odds were so good for June. For a five-dollar bet, I could collect as much as five hundred if you were to marry around the middle of the month—say the sixteenth. It's a Saturday. Weekends are always best for weddings, don't you think?"

Kate wasn't about to answer that. "You know, I suspect this whole thing is illegal. Each and every one of you should thank your lucky stars I don't call the sheriff."

"He's betting himself—on March. Said his own wedding anniversary is March tenth and he thinks Luke will be able to persuade you early in the spring. According to Fred, the sheriff figures that once Luke gets you to agree, he won't wait around for a big wedding. He'll want to marry you before you can change your mind."

Kate sent her a furious look. "If you're telling me this to amuse me, you've failed miserably."

"I'm sorry, Kate, I really am. The only reason I went into the feed store was so I could assure you the whole betting thing was over, but I can't and—"

"Instead you placed a bet of your own."

"I feel guilty about that," Linda admitted, her voice subdued.

"Why don't we both forget it and concentrate on the Thanksgiving play?" Instead of upsetting herself with more talk of this wedding lottery, Kate preferred to do something constructive with her time.

"I might be able to make it up to you, though," Linda murmured, fussing with the cuffs of her long-sleeved blouse.

"Whatever it is will have to be good."

"It is." Linda brightened and pulled a slip of paper from her purse. "I got this information from a friend of a friend, so I can't confirm how accurate it is, but I *think* it's pretty much for sure."

"What's for sure?" she asked when Linda handed her the paper. A local phone number was carefully printed on it.

Linda's sheepish look departed. "It's Mrs. Jackson's number—she's the manager of the apartment complex on Spruce Street. They may have a vacancy coming up next week. If you're the first one to apply, you might have a decent chance of getting it."

"Oh, Linda, that's great!"

"Am I forgiven?"

Kate laughed. "This makes up for a multitude of sins."

"I was counting on that."

Kate called five times before she got through. Mrs. Jackson seemed surprised to be hearing from her.

"I thought you were marrying that Rivers chap," the elderly woman said. "Can't understand why you'd want to rent an apartment when you're engaged to that man. The whole town says it's just a matter of time."

"Mrs. Jackson," Kate said loudly, because everyone knew the old woman was hard of hearing, "could I look at the apartment soon?"

"Won't be cleaned up for another day or two. I'll let you know once it's ready to be shown, but I can't help feeling it's a waste of time. Don't know what's wrong with you young women these days. In my day, we'd snap up a good man like Luke Rivers so fast it'd make your head spin."

"I'd still like to see the apartment," Kate said.

"Saturday, I guess. Yes, Saturday. Why don't you plan to come over then? I'll need a deposit if you decide to take the place."

"Will a check be all right?"

"Good as gold when it's got your name on it," Mrs. Jackson said, chuckling. "Don't suppose you have any season or month you're particularly partial to for weddings, would you?"

"No, I can't say I do."

"Well, me and Ethel Martin think you and that Rivers fellow will tie the knot in April. April seems a mighty nice month for a country wedding."

"I'm sure it is," Kate said, clenching her teeth.

"Good. Now listen, soon as the word gets out, someone else'll be wanting that apartment, so if you aren't here by noon Saturday, I'm going to have to give it to whoever shows up. You understand?"

"I'll be there before noon."

"See you then."

"Goodbye, Mrs. Jackson."

"You keep thinking about April, you hear?"

"Yes, I will," Kate murmured, rolling her eyes as she replaced the receiver.

   That night, Luke stopped in shortly after Kate had finished dinner, which consisted of a sandwich eaten while
she emptied the living-room bookcases. She filled box
after box with books, her own and her father's, as well as
complete sets of Dickens, Thackeray and George Eliot that
had belonged to her mother. The physical activity gave
her time to think. She'd realized the night she had dinner
at the Franklins' that she wasn't in love with Clay. That
same evening, Kate had also realized how much Luke had
done for her in the weeks following her broken engagement. It troubled her to acknowledge how unappreciative
she'd been of his support.

   At Clay's wedding, she'd only added to the problem by
asking Luke to marry her. He'd been willing to comply,
willing to continue taking care of her through these difficult emotional times. In his own way, he did love her;
Kate didn't question that. But he seemed far more concerned with protecting her from the harsh realities of life.

   All the talk about weddings had brought the subject to
the forefront of Kate's mind. She tried to picture what her
life would be like if she were to marry Luke. From the
night of Clay's wedding, Luke had been telling her she
was in love with him. It came as a shock to realize how
right he was. She *did* love him, a thousand times more
than she'd ever dreamed.

   Luke claimed he loved her, too. If that was true, why
was she fighting him so hard? For one thing, Luke had
delivered his declaration of love in such a matter-of-fact,
unromantic way, it was hard to believe he really meant it.
If she could be sure that his feelings were rooted in more
than sympathy and physical attraction, she'd feel more
confident. But Luke kept trying to shield her, as though
she were a child. Now that she was moving into a place
of her own, she'd be able to analyze her changing emo-

tions more objectively. She'd be completely independent, away from the environment they'd always shared. Once they were apart, once it was clear that she could manage by herself, Luke would be free to pursue a relationship with her as an equal, an adult woman—not a little girl who needed looking after.

"I see you're at it again," he said, standing in the doorway between the kitchen and the living room.

"Luke—" she slapped her hand over her heart "—you startled me!" Her thoughts had been full of him and then suddenly he was there.

As he did more and more often of late, Luke was frowning, but Kate wasn't going to let that destroy her mood. She was thrilled with the prospect of moving into her own apartment and settling into a different kind of life.

"I have good news. I'm going to look at an apartment on Saturday morning." She dragged a heavy box of books across the carpet. "So," she said, huffing, "I'll probably be out of here sooner than we figured."

Luke interrupted her, effortlessly picking up the cardboard box and depositing it on the growing stack at the far side of the room.

"Thanks," she murmured, grateful for his help.

"You shouldn't be doing this heavy work by yourself."

"It's fine," she said, rubbing the dust from her hands. "The only trouble I'm having is with these books. We've got so many."

"Kate, dammit, I wish you'd listen to reason."

"I'm being reasonable," she said, fixing a reassuring smile on her face. "All I'm doing is giving you what's rightfully yours."

Luke's frown grew darker, and he dragged a hand through his hair. "Listen, I think we may have more of a problem with Fred Garner than I thought."

"Yes, I know," Kate said, already filling the next box. "Linda told me after school that he's doing a thriving business."

Luke knelt on the floor beside her. "You're not upset?"

"Would it do any good? I mean, you obviously did your best and that just seemed to encourage the betting. As far as I can see, the only thing that will resolve this issue is time." She kept her gaze averted and added, "When six months pass and we're still not married, everyone will accept that nothing's going on between us."

"Nothing?" Luke asked bitterly.

Hope stirred briefly within her. "I like to think we'll always be friends." An absent smile touched her lips. "Now that I've decided to distance my emotions from this lottery nonsense, I find it all rather comical. You should do the same."

"This amuses you?"

"The good citizens of Nightingale are amused. Everyone seems to assume that because Clay and Dad both got married and the ranch has been sold, I should swoon into your arms."

"Personally, I don't think that's such a bad idea."

"Oh?" She chuckled and tucked a few more books in the box. Her heart was racing. If Luke was ever really going to declare his love, it would be now. "That wasn't the message I got the other night. I tried to have a serious talk with you about my evening with Clay and Rorie, and all you could do was glower at me." She glanced up, shaking her head. "Like you're doing now."

Luke walked away from her. He stood staring out the window, although Kate suspected the view was of little interest to him. "I just wish you'd be sensible for once in your life," he snapped.

"I didn't know I had a habit of not being sensible," she

said conversationally, disheartened by his attitude. She rose and walked over to the larger bookcase, but even standing on her toes, she couldn't quite reach the trophies stored on the top shelf. Not to be defeated, she rolled the ottoman in front of the empty bookcase and climbed onto the thick cushioned seat. She stretched up and her fingers were about to grasp the first trophy when she heard Luke's swift intake of breath.

"Kate!"

Just as he spoke the ottoman started to roll out from under her. She flailed her arms in a desperate effort to maintain her balance.

Kate had never seen Luke move faster. His hands closed around her waist in an iron grip. Her cry of alarm caught in her throat as she was slammed against his solid chest.

"Of all the stupid, idiotic things I've ever seen—"

"I would've been perfectly fine if you hadn't called my name." Her heart was pounding so hard she could barely breathe.

Luke's hold relaxed. "You're all right?"

She nodded.

He closed his eyes, exhaling a ragged sigh. When he opened them, he assessed her carefully; apparently he concluded that she was unhurt because he gave her an impatient little shake. "Whatever possessed you to climb up on that ottoman in the first place?" he demanded.

"I couldn't reach the trophies."

"Couldn't you have asked me to get them for you? Why do you have such a difficult time accepting help from me?"

"I don't know," she admitted softly.

Still he held her and still Kate let him, trying to resist the comfort she felt in his arms. Her hands were braced against his powerful shoulders, but then she relaxed, unconsciously linking her fingers behind his neck.

Neither moved for a long moment.

Slowly Luke ran a provocative finger down the length of her cheek, and Kate's eyes drifted shut. She felt herself drawn inexorably toward him. Her lips parted and trembled, awaiting his kiss. When she realized what she was doing, she opened her eyes and broke away from him so quickly that she would've stumbled had his hands not righted her.

Embarrassed now, she stepped back. Luke brought down the trophies and handed them to her, but she saw that his eyes had become distant and unreadable.

"That's enough packing for tonight," she murmured, her voice breathless even while she struggled to sound cheerful and bright.

He nodded slightly, then without another word stalked from the room. Kate didn't know what possessed her to follow him, certainly the last thing she should have done.

"Luke?"

He stopped halfway through the kitchen and turned toward her. His eyes were steely and intense, and just seeing that harsh edge drove her to take a step backward in retreat.

"You wanted something?" he asked when she didn't immediately explain.

"Just to say…" She could barely talk coherently. It occurred to her to ask if he loved her the way a man loves his wife, but she lacked the courage. "I thought maybe, I mean, I wanted to know if there was anything I could do for you before I left the house. Paint the living room…or something?"

"No."

Briefly she toyed with the idea of following him outside. For all his words about wanting her to stay, he couldn't seem to get away from her fast enough. The thought of not having Luke for her friend anymore felt crippling. Her pride was the problem. Luke had told her repeatedly that she needed him, and she knew now that she did. But not in the way he meant. Not just as a friend who was willing to offer her the protection and peace of marriage, a friend who felt obliged to take care of her.

"I don't want you to move from the ranch," he said.

Her heart was begging him to give her a reason to stay—the reason she longed to hear. "Luke, please accept that I'm only doing what I think is best for my life."

"I know that, but dammit, Kate, why are you being so stubborn? Why do you resist me when all I want is to make things easier for you? We could be married, and you could settle down in the house, and nothing needs to change. Yet you insist on causing all this turmoil in your life."

There wasn't anything Kate could say.

"You can't tell me we aren't physically attracted to each other. The electricity between us is powerful enough to light up Main Street."

"I…know."

"Say it, Kate. Admit that it felt good when I held you just now."

"I…"

Luke reached for her then, and Kate felt as if she'd lost some strategic battle. When his mouth found hers, her stomach tightened and fluttered wildly. Against her will, her lips parted, and before she understood what was happening she slid her arms tightly around his hard, narrow waist, wanting to hold on to him forever.

Luke moaned, then suddenly tore his lips from hers. She felt a tremor go through him before he raised his head and gazed tenderly into her face, his eyes dark and gentle.

"Is it so difficult to say?" he asked.

Nine

"This is the second bedroom," Mrs. Jackson was saying as she led Kate through the vacant rooms. From the moment she'd walked in the door, Kate had known that this apartment would suit her needs perfectly.

"I can't understand why you'd be wanting a two-bedroom place, but that's none of my business," Mrs. Jackson went on. Her hair was tightly curled in pink plastic rollers. To the best of her ability, Kate couldn't remember ever seeing the woman's hair *without* rollers.

"What did that Rivers fellow say when you told him you were moving into town?" She didn't wait for a response, but cackled delightedly. "Frankly, I wasn't sure you'd show up this morning. My friend Ethel and me talked about it, and we figured Rivers would tie a rope around you and hightail it to Nevada and marry you quick. Offhand, I can't remember who's got money on November."

"You said to be here before noon," she murmured, ignoring the other comments.

"Well, if Luke didn't stop you, I expected that snowstorm would, the one the weatherman's been talking about for the last two days."

"Do you really think it's going to snow?" Kate asked

anxiously. The sky had been dark all morning, and the temperature seemed to be dropping steadily. Normally Kate wouldn't have chanced driving into town by herself with weather conditions this uncertain, but if she hadn't come, she might have missed getting the apartment.

"If I was you, I'd stick around town for a while," Mrs. Jackson advised. "I'd hate the thought of you getting trapped on the road in a bad storm."

"I'm sure I'll be all right." She'd driven her father's four-wheel-drive truck, and even if the storm did materialize, she shouldn't have any trouble getting home. The Circle L was only twenty minutes away, and how much snow could fall in that time?

"Would you like me to write you a check now?" Kate asked, eager to be on her way.

"That'd be fine. There's still some cleaning to be done, but it'll be finished before the first of the month. Fact is, you can start moving your things in here next week if you want."

"Thanks, I appreciate that."

Mrs. Jackson bundled her coat around her thin shoulders as they stepped outside. She glanced at the sky and shook her pink-curlered head. "If you are going home, I suggest you do it quick. I don't like the look of them clouds."

"Then I'd better write that check and head out."

No more than five minutes later, Kate was sitting in her father's truck. The sky was an oyster gray and darkening by the minute. Shivering from the cold, she zipped her jacket all the way up to her neck and drew on a pair of fleece-lined leather gloves.

Kate started the engine and shifted the gears. The radio was set on her dad's favorite country station and the music played softly. When she left the outskirts of town, she hit a couple of rough patches in the road and bounced so high her head nearly banged into the roof of the cab. After that she kept her speed down. She drove at a steady pace, her gaze focused on the road ahead, scanning the horizon for any sign of snow.

When she was about ten miles from the ranch, the storm began. Light, fluffy flakes whirled around the windshield. The morning sky darkened until it resembled dusk and Kate was forced to turn on the headlights.

A love song came on the radio, one the band at the Red Bull had played that fateful Friday night. The night Luke had lifted her in his arms and carried her off the dance floor. Embarrassed by the memory, she reached for the radio dial, intending to change the station.

She didn't see the rock that had rolled onto the road, not until she was almost on top of it, and then it was too late. Her instincts took control. She gripped the wheel with both hands, then swerved and slammed into the embankment. The truck stopped with a sudden jerk, and the engine went dead.

For a stunned moment, Kate couldn't breathe. Her heart was in her throat and her hands clenched the steering wheel so tightly her fingers felt numb.

Finally, when she was able to move, Kate released a long, shaky breath, grateful the accident hadn't been worse. She took a moment to compose herself and tried to restart the engine, but nothing happened. Twice more she tried to get the engine to kick over, but it wouldn't even cough or sputter.

Frustrated, she smacked the cushioned seat with her gloved hand and closed her eyes. The snow was coming down thick and fast now.

"Don't worry," she muttered, opening the door and climbing out. "Stay calm." Although everything Kate knew about the internal workings of engines would fit on a Post-It note, she decided to see if she could find the problem.

The snow and wind struck at her viciously, as though to punish her for not listening to Mrs. Jackson and staying in town.

After considerable difficulty locating the latch, Kate raised the hood. With a prayer on her lips, she looked everything over, then touched two or three different parts as if that would repair whatever was broken. Certain that she was destined to sit out the storm huddled in the cab, she returned and tried the key again.

The engine gave one sick cough and promptly died.

"Damn!"

Nothing remained but to sit and wait for someone to drive past. Leaving the truck and attempting to make her way to the house would be nearly as insane as driving around in a snowstorm in the first place.

Kate could almost hear Luke's lecture now. It would be hot enough to blister her ears. All she could do was hope her father never found out about this—or she'd get a lecture from him, too.

A half hour passed and, hoping against hope, Kate tried the engine again. Nothing. But it was snowing so hard now that even if the truck had started, she probably wouldn't have been able to drive in these conditions. She tried to warm herself by rubbing her hands and hugging her arms close to her body. It had become cold, the coldest weather she could remember.

With very little to take her mind off the freezing temperature, she laid her head back and closed her eyes, trying to relax. There was nothing to do but sit patiently and wait....

She must have dozed off because the next thing she

knew, the truck door was jerked open and her arm gripped in a sudden, painful hold.

"Have you lost your mind?" The fury in Luke's voice was like a slap in the face.

"Luke… Luke." She was so grateful to see him that she didn't question where he'd come from or how he'd found her. It all felt like a dream. Moving was difficult, but she slid her arms around his neck and hugged him, laughing and crying at the same time. "How did you ever find me?"

"Don't you realize I was about to have heart failure worrying about you?"

"You're sick?" Her mind was so muddled. Of course he'd be worried. How had he known where she was? And he seemed so angry, but that was nothing new. For the past few days, he'd been continually upset with her.

Her arms tightened around his neck and she breathed in his fresh, warm scent. When she sat up and looked around, she was shocked by how dark it had become; if it weren't for the blowing, swirling snow, the stars would be twinkling. The storm had abated somewhat, but not by much.

"I can't believe you'd do anything so stupid." His voice was low and angry, his face blanched with concern. "Don't you know you could've frozen to death out here? If you don't want to consider your own life, then what about Devin away on his honeymoon? If anything happened to you, he'd never forgive himself."

Kate bore up well under Luke's tirade, refusing to cry even though she was trembling with shock and cold and the truth of his words. As for the part about being frozen, she was already halfway there, but he didn't seem to notice that.

"Kate, I don't know what I would've done if you'd left the truck and tried to make it back to the house on foot."

"I knew enough to stay here at least." She'd been a fool

not to have taken the danger more seriously. "I'm sorry," she whispered.

He pulled her to him and held her so tight she couldn't move. His face was buried in her hair, one ungloved hand gently stroking her forehead, her cheek, her chin, as if he had to touch her to know he'd found her safe. When he lifted his head, he gazed into her eyes, his own dark and filled with unspoken torment. "Are you all right?"

She nodded and tried to talk, but her teeth began to chatter. Luke shrugged out of his coat and draped it over her shoulders.

"Tell me what happened."

"I swerved to miss a rock and hit...the embankment. It was already snowing and I...the song... I changed stations and that's when it happened... I don't know what I did, but after I turned so sharply, the truck wouldn't start."

"I've got to get you to the house." He half carried her to his truck and placed her in the passenger seat. He climbed into the driver's side and leaned over to wrap a warm blanket around her, then began to rub some warmth back into her hands.

"What about Dad's truck?" Kate asked, shocked by how tired and weak she felt.

"We'll worry about that later. I'll send someone to fix it when the storm's over."

The blast from the heater felt like a tropical wind and Kate finally started to relax. She was terribly cold but dared not let Luke know.

All the way back to the ranch he didn't say a word. Driving was difficult, and she didn't want to disturb his concentration. So she sat beside him, her hands and feet numb despite the almost oppressive warmth, and her eyes heavy with weariness.

Several of the ranch hands ran toward the front porch

when Luke pulled into the yard. Kate found the flurry of activity all centered on her disconcerting, but she tried to thank everyone and apologized profusely for the concern she'd caused.

If Luke had been impatient and demanding when he rescued her, it didn't compare to the way he rapped out orders once she was inside the house.

"A bath," he said, pointing toward the bathroom as if she'd never been there before. "Warm water, not hot."

Bill Schmidt, Luke's newly appointed foreman, followed them to the doorway of the tiny room, looking pale and anxious. Kate felt so weak that she simply stood, leaning against the sink, while Luke ran the bathwater, testing it several times to check the temperature.

"It's stopped snowing. Do you think I should contact one of her female friends? Maybe Miz Franklin?" Bill asked, shifting awkwardly from foot to foot. When Luke nodded, Bill charged out of the house, slamming the door behind him.

Luke turned off the bathwater and straightened. He shook his head, arms limp and at his sides, mouth stern and tight. "Kate, Kate, what could have possessed you to drive in from town during the worst storm of the year? Can you imagine what went through my mind when I was looking for you?"

It took all her strength just to manage a few words. "How'd...you know...where I was?"

"You told me you were going to town to look at an apartment on Saturday. Remember? When you weren't back after the blizzard hit, I called around town until I learned you were renting one of the apartments on Spruce Street. Mrs. Jackson told me she'd warned you herself and that you'd left a few hours earlier. Also that she's fond of

April because of all the flowers, whatever the hell that means."

"I'm...sorry I worried you."

His hands gripped her shoulders and the anguish he'd endured during the past few hours was written plainly on his face. The anger and pain in his eyes told her about the panic he'd felt. A rush of emotion crossed his expression and he pulled her close, wrapping his arms around her.

He didn't speak for a long moment. Instead, quietly, gently, he stroked her hair as he dragged in several deep breaths.

Kate's heart pounded wildly in her chest. She longed to look at him, to gaze into his eyes again. She was puzzled by the intensity she'd seen there. Fear, yes, doubt and anger, too, but there was something more, something deeper that she didn't recognize.

She longed to tell him she loved him, just the way he claimed she did, but the thought didn't make it to her lips. Love was a strange, unpredictable emotion, so painful and difficult. Her eyes held his and she tried to smile, but her mouth wouldn't cooperate.

Her fingertips mapped out the lines of his face, as she strove to reassure him with her touch when her words couldn't. He captured her wrist and brought her palm to his lips.

She'd just opened her mouth to speak, when Bill Schmidt came crashing into the room. "Rorie Franklin will be over as soon as she can."

"Thanks, Bill," Luke said without looking away from Kate.

"Uh, I'll be leaving now, if you don't need me."

"Fine. Thanks again for your help."

"No problem. Glad you're all right, Kate." He touched his hat and then was gone.

"Someone should help you out of those clothes," Luke said, half smiling, "and I don't think I should be the one to do it."

"I'm fine. I can undress myself."

Luke didn't seem inclined to challenge her statement. She floated toward the bathroom door and ushered him out, then shut it softly.

Once she started undressing, she discovered that Luke hadn't been too far wrong when he'd suggested she needed help. By the time she sank into the warm water, she was shivering, exhausted and intensely cold again. But the water felt wonderful, although it stung her tender skin. When the prickling sensation left her, she was almost overwhelmed by the sensation of comfort. She sighed deeply, closed her eyes and lay back in the tepid water.

"Kate," Luke called from the other side of the door, "are you okay in there?"

"I'm fine."

"Do you need anything?"

"No," she assured him.

A sudden thought made her bolt upright, gasping. *Luke could have died searching for me.* She closed her eyes and whispered a prayer of thanks that the events of this traumatic afternoon had turned out as they had.

She must have sobbed because Luke called out, "What's wrong? It sounds like you're crying."

"You…could have died trying to find me."

"I didn't."

"I know," she said hoarsely, biting her lip. "I'm glad. I wouldn't want you to die."

"That's encouraging," he answered with a soft laugh.

Dressed in her flannel pyjamas and long robe, her hair hanging wetly against her shoulders, Kate let herself out of the bathroom. She looked like something the cat had proudly dragged onto the porch, but at least she felt better. A thousand times better.

Luke was sitting in the kitchen, nursing a shot glass of whiskey. Kate had very rarely seen Luke drink straight liquor.

"I blame myself," he muttered. "I knew about the storm and didn't warn you."

"Warn me? That wouldn't have made any difference. I would've gone into town anyway. I had to be there before noon if I was going to get the apartment. You couldn't have stopped me, Luke. You know that."

Luke shook his head grimly. "What I can't understand is why moving away from here is so all-fired important that you'd risk your fool neck to do it."

"Mrs. Jackson said she'd have to give the apartment to someone else if I wasn't there."

"She wouldn't have understood if you'd phoned? You had to go look at it in a blizzard?" He urged her into a chair and poured a cup of hot coffee, adding a liberal dose of whiskey before handing her the cup.

"I already told you I couldn't wait. Besides, it wasn't snowing when I drove there," Kate said patiently. "Please don't be angry, Luke." She reached for his hand, needing to touch him.

He clutched her fingers with his own. "Kate, if anything should convince you we ought to get married, this is it. You need me, Princess, can't you see that?" He released her hand to brush the damp curls from her forehead. "How many times do I have to tell you that before you'll believe it?"

"Oh, Luke," she moaned, feeling close to tears.

"I want to take care of you, Kate. What nearly happened today, plus the fiasco with Eric Wilson, should tell you something."

She stared at him, feeling lost and disoriented. "There are women in this community, women my age, who already have children." Even as she spoke, she knew she wasn't making sense.

Luke blinked in confusion. "You want children? Great, so do I. In fact, I'm hoping we'll have several."

"That's not what I meant," Kate said, exasperated. She tried again. "These women don't live with a guardian." Was that clearer? she wondered.

"Of course they don't—they're married," Luke countered sharply.

Kate shut her eyes. "Don't you understand? I'm old enough to be on my own. I don't need someone to protect me."

"We're not discussing your age."

"You don't *love* me," she blurted. "You feel sorry for me, that's all. You think because Clay's married to Rorie and...and Dad married Dorothea that I don't have anyone. But I do! There's Linda and lots of other friends. I've got a good life. I don't need to get married."

Luke sprang from the chair and walked to the sink, pressing both hands against the edge, hunching his shoulders, his back toward her. He said nothing for several minutes and when he finally spoke, his voice was cool, detached. "All I can say is that you must feel a lot more strongly about this than I realized. Apparently you're willing to risk your life to get away from me."

"I didn't go to town knowing I was in any danger," she objected, but he didn't seem to hear.

"Then leave, Kate. I won't try to keep you any longer, despite the fact that I love you and want to marry you. If you want your independence so badly, then take it."

"Luke, please, you don't love me—not the way you should."

"Oh, and what do you know about that? Obviously nothing."

"I know you keep saying you want to take care of me."

"That's so wrong?"

"Yes! A woman needs more. She needs to be an equal. She—"

"My love and my life are all I've got to offer you, Kate," he broke in. "It's a take-it-or-leave-it proposition."

"That's not fair," she said. "You make it sound as though I'm going to live my life alone if I don't marry you within the next ten minutes."

Slowly he turned to face her. His eyes were piercing and as dark as she'd ever seen them. "Fine. You've made your choice. I'm not going to stand here arguing with you. It's over, Kate. This is the last time we'll talk about marriage."

She tried to say something, but couldn't think coherently. Even if she'd been able to work out her thoughts and give them voice, she doubted Luke was in any mood to listen. He avoided looking at her as he stalked out of the house.

A fire was blazing in the fireplace and Kate stretched out on the nearby sofa, intending to mull over Luke's words. But her eyes felt as heavy as her heart, and almost as soon as she laid her head on the pillow, she was asleep.

Someone working in the kitchen stirred Kate to wakefulness, and when she glanced at her watch she was shocked to see that she'd slept for almost two hours.

Her heart soared when she thought it must be Luke. He'd been so angry with her earlier, although she supposed his anxiety about finding her in the snowstorm explained his attitude. She hoped they could clear the air.

But it wasn't Luke. Instead, Rorie peered into the living room, her eyes concerned.

"I hope you don't mind. Luke let me in."

"You're always welcome here, Rorie, you know that."

"Bill Schmidt called with an incredible story about you being lost in the storm. I could hardly believe it. Clay drove me over as soon as he could, but to be honest I don't know who was worse off—you or Luke."

At the mention of his name, Kate lowered her gaze to the multicolored quilt spread across her lap. Idly she smoothed the wrinkles, trying not to think about Luke.

"How are you feeling?"

"I'm okay. I just have a headache."

"A bad one from the look of you. I've never seen you this pale."

Kate's hands twisted the edge of the homemade quilt. "Luke was furious with me for going into town—I found an apartment, Rorie. He said it was over between us." She began to cry. "He said he'd be glad when I was gone and that he'd…never bother me again." By the time Kate had finished, her voice was reduced to a hoarse whisper.

"I see," Rorie murmured.

"I don't even recognize Luke anymore. We used to be able to talk to each other and joke together, but lately we can't seem to discuss anything in a rational manner. I've tried, Rorie, I really have, but Luke makes everything so difficult."

"Men have a habit of doing that."

"I wanted to tell Luke about the night I had dinner with you and Clay and—" She stopped abruptly when she realized what she'd almost said.

"What about it?" Rorie coaxed.

"It's just that I'd dreaded the evening because I was afraid of being with Clay again. I'm sorry, I don't want to upset you, Rorie, but I loved Clay for a long time, and getting over him was much harder than I thought it would

be. Until the night we were all together." The words came
rushing from her. "I saw Clay with you and I assumed I'd
feel all this pain, but instead I felt completely free. You're
both so happy, and I knew, then and there, that I never
loved Clay the way you do. True, I adored him for years,
but it was more of an adolescent infatuation. Clay was part
of my youth. When I understood all these things about myself, all these changes, I felt such hope, such excitement."

"Oh, Kate, I'm so pleased to hear that." A shy smile
dented Rorie's cheeks.

"I wanted to explain all this to Luke, but I never got
the chance, and now it's all so much worse. I don't know
if we'll ever be able to talk to each other again."

"Of course you will."

"But he sounded so angry."

"I'm sure that's because of his concern for your safety."

"I can't talk to him," Kate repeated sadly. "At least not
yet and maybe not ever…"

"Yes, you will, and it'll be sooner than you think," Rorie
said. "You won't be able to break off all those years of
friendship, and neither will he. He'll be around in a day
or two, ready to apologize for being so harsh. Just you
wait and see."

Kate shook her head. "You make it all seem so easy."

"Trust me, I know it isn't. When I think back to the way
things went between Clay and me, I empathize all the more
with what you're going through now."

Kate remembered the dark days following Clay's visit to
California. Neither Rorie nor Clay had ever told her what
happened. Clay had gone to San Francisco, intending to
bring Rorie back with him, and instead had returned alone.

"Maybe we need to get away from each other for a
while," Kate said. "Maybe if we aren't in such close prox-

imity, we'll be able to sort out what we really feel for each other."

"When are you moving to town?"

"Monday," Kate said, looking at the cardboard boxes stacked against the opposite wall.

"Do you need help? Skip, Clay and I could easily lend a hand."

"That would be wonderful."

The rest of the weekend passed in a blur. Kate didn't see Luke once. So much for Rorie's assurances that he'd come by soon to talk everything out. Apparently he meant what he'd said.

Monday morning, when she was about to leave for school, Kate paused before she got into her car, deciding she should at least say goodbye to Luke before she moved out.

Luke wasn't in the barn, but Bill Schmidt was.

"Good morning, Bill."

"Howdy, Kate," he said with a wide grin. "Glad to see there's no ill effects from your accident."

"None, thanks. Is Luke around?"

Bill settled his hands in the pockets of his bib overalls. "No. Thought you knew. He left yesterday afternoon for New Mexico to look at some new equipment. He won't be back until Thursday."

Ten

Kate was carrying the last of the cardboard boxes to the recycling bins outside the apartment building on Thursday evening when she saw Luke's pickup turn onto Spruce Street. He came to a grinding halt at the curb, vaulted out of the cab and stood there scowling. His features were contorted, but for the life of her Kate couldn't understand why he was so irritated. Didn't he *tell* her to move? Wasn't this what he wanted?

She was about to make her presence known, but before she could act, Luke brought his fist down on the bonnet. She heard the sound from where she was standing. It must have smarted because he rubbed his knuckles, gazing intently at the redbrick building. Then, tucking his hands in the back pockets of his jeans, he squared his shoulders and strode toward it. He stopped abruptly, then retreated to his truck. Opening the door, he balanced one foot on the side rail, as if he was about to leap into the cab.

Kate leaned forward on the tips of her toes and stretched out her hand to stop him. It took everything in her not to rush forward. She was afraid she'd burst into tears. Viewing Luke's behavior had touched something deep within her.

If Luke had planned to drive away, he apparently

changed his mind, because he slammed the door shut and resolutely faced the building again.

Knowing that the time to make her move was now, Kate casually turned the corner.

"Kate."

"Luke," she said, pretending surprise.

For a moment, Luke didn't say a word. "I just got back to the ranch and discovered that the main house was empty. I thought you'd be there when I returned."

"Mrs. Jackson said I could have the apartment Monday, and since Rorie, Clay and Skip were able to help me move, I couldn't see any reason to delay."

"You might've told me."

Kate lowered her eyes, feeling a little guilty, since they'd parted on such unfriendly terms. "I tried, but you'd already left for New Mexico."

"Bill did say you wanted to talk to me," he conceded.

"Would you like to come inside?" she asked, opening the door for him.

"All right." He sounded reluctant.

Once in the apartment they stood looking at each other, and Kate felt suddenly awkward. Luke's eyes were dark and luminous and his face had never seemed so dear to her—familiar, yet in some exciting new way, not fully known. She would've liked nothing better than to walk into his arms. She wanted to tell him how sorry she was about the way they'd parted, to tell him she was ready to accept his proposal on any terms. But her pride made that impossible.

"Nice place," he said when the silence became painful. He tucked his fingers in his back pockets again.

"Can I take your coat?"

"Please." He took it off and gave it to her.

She motioned toward the sofa. "Would you like to sit down?"

He nodded and sat on the edge of the cushion. Leaning forward, he balanced his hands between his knees and rotated his hat with his fingers. Luke had sat on this very same sofa a thousand times, but he'd never looked as uncomfortable as he did now.

"I came to apologize for the last time we spoke."

"Oh, Luke," she whispered, sitting in the overstuffed chair across from him. "I felt bad, too. Why do we argue like that? Some days I feel we're growing further and further apart, and I don't want that."

"I'd like to suggest we put an end to this nonsense, but you've made your views plain enough."

"You still want to take care of me?"

"I don't think that's so wrong."

"I know." She sighed, tired of repeating the same arguments. "But I'm fully capable of doing that myself."

"Right," he said with deadly softness. "You took care of yourself pretty well during that snowstorm, didn't you?"

"Why don't you throw Eric Wilson in my face while you're at it? I thought you came because you regretted our last argument, but it looks to me as if you're trying to start another one."

"All right," he shouted, "I'll stop! You asked me not to bring up the distasteful subject of marriage and I agreed. It's just that—" He clamped his mouth shut. "We're better off dropping the subject entirely," he finished stiffly.

"I hate when we argue," Kate said.

"So do I, Princess."

Although his tone was light, Kate heard the distress in his voice. It filled her with regret, and she longed for something comforting to say, something that would ease this awkwardness between them, and restore a sense of balance to their relationship.

"Do you need anything, Kate?"

"No. I'm fine," she rushed to assure him. She might occasionally date the wrong men and take foolish risks in snowstorms, but she could manage her own life!

Luke glanced around the room, then slowly nodded as if accepting the truth of her words.

"It was kind of you to stop by... I mean, it's good to see you and I really am grateful you wanted to clear the air, too."

"Are you saying you missed me while I was away?"

She had, terribly, but until that moment, Kate hadn't been willing to admit it, even to herself. Unconsciously she'd been waiting for Thursday, hoping to hear from Luke—but not really expecting to. For the past few days, she'd worked frantically to unpack her things and make her apartment presentable. And all along it had been an effort to prove to Luke how efficient and capable she actually was. After falling on her face so many times, she wanted this transition from the ranch house to her first apartment to go off without a hitch. It was a matter of pride.

They were like polite strangers with each other. Kate couldn't think of a single clever remark or probing question to reduce the tension between them.

"Have you eaten?" Luke asked brusquely. "I thought I'd take you to dinner. I realize I'm not giving you much notice and I read somewhere that women don't like a man to take things for granted, so if you don't want to go, I'll understand."

He sounded as though he assumed she'd reject his invitation. "I'd love to have dinner with you," she said, unable to hide a smile.

Luke seemed shocked by her easy acquiescence.

Kate stood up, stretching luxuriously. "If you'll give me a moment, I'll freshen up." She couldn't keep the happiness out of her voice.

Luke rose then, and his presence seemed to dwarf her small living room. Only a few scant inches separated them. With one finger, he tilted up her chin and looked deep into her eyes. "You honestly missed me?" he whispered.

For some reason, her throat squeezed shut and Kate was forced to answer him without words. She cradled his face between both hands and gazed up at him, nodding fervently.

Luke's eyes darkened and she thought he meant to kiss her. Just when she was prepared to slip into his arms and raise her mouth to his, he pulled loose from her light grasp and stepped back. Kate swallowed her disappointment.

"I was thinking about that pizza parlour in Riversdale," he said gruffly.

"Pizza would be wonderful," Kate said.

"Then it's settled."

Kate didn't bother to change clothes, but ran a brush through her hair and refreshed her make-up. A few minutes later, she was ready to leave. Luke stood at the door, and as she approached him, his appreciative look sent small flutters of awareness through her body.

Companionably they drove the thirty miles to Riversdale. By unspoken agreement they avoided any subject that would cause them to disagree.

The restaurant, Pizza Mania, was known throughout the county for its excellent Italian food. The room was dimly lit, and the wooden tables were covered with red-checkered cloths. Since it was a weeknight, the restaurant wasn't especially busy.

Luke guided her to a table in the middle of the homey room. Service was prompt and they quickly placed their order for a large sausage-and-black-olive pizza. Kate also ordered a raw vegetable platter with yogurt-herb dip, and she laughed at the disdainful expression on Luke's face. Then she laughed again.

"What's so funny now?"

"I was remembering the last time I ate pizza from here. It was when Rorie had just arrived, and she and I were making dinner for Clay and Skip. I made a lemon meringue pie and Rorie spent the entire afternoon preparing this fancy seafood dish."

"Where does the pizza come in?"

Kate told Luke about the disastrous dinner, and he smiled slightly, shaking his head. "Rorie must've been devastated."

"Actually she was a pretty good sport about the whole thing. We called Pizza Mania, ordered two large pizzas that Skip offered to pick up, and afterward we sat around the piano for a while."

That night was when she'd realized how hard Clay was fighting not to fall in love with Rorie. All evening he'd tried not to even glance in her direction. Then, later, when he drove Kate home, he'd said barely a word and gently kissed her cheek after he'd walked her to the door. A peck on the cheek, the way he'd kiss a younger sister.

"What's wrong?" Luke asked.

"Nothing." Kate summoned a smile. "What makes you ask?" She was relieved at the appearance of their vegetable appetizer, immediately reaching for a carrot stick.

"Your eyes looked kind of sad just now."

Kate concentrated on munching her carrot, astonished at the way Luke so often seemed to know what she was thinking. But then, sometimes he didn't.... "That night was when I knew I was losing Clay to Rorie. My whole world was about to fall apart and I felt powerless to do anything about it. It didn't mean I stopped trying, of course—it hurt too much to accept without putting up a fight." She paused and helped herself to a zucchini strip. "Enough about me. It seems I'm the only one we ever discuss. How was your trip to New Mexico?" she asked brightly, determined to change the subject.

"Good." He didn't elaborate. His eyes held hers, the mood warm and comfortable. "There are going to be a few changes around the Circle L in the coming months. I don't want you to be surprised when you find out I'm adding a couple of outbuildings and doing some remodelling on the house."

Although he spoke in a conversational tone, Kate wasn't fooled. "The Circle L belongs to you now. I expect there'll be plenty of changes, but don't worry about offending me or Dad."

He nodded and his eyes brightened with his dreams for the future. "I intend to turn it into one of the top cattle ranches on the West Coast."

"I'm sure you'll do it, Luke." And she was.

He seemed pleased by her confidence in him. Kate couldn't help believing in Luke. In the ten years he'd worked for her father, he'd initiated several successful breeding programs. With each passing year, Devin had turned more and more of the ranch business over to Luke. Her father had become a figurehead. Kate had often heard Devin say that he couldn't understand why Luke would continue working for him when he was completely capable of maintaining his own spread. At one time, Kate had thought money was the issue, but that obviously wasn't the case.

"Why'd you delay buying your own ranch for so long?" Kate asked, just as their pizza arrived. Their waitress remained standing at their table and studied them so blatantly that Luke turned to her.

"Is something wrong?" he asked sharply.

"No...not at all. Enjoy your dinner." She backed away from their table and hurried over to the counter, where two other employees were waiting. Almost immediately the three of them huddled together and started whispering.

Luke chose to ignore their waitress's strange behavior and lifted a steaming piece, thick with melted cheese and spicy sausage, onto her plate. Then he served himself.

"Now, where were we?" Luke murmured.

"I asked why you didn't buy your own ranch before now."

"You don't want to know the answer to that, Princess."

"Of course I do. I wouldn't have brought it up otherwise," she insisted.

"Fine." Luke settled back in his chair. He looked at her, eyes thoughtful. "I had a minor problem. I was in love with the boss's daughter and she was crazy about me, only she didn't know it. In fact, she'd gotten herself engaged to someone else. I was afraid that if I moved away she'd never realize how I felt—or how she did—and frankly, I didn't think I could ever love anyone the way I do her."

Kate focused her attention on her meal. The lump in her throat was almost choking her. "You're right about... me not loving Clay," she told him softly. No matter how hard she tried, she couldn't raise her eyes high enough to meet his.

"What did you say?"

"I... You were right about me and Clay. I could never feel for him the things a wife should feel for her husband. I'd adored him for years, but that love was just a teenage fantasy."

She was well aware of the seriousness of her admission. The room seemed to go still; the music from the juke box faded, the clatter from the kitchen dimmed and the voices from the people around them seemed to disappear altogether.

"I didn't think I'd ever hear you admit that," Luke said, and his face filled with tenderness.

"I tried to tell you the night after I had dinner with Clay and Rorie, but you were so angry with me...because I was moving." She laughed, hoping to break the unexpected tension that had leaped between them.

"Does this also mean you're admitting you love *me*?"

"I've never had a problem with that—"

Kate was interrupted by an elderly man who strolled up to their table. With considerable ceremony, he lifted a violin to his chin and played a bittersweet love song.

"I didn't know they had strolling violinists here," Kate said when the man had finished. Everyone in the restaurant stopped to applaud.

"This next song is dedicated to the two of you," the man announced, "that the love in your hearts will blossom into a bouquet of *May* flowers."

It wasn't until he'd finished the third song that Kate noticed he didn't go to any of the other tables. He seemed to be playing only for them. Some of the customers had apparently noticed this, too, and gathered behind Luke and Kate in order to get a better view of the musician.

"Thank you," Kate said as the last notes faded.

The man lowered his instrument to his side. "You two have become quite a sensation in Nightingale and beyond. We at Pizza Mania are honored that you've chosen our restaurant for a romantic evening. We want to do our part to bring you together in wedded bliss."

"And you're suggesting the month of May?" Kate asked, referring to his comment about a bouquet of flowers.

"That would be an excellent choice," the violinist said, grinning broadly.

"It's time we left," Luke said, frowning. He pulled out his wallet, but the violinist stopped him. "Please, your pizza's on the house. We are delighted that you chose to dine in our humble establishment."

From the tight set of Luke's mouth, Kate could tell he wanted to argue, but more urgent was his need to escape. He took her by the hand and charged for the door.

"Your leftover pizza!" Their waitress ran after them, handing Luke a large white box as she cast Kate an envious glance.

Luke couldn't seem to get out of the car park fast enough. Kate waited until they were on the road before she spoke. "So this is the first time that's happened to you?"

Luke laughed shortly. "Not really, only I didn't pick up on it as quickly as you did. Several people have made odd comments about certain months, but until now, I didn't get what they were actually saying."

"It's funny when you think about it. Half the county's got money riding on our wedding day, and Fred Garner's making a killing raising and lowering the odds." Suddenly the lottery was the most hilarious thing Kate had ever heard of, and she started to laugh. She slumped against the side of the cab, holding her sides. She was laughing so hard, her stomach hurt. Tears ran down her cheeks and she wiped them away as she tried to regain control. The wedding lottery and everyone's interference wasn't all *that* funny, but Luke's disgruntled reaction was.

"Come on, Luke," she said, still chuckling. "There's a lot of humor in this situation."

He snorted.

"Don't be such a killjoy. I've been getting free advice from the butcher, Sally Daley, the paperboy and just about everyone else in town. It's only fair that you put up with a few of their comments, too."

"One might think you'd take some of that free advice," he muttered.

"What?" she cried. "And ruin their fun?"

Luke was oddly quiet for the remainder of the trip into Nightingale. He stopped at her building, walked her to her door with barely a word, then turned and walked away. No goodnight kiss, no mention of seeing her again.

This was the last thing she'd expected. For the entire drive home, she'd been imagining how good it would feel when Luke kissed her. She'd decided to invite him in for coffee, hoping he'd accept. But this was even worse than Clay's peck on the cheek all those months ago.

"Luke…"

He stopped abruptly at the sound of her voice, then turned back. His eyes seemed to burn into hers as he came toward her, and she stumbled into his arms. His mouth, hot and hungry, sought hers in a kiss that scorched her senses.

His fingers plunged into her hair, releasing the French braid and ploughing through the twisted strands of blond hair.

Instinctively Kate reached up and slid her arms around his shoulders, feeling so much at home in his arms that it frightened her. She trembled with the knowledge, but she didn't have time to analyze her feelings. Not when her world was in chaos. She clung to him as though she were rocketing into a fathomless sky.

Luke broke away from her, his face a study of hope and confusion. "I never know where I stand with you, Kate." With that, he stroked her hair and quickly returned to his truck.

Kate was still reeling from the effects of Luke's kiss. If

she hadn't leaned against her door, she might have fallen onto the walkway, so profound was her reaction.

"Luke," she called, shocked by how weak her voice sounded. "Would you like to come inside for coffee? We could talk about…things."

Slowly a smile eased its way across his handsome features. "I don't dare, Princess, because the way I feel right now, I might not leave until morning. If then."

Flustered by his words, Kate unlocked her door and let herself inside.

She gulped a deep breath and stood in the middle of the living room with her hand over her rampaging heart. "You're in love with him, Kate Logan," she told herself. "Head over heels in love with a man and fighting him every step of the way."

Groaning, she buried her face in her hands. She didn't understand *why* she'd been fighting him so hard. She did realize that Luke wouldn't have spent years building up her father's ranch if he hadn't loved her. He could have left anytime, gone anywhere to buy his own ranch, but he'd stayed at the Circle L. He honestly loved her!

Now she knew what she wanted, but she didn't know what to do about it.

She guessed Luke was planning to court her, to use that charming old-fashioned term. If so, one more dinner with him would be enough. They'd be officially engaged by the end of the evening. She'd bet on it!

To her disappointment, Kate didn't hear from him the following day. Fridays were generally busy around the ranch, so she decided the next move would have to come from her.

Early Saturday morning she compiled a grocery list, intent on inviting Luke over for a home-cooked meal. She was reviewing her cookbooks, searching for a special dessert recipe, when she was suddenly distracted by the memory of their kiss. Closing her eyes, she relived the way she'd felt that night. She smiled to herself, admitting how eager she was to feel that way again.

If only she'd been listening to her heart instead of her pride...

She tried phoning Luke, but there was no answer, so she decided to do the shopping first. She put on her coat, hat and gloves, and walked the few blocks to the Safeway store.

It must've been her imagination, but it seemed that everyone stopped to watch her as she pushed her cart down the aisles.

When she'd finished buying her groceries, she headed over to the pharmacy and bought a couple of scented candles. Once again, everyone seemed to stop and stare at her.

"Kate," Sally Daley said, hurrying toward her. The older woman was shaking her head, eyes brimming with sympathy. "How are you doing, dear?"

"Fine," Kate said, puzzled.

Sally's mouth fell open. "You don't know, do you?"

"Know what?"

"Luke Rivers took Beth Hammond to dinner yesterday, and the two of them danced all night at the Red Bull. Why, everyone in town's talking about it. People are saying he's lost patience with you and is going to marry Beth. Really, dear, every woman in town thinks you'd be crazy to let a man like Luke Rivers get away."

Kate was so shocked she could hardly breathe. "I see," she murmured, pretending it didn't matter.

"You poor child," Sally said compassionately. "Don't let your pride get in the way."

"I won't," Kate promised, barely able to find her voice.

"I do worry about you, Kate. I have this terrible feeling that you're going to end up thirty and all alone."

Eleven

Thirty and all alone. The words echoed in Kate's mind as she walked the short distance to her apartment. Tears burned her eyes, but somehow she'd dredged up the courage to smile and assure Sally that Luke was free to date whomever he pleased. In fact, she'd even managed to laugh lightly and say that she hoped Luke's dating Beth would finally put an end to all this wedding-lottery nonsense.

Moving at a fast pace, she kept her head lowered and went directly back to her apartment, clutching her purchases. By the time she let herself in the door, her face was streaked with tears.

No doubt Sally would spread the story of her meeting with Kate all over town by evening. Not that it made much difference. By now, the residents of Nightingale should be accustomed to hearing gossip about her and Luke.

Luke. At the mere thought of him, her heart constricted painfully. He'd given up on her and now she'd lost him. Only it hurt so much more than when Clay had broken their engagement.

Wiping the tears from her eyes, she struggled to take in everything that had happened in the past few weeks. It seemed every time she found her balance and secured her footing, something would send her teetering again. Would it never end? Was her life going to be an endless struggle of one emotional pain after another?

She set her bags on the floor, and without bothering to remove her coat, slumped into the overstuffed chair.

"Okay," she said aloud. "Luke took Beth Hammond out to dinner and dancing. It doesn't have to mean anything."

But it did. In her heart Kate was sure Luke planned to do exactly as Sally suggested. He'd made it plain from the first that he wanted a wife, and like a fool Kate had repeatedly turned him down. He loved her, or so he claimed, and Kate had doubted him. Now she wondered if perhaps he didn't love her enough. But over and over again, Luke had insisted she needed him—and he'd been right.

Closing her eyes, she tried to picture her life without Luke. A chill ran down her spine as an intense wave of loneliness swept over her.

Someone pounded at the door, but before Kate could answer it, Luke strode into the apartment. Having to face him this way, when she was least prepared, put her at a clear disadvantage. Hurriedly she painted on a bright smile.

"Hello, Luke," she said, trying to sound breezy and amused. "What's this about you and Beth Hammond?"

"You heard already?" He looked stunned.

"Good heavens, yes. You don't expect something like that to stay quiet, do you?"

"When...who told you?"

"I went to the grocery store and ran into Sally Daley."

"That explains it," he said, pacing her carpet with abrupt, impatient steps. He stopped suddenly and turned to study her. "It doesn't bother you that I'm seeing Beth?"

"Not at all," she lied. "Should it? Would you like some coffee?"

"No."

Desperate for a chance to escape and compose herself, Kate almost ran into the kitchen and poured herself a cup, keeping her back to him all the while.

"You seem to be downright happy about this," he accused, following her into the small, windowless room.

"Of course I'm pleased. I think it's wonderful when two people fall in love, don't you?"

"I'm not in love with Beth," he said angrily.

"Actually I think dating Beth is a wonderful way to kill all the rumors floating around about us," she said, finally turning toward him. She held her coffee cup close.

Rubbing his neck, Luke continued his pacing in the kitchen. "I thought you might be…jealous."

"Me?" She refused to admit she'd been dying inside from the moment Sally had told her. "Now why would I feel like that?"

"I don't know," Luke barked. "Why would you?"

Before Kate could answer, he stormed out of the apartment, leaving her so frustrated she could have cried.

"You should've told him how you feel," she reprimanded herself. "Why are you such a fool when it comes to Luke Rivers? Why? Why? Why?"

"I saw Luke yesterday," Rorie said, watching Kate closely as they sat across from each other in a booth at Nellie's.

"That's nice," she said, pretending indifference and doing a good job of it.

"He was with Beth Hammond."

Kate's breath caught in her throat at the unexpected rush of pain. "I…see."

"Do you?" Rorie inquired. "I swear I could shake the pair of you. I've never met two more stubborn people in my life. You look like one of the walking wounded, and

Luke's got a chip on his shoulder the size of a California redwood."

"I'm sure you're mistaken." Kate concentrated on stirring her coffee and avoided Rorie's eyes. Her heart felt like a ball of lead.

"When's the last time you two talked?"

"A couple of days ago."

"Honestly, Kate, I can't understand what's wrong with you. Clay and I thought…we hoped everything would fall into place after you moved to the apartment. Now it seems exactly the opposite has happened."

"Luke's free to date whomever he pleases, just the way I am."

"There's only one person you want and that's Luke Rivers and we both know it," Rorie said with an exasperated sigh. "I shouldn't have said that. It's just that I hate the idea of you two being so miserable when you're in love with each other."

"Is love always this painful?" Kate asked, her question barely audible.

Rorie shrugged. "It was with Clay and me, and sometimes I feel it must be for everyone sooner or later. Think about it, Kate. If you really love Luke, why are you fighting the very thing you want most?"

"I don't know," she admitted reluctantly.

When they parted shortly afterward, Kate felt a new sense of certainty and resolve. She *did* love Luke and if she didn't do something soon, she was going to lose him.

She drove to the Circle L, her heart in her throat. Luke's truck was parked behind the house, and she left her car beside it, hurrying through the cold to the back door. Luke didn't respond to her knock, which didn't surprise her, since it was unusual for him to be in at this time of day.

But she couldn't find him outside, either, and even Bill didn't know where he was.

Making a rapid decision, she let herself into the house and started preparations for the evening meal. It gave her a way of passing the time. Dinner was in the oven and she was busy making a salad, when the back door opened and Luke walked into the kitchen.

Apparently he hadn't noticed her car because he stopped dead, shock written on every feature, when he saw her standing at the sink.

Kate held her breath for a moment, then dried her hands on the dish towel she'd tucked into her waistband. She struggled to give the impression that she was completely at ease, tried to act as though she made dinner for him every evening.

"Hello, Luke," she said to break the silence that had been growing heavier by the second.

He blinked. "I suppose you're looking for an explanation."

Kate wasn't sure what he meant.

"Taking Beth out on Friday night was a mistake."

"Then why'd you do it?"

"So you'd be jealous. The night you and I went out, I was furious at the way you started laughing, and talking as if you were never going to marry me. I wanted you to know you weren't the only fish in the sea. Only my plan backfired."

"It did?" Not as far as Kate was concerned—she'd been pretty darn worried.

"That wasn't all that went wrong. Beth saw I was in town on Saturday and started following me," he explained. "I swear I had no intention of seeing her again, but before I knew it, her arm was linked with mine and we were strolling through the middle of town together."

"Beth's a nice girl."

He frowned. "Yes, I suppose she is. I'd forgotten it doesn't bother you who I date. You've never been one for jealousy."

"I was so jealous I wanted to die."

"You were? You could've fooled me."

"Believe me, I tried to," Kate murmured.

"So what are you doing here?"

"I made dinner," Kate said sheepishly. She'd admitted how she felt about Luke seeing Beth and she couldn't stop there. "I've got pork chops in the oven, along with scalloped potatoes and an acorn squash," she rattled off without pausing for breath. Then, gathering her resolve, she casually added, "and if you're still asking, I'll marry you."

Luke stared at her. When he finally spoke he sounded strangely calm. "What did you just say?"

"There's pork chops and potatoes and—"

"Not that. The part about marrying me."

She struggled to hold on to what remained of her tattered pride. "If you're still asking me to marry you, the answer is yes."

"I'm still asking."

Kate dropped her gaze. "You've been right about so much. I do need you. I guess I was waiting for you to admit you needed *me,* only you never did."

Luke rubbed a hand over his face. "Not need you?" he repeated, his voice filled with shock and wonder. "I think my life would be an empty shell without you, Kate. I couldn't bear the thought of living one day to the next if you weren't at my side to share everything with me—all the good things that are in store for us. I've waited so long, Kate."

"You do love me, don't you?" she whispered.

For a long, long moment Luke said nothing. "I tried not to. For years I stood by helplessly, watching you break out in hives with excitement every time you saw Clay Franklin. I realized it was a schoolgirl crush, but you never seemed to get over him. Instead of improving, things got worse. How could I let you know how I felt?"

"Couldn't you have said something? Anything?"

A flicker of pain crossed his face. "No. You were so infatuated with Clay I didn't dare. It wouldn't have done any good—although God only knows how you managed not to figure it out yourself. The first day Rorie met me, she guessed."

"Rorie knew all along?"

Luke shook his head in bewildered amusement. "We were quite a pair a few months back—Rorie in love with Clay and me crazy about you. All this time, I thought I'd kept my feelings secret, and then I discovered everyone in town knew."

"Beth Hammond didn't."

"No, but she should have. I've never wanted anyone but you, Kate Logan. I haven't for years. Somehow I always kept hoping you'd see the light."

"Oh, Luke." She took a step toward him, her eyes full of emotion. "Are you going to stand way over there on the other side of the room?"

For every step Kate took, Luke managed three. When they reached each other, she put her arms around his waist, hugging him tight. She felt the beating of his heart and closed her eyes, succumbing to the wave of love that seemed about to overwhelm her.

Luke's hand was gentle on her hair. "Do you love me, Kate?"

She couldn't speak, so she nodded her head wildly. Her hands framed his face and she spread light, eager kisses over his mouth and nose and eyes, letting her lips explain what was in her heart.

"I love you," he whispered. "If you marry me, I promise I'll do everything I can to make you happy." His eyes shone with delight and a kind of humility that touched Kate's very soul. Gone was the remoteness he'd displayed so often these past few weeks.

"Oh, Luke, I can hardly wait to be your wife," she said. "Didn't you say something about a December wedding?"

"Kate, that's only a few weeks from now."

"Yes, I know. But Christmas is such a lovely time of year for a wedding. We'll decorate the church with holly, and all the bridesmaids will wear long red dresses...."

"Kate, you mean it, don't you?" His voice was low and husky.

"I've never meant anything more. I love you, Luke Rivers. We're going to have a wonderful life together."

He kissed her then, with a hunger that spoke of his years of longing. Dragging his mouth from hers, he buried it in the curve of her neck.

"I want children, Kate. I want to fill this home with so much love that the walls threaten to burst with it."

For a breathless moment, they did nothing more than gaze at each other as they shared that dream.

Kate smiled up at him, and as her hands mapped his face, loving each strong feature, she was astonished at how easily this happiness had come to her once she'd let go of her pride.

Luke's mouth settled on hers, his kiss almost reverent, as though he couldn't yet believe she was in his home and eager to be his wife.

As Kate wrapped her arms around his neck, her glance fell on the calendar. She seemed to recall that Pastor Wilkins had placed a sizeable wager on the fifteenth of December. That sounded good to Kate.

Very good indeed.

Epilogue

The sun shone clear and bright in the late-July afternoon, two years after Rorie Campbell's car had broken down near Nightingale. Kate was making a fresh pitcher of iced tea when Rorie knocked on the back door.

"Come on in," Kate called. "The screen door's unlocked."

A moment later Rorie entered the kitchen, looking slightly frazzled. "How did your afternoon at the library go?" Kate asked, as she added ice cubes to the tall pitcher.

"Very well, thanks."

"Katherine's still sleeping," Kate told her.

Rorie's eyes softened as she gazed out at the newly constructed patio where her baby slept under the shade of the huge oak tree.

"It was such a lovely afternoon I kept her outside." Kate wiped her hands dry. She poured them each a glass of iced tea, and carried a tray of tea and cookies onto the patio.

The nine-month-old infant stirred when Rorie stood over the portable crib and protectively placed her hand on the sleeping baby's back. When she turned, her eyes fell on Kate's protruding abdomen. "How are *you* feeling?"

"Like a blimp." Kate's hands rested on her swollen

stomach. "The doctor told me it'll probably be another two weeks."

"Two weeks!" Rorie said sympathetically.

"I know, and I was hoping Junior would choose this week to arrive. I swear to you, Rorie, when you were pregnant with Katherine you positively glowed. You made everything seem so easy."

Rorie laughed. "I did?"

"I feel miserable. My legs are swollen, my hands and feet look like they've been inflated. There isn't a single part of my body that's normal-sized anymore."

Rorie laughed again. "The last few weeks are always like that. I think the main difference is that Katherine was born in October, when the weather was much cooler."

With some difficulty Kate crossed her legs. "I only hope our baby will be as good-natured as Katherine. She barely fussed the whole time she was here."

"Her uncle Skip thinks she's going to start walking soon."

"I think he's right." Pressing a hand to her ribs, Kate shifted her position. She was finding it difficult to sit comfortably for longer than a few minutes at a time.

"Oh—" Rorie set her iced tea aside "—I almost forgot." She hurried back to the kitchen and returned with a hardbound children's book. "I received my first copies of *Nightsong's Adventures* in the mail yesterday. Kate, I can't even begin to tell you how thrilled I was when I held this book in my hands."

Kate laid the book on her lap and slowly turned the pages. "The illustrations are fantastic. They really fit the story."

"The reviews have been excellent. One critic said he expected it to become a children's classic, which I realize is ridiculous, but I couldn't help feeling excited about it."

"It isn't ridiculous, and I'm sure your publisher knows that, otherwise they wouldn't have been so eager to buy your second book."

"You know, the second sale was every bit as exciting as the first," Rorie said with a smile.

"Just think, in a few years our children will be reading your stories and attending school together. They're bound to be the best of friends."

Before Kate could respond, the baby woke and they watched, delighted, as she sat up in the portable crib. When she saw her mother sitting next to Kate, she smiled, her dark eyes twinkling. She raised her chubby arms, reaching for Rorie.

Rorie stood and lifted Katherine out of the crib, kissing the little girl's cheeks. "I'd better get her home. Thanks so much for watching Katherine for me. I promised I'd pinch-hit for the new librarian if she ever needed me, and I didn't think I could refuse her even though it was at the last minute."

"It wasn't any problem, so don't worry. And tell Mary she should visit her sister more often so I get the opportunity to babysit every once in a while."

"Call me later and let me know how you're feeling."

Kate nodded.

Ten minutes after Rorie and Katherine left, Luke drove up and parked behind the house. Standing on the porch, Kate waved to her husband.

Luke joined her, placing an arm around what once had been a trim waist, and led the way into the kitchen. "You okay?" His gaze was tender.

Kate wasn't sure how to answer that. She was miserable. Excited. Frightened. Eager. So many emotions were coming at her, she didn't know which one to mention first.

"Kate?"

"I feel fine." There was no need to list her complaints, but all of a sudden she felt *funny*. She didn't know any other way to describe it. As Rorie had said, there were a dozen different aches and pains the last few weeks of any pregnancy.

Luke kissed her, his mouth soft. "Did you have a busy day with Katherine?"

"She slept almost the entire time, but I think Rorie knew she would." Leaning forward, Kate kissed her husband's jaw. "I made some iced tea. Want some?"

"Please."

When Kate reached inside the cupboard for a glass, a sharp pain split her side. She let out a cry.

"Kate?"

Clutching her swollen abdomen, Kate stared at Luke. "Oh, my goodness. I just felt a pain."

Luke paled. "You're in labor?"

Smiling, wide-eyed, she nodded slowly. "I must be. I didn't expect them to start off so strong."

In an instant, Luke was across the kitchen beside her. "Now what?"

"I think I should call the doctor."

"No." Luke's arm flew out as if that would halt the course of nature. "I'll call. Stay there. Don't move."

"But, Luke—"

"For heaven's sake, Kate, don't argue with me now. We're about to have a baby!"

He said this as if it were a recent discovery. As he reached for the phone, she saw that he'd gone deathly pale. When he finished talking to the doctor, he gave her a panicked look, then announced that Doc Adams wanted them to go straight to the hospital. As soon as the words left his mouth, he shot to the bedroom, then returned with her suitcase. He halted abruptly when he saw she'd picked up the phone.

"Who are you calling?"

"Dad and Dorothea. I promised I would."

"Kate, would you let me do the phoning?"

"All right." She handed him the receiver and started toward the bedroom to collect the rest of her things. If he thought that talking on the phone was too taxing for her, fine. She'd let him do it. The years had taught her that arguing with Luke was fruitless.

"Kate," he yelled. "Don't wander off."

"Luke, I just want to get my things before we leave." A pain began to work its way around her back and she paused, flattening her hands across her abdomen. She raised her head and smiled up at her husband. "Oh, Luke, the baby..."

Luke dropped the receiver and rushed to her side. "Now?"

"No." She laughed and touched his face. "It'll be hours yet. Oh! I just felt another pain—a bad one."

He swallowed hard and gripped both her hands in his own. "I've been looking forward to this moment for nine months, but I swear to you, Kate, I've never been more frightened in my life."

"Don't worry." Her hands caressed his face and she kissed him, offering what reassurance she could.

He exhaled noisily, then gave her a brisk little nod. Without warning, he lifted her in his arms, ignoring her protests, and carried her out the door to the truck. Once he'd settled her in the seat, he returned to the house for her bag.

"Luke," she called after him, "I really would like to talk to Dad and Dorothea."

"I'll phone them from the hospital. No more arguing, Kate. I'm in charge here."

Only another sharp pain—and her regard for Luke's feelings—kept her from breaking out in laughter.

Ten long hours later, Kate lay in the hospital bed, eyes closed in exhaustion. When she opened them, she discovered her father standing over her. Dorothea was next to him, looking as pleased and proud as Kate's father. Devin took his daughter's hand in his own and squeezed it gently. "How do you feel, little mother?"

"Wonderful. Did they let you see him? Oh, Dad, he's so beautiful!"

Her father nodded. For a moment he seemed unable to speak. "Luke's with Matthew now. He looks so big sitting in that rocking chair, holding his son."

"I don't think I've ever seen Luke wear an expression quite like that before," Dorothea murmured. "So tender and loving."

Devin concurred with a nod of his head. "When Luke came into the waiting room to tell us Matthew Devin had been born, there were tears in his eyes. I'll tell you, Kate, that man loves you."

"I know, Dad, and I love him, too."

Devin patted her hand. "You go ahead and rest, Princess. Dorothea and I'll be back tomorrow."

When Kate opened her eyes a second time, Luke was there. She held out her hand to him and smiled dreamily. "I couldn't have done it without you. Thank you for staying with me."

"Staying with you," he echoed, his fingers brushing the tousled curls from her face. "Nothing on earth could have kept me away. I would've done anything to spare you that pain, Kate. Anything." His voice was raw with the memory of those last hours.

Her smile was one of comfort. "It only lasted a little while and we have a beautiful son to show for it."

"All these months when we've talked about the baby," he said, his eyes glazed, "he seemed so unreal to me, and then you were in the delivery room and in so much agony. I felt so helpless. I wanted to help you and there was nothing I could do. Then Matthew was born and, Kate, I looked at him and I swear something happened to my heart. The love I felt for that baby, that tiny person, was so strong, so powerful, I could hardly breathe. I thought I was going to break down right there in front of everyone."

"Oh, Luke."

"There's no way I could ever thank you for all you've given me, Kate Rivers."

"Yes, there is," she said with a smile. "Just love me."

"I do," he whispered, his voice husky with emotion. "And I always will."

* * * * *

WOODROSE MOUNTAIN

To all the teachers, aides and physical, occupational and speech therapists who have been such a valued part of our life, working tirelessly to help children reach beyond their abilities. Thank you!

One

On a warm summer evening, the homes and buildings of Hope's Crossing nestled among the trees like brightly colored stones in a drawer—a brilliant lapis-lazuli roof here, a carnelian-painted garage here, the warm topaz of the old hospital bricks.

Evaline Blanchard rested a hip against a massive granite rock, taking a moment to catch her breath on a flat area of the Woodrose Mountain trail winding through the pines above the town she had adopted as her own.

From here, she could see the quaint old buildings, the colorful flower gardens in full bloom, Old Glory hanging everywhere. At nearly sunset on a Sunday, downtown was mostly quiet—though she could see a few cars parked in the lot of the historic Episcopalian church that had been the first brick structure in town, back when Hope's Crossing was a hustling, bustling mining town with a dozen saloons. Probably a Sunday-evening prayer service, she guessed.

Farther away, she could see more cars and a bustle of activity near Miners' Park and she suddenly remembered a bluegrass band was performing on the outdoor stage there for the weekly concert-in-the-park series.

Maybe she should have opted for an evening of music

in the park instead of heading up into the mountains. She always enjoyed the concerts on a lovely summer night and the fun of sitting with her neighbors and friends, sharing good music and maybe a glass of wine and a boxed dinner from the café.

No, this was the better choice. As much as she enjoyed outdoor concerts, after three days of dealing with customers nearly nonstop at the outdoor art fair she had just attended in Grand Junction, she had been desperate for a little quiet.

Next to her, Jacques, her blond Labradoodle, stretched out on the dirt trail with a bored sort of air, tormenting a deerfly with the effrontery to buzz around his head.

"You don't have any patience when I have to stop to catch my breath, do you?"

He finally took pity on the fly—sort of—and swallowed it, then grinned at her as if he had conquered some advanced Jedi Master skill. Mission accomplished, he lumbered to his big paws and looked at her expectantly, obviously eager for more exercise.

She couldn't blame him. He had been endlessly patient during three days of sitting in a booth. He deserved a good, hard run. Too bad her glutes and quads weren't in the mood to cooperate.

Finally she caught her breath and headed up again, keeping to a slow jog. Despite the muscle aches, more of her tension melted away with each step.

She used to love running on the beach back in California, with the sea-soaked air in her face and the thud of her jogging shoes on the packed sand and the sheer, unadulterated magnificence of the Pacific always in view.

No ocean in sight here. Only the towering pines and aspens, the understory of western thimbleberry and wild roses, and the occasional bright flash of a mountain blue-bird darting through the bushes.

She was content with no sound of gulls overhead. She still loved the ocean, without question, and at times yearned to be alone on a beach somewhere while the surf pounded the shore, but somehow this place had become home.

Who would have expected that a born-and-bred California girl could find this sort of peace and belonging in a little tourist town nestled in the Rockies?

She inhaled a deep, sage-scented breath, more tension easing out of her shoulders with every passing moment. It had been a hectic three days. This was her fourth outdoor arts-and-crafts fair of the season and she had one more scheduled before September. Her crazy idea to set up a booth at summer fairs across Colorado to sell her own wares and those of the other clients of String Fever—the bead store in Hope's Crossing where she worked—had taken off beyond her wildest dreams.

She was especially pleased, since all of the beaders participating had agreed to donate a portion of their proceeds to the Layla Parker memorial scholarship fund.

Layla was the daughter of Evie's good friend Maura McKnight-Parker and she had been killed in April in a tragic accident that had ripped apart the peace of Hope's Crossing and shredded it into tiny pieces.

Outdoor art-and-crafts fairs were exciting and dynamic, full of color and sound and people. But it was also hard work, especially when she worked by herself. Setting up the awning, arranging the beadwork displays, dealing with customers, running credit cards. All of it posed challenges.

Over the weekend, she'd had to deal with two shoplifters and the inevitable paperwork that resulted. This Sunday-evening run was exactly what she needed.

Finally tired, her muscles comfortably burning, she took the fork in the trail that headed back to town, her cross-trainers stirring up little clouds of dirt with every step. She'd forgotten her water bottle in her haste to get up on the cool trail after the drive and suddenly all she could think about was a long, cold drink of water.

The return trip took her and Jacques down Sweet Laurel Road, past some of the small, wood-framed older houses that had been built when the town was raw and new. She saw Caroline Bybee out watering her gorgeous flowers, her wiry gray braids covered by a big, floppy straw hat. Evie waved to her but didn't stop to talk.

The air smelled of a summer evening, of grilling meat from a barbecue somewhere, onions being cooked in one house she passed, fresh-mown grass at another, all with the undertone of pine and sage from the surrounding mountains.

By the time she turned at the top of steep Main Street and headed past the storefronts toward her little two-bedroom apartment above String Fever, she was hungry and tired and only wanted to put her feet up for a couple of hours with a good book and a cup of tea.

String Fever was housed in a two-story brick building that once had been the town's most notorious brothel, back in the days when this particular piece of Colorado was full of rowdy miners. She cut through an alley that opened onto the lovely little fenced garden behind the store, enjoying the sweet glow of the sunset on the weathered brick.

Jacques gave one sharp bark when she reached the gate into the garden, barely big enough for some flowers, a patch of grass and a table and four chairs where the String Fever employees took breaks or the kids of Claire Bradford—soon to be Claire McKnight—could hang out and do homework when their mother was working.

Evie really needed to think about moving into a bigger place where Jacques could have room to run. When she had moved into the apartment above the store, she'd never planned on having a dog, especially not a good-size one like Jacques. She had only intended to foster him for a few weeks as a favor to a friend who volunteered at the animal shelter, but Evie had fallen hard for the big, gentle dog with the incongruously charming poodle fur.

"Hold on, you crazy dog. You're probably as thirsty as I am. I can let you off your leash in a minute."

She pushed through the gate, then froze as Jacques instantly barked again at a figure sitting at one of the wrought-iron chairs. The shade of the umbrella obscured his features and her heart gave a well-conditioned little stutter at finding a strange man in her back garden.

Back in L.A., she probably would have already had one finger on the nozzle of her pepper spray and one on the last "1" in 9-1-1 on her cell phone, just in case.

Here in Hope's Crossing, when a strange man showed up just before dark, she was definitely still cautious but not panicky. Yet.

She peered through the beginnings of pearly twilight and suddenly recognized the man—and all her alarm bells started clanging even louder. She would much rather face a half dozen knife-wielding criminals out to do her harm than Brodie Thorne.

"Evening," he said and rose from the table, tall and lean and dark amid the spilling flowerpots set around the pocket garden.

Jacques strained against the leash, something he didn't normally do. As she wasn't expecting it and hadn't had time to wrap her fingers more tightly around it, the leash slipped through and Jacques used his newfound freedom to rush eagerly toward the strange man.

The distance was short and she'd barely formed the words of the *sit* command before the dog reached Brodie. Given her experience with the annoying man, she braced for him to push the dog away with some rude comment about how she couldn't keep her dog under any better control than her life, or something equally disdainful. Instead, he surprised her by scratching the dog between his Lab-shaped ears.

She didn't want him to be kind to dogs. It was a jarring note in an otherwise unpleasant personality.

Her relationship with Brodie had gotten off to a rocky start from the moment she'd started an email friendship with his mother nearly three years ago on a beading loop, a friendship that had finally led Evie to Hope's Crossing and String Fever, the store Katherine had opened several years ago and eventually sold to Claire Bradford.

His mother had become a dear friend. She had offered unending support and love to Evie during a very dark time and Evie adored her. She owed Katherine so much. Being polite to her abrasive son was a small enough thing, especially since Brodie had troubles of his own right now.

"Sorry. Have you been waiting long?" she asked after an awkward, jerky sort of pause.

"Ten minutes or so. I was about to leave you a note when I heard you coming down the alley."

She didn't feel at all prepared to talk to him, especially when she couldn't focus on anything but her thirst. "I'm sorry, but I didn't take my water bottle on my run and I desperately need a drink. Can you give me a minute?"

"Sure."

"Do you want to come up or wait for me down here?"

"I'll come up."

On second thought, she should have phrased that differently. *How about you wait here where it's safe and stay*

the heck out of my personal bubble. Alas, too late to re-
scind the invitation now.

She led the way up her narrow staircase, aware with
each step of the man following closely behind her. She
wasn't used to men in this space, she suddenly realized.
Yes, she had dated a few times since she'd come to Hope's
Crossing, but nothing serious and nobody she would consider inviting up to her personal sanctuary.

For the most part, her life was surrounded by women.
She worked in a bead store, for heaven's sake, a location
not usually overflowing with an overabundance of tes-
tosterone. If she wanted to date, she was going to have
to put a little effort into it. Now that she almost thought
she'd begun to finally achieve some level of serenity after
the last rough two years, maybe it was time she did something about that.

If she *were* to start thinking seriously about entering
that particular arena again, she could guarantee with absolute certainty that the words *Brodie Thorne* and *dating*
would never appear in the same context in her head—even
though he was gorgeous, if one went for the sexy, dark-
haired, buttoned-down businessman type.

Which she so didn't.

She pulled her house key out of the small zipper pocket
on the inside waistband of her leggings and unlocked the
door. As soon as it swung open, she winced. She had forgotten the mess she'd left behind when she headed up into
the mountains immediately after her return to town—the
jumble of boxes and bags and suitcases. She really ought
to have left Brodie down in the garden with Jacques.

Brodie raised an eyebrow at the mess—or perhaps at her
eclectic design tastes, with the mismatched furniture covered in mounds of pillows, the wispy curtains on the windows and the jeweled lampshades she'd created one winter

night when she was bored. It was a far cry from her sleek little house in Topanga Canyon or her childhood home, a sprawling mansion in Santa Barbara, but she loved it.

Brodie lived in a huge designer cedar-and-glass house up the canyon high on the mountain, she remembered. She could only imagine what he must think of her humble apartment—and the fact that she could spend even an instant being embarrassed about her surroundings sparked anger at herself and completely unreasonable annoyance at him.

"Sorry. I'm in a bit of a mess. I only arrived back in town an hour ago from an art fair in Grand Junction. I'm afraid I only stopped here long enough to unload the car before Jacques and I took off for a run."

She moved her suitcase out of the way so he could enter the living room and immediately the space seemed to shrink in half. Good thing she'd left Jacques down in the garden or she wouldn't have room to breathe, with two big, rangy males in her small quarters.

"No problem."

He moved inside the room but didn't sit down. For a man who usually seemed self-assured to the point of arrogance, he seemed ill at ease for some reason. She couldn't define why she had that impression. Maybe the sudden tension of his shoulders or some wary look in his eyes.

She swallowed and was instantly reminded of the reason she had come upstairs in the first place. She was parched. After crossing to the refrigerator in the open kitchen, she opened the door and pulled out her filtered pitcher. "Can I get you something? Water? Iced tea or a Coke?"

"I'm good."

She closed the door and took a long, delicious drink, playing for time as much as quenching her thirst.

Why was Brodie standing in her apartment looking restless and edgy? She couldn't begin to guess. In the year since she'd arrived in Hope's Crossing, she'd barely exchanged a handful of terse words with him, and most of their interactions had been in some public hearing or other where she was speaking out about his latest plan to turn the charming community into a carbon copy of every other town.

A social call was completely unprecedented.

What had she done lately that might have annoyed him enough to come looking for her? She'd been too busy during the summer with the art fairs to be around town much. Maybe he was still smarting from the last time she'd taken him on at a planning commission meeting over one of his developments she considered an environmental blight.

She was painfully aware of the damp neckline of her performance T-shirt and her tight leggings, which she suddenly realized must have given him quite an eyeful of her butt as he'd followed her up the stairs.

Hiding her discomfort, she lifted her ponytail off her neck in the hot, closed air. The room felt like a sauna. She set her glass down on the counter and hurried to open a window, wishing she'd had the foresight to do that before she headed out with Jacques for the peace and cool of the mountains.

"You don't have air-conditioning up here?"

Evie shrugged, instantly on the defensive about her employer and landlady and, most important of all, good friend. "Claire wanted to install it earlier in the summer but I wouldn't let her. A fan in the window is usually sufficient for me on all but the hottest summer afternoons and I can always sit down in the garden if it's too stuffy up here."

She turned on the box fan placed in one of the three windows that overlooked Main Street. The air it blew in wasn't much cooler but at least the movement of it served to make the room feel less stuffy.

"I'm assuming you aren't here to discuss my ventilation issues, Brodie."

He glanced out the window at the gathering dusk, his jaw tight, as if he were steeling himself for something particularly unpleasant, and her curiosity ratcheted up a notch.

"I want to pay for your services."

O—kay. She blinked. The building that housed String Fever and her apartment above it had been a bordello in the town's wilder days but she was almost positive Brodie didn't mean that like it sounded.

She was also quite sure she should ignore the little quiver low in her belly as her imagination suddenly ran wild.

She sipped at her water again. "Did you want to commission some jewelry? Is it a gift for Taryn?"

"It's for Taryn. But not jewelry." Again, that hint of discomfort flashed in his expression and just as quickly, he blinked it away. "You haven't talked to my mother, have you?"

"No. Not since before I left town Thursday."

"Then you probably haven't heard the news. Taryn is coming home."

Some of her tension lifted, replaced by instant delight. "Oh, Brodie. That's wonderful!"

She might heartily dislike the man but she could still rejoice at such terrific news, for Katherine's sake if nothing else. "Isn't this sudden, though? I'm stunned! Last week when your mother came into the store, she said Taryn would be at the rehab facility at least another couple of months. How wonderful for you that she's so far ahead of schedule!"

"One would think."

She frowned at his tone, his marked lack of excitement. "You don't agree."

"I would like to."

"It's been more than three months since the accident. Aren't you overjoyed?"

"I'm happy my daughter is coming home. Of course I am." His voice was clipped, his words as sharp as flat-nose pliers.

"But?"

He released a long breath and shifted his weight. "The rehab facility is basically kicking her out."

"Kicking her out? Oh, surely not."

"They don't phrase it quite that bluntly. More a kindly worded suggestion that perhaps the time has come for us to seek different placement for Taryn."

"Why on earth would they do that?"

"The rehab doctors and physical therapists at Birch Glen have reached the consensus that Taryn has reached a pla-teau there. She refuses to cooperate with them, to the point that she's become unmanageable and refuses to even go to therapy anymore."

"It's their job to work around her plateau and take her treatment to the next level." Nearly a decade as a physical therapist had proven that over and over. She couldn't count the number of times she thought she had taken a patient as far as she could, had managed to push them to the limit of capability, only to discover a new exercise or stretch that made all the difference.

"Birch Glen is the most well-regarded rehabilitation facility in Colorado. As such, they have a lengthy wait-ing list of patients who actually want to be there and the staff would like to focus on people willing to be helped. It's not malicious. Everyone is very sorry about the situ-ation, blah blah blah. The director just gently suggested Birch Glen had helped Taryn as far as she would let them and perhaps staff members at a different facility might be better able to meet her needs at this time."

Evie could understand that. Sometimes patients and therapists couldn't gel, no matter how hard each side tried. "That must be aggravating for you—and especially for Taryn. I'm sorry, Brodie. I've heard of several excellent rehabilitation centers in the Denver area. Perhaps therapists with different personalities and techniques can find a way to challenge and motivate her."

"We're dealing with a fifteen-year-old girl who's suffered a severe brain injury here. She's not being rational."

"Is she talking now?" Last she'd heard from Katherine, the girl was reluctant to say much since each word seemed to be a struggle.

"Her speech is coming along. Better than it used to be, anyway. Taryn has managed to communicate in her own determined way that she wants to come home. That's it. Just come home." He sighed. "She's made it abundantly clear she won't cooperate anywhere else—not even the best damn rehab unit in the country. All she wants is to come home to Hope's Crossing."

He showed such obvious frustration, she couldn't help feeling sorry for him. Yes, she might dislike the man personally and, in general, find him arrogant and humorless. It was more than a little tough to reconcile those first— and second and third—impressions with the image of a devoted father who had dedicated all his resources to helping his daughter heal in the three months since the car accident that had severely injured her and killed another teen.

"Taryn's basically throwing a temper tantrum like a three-year-old," he went on.

"She's been through hell."

"Granted. And as much as I want to ignore her wishes and continue with the status quo or find her another rehab facility, I have to listen to what she's telling us. She's not progressing and a few of the members of her care team have suggested giving in to what she wants—bringing her home and starting a therapy program here."

His words suddenly echoed through her mind. *I want to hire your services,* he had said. Suddenly, ominously, all the pieces began to click into place.

"And you're here because?" she asked, still clinging to the fragile hope that she was far off the mark.

He looked as if he would rather be using those flat-nose pliers she'd thought of earlier to yank out his toenails than to find himself sitting in her living room, preparing to ask her a favor.

"It was my mother's idea, actually. I'm sure you can imagine the level of care required if we truly want to bring Taryn home. For this kind of program, she's going to need home nursing and an extensive program of rehab thera-pies—physical therapy, occupational therapy, speech. She still can't—or won't—take more than a step or two on her own and as a result of her injuries she has very limited use of her hands, especially her left one. Right now she struggles to even feed herself. Doctors aren't sure what, if any, skills she might regain."

Brain injuries could be cruel, capricious things. In an instant, a healthy, vibrant girl who loved snowboarding and hanging out with her friends and being on the cheer-leading squad could be changed into someone else entirely, possibly forever.

He shoved his hands in his pockets. "The people at Birch Glen are telling me I really need someone to coor-dinate Taryn's care. Someone who can work with all the therapists and the home-nursing staff and make sure she's receiving everything she needs."

Evie braced herself for him to actually come out and say the words he had been talking around. She pictured another fragile girl and those raw, terrible weeks and months after she died and everything inside Evie cried out a resounding *no* to putting herself through that again.

"My mother immediately suggested you as the perfect person to coordinate her care. I'm here to ask if you'll consider it. "

And there it was. She drew in a breath that seemed to snag somewhere around her solar plexus.

"I'm a beader now," she said tersely.

"But you're also a licensed rehab therapist. My mother told me you even maintained Colorado certification after you moved."

And hadn't that been one of her more stupid impulses? She'd tested mainly as a challenge to herself, to see if she could, but also in case anyone raised objections to her volunteer work at the local senior citizens' center. Now she deeply regretted it.

"Simply because I'm capable of doing a thing doesn't mean I'm *willing*."

Good heavens, she sounded bitchy. Why did he bring out the worst in her?

His already cool eyes turned wintry. "Why not?"

A hundred reasons. A thousand. She thought of Cassie and those awful days after her death and the hard-fought serenity she now prized above everything else.

"I'm a beader now," she repeated. "I've put my former career behind me. I've got commitments. Besides working for Claire at the store, I've got several commissioned projects I've agreed to make, not to mention another art fair over Labor Day weekend. What you're asking is completely impossible."

"*Nothing* is impossible. That's not just a damn T-shirt slogan."

He rose from the couch and moved closer to her and Evie had to fight the urge to back into the fireplace mantel. "This is my daughter we're talking about," he growled. "After the accident, not a single doctor thought Taryn would even survive her head injuries. When she didn't come out of the coma all those weeks, some of them even pushed me to turn off life support. No chance of a normal life, they told me. She'll only be an empty shell. But she's *not*. She's the same stubborn Taryn inside there!"

His devotion to his child stirred her. She had to respect it—but that didn't mean she had to allow herself to be sucked under by it.

"That isn't what I do anymore, Brodie. Perhaps her care center can recommend someone else in the area who might help you."

"I'll pay whatever you want."

He named a figure that made Evie blink. For one tiny moment she imagined splitting the amount between the scholarship fund here in Hope's Crossing and the charitable foundation she supported in California that facilitated adoptions of difficult-to-place special needs children.

No. The cost to her would be far too great.

"I'm sorry," she said firmly. "But I'm not part of that world anymore."

"By choice."

"Right. My choice."

His eyes looked hard suddenly, glittering blue agate. "Does it mean nothing to you that a young girl needs your help? *Taryn* needs your help? You could change her life. Doesn't that count for anything?"

Oh, he definitely didn't fight fair. How could the blasted man know so unerringly how to gouge in just the exact spot under her heart to draw the most blood?

She wouldn't let him play on an old guilt that had nothing to do with his daughter. "You'll have to find someone else," she said.

"What if I increase the salary figure by twenty percent?"

"It doesn't matter how much you offer. This isn't about money. You should really look for someone with more experience in the Colorado health system."

Any politeness in his facade slid away, leaving his features tight and angry. "I told my mother you wouldn't do it. I should have known better than to even ask somebody like you for help. I'm sorry I wasted my time and yours."

And the arrogant jerk raised his ugly head. *Somebody like you*. What did that mean? Somebody with a social conscience? Somebody who opposed his efforts to turn the picturesque charm of Hope's Crossing into just another cookie-cutter town with box stores and chain restaurants?

"Next time you should listen to your instincts," she snapped.

"There won't be a next time. You can be damn sure of that."

He stalked toward the door, jerked it open and stomped down the stairs.

After he left, Evie pressed a hand to the sudden churn in her stomach. Only hunger, she told herself. What did she expect, when she hadn't eaten except for a quick sandwich on the road six hours ago?

She sank down onto a chair. Not hunger. Brodie Thorne. The man made her more nervous than a roomful of tax attorneys.

Maybe she should have said yes. She adored Katherine and owed her deeply. And Brodie was right. Despite the difference in their ages, she had been friends of sorts with Taryn, who used to frequently come into String Fever before her accident, full of dreams and plans and teenage angst.

Evie wanted to help them, but how could she possibly? The cost would be far too dear. Since coming to Hope's

Crossing, she had worked hard to carve out a much healthier place than she had been in the day she had arrived, lost and grieving, wrung dry.

She knew her limitations. Hard experience was a pretty darn good teacher. She threw everything inside her at her patients—her energy, her strength, her passion. She lost all sense of professional reserve, of objectivity.

After Cassie and the emotional fallout from her death, Evie knew she didn't belong in that world anymore, no matter whom she had to disappoint.

Brodie had to exert every bit of his considerable self-control to prevent himself from slamming the door behind him as he stalked down the stairway and back out to the garden behind her apartment.

His temper seethed and bubbled and he wanted to rip out a flower or two. Or every last freaking one.

Her dog—half poodle, half Labrador and all unique, just like her—woofed a quick greeting and headed for him, tail wagging. Brodie scratched the dog between the ears and released a breath, some of the tension seeping away here in the summer evening with a friendly dog offering quiet comfort.

A little of his tension. Not all of it. What the hell was he supposed to do now? Yeah, maybe it had been stupidly shortsighted of him, but despite what he had said up there, he'd never truly expected her to say no.

Ironic, really. He hadn't wanted her involved in Taryn's home-care program in the first place. He thought his mother was crazy when she first suggested it a few weeks ago, after the director of the Birch Glen rehab center had first rather gently suggested Taryn's placement there might not be working out.

Evaline Blanchard was a loose screw. She kept her long,

blond wavy hair wild or in braids, she favored Teva sandals to high heels, she always had some sort of chunky jewelry on that she had probably designed herself. Most of the time she wore flowing, flowery sundresses as if she was some kind of Mother Earth hippie—except when she was wearing extremely skintight exercise leggings, he amended. His body stirred a little at the memory, much to his chagrin.

He didn't *want* to be attracted to Evie Blanchard. She was a bleeding heart do-gooder who seemed to spend her spare time trying to think of ways to mess with things that weren't broken. Everything about her grated on him like metal grinding on metal.

When she first came to town, he had entertained the idea that maybe she was some kind of grifter trying to run a con on his too-trusting mother. Really, what woman in her right mind would decide to pick up and move across three states—leaving what had apparently been a lucrative rehab therapy career—on the basis of an email friendship alone?

Either she was the most patient shyster he'd ever heard of or she had genuinely moved to Hope's Crossing for a new start. She had been in town a year and seemed to have settled in comfortably, becoming part of the community. His mother and all her friends certainly adored her, anyway.

He scratched the dog one last time, then headed out the wrought-iron gate and through the alley toward Main Street.

Evie Blanchard might not be a con artist but he still took pains to avoid her. She had a particular way of looking at a man that made him feel edgy and tense, condemned before he even opened his mouth. He knew her opinion of him. That he was a bully with a big checkbook who liked to have his way around town. He was the big, bad developer who wanted to ruin Hope's Crossing.

Not true. He loved this town. He had made his home here, had brought his three-year-old daughter here after his hasty mistake of a marriage had fallen apart. And now he was bringing Taryn home again to heal. Didn't that count for something?

Not to Evie Blanchard, apparently. She obviously disliked him intensely. It didn't help that every time they had appeared on opposite sides of some planning commission meeting or public hearing or other, she would be giving some eloquent opposition to whatever he was working on and he would be appalled by the hot surge of completely inappropriate lust curling through his gut.

Of course, he couldn't tell his mother that. He didn't even like admitting it to *himself.*

He would prefer to keep a healthy distance from Evie Blanchard and her wavy blond hair and her lithe figure, which definitely filled out her tight running leggings in all the right ways.

Too bad his mother had convinced him she was absolutely the best person to help his daughter right now.

Katherine's arguments had been persuasive, full of journal articles Evie had written a few years earlier, media reports about the amazing progress she'd made with some of her patients, even references from parents of her former clients. His mother had done her homework and had presented all her findings to him with a satisfied flourish. After reading through her dossier on Evie's time as a physical therapist in California, he had to admit he had been impressed. Now he didn't know if he could be satisfied with anyone else.

Brodie sighed as he headed toward his car, parked in the lot behind the Center of Hope Café. He spotted Dermot Caine, owner of the café, heading to the Dumpster out back with a garbage bag in each hand. Brodie waved and Dermot called out a greeting.

"Is it true your girl's coming home?" the other man asked, a hopeful expression on his sunbaked features.

"That's the plan. She still has a long way to go." He really wished he didn't have to add that disclaimer whenever he talked to anyone in town, but the people of Hope's Crossing had seen enough disappointment and sorrow over the last three months. He didn't want anyone to set unreasonably high expectations.

"You give her a big hug from me, won't you? That little girl's a trouper. If anything sounds good to her—one of my huckleberry pies, some of that chocolate mousse she always liked—you just say the word and I'll personally deliver it."

"Will do. Thanks, Dermot." There had been a time when the owner of the diner considered Brodie nothing but a troublemaker with a chip on his shoulder. Brodie had worked hard to overcome his rep around town over the years and it was heartening to see Dermot's concern for his daughter.

"I mean it. Everyone in town is praying for that little girl. She's a miracle, that's what she is, and we can't wait to have her back."

"I appreciate that. I'm sure Taryn does, too."

All of Hope's Crossing was invested in her recovery. That was a hell of a lot of pressure on a fifteen-year-old kid who couldn't string more than a couple of words together at a time.

Brodie headed toward his SUV, a grim determination pulsing through him. Evie Blanchard was still his best hope.

He wasn't about to give up after one measly rejection.

He had never been a quitter, not in the days when he used to ski jump and had trained for the Olympics, nor in his business endeavors. He sure as hell wasn't going to quit on his little girl.

He had failed her enough as a single father, starting with his lousy choice of her mother, who had jumped at the chance to escape them as soon as she could, leaving him with a three-year-old kid he was clueless to raise. With a great deal of help from his mother, Brodie had worked hard to give Taryn a stable life, with all the comforts any kid could want.

What he hadn't given her was much of himself. The last few years, their relationship had been stilted and awkward, filled with fights and tantrums. He found out as she hit about thirteen that he knew diddly-squat about teenage girls and their mood swings. Somehow in all the lecturing and grounding and disappointments, he had missed the signs that Taryn had strayed dangerously off track, running with a bad crowd, drinking, even burglarizing stores.

He might have been earning a failing grade as a parent before the accident—something he was used to from his own school days—but he refused to let her down now. He was determined to find the absolute best person to spearhead her rehabilitation program on the home front. Like it or not, Evie Blanchard appeared to be that person.

So what if he found her grating and confrontational on a personal level? He was a big boy. He would get over it, especially if she could help him give his daughter her best chance at a full recovery.

Two

Evie awoke early the next morning tired and gritty-eyed. Jacques stuck his nose into the curve of her neck and she laughed hoarsely.

"Yeah, okay. I know what you want," she muttered. She sat up gingerly, her body aching a little from the long weekend. Jacques needed to go out and an early-morning hike up the Woodrose trail would be just the thing to shake the cobwebs away.

She dressed quickly, especially since the dog was prancing around anxiously by now, and ten minutes later she grabbed the dog's leash and they headed out just as the sun peeked above the mountains.

By the time they reached the trailhead to Woodrose Mountain, both of them were a little more settled. The trail was wet from a predawn storm and she wondered if it were possible to become intoxicated from the scent of rain-washed sage and tart pine.

The farther she hiked up the trail, the more stunning the view. It never failed to move her. Hope's Crossing looked small, provincial, especially with the vast shadows of mountain ranges rippling out in every direction.

The quiet stillness was a far cry from the traffic and

craziness of L.A.—and she wouldn't trade it for anything. When she arrived in Hope's Crossing, she had been battered and lost. Somehow here in this space where she could breathe and think, she had reconnected with herself, and the aches and pains and scabs of grief and self-doubt had begun to heal.

Not completely. She sighed, lifting her face to the sun just barely cresting the mountains. Just when she thought she was finally in a good and healthy place, content with the world and her place in it, reality had smacked her upside the head like an unexpected branch stretching across her life's trail.

Despite her exhaustion from the busy weekend, she hadn't slept well, her dreams fragmented and jagged, a tangle of memories and ghosts. No surprise whom to blame. Brodie Thorne's unexpected request had ricocheted through her mind all night.

She felt like a coward for saying no to him but she knew she wasn't. It had taken great courage to walk away from a career, a home, friends she loved, in search of something she knew she could no longer find in L.A. She had worked too hard to achieve homeostasis—harmony, balance, equilibrium, whatever word fit best. Although some part of her felt guilty for saying no to him and refusing to help with Taryn's rehabilitation, she knew it had been the most healthy answer she could have offered.

After she and Jacques had both worked out their edginess, she headed back down the mountainside, passing a couple of tourists who were obviously continental, with their walking sticks and their Birkenstocks and that indefinable élan. They greeted her in heavily accented English then said something quickly to each other in musical French, gesturing toward Jacques, with his Labrador body and his wool-like poodle coat, which she kept groomed short in the summer for his comfort. He gave them a regal nod before padding down the trail behind her and Evie smiled, rubbing his head with affection. Boy, she loved this mutt.

Back at her apartment, she spent the morning working on the instructions for a couple of bead designs she planned to submit to an industry magazine, then grabbed a quick sandwich before heading for work.

It was impossible not to compare her commute now— sixteen narrow steps down the back stairway and then through the String Fever rear entryway—to the endless lifetime she used to spend in the stop-and-go nightmare of Southern California traffic.

A teenage girl was poring over the wires, and a couple of young mothers sat in the reading corner leafing through the bead pattern books while their children explored with the toys Claire had provided in the playroom.

Evie's employer was on the telephone in her small office. Through the open doorway, Claire Bradford waved at her as she crossed to the rack hanging behind the big worktable for the multipocketed half apron that came in so handy for holding her beading tools.

By the time she returned, Claire had finished her phone call. She glowed today, her eyes shining and her smile bright and cheerful. She wore her new happiness like a brilliant tiara and Evie was thrilled for her. Claire was the most generous, giving woman she knew, always reaching out to lift someone else. Though she didn't seem bitter that her ex-husband had married someone ten years younger shortly after their divorce and seemed to flaunt it in her face by settling into Hope's Crossing with his bride, Evie knew it must have stung.

Riley McKnight made Claire happy. Everyone in town could see that, and the man plainly adored her.

"You're not supposed to be here for—" Claire checked her watch with its band of gorgeous pink-toned Murano art glass "—another hour."

Evie smiled. "I wanted to double-check the kits for my class tonight."

"Probably a good idea. We had a rush on last-minute sign-ups over the weekend. I think we added six more Saturday alone. Your classes are always full. Face it, honey, you're a rock star among the beaders of Hope's Crossing."

Evie laughed. "That's something, right?"

"I hope we're going to have enough room at the worktable. Let me know if you think you'll need a second one. So how was Grand Junction?"

"Much better than I expected. So good, in fact, we're going to have a crazy time replenishing the inventory before the last show over Labor Day weekend."

"I'll put out a notice by the checkout that you'll be taking consignment items. This is a great thing you're doing, Evie. I can't believe how the scholarship fund has grown in just a few months. Between the ginormous amount we collected at the benefit auction in June and the money that's come in since then because of everything you're doing, as well as the other fundraisers around town, we might have enough of an endowment to be able to fund a couple of scholarships a year in Layla's memory. You're doing a wonderful thing, Evie."

"I'm not doing much. You're the one handling all the organizational legwork. Selling jewelry is the fun part."

"I've done arts-and-crafts fairs before. Parts of it are fun but it's hard, intense work."

"So far I'm enjoying it. Almost done now. Only the Labor Day festival in Crested Butte." She quickly shifted the subject. "How are the wedding plans coming?"

"Whose?"

Evie laughed. "Um, yours. What wedding did you think I meant?"

"As far as certain people are concerned, the Beaumont-Danforth nuptials are the only game in town, even though it's still nine months away. Gen Beaumont has been in once a day, looking for that order of art glass she placed last week for the jewelry sets she's making for her bridesmaid gifts. I keep telling her it takes two weeks for delivery but she seems to think she can make the process move faster by sheer force of will."

"If anyone could manipulate the space-time continuum, Genevieve Beaumont would get my vote."

Claire's laugh had a wild edge. "I think I speak for all the merchants in Hope's Crossing when I say how happy I will be when her wedding is a distant memory."

Genevieve Beaumont was the daughter of the Hope's Crossing mayor and the town's most prominent attorney. Her society wedding had been in the works for months. It was supposed to be a lovely fall wedding, set for October, but Gen had postponed it after the tragic accident that had impacted the entire town three months earlier.

"Have you had any time to plan your own?" Evie asked.

"It's coming. We're looking at December now, with a small, intimate dinner and dance afterward in the Silver Strike ballroom."

"Lovely. I can picture it now. Everything silver and white and blue, with fairy lights and acres of tulle."

Claire's features turned dreamy for just a moment before she shrugged. "I've already done the big-reception thing once. I don't want to go overboard this time around."

"Riley hasn't, though."

"He doesn't care. He would run off to Vegas tomorrow if his mother and sisters wouldn't kill us later."

Evie smiled, though she was disconcerted by a sudden, completely unexpected twinge of envy at Claire's bubbly happiness.

Where did that come from? She wasn't jealous of Claire. Absolutely not. While she was certainly delighted for her friend, Evie wasn't in the market for a relationship. Hadn't she just decided the night before that she was completely happy with her single, unencumbered life here? She had Jacques for company and he was far more comfortable than any romantic entanglement of her experience.

"You both deserve a lovely wedding. You know I'm here for whatever help you need," she assured Claire.

"Be careful what you offer." Claire laughed. "I might take you up on it when the date gets closer."

"You know perfectly well I wouldn't have offered if I didn't want to help."

Claire started to answer but paused when the teenage girl approached them, her plump features hesitant. "Sorry to interrupt. I can come back."

"Not at all," Evie said quickly. "Hannah, right? You're friends with Lara, who works here sometimes."

"Not really. We just know each other from school and stuff."

Something about the girl's unease, her hesistance bordering on gawky awkwardness, tugged at Evie's heart.

"How can we help you?" Claire asked just as the phone in the office rang.

"I've got this," Evie answered. "Go ahead and take the call."

"It's probably Gen again," Claire said with a reluctant sigh, but she crossed the showroom to the phone at her desk.

"If you're busy or whatever, I can come back another time."

"Not at all," Evie assured the girl. "I'm all yours. How can I help you?"

"I don't know anything about beading but I think it looks kind of neat. I'd like to learn, I guess. I was thinking about trying to make some earrings for my mom. It's her birthday next week."

"Lovely!"

"She's been, you know, kind of sad lately and I sort of thought, you know, that some new earrings would cheer her up."

Kirk. That was her last name, Evie suddenly remembered. Hannah Kirk. Evie didn't know the family well but she suddenly recalled the buzz around town had it that Hannah's father had walked out on them right after Christmas for another woman, leaving her mother to struggle alone with Hannah and three younger siblings.

If rumor could be believed, the Angel of Hope—the mysterious benefactor who had been busy around town for the last six months or so helping families hit hard by the poor economy or by health concerns or family issues—had paid more than one visit to the Kirks since Christmas. She hoped so. Gretchen Kirk and her children were just the sort of down-on-their-luck family that deserved a helping hand.

"Your mother will love new earrings, especially handmade ones."

"It was just a crazy idea. Like I said, I don't really know what I'm doing or anything. I would need a lot of help."

"You've come to exactly the right place." Evie smiled. "We love to help beaders, trust me. Especially beginning beaders. We've got a worktable here with all the supplies and tools you need and there's always someone around who can give you a hand with any project."

Hannah's face lit up with relief. "Really? That would be great. Thanks. Thanks a lot. You're right, my mom will love them, I think."

"Moms go crazy for the handmade stuff. Trust me on

this. Do you want to get started now? We can look through the beads and get an idea of colors that your mom likes to wear, if you want."

Hannah pulled out an older sort of flip phone and looked at the time on it. "I'd better go. I have to go to work. Um, I work at the shave-ice stand over by the hardware store and afternoons are kind of busy for us. Can I come back another time?"

"Sure. If I'm not here to help you, Claire should be or one of our other resident beaders. You think about what kind of earrings your mom likes and we'll look through the books and come up with some killer designs."

"Something easy, though, right?"

"Sure thing."

"Thanks. That's really nice of you." Hannah's sweet smile transformed her rather plain, round features into someone young and bright and pretty. "I don't have much money, though. I can probably only make one pair."

"We'll figure something out. We've probably got some overstock we can swing a good deal on." If Claire objected—though Evie knew she wouldn't—Evie had samples from her own huge inventory of beads she would be willing to donate to the cause.

"I'll see you later, okay?"

The girl smiled again, looking much happier than she'd been earlier. "Great. Thanks. Thanks a lot."

She headed for the door and reached to pull the handle just as it was pushed in from the other side and Katherine Thorne walked into the store.

Evie's stomach plummeted, all her angst of the long, sleepless night returning in spades.

While Katherine always looked elegant and put-together, from her streaky ash-blond hair, cut in a chin-length bob, to her strappy sandals and blush-painted toenails, the last three months since her granddaughter's accident had definitely taken a toll. She was thinner than ever, her sixty-year-old skin showing a few more wrinkles.

The little happy buzz Evie had been enjoying at the prospect of helping a very needy young girl make a birthday present to lift her mother's spirits fizzled away. Saying no to Brodie Thorne had been as easy as adding beads to a basic earring headpin, something she could do in her sleep. Katherine's inevitable disappointment was a different matter altogether.

Hannah brushed by her with a flash of that hesitant smile, and Katherine closed the door behind her while Evie tried to come up with some excuse to avoid her dear friend. She could always use the other customers as a reason but with Hannah gone, that left only the two young mothers who, unfortunately, seemed perfectly at ease poring over magazines while their children giggled in the play space.

Evie was stuck. With as much grace as she could muster, she greeted Katherine with their customary warm embrace, sweet with the scent of blooming fresh-cut flowers from the Estée Lauder Beautiful fragrance Katherine used. The other woman felt fragile somehow, her bones sharp and defined. She wasn't eating like she should, Evie fretted. How much more of a burden would Katherine take on after her granddaughter returned to Hope's Crossing for rehab?

"How was your trip, my dear?" Katherine asked.

She pulled away. "Great. They had big crowds this year and people were actually willing to spend money again."

"I did that show once or twice and always loved it."

She didn't seem angry. No yelling or asking how Evie could disappoint her like that. Maybe she didn't know what Brodie had asked of her—or that Evie had refused.

No. She couldn't believe that. Katherine had a purposeful look in her eyes and Evie wasn't naive enough to think she was only here to look at beads.

They traded pleasantries for a few more moments until Evie could barely wade through the murky currents of subtext between them.

Finally she sighed. "All right. Have pity on me, Kat. You might as well come out with it. Brodie knows exactly what he's doing, doesn't he, sending you in as his reinforcement?"

Katherine sniffed. "I'm sure I don't know what you're talking about."

"Ha." Evie straightened some of the inventory hanging on the wall, just to keep her hands busy and for an outlet to the tension in her shoulders. This was what had kept her restless and uneasy through the night, this terrible fear that she would be forced to choose between her self-preservation or losing a dear, dear friend.

In a way, Katherine had become a surrogate mother to her. After Cassie's death, their email correspondence had provided a spark of life, of hope. When Katherine encouraged Evie to come to Colorado for a few weeks as her guest, she had jumped at the chance and instantly fallen in love with the town and the people here.

Most of them, anyway.

"You want me to believe Brodie didn't send you."

"No. In fact, he told me not to come."

"Yet here you are."

"Only because we're desperate, my dear. Brodie and I both want the absolute best care available for Taryn. Surely you can understand that."

Oh, she hated this. "Any parent would want the same."

"You're the best," Katherine said simply. "Can you blame us for wanting your help?"

"Whatever I might have once been is a long road away.

That's not me anymore, Katherine. I'm a beader. I make jewelry."

"I thought you might make an exception in this case, if not for Brodie than maybe for me and especially for Taryn."

The tension in Evie's shoulders tightened to a fine and exquisite pain. No wonder Katherine made such a good Hope's Crossing Town Council member. She knew exactly which buttons to push.

"Not fair," she murmured.

"I know." Katherine looked unapologetic. "My son is not the only ruthless one in the Thorne family."

Evie was trapped in an unwinnable dilemma. Refuse and hurt a dear friend. Accept and hurt herself.

Claire's approach was a welcome reprieve. "Katherine! I didn't hear you come in. Hello, darling! How's Taryn?" she asked instantly.

Katherine aimed a quick look at Evie and then turned back to Claire. Evie's tension tightened a few more screws.

"She's coming home at the end of the week."

Claire's mouth sagged open and a fierce joy lit up her lovely, serene features. "You're kidding! I never heard a word. This is fabulous! We need to celebrate! Fireworks, confetti. Throw a parade or something!"

Katherine shook her head slightly, squeezing Claire's fingers. "I'm afraid we're not breaking out the champagne yet. The doctors and therapists in Denver are basically kicking her out of the rehab center, saying they've done all they can with her. She's become what the experts call a recalcitrant patient."

A little of Claire's ebullience faded but she was enough of a natural optimist that Evie could tell she wouldn't let that minor setback completely dim her happiness. "Well, it will be wonderful to have her back in Hope's Crossing anyway, right? What can we do? Do you have any idea yet what Brodie's going to need help with at first?"

Claire's instant willingness to step forward, no matter the cost, left Evie feeling small and ashamed. That was always her friend's way, always thinking about what she could do to help someone else. As much as she loved Claire, sometimes she privately thought her friend carried that whole give-of-yourself thing a little too far.

Katherine hugged the other woman again. "We don't know yet. We have so many details to figure out. We've been looking ahead to this day for some time. Over the last month or so, Brodie has been having Paul Harris do some work on the house, knock out a couple walls to put in a roll-in shower, install a couple of ramps, a lift system, that sort of thing."

Katherine's gaze slanted quickly toward Evie. That tension gripped her and she drew in a ragged breath. *Here we go.*

"Actually, we're trying to persuade Evie to help us set up a home-based rehab program."

Claire gasped, her eyes bright. "Oh, brilliant!"

"That's exactly what Brodie and I think. I'm afraid Evie isn't as convinced."

Claire's gaze zinged from one of them to the other and Evie knew precisely the moment she picked up the undercurrents of tension seething between them.

"Is it the store?" she asked. "If that's the case, don't you worry about us for a moment, Evie. I know I said you're a beading rock star and all that but we can get along here at the store without you if we have to, especially when it's for such a good cause. I've got a couple of teenage girls who've been in a half dozen times since the beginning of the summer with their résumés, looking for part-time work. I can use them until school starts in a few weeks and then figure something else out. You take as long as you need with Taryn."

"Actually, that's one of the reasons I stopped in," Katherine said smoothly. "I don't want you to think we're trying to steal Evie away from String Fever during the rest of the busy summer tourist weeks before the shoulder season. I wanted to offer a trade."

When Evie was a girl, their nanny used to take her and her younger sister to the park near their home in Santa Barbara. Lizzie would beg her to come with her on the merry-go-round and Evie would always eventually relent, though she always hated that out-of-control feeling, that whirling, churning, wind-tossed disorder. This conversation felt very much as if she was clinging tightly to the bars, trying to keep from being flung into chaos.

Claire smiled at Katherine. "Tell me more."

"I want to apply for a temporary job as Evie's substitute here at the store," Katherine said. "I can even take over some of her classes. That would free her schedule so she can work with my granddaughter."

Evie fought the urge to close her eyes. She was well and truly trapped now. Claire looked delighted at the offer. Why wouldn't she be? Katherine was the founder and original owner of String Fever. She'd sold the store to Claire a few years ago after Claire's divorce. Nobody in town— least of all Evie—knew more about beads than Katherine.

"Again, brilliant, Kat. You're a genius."

"I was going to say, positively Machiavellian," Evie muttered.

Claire looked startled but Katherine only gave a smug sort of smile. "When I have to be, my dear."

"You *don't* have to be in this case. I'm a beader now, not a physical therapist," she repeated for what felt like the umpteenth time. "I have no experience here in Colorado."

"But you are licensed, right?"

"Katherine. You know why I quit."

For the first time, she saw a glimmer of sympathy in the older woman's eyes but it quickly hardened into more of that steely determination. How could Evie blame her? She understood Katherine's perspective. Her granddaughter was facing months—possibly years—of painful, difficult rehabilitation with no guarantee of a rosy recovery.

Evie could empathize. She would have done anything to help those she loved, would have traded on every possible friendship to help Liz after the fire that had severely burned her and their mother.

And Cassie. In the two years she had with her daughter, she had fought fiercely to provide the best possible care but in the end none of her efforts had worked.

"I know. I'm sorry. You know that. But we need you, Evie."

Claire looked from one of them to the other, her expression confused. "I don't understand," she said. How could she? Evie had never shared all her reasons for leaving her practice in L.A. As far as Claire knew, she had dropped out of her practice and moved to Colorado only because she needed a change.

Katherine knew, however. She had been there to comfort and lift Evie through a very dark and ugly time. Evie heartily wished she could do the same now for her friend.

"I understand your reluctance, my dear," Katherine went on. "This is a big commitment with a great deal of pressure attached to it."

"You know that's not it. If I could help you, I would."

Katherine nodded and to Evie's dismay, her friend pulled her into another hug. "I do understand," she murmured. "I'm sorry I've put you in a difficult position."

"You're the only one I would consider coming out of

retirement—or whatever you want to call it—to help. You know that, don't you?"

Katherine eased away. "I do. And I'm going to presume on our friendship terribly to ask you one more favor."

Evie braced herself.

"Will you at least consider helping us for a week or two, just while we find our feet and start a treatment plan for Taryn?" Katherine asked. "With your knowledge and experience, you can make sure Brodie has retrofitted the house with everything we might need for her care. A few weeks would give us a little breathing room so we can take our time looking for the best possible person for the job."

The request was reasonable and certainly made sense. Refusing to give up a few weeks of her life for her dear friend would make her sound churlish. Immature, even.

"When is Taryn being transferred from Birch Glen?" she asked, doing her best to keep the weary resignation from her voice.

To Katherine's credit, not so much as a trace of victory flashed in her expression, even though she must have known Evie couldn't say no. "Friday."

"I suppose I could give you a week or two, as long as you can help Claire with my responsibilities here."

Claire squeezed her arm. "Of course. Take as long as necessary. Whatever Taryn needs."

"Just a few weeks. No more than that. I'll help you hire another therapy coordinator and set up the treatment plan, but that's all."

She could handle anything for a few weeks, couldn't she?

"That should be plenty of time to point us in the right direction." Katherine pressed her cheek to Evie's, filling her senses with flowers and guilt. "Thank you so much. I know it's difficult for you and I'm very sorry, but believe me, we're so grateful. I don't know how we'll ever repay you for this."

"You don't owe me anything, Katherine," she answered, taking a subtle step back. "Tell Brodie to donate whatever fee he would have paid someone else for those few weeks to the scholarship fund."

At least something good should come of this, she thought, as Katherine and Claire began discussing another fund-raising event the high school student body officers wanted to sponsor for the Layla memorial fund.

Evie let their conversation drift around her, focusing instead on double-checking the kits for her class that evening to help beat off the residual twinges of panic. After a few moments, one of the mothers asked a question about their display of Greek worry beads and Evie was grateful to help the customers, an excuse to leave her friends and the heavy weight of their expectations.

"They're called *komboloi*," she explained. "Traditionally, they're made with an odd number of beads and then a metal spacer in between. Touching them at various times throughout the day is believed to help with relaxation and stress management."

"I certainly need that," the woman said, rolling her eyes at her busy preschooler in the play area.

Evie smiled. "They're easy to make and they can really relieve tension. There's something very soothing about working the beads between your fingers. Lots of people even put them on their key chains. Want to try one?"

The two women exchanged glances. "Sure. Sounds like fun," the other young mother said.

"You can use any kind of bead, though usually people use amber or coral because of their soft, comforting texture."

Evie pointed them toward the beads, then went to gather

the basic supplies for them. While she was helping them, she would make one for herself, she decided on impulse. It had been too long since she had crafted a piece simply for her own enjoyment—and she had a very strong feeling she was going to need all the stress management tools she could find in the coming two weeks.

Three

Brodie's house in the exclusive gated Aspen Ridge community wasn't quite what Evie had imagined.

Given her preconception of the man as someone who always wanted something bigger and better than anyone else—at least in the various businesses and developments he owned around Hope's Crossing—she had expected something opulent and overwhelming. The house was certainly vast and sprawling, with soaring windows and cedar-plank walls, unusual curves and angles. But the landscaping was tasteful and seemed to focus on native plants and trees and granite boulders. Whoever designed the place had managed to adapt it nicely to its surroundings, nestled into the hollow of a foothill.

His view was spectacular, she would definitely give him that. Even from her favorite spot on the Woodrose Mountain trail, she couldn't see as far as Silver Strike Canyon but from various places on the property, he would have a clear vantage point of both the town below and the higher ski resort in the canyon.

She might have allowed herself to enjoy the view a little more in the stretched-out shadows of late afternoon but she wasn't exactly in the mood for restful Zen-like contemplation of the mountains—not when she stood on Brodie's doorstep holding a basketful of therapy-equipment catalogs.

Oh, she didn't want to be here. Three days after Katherine had laid on the emotional blackmail, Evie wasn't any more comfortable with her decision to help Taryn transition to a home-based program. She didn't want to be dragged into this world again, not after she had fought so hard to find peace outside of it.

She would simply have to be tough and determined and remind herself that this was all only temporary. For a few weeks she could be tough and detached, clinical even. She could keep her emotions contained and safe, despite her relationship with Katherine.

It was only a job, right?

With that thought firmly in mind, she rang the doorbell and waited, expecting some housekeeper or secretary to open the door. When it opened a moment later, she was greeted by the unexpected sight of Brodie standing in the doorway wearing jeans and a white-cotton dress shirt with the sleeves rolled up to midforearm.

His dark hair was slightly messy as if he'd just run his hands through it and he had that typical afternoon shadow that made him look somehow rakish and dangerous. Throw in a sword and an eye patch and maybe switch out the tailored cut of his white shirt for one with flowing sleeves and she could definitely see him sailing the high seas with Jack Sparrow and friends.

Yum.

That was the only word that seemed to register in her brain for about half a second, until he spoke and shattered, like a well-placed cannon blast, all those half-formed pirate fantasies.

"Evaline. Hello. I wasn't expecting you." His tone was

stiff, formal, as if he were greeting unwelcome gate-crashers at some highbrow society function, and she had to fight down her instinctive sharp retort.

"Katherine asked me to stop by and check on the renovations in Taryn's bedroom and bathroom so I'll know what equipment we might need to order eventually."

"Right. Of course." He thawed enough to give her a half smile. "She mentioned you might stop by to check things out. It's a great idea, one I should have thought of earlier."

He held the door open wider for her. "Come in. The truth is, I'll be glad to have your perspective on what we've done in her rooms, to see if we've missed anything."

Brodie inclined his head in the direction of the hammering she could hear coming from the far reaches of the house. "The crews might be working all night to wrap things up before tomorrow but at least they're down to the finished carpentry now. Come in. We can work our way around the dust."

She gazed at that door and the muscled arm holding it open, aware of the tiniest flicker of nervous hesitation. Stupid. It was only a doorway and this was only a job. A few weeks, that's all, and then she could go back to her happy place, among the good and kind beaders of Hope's Crossing.

When she finally forced herself to move forward, Brodie ushered her into a welcoming two-story foyer decorated in the Craftsman style—clean lines, tasteful use of wood and stone, a stunningly understated burnished glass chandelier that had probably cost a fortune.

The house was appealing and warm, just as she should have expected. No one ever said the man was a tasteless boor. His sporting-goods store managed to be stylish without seeming trendy and she had heard that several of the restaurants he owned in Hope's Crossing had won design awards.

He led the way down a long hallway decorated with photographs of places she recognized around Hope's Crossing. The bridge near Sweet Laurel Falls, moonlight reflecting on Silver Strike Reservoir, a moose standing in a pond she had walked past often on Woodrose Mountain, moss dripping from his antlers.

While one part of her mind was enjoying the photographs, the therapist side of her brain she could never quite silence was thinking that this long space with the polished-wood floors might be a perfect place to practice walking with Taryn.

"I've moved her bedroom down to the main level," Brodie said when they neared a doorway at the end of the hall. Behind the extrawide door, the sounds of construction intensified.

"That seems logical."

"You and I might agree but I'm afraid Taryn likely won't see it that way. She loved her room upstairs and I have a feeling she's likely to pitch a fit about the new digs. Just one more major change for her."

"Some things can't be helped. She'll get over it."

"I'm shocked. You actually agree with me about something?"

She smiled a little. "Don't worry. I won't let it become a habit. In this case you're right. It makes perfect sense to keep her room on the ground floor for now."

"For now. Right." He frowned. "I'd like to tell her she can move back up to her room eventually, but that's one more promise I can't make Taryn right now. It seems cruel to promise her that when we don't know if she'll ever be out of that wheelchair."

Somehow she sensed this was important to him. Only

)gical. He was a very active, very physical man. One of is many businesses was a sporting-goods store and Brodie ad even been a former competitive ski jumper at one time.

Katherine had told her once that Brodie and Taryn in-:racted most through skiing together in the winter, hiking nd mountain biking in summer. No doubt the prospect of is daughter never being able to join him again in those ctivities would seem a crushing blow. She only hoped he vouldn't pin unrealistic hopes on Taryn and could keep roper perspective. Walking again was only one of Taryn's nany hurdles.

As he opened the door, the scent of fresh paint wafted ut and the thuds and bangs grew louder. She had a quick mpression of a roomy, bright space with large windows nd a light-grained wood floor. The room was painted vhite with some lavender trim and one wall of mirrors eflected the mountain scene out the window.

The construction workers apparently were installing arge eye-hooks from the ceiling at various intervals, which vould be perfect for hanging a pommel or swing. Around he corner from the therapy space, set in its own good-,ize alcove, was a sleeping area, complete with a hospi- al bed covered in a fluffy lavender comforter. A padded reatment-table just right for stretching ran the length of)ne wall and she could see a wheeled lift in one corner or helping to transfer Taryn from the wheelchair to dif- ferent positions. The workmen were putting the finishing ouches on a built-in cabinet in one wall with open shelves hat would be perfect for storing odds and ends like exer- :ise bands, hand weights, small weighted balls.

She had worked in world-class therapy facilities that veren't as well equipped.

"Wow." It was all she could say.

"We ended up taking out a couple of walls between

rooms down here to make an extra-large space. Most o
the work was focused on the bathroom, where we put in
roll-in shower and a lift tub."

"This looks really great, Brodie. Perfect."

"I hope we've considered everything, at least structu
ally. If you think of any equipment we need, just say th
word. I've got a treadmill and stationary bike in the e
ercise room upstairs and we can bring those down, or
you'd like a different kind, we can get that, too. I've als
got plans to have an all-season cover installed over the po
and hot tub out back so Taryn can continue to use ther
for therapy after the weather changes."

Evie didn't want to admit it, even to herself, but sh
was touched that Brodie was going to so much effort an
expense for his daughter. Despite her best intentions, sh
was finding it a little hard to dislike a man who was s
obviously committed to doing all he could to return hi
injured daughter to her previous abilities.

"Offhand, the only need I can see immediately is per
haps a table and some chairs in here so the occupationa
therapist can work on fine motor skills during her visits.

"Oh, right. I hadn't even thought of that. We've got on
down the hall in the media room I can bring up."

She held out the basket, feeling a little like Red Ridin
Hood offering goodies to the Big Bad Wolf. "I've brough
some catalogs with basic items that will probably be use
ful. Therapy balls, pommels, that sort of thing. I've marke
them with sticky notes. There are a few other things yo
may want to consider down the line but I suggest you giv
me and the O.T. a chance to work with Taryn for a fev
days and assess a baseline before you make any decisions.

"Great." He took the basket from her, leaning a hi
against the padded table while he leafed through the cat
alogs.

She found it interesting that even during a moment of apparent ease, when he was only looking through catalogs, he seemed restless. His toe tapped a little, he shifted his weight, he flipped a page and then back. It occurred to her she had never seen the man completely still. Was it her imagination or was that just Brodie?

She wasn't here to wonder about him, she reminded herself, and forced herself to wander the room taking mental measurements. As soon as she shifted gears, her mind began to spin with ideas about how she could utilize the space for therapy.

This all seemed natural, right, as if the clinical part of her brain had simply been hibernating, waiting for the first chance to emerge and stretch in the sunlight again.

She should have known she couldn't just twist a valve shut on years of training and experience. It was part of who she was. She had loved being a therapist, helping children in need because of accident or illness regain skills they had lost or achieve new milestones.

Until Cassie's death, she had been extremely content in her career and had enjoyed knowing she was good at what she did.

Everything had changed when her adopted daughter died. What had always given her such satisfaction and fulfillment suddenly became a harsh reminder of her own failures. After the funeral, she had returned to work but quickly discovered that the passion and drive so necessary in a dedicated physical therapist seemed to have shriveled away. After a few weeks, she had known she couldn't do it anymore. Her patients deserved more than someone going through the motions. If she couldn't force herself to stretch past the pain—and if she was no longer able to find that joy and passion again—she had reached the grim conclusion it was time to walk away.

Apparently it wasn't as easy as she'd thought to turn her back on the career path she had once loved.

"Can you give me your honest opinion?" Brodie asked sliding the catalog back in the basket with the others.

"That's usually not a problem for me." She gave him a wry smile. "If anything, I can sometimes be a little too brutal."

"Brutal is just what I need right now. Most of the doctors give platitudes and best-case scenarios. How the brain still is a big mystery and we have to wait and see, blah-blah-blah. It's been more than three months and I need more than that. I know you've visited Taryn in Denver and I'm sure you've seen similar brain injuries to hers. When all is said and done and we've thrown all the intensive therapy we can at her, let's be realistic. What are our chances for a full recovery?"

Oh, the dreaded question. Her stomach muscles tightened and she cursed that she'd ever allowed herself to be dragged here. Yes, she might have been hibernating. But right now she couldn't help wishing she could curl up back in her warm cave where she was safe, and slide back into sleep.

"I haven't seen Taryn yet from the perspective of a therapist, Brodie. Even if I had, I'm not sure I could answer that adequately. For one thing, *full recovery* is very subjective. Will she ever be exactly as she might have been if the accident had never happened? Probably not. That's the cold, hard truth. People who have suffered traumatic brain injuries often have things they have to struggle with the rest of their lives. But does that mean she won't be able to lead a functional, successful life? I'm sure the doctors at the rehab facility have given you a much more comprehensive outlook than I ever could."

"They won't tell me anything. Just about how the brain

is still a big mystery, how every case is individual, how it's a miracle she even survived the accident."

"Six weeks ago, she was in a coma. Think about how far she has come!"

"Has she? Sometimes it doesn't feel like it."

"Tell that to Maura, why don't you?" She tried to keep the anger out of her voice but she was certain some of it filtered through, especially when a muscle in his jaw tightened at the reminder of Maura's daughter, Layla, who hadn't survived the same accident that had injured Taryn.

"Taryn is alive. I know. I get it. She survived and I'm deeply grateful for that. But I can't help wondering what quality of life she's going to have."

Though his features were stony, she heard the pain filtering through his voice and her anger faded. Whatever she might think of him, Brodie was a concerned father, worried for his daughter's future and frustrated by the slow pace of her recovery. Evie had spoken with many such parents in her career and had been one herself for a few brief years.

Though she knew it would be far easier for her to keep a comfortable distance if she could nurture her dislike of him, she was sympathetic to his concerns.

Acting out of habit rather than conscious thought, she touched his bare forearm beneath the rolled sleeve of his shirt. A tiny spark jumped from his warm skin to hers and she pulled her hand away quickly.

"By the looks of things here, she's going to have the very best quality of life you can provide for her. She has you and she has Katherine in her corner, along with the prayers of everyone else in Hope's Crossing, which is no small thing."

He didn't look convinced. "We're doing all we can. I just hope it's enough."

"You're bringing her home tomorrow, then?"

"That's the plan."

She didn't miss the glint of apprehension in his eyes. Again, she was aware of a pang of sympathy. The first night she took Cassie home, she had been terrified. Despite years of training and working with children who had similar disabilities, the idea of being responsible for this fragile person had been overwhelming.

"Have Katherine call me when you leave the care center and I'll meet you here when you arrive. I'd like to get started right away."

Surprise widened those startling blue eyes. "You don't think she'll need a rest? The drive from Denver might be rough on her, especially sitting in her wheelchair in the van for an hour."

"I expect it will be tiring for her. That's why I'd like to start working her muscles right away."

"Whatever you think best." He didn't bother to hide his doubt.

"You asked me to do this, remember? You're going to have to trust my judgment on some things."

It wouldn't be easy, for either one of them. Brodie was a man of strong opinions—their limited contact before this week had made that crystal clear.

"Actually, I would like to make one thing clear," she continued. "I've agreed to help you only as a stopgap while you're looking for someone else to fill the position."

"Believe me, I haven't forgotten. You want to get back to your beads as soon as you can."

She refused to let herself flinch at the hint of disdain in his voice. Let him think what he wanted about her motives. She didn't care. "While I'm only planning to be working with Taryn for a few weeks, I see my role as laying the groundwork for subsequent therapies."

"I fully concur." He was back to being the stiff, formal

businessman, which she found something of a relief. That Brodie was much easier to categorize than the one who engendered empathy and compassion.

"Good. That makes this easier."

He looked wary. "Makes what easier?"

"I need a promise from you before Taryn comes home tomorrow."

"You're going to have to be a little more specific. I learned a long time ago that the devil was in the details. What sort of promise?"

"I need to be certain I have full authority to do whatever I think is best for her care. I can't have you coming in and questioning everything I do. If you have concerns about my methods, of course we can discuss those and you're more than welcome to sit in all day as I work with her if you'd like."

She really, really hoped he wouldn't do that. She could imagine few things more disconcerting than having to work with Taryn while the girl's entirely too gorgeous father watched from the sidelines. "But I need to know you're not going to micromanage what I do here."

"Full authority. I don't even give my chief operations officer full authority."

"It all comes down to trust. If you can't trust me to do what I think is best for Taryn, this isn't going to work out, even for the short term. You would be better coordinating her care yourself."

"You're asking a great deal."

"Too much?"

He appeared to be consider. "I suppose it's fair, especially since my mother basically guilted you into agreeing to help us anyway."

She laughed. "Big of you to admit you sicced Katherine on me."

"I didn't get where I am today by refusing to capitalize on my advantages. My mother was my ace in the hole. I knew you could say no to me without blinking, but she has a true talent for getting her way."

"Good to know she passed something on to the next generation."

He laughed softly and her stomach muscles shivered. "Along with blue eyes, healthy tooth enamel and a particular fondness for artichokes," he said.

Oh, this was bad. Really, really bad. Not only did she have to once more confront a life's calling she thought she'd left behind, but working with Taryn was bound to put her into repeated contact with Brodie.

A few days ago, she had thought that wouldn't matter. She had assumed that nothing could induce her to soften toward a man she disliked so instinctively. She was beginning to have the very uneasy feeling she might have been a smidge optimistic in that blind confidence in her ability to resist the man.

What was it about Evie Blanchard that seeped under his skin like water wearing away at shale?

Fifteen minutes later, Brodie watched her drive through the gates and back toward town in her sporty little Honda SUV and wondered how one small, slender woman could leave him feeling as if he'd just tangled with a badger in a bad mood.

Every time he was with her, he felt itchy and off balance and he didn't like it. A big part of it was this inconvenient attraction. Intellectually, he knew damn well he shouldn't be so drawn to her. It made no sense at all, especially when they approached the world from completely different stratospheres when it came to, oh, just about everything. Politics, philosophy, business. Probably because of the attention deficit disorder he still battled, he craved order in his life, neat and organized structure to help him cope with the chaos that was his mind sometimes.

In contrast, Evie's personality was like the beads and bangles she tended to favor—colorful, splashy, unique.

He knew his reaction to her was purely physical. Something about that lithe body, her delicate, sun-kissed features, all that sumptuous, silky honey-blond hair just reached into his gut and twisted hard.

Having her here in his house for the next few weeks would be an exercise in self-restraint, especially when his unruly mind drifted into all kinds of unwelcome areas, like wondering just what she would do if he gave in to temptation and tasted that mobile, fascinating mouth of hers.

If he tried it, he didn't doubt she would probably shut him down faster than that pissed-off badger would go for his throat if he ventured into its personal space.

He couldn't afford to antagonize her any more than he seemed to do just by simply breathing. The woman knew her stuff. His mother was right. He hadn't even seen her work with Taryn yet but he sensed knowledge and competence in the cool appraisal she'd given the renovations to the house.

He was impressed, despite his instinctive objections, by her firm assurance that she planned to begin working immediately with Taryn. How could he help but respect her willingness to jump right in, especially when she was still quite obviously reluctant to take on Taryn's therapy.

Absolute authority, Evie had demanded he give her. He shook his head, watching as her little SUV headed down the hill. That wasn't going to be an easy thing to surrender but he understood the wisdom of it. In every one of his endeavors, someone needed to be the boss. Sometimes he refused to relinquish that role but most of the time he had seen the wisdom and efficiency in handing it off to someone else he trusted. Like it or not, this was going to have to be one of those times. If he second-guessed every decision, she might bolt before the two weeks were up.

Already, he could tell he wasn't going to be satisfied with her agreement to only help Taryn transition to a home program. He wanted her here permanently. She was the best choice to help Taryn; he knew it in that same gut that responded so physically to Evie as a beautiful woman—which meant he would have to do everything in his power to convince her to stay beyond that initial two weeks.

What choice did he have? She was absolutely right. He intended to do every freaking thing possible to make sure his daughter had the best chance at a normal life, no matter what the cost.

Four

Home.

She was almost home.

Taryn looked out the window of the van. Town. Trees. Mountains.

Home.

She was glad. So glad.

She shifted, back aching from the wheelchair.

"We're almost there, baby." Her dad spoke from the front seat.

"Only a few more miles." Grandma smiled. She looked pretty. Tired.

No more hospital. Her friends. Her room.

Normal.

She heard the word just right in her head but she when she tried to talk, she could only make a stupid sound. "Noorrmmm."

Grandma smiled again. "You're going to be surprised. Your dad's been so busy fixing things up for you. You've got a beautiful new room downstairs with a roll-in shower in the bathroom and your own private workout space."

She frowned. "No. Up." She thought of posters on the wall, her pillow couch, purple walls. Her room.

Her dad turned, frowning. "We don't have an elevator yet and you're a ways from tackling the stairs, kiddo. This will be better."

She wanted her room. Window seat, canopy bed, everything. She wanted to argue but the words caught. "No. Up."

"Wait until you see your new room, Taryn." Dad's smile was fake, too big. "We painted the trim your favorite color and it has a really nice view. I think you're going to love it."

She shook her head. She wouldn't.

This wasn't right. She was going home but it wasn't the same. Out the window, she saw trees, flowers, mountains.

Home.

Everything *else* was normal. Not her. Not anymore. Never again.

She was broken.

In the rearview mirror, Brodie watched his daughter's chin tremble and he thought she would cry. He'd been afraid of this. She wanted her regular room, her regular life. That she couldn't have those things right now would be one more stark reality-check for a girl who had endured far too many already.

He kept his gaze on the road as he drove the wheelchair-accessible van he'd purchased for an ungodly amount from a dealership in Loveland just a few days earlier, but he allowed himself occasional glances at Taryn in her wheelchair—secured by latches to the lowered floor behind the driver and passenger seats—until finally the distress in her features eased a little.

She was still pretty, his baby girl. Her facial features might seem a little more slack than before the accident and she would always have faint traces of scars but most of them were beneath her hairline.

Her hair was short since they'd had to shave it during

her various procedures, but it was dark and impishly curly, and her eyes were still the same blue of the sky just before a twilight thunderstorm. He wondered if others would see the courage and strength inside her or if they would only register the wheelchair, the scars, the halting, mangled words.

"Oh, it will be nice to be home," Katherine said from the seat beside him.

She gazed out the window as if she'd been away for years and he was grateful all over again for his mother's sacrifices for him and his daughter. After the accident, Katherine had basically given up her own life and moved to Denver to stay at Taryn's bedside around the clock. He had spent as much time at the hospital as he could and had turned many of his business responsibilities over to his associates at Thorne and Company. He had eventually set up a mobile office at the apartment they had rented near the hospital and had scrambled the best he could to keep everything running smoothly.

"Look at that," Katherine suddenly exclaimed.

He followed the direction she was pointing and saw a six-foot-long poster driven with stakes into a grassy parking strip near Miners' Park. "Welcome Home, Taryn," he read. A little farther, splashed in washable paint in the window of a fast-food restaurant, was the same message.

On the marquee at the grocery store that usually broadcast the latest sale on chicken legs or a good buy on broccoli was another one. "We love you, Taryn."

And as they headed through town, he saw another message in big letters on the street, "Taryn Rocks!"

The kids at the high school had probably done it, since it was similar to the kind of messages displayed during the Paint the Town event of Homecoming Week.

He was grateful for the sentiment, even as a petty little

part of him thought with some bitterness that the message might have been a little more effective if a few of them could have been bothered to visit her on a regular basis in the hospital.

That wasn't completely fair, he knew. The first few weeks after she'd come out of a coma, Taryn had been inundated with visitors. Too many, really. The cheerleading squad, of which she was still technically a part, the captains of the football team, the student body officers.

Eventually those visits had dwindled to basically nothing, until the last time anybody from Hope's Crossing High School stopped in to see her had been about a month ago.

He supposed he couldn't really blame the kids. It was obvious Taryn wasn't the same social bug she had been. She couldn't carry on a conversation yet, not really, and while many teenagers he knew didn't particularly need anybody else to participate when they jabbered on about basically nothing, it would have been a little awkward.

This gesture, small though it might have been, was *something*. He could focus on that, he thought as his mother pointed out all the signs to Taryn, who smiled slightly at each one.

Though he could have easily circumvented driving through the main business district of downtown to reach their home in the foothills, he could tell the outpouring of support had touched Katherine. This was a small thing he could give his mother to thank her for all her help these last weeks. A few more moments of driving wouldn't hurt.

More Welcome Home signs hung on several of the storefronts downtown, including the bead store, the café and even Maura Parker's bookstore.

"We should have put something up at the sporting-goods store and the restaurants," he said. "I didn't think about it. I'm glad someone else in town did."

"We've had a few other things on our minds."

"True enough." He smiled, grateful all over again for her steady strength these last few months. He would have foundered on the rocks and sunk without her.

He had always loved his mother but that natural emotion had sometimes been tempered over the years by a low, vague simmer of anger he hadn't really acknowledged. Why would someone as kind and giving as his mother ever stay with a man like his father, a hard, uncompromising man with no sense of humor about life and little patience for a son with learning deficits and a gnat-short attention span?

That frustration seemed far away and unimportant now when he considered all Katherine had done for Taryn since the accident. He supposed an adult child never really understood or appreciated the best qualities of a parent until they had walked a difficult road together.

She was growing older. It was a sobering reality made more clear in the harsh afternoon sunlight when he saw new lines around her mouth, a few gray streaks she usually ruthlessly subdued with artful hair color.

"You ought to think about taking a trip somewhere in the next few months," he said suddenly. "A cruise or a trip back to Provence or something. Lord knows you deserve it and we can certainly hobble along without you for a month or so."

"Maybe next spring, when things settle down a little."

Spring seemed a long way off to him right now. The aspens were already turning a pale gold around the edges and in only a few months Hope's Crossing would be covered in snow and the skiers would return like the swallows at Capistrano.

"Ice." Taryn suddenly spoke up.

Considering what he'd just been thinking about, he wondered if she had somehow read his mind.

"It's August, sweetheart," he answered. "No ice around, at least for a few more months." The idea of coping with the wheelchair ramp around town in the snow was daunting but maybe by then they wouldn't need this van.

"Ice!" she said more urgently, looking out the van window with more animation than he'd seen since they had left the care center. He sent a quick, helpless look to his mother, who shrugged, obviously as baffled as he was.

An instant later, they passed a little stand shaped like a Swiss chalet, planted in a small graveled parking lot on the outskirts of downtown. A few people sat under umbrella-topped tables holding foam cups and, as he caught them out of the corner of his gaze, a light switched on.

"Oh! Ice! Shave ice!" he exclaimed.

Taryn gave her tiny, lopsided smile and nodded and he felt as if he'd just skied a black-diamond run on pure, fresh powder.

Though he was impatient to get her home and begin the next phase of this crazy journey they'd traveled since April, Taryn had asked him for something. She had actually communicated a need and, more importantly, he'd understood it. It seemed like a red-letter moment that ought to be celebrated—despite the fact that she wouldn't be able to hold the cup by herself or feed herself the treat.

"You want a shave ice, you've got it, sweetheart."

He turned the van around and by some miracle, he found a fortuitous parking space a moment later, sandwiched between a flashy red convertible with rental plates and a minivan with a luggage bag bungeed to the roof. The summer tourists were still out in force, apparently. He'd missed most of the onslaught while relocated in Denver.

"What flavor?"

Her brow furrowed as she considered her options and then she gave that smile that was a lopsided shadow of her former mischievous grin. "Blue."

He had to guess that meant raspberry. That had been a favorite flavor of hers before the accident and he was heartened at this evidence that, while so many things had changed about his daughter, he could still find traces inside of all the things that made her Taryn.

He opened his car door. "Mom? Do you want one?"

Katherine looked elegantly amused. "I think I'll pass today. But thank you."

The afternoon was warm but mountain-pleasant compared to the heat wave they'd left down in Denver. Hope's Crossing consistently enjoyed temperatures about ten degrees cooler than the metro area, one reason tourists even from the city enjoyed coming to town, to visit the unique shops and eat in the town's many restaurants.

He recognized the teenager working at the shave-ice stand as one of Taryn's friends from elementary school, Hannah Kirk. Before he had moved up to the Aspen Ridge area, the girl and her family had been neighbors.

"Hi, Hannah."

She set down the washcloth she had been using to wipe down the counter, probably sticky from an afternoon of serving up syrupy treats. "Hi, Mr. Thorne," she said. "How's Taryn? I heard she might be coming home today."

"She is. Right now, in fact. She's in the van over there. We were just driving past on our way home and she asked for a shave ice."

Hannah beamed. "She asked for a shave ice? That's great. I heard she couldn't talk," she faltered, the excitement on her slightly round features fading to embarrassment, as if she was afraid she'd just said something rude. "Sorry. I mean..."

"She *can* talk. It's still a little tough to understand her sometimes so she just doesn't say much. Only the important things. I guess she really wanted a shave ice."

"I can sure help you with that. What size?"

"Let's go with a medium. She wanted blue raspberry. I'll take a peach coconut, medium."

He knew it was straight sugar but he figured every once in a while a guy was entitled to enjoy something lousy for him. Why that made him suddenly think of Evie Blanchard, he didn't want to guess.

While he waited for Hannah to run the ice in the grinder—a process that seemed to take roughly the equivalent time to carve a masterpiece out of marble—he stood beside the faux chalet, looking at Main Street. The town looked warm and comfortable in the afternoon sunlight, full of parents pushing strollers, an elderly couple walking arm in arm, a couple of joggers with their white iPod earbud tethers dangling.

He loved Hope's Crossing. When he was a kid, he couldn't leave fast enough and thought it was a town full of provincial people with small minds and smaller dreams. But this was the place he'd come to after his marriage had fallen apart, when he had been a lost and immature twenty-four-year-old kid suddenly saddled with a three-year-old girl he didn't know what the hell to do with.

If his father hadn't just died, he wasn't sure he would have come home, even as desperate as he'd been for his mother's help with Taryn. Raymond Thorne's massive heart attack at that particular juncture of Brodie's life was probably the bastard's single act of kindness toward him.

He was mulling that cheerful thought when a teenage boy with streaked blond hair rode up on a high-dollar mountain bike wearing board shorts and a black T-shirt with a vulgar picture on the front.

"Hey, Hannah-banana. Give me a medium watermelon."

Raw fury curled through Brodie. He could taste it in the back of his throat, sharp and acrid. He hated this kid with every microcell of his heart and it took all the discipline he'd learned in his ski-jumping days to keep from grabbing the kid and shoving his face into that freezer full of ice beside the stand.

He stepped around the side of the fake little chalet and had the tiny satisfaction of seeing the kid's features go a little pale under his summer tan.

"Nice bike," he said to Charlie Beaumont, the son of a bitch who had ruined Taryn's life.

The kid looked as if he would rather be anywhere else on earth, as if he were tempted to climb back onto his bike and race away. Hot color washed up to replace his paleness and he didn't meet Brodie's gaze.

"Mr. Thorne," he muttered.

Brodie could think of a hundred things he would like to say to this kid, whose position of wealth and privilege apparently led him to think he could destroy lives around him with impunity from his choices.

Charlie's father was the mayor of Hope's Crossing and one of the town's most powerful members. He was also an attorney who—along with his partners—was doing everything he could to keep his son from having to atone for his stupid choices.

Because of this little punk, his baby girl's life had been decimated. While he rode around town flaunting his five-thousand-dollar mountain bike and buying iced treats, Taryn was forced to endure countless procedures and shots, to be unable to communicate even the most basic of needs, to spend her days in a wheelchair when she should be dancing and running and enjoying life as a teenage girl.

Shoving him into the freezer was too good for him.

"Um, how's Taryn?" Charlie finally asked.

Brodie had to admit, the kid showed balls to pretend concern. "Do you really care? I didn't notice you coming to the hospital anytime during the last three months."

At least he had the grace to look embarrassed. "I wanted to. I just…my parents, uh, didn't think I should."

"Right. Wouldn't want you to face something as inconvenient as your conscience, would we?"

If possible, Charlie's features turned an even deeper shade of red. Brodie would have liked to say something cutting and harsh but a family of tourists in shorts and ball caps came up behind Charlie and the moment passed. What was the point anyway? Yelling at the kid wouldn't help Taryn and probably wouldn't make Brodie feel any better.

Hannah Kirk called his name just a moment later. "Here you go, Mr. Thorne. You tell Taryn we're all praying for her, okay?"

He forced a polite smile, biting down the urge to point out that prayers hadn't done a hell of a lot of good so far.

"I'll tell her. And thank you for the shave ice. I'm sure she'll enjoy it."

Hannah hesitated. "Would it be okay if I stopped by to bring her another one sometime, now that she's home?"

It was nice of her to offer, especially as their friendship seemed to have withered away after grade school. "I think she'd like that," he answered.

Charlie was apparently following their conversation. "Wait. She's home?" he asked.

"Didn't you see the signs all over town?" Hannah asked, with a touch of pugnacity that seemed out of character for her. "Mr. Thorne is taking her home now. That's why he bought her a shave ice here instead of in Denver."

An interesting mix of emotions crossed Charlie's features. He looked happy and miserable and wary at the same time. "So she's okay?"

Chief McKnight probably wouldn't arrest him if he "accidentally" dumped a shave ice on the punk's head, would he? "Right," he growled. "If you call needing twenty-four-hour care, not being able to get out more than a few words, not having the motor control to feed herself this shave ice, *okay,* then yes. I guess she's *okay.* Unlike Layla Parker."

It was a cruel thing to say, he knew, and he felt small for it when Charlie hissed in a breath as if Brodie had cold-cocked him like he wanted to. The kid stared at him for a long moment then climbed back onto his mountain bike and pedaled away without taking the icy treat Hannah was reluctantly fixing for him.

Brodie stood like an idiot for a moment watching after him, then shook his head. He tried to put the encounter out of his mind as he headed back to the van. This was a good day, right? Taryn was going home. That was the important thing, not some little shit with an entitlement complex.

At the van, he slid open the left rear door—the one without the ramp—set his own shave ice in the drink holder and then scooped a spoonful of the sugary treat for Taryn.

"Here you go, honey. Blue. Just like you wanted."

She gave that lopsided smile again, the one doctors warned him might be permanent, and opened her mouth for a taste.

"Mmmm," she said, so he gave her another one, wiping her face a little where some of the flavored ice dribbled out.

"Is that good for now?" he asked after a few more tastes. "I can give you more when we get home."

"Yeah," she answered, smiling again, and his heart ached with love for her. He hated that it had taken a tragic accident stunning the entire town to remind him how much.

"Everything okay?" his mother asked when they were

once more heading up the causeway toward his neighborhood above the main section of town.

"Why wouldn't it be?" He focused on the drive instead of the jumble of emotions he didn't know what to do with. Anger at Charlie, love for his daughter, fury at this whole damn situation.

"You seem tense."

In the rearview mirror, he could see Taryn gazing out the window, not paying attention to their conversation, so he decided to tell his mother the truth.

"Charlie Beaumont was behind me in line at the shave-ice stand." He pitched his voice low.

Katherine didn't seem to think this was all that earth-shaking an event. "What did you do?"

"He's still in one piece, if that's what you're asking."

His mother's smile had a bittersweet edge. "Glad to hear it. I think enough people have suffered from one boy's foolish mistakes, don't you?"

Except Charlie. The kid hadn't suffered one damn bit. By one of those weird quirks of physics and sheer stupid luck, he'd emerged from the accident completely unscathed—and Brodie was quite sure one part of him would never be content until the kid paid somehow for all the lives he'd ruined.

She could be Switzerland.

Think the Matterhorn, lederhosen, those ten-foot-long trumpety thingies.

Above all, neutrality.

Evie stood inside the sprawling Thorne home, wondering at the delay. Katherine had texted her thirty minutes earlier to say they were arriving in Hope's Crossing. They should have been here fifteen minutes ago but maybe they stopped somewhere along the route to enjoy the outpouring of support from the town.

She wasn't sure how word had trickled out but by now everybody seemed to know. Maybe the Chamber of Commerce had started a phone tree or something, because nearly every store in town had some kind of sign in the window or on their marquee and it seemed everyone who came into the store wanted to talk about Taryn's homecoming.

Evie only hoped Brodie would take that support in the light it was intended, as a manifestation of the good wishes of people in town and not as some expression of pity. Somehow she doubted the latter would sit well with him.

"Can I get you something to drink while we wait? A soda or some tea?" Mrs. Olafson, Brodie's scarily efficient housekeeper, hovered in the doorway. She was squat and apple-cheeked and had seemed stern at first glance. A bit on the terrifying side, actually, but Evie could see by her frequent glances down the driveway that the housekeeper was eagerly anticipating Taryn's return.

"I'm great," she said, her tone gentle. "Why don't you sit down and wait for her with me?"

"I couldn't. I should be working on the salad for dinner."

"Dinner is still a few hours away. Please. Sit."

Mrs. Olafson looked reluctant but she finally perched on the edge of the teak bench beside the front door.

"How long have you worked for the Thornes?" Evie asked. She had seen the older woman around town but their circles hadn't really connected before and she had yet to take the chance to get to know her. They would be working in close proximity the next few weeks. No harm in trying to be friendly and learn more about Mrs. Olafson, other than that she rarely smiled and always pulled her hair into a rather severe steel-gray bun at the base of her neck that made Evie think of her elementary school lunch ladies or perhaps the stereotypical warden at a women's prison.

"Almost five years. My husband was a chef and Mr. Thorne hired him to work one of his restaurants up at the ski resorts."

"Oh, is that where you learned to cook so well?"

"I taught him everything he knew," the other woman said, the first hint of a smile Evie had seen just barely lifting the corners of her mouth. It faded quickly. "We moved from our home in Minneapolis just six weeks before he was diagnosed with liver cancer."

"Oh. I'm so sorry."

The other woman shrugged. "I thought for sure Mr. Thorne would fire him but he didn't. He continued to give him a paycheck even when he couldn't work anymore. After David died, Mr. Thorne asked if I would like to come to work for him, helping him with the house and with Taryn. I've been here ever since." She fidgeted with her apron, her pale blue eyes darting to the driveway again. "He's a very good man, Mr. Thorne. Though I've always been a good cook, I had no real job experience at all. I married young and all I'd ever done was be a mother to my boys, who are both in college now. Mr. Thorne didn't care about that. He hired me anyway."

She should never have asked. Evie fidgeted. She didn't want to hear these glowing words of praise for Brodie. It made him seem kind and generous, not the stiff, unpleasant man she'd always thought him to be.

"It seems to me a lifetime of taking care of your family made you eminently qualified to handle things here. If those delicious smells coming from the kitchen are any indication, I'm sure you do your job exceptionally well."

The woman seemed to warm a little, some of the reserve in her expression thawing. "I try. I don't have any experience with therapy either but if you need my help with Taryn in any way, I can always offer an extra set of hands."

"Thank you. I might take you up on that."

She knew Brodie had hired personal nurses to be help with Taryn's medical needs, but the plan for now was for Evie to work with the girl on an intensive physical therapy program six hours a day, between the hours of ten and four, until Brodie could find someone to replace her. In addition, an occupational therapist who had worked with Taryn at the rehab facility would come to the house three times a week for two hours at a time. Evie would reinforce the skills she was working on during her own time with Taryn on the other days.

Only a few weeks. She could handle this, she reminded herself.

She had dreamed of her adopted daughter the night before, of Cassie's sweet smile and loving heart and endless eagerness to please.

They had been lying in the hammock under the trees behind her bungalow in Topanga Canyon, telling stories and humming silly little tunes and listening to the creek murmuring by and the wind in the trees. Cassie had been laughing and joyful, just as Evie remembered her—and then she had awakened to the grim awareness that her daughter was gone.

It had been nearly two years since she died and the grief still seemed so much a part of Evie, despite the peace she had found in Hope's Crossing. The raw pain of it had eased over the last year during her time here and she had begun to think that perhaps she was finally growing a protective scab over her heart.

The trick was going to be preventing Taryn Thorne and her entirely too appealing father from ripping it away.

Switzerland. Stoic and aloof, with no trace of emotional

involvement. She could do it, even when her friendship with Katherine complicated the situation.

She was still trying to convince herself of that when a silver minivan pulled into the circular driveway.

"Oh. She's here," Mrs. Olafson breathed. Evie smiled and squeezed the woman's hand, then rose to greet them.

Brodie seemed to hesitate a moment in the driver's seat before hitting the button for the power ramp and Evie was aware of another unwanted pang of sympathy. She remembered well that panicky *what now* the first night she'd taken Cassie home after Meredith's funeral, when she had to shift instantly from friend and therapist to parent.

That compassion urged her forward with a broad smile of welcome, down the gleaming new graded concrete walkway that had been artfully designed to accommodate a wheelchair. "Hi. Welcome home! How was your drive?"

He blinked a little as if he hadn't expected such an effusive greeting. "Good. She's been a real trouper but I'm sure she's tired."

Mrs. Olafson had followed her toward the van. "Mr. Thorne, the home-nursing company called and said their nurse was running late. She should be here in another hour."

"Thank you, Mrs. O."

He stood helplessly for just a moment as if not quite sure what to do next. Evie wanted to hug him and whisper that everything would be okay. As the mental image formed in her mind she almost laughed. She could just imagine how he would react to that.

Instead, she took charge, leaning in and placing a hand on the armrest of the wheelchair. "Hi, Taryn. Remember me? Evie Blanchard from the bead store?"

The girl nodded and her mouth stretched into a half smile. "Hi."

What are you doing here? Though Taryn didn't say the words, Evie could see them clearly in her eyes. One lesson she'd learned well with her patients was how to read all kinds of nonverbal cues and right now Taryn was completely confused by her presence.

"You want to know why I'm here, right?"

Taryn dipped her chin down and then back up again, which Evie took as agreement.

"Great question. I'm not sure if you knew this but back before I came to Hope's Crossing and started working for Claire at the bead store, I was a physical therapist in California. Your dad and grandmother have asked me to help set up your home therapy program with the aides and nurses who will be working with you. Is that okay?"

She lifted one shoulder, though she didn't look thrilled at the idea of therapy.

"I would guess you're ready to head inside, aren't you? I know my butt is always tired after I've been sitting in the car for a while. Let's go stretch out, shall we?"

"O—kay."

"I'll bring your shave ice," Katherine said.

"Shave ice. Yum. And blue. My favorite."

"We saw that little shack near the end of Main Street on our way here and Taryn made it clear she had to have one."

That must have been the reason for the delay, Evie thought. At this evidence that Brodie wasn't so impatient and inflexible he couldn't fulfill one of his daughter's wishes, she felt a little scrape against that scab over her heart, like a fingernail prying up the edge.

Evie stepped back while Brodie wheeled the chair down the ramp and pushed Taryn toward the front door. When he turned her through the doorway leading to her suite of rooms, Taryn jerked her head back toward the stairway. "My room. Up."

"T, we talked about this. For now you've got new digs down here."

"No. My room."

Brodie shot Evie a frustrated plea for help and she stepped forward. "You want your old bedroom up there?"

Taryn nodded firmly.

"Then you're the one who will have to work your tail off to get there. Are you ready for that?"

"Yeah," Taryn said, a rather militant light in her eyes that heartened Evie.

"Excellent. I am, too."

"Come on, sweetheart," Katherine said. "Let me show you your new room."

Her grandmother pushed the wheelchair down the hall and, though Evie wanted to start working with the girl right away, she was aware of that twinge of unwanted compassion for Brodie as he watched his mother and daughter together—a stark, hopeless expression on his features.

She again wanted to comfort him, to promise him everything would be okay, but she wouldn't lie to him.

"Did Taryn enjoy the shave ice?" She gestured to the cup Katherine had handed him when she'd taken over pushing the wheelchair.

"She only had a few tastes but I think so. I, on the other hand, could have done without the company."

When she gave him a blank look, he shrugged. "I saw that little prick Charlie Beaumont at the shave-ice stand. And before you ask, no, I didn't punch him—though I'll be honest, I almost dumped my peach coconut on his head."

"Admirable restraint," she said with a smile. She decided not to tell him she felt a little sorry for the kid, who had been vilified by everyone in town.

"On a lighter note, I also talked to one of Taryn's

friends. She'd like to come visit sometime. Since you have requested absolute power, I guess that's your call."

"I don't need absolute power," she muttered.

"Visitors weren't really a problem in Denver where we were nearly two hours away. She didn't have that many visitors after the first few weeks out of the coma. Now that she's home, I anticipate more of her friends may want to drop in. What do you think?"

"Why do you consider it an issue?"

He inclined his head toward the suite of rooms. "You saw her. She can't carry on much of a conversation with anyone. I thought maybe it might be hard on Taryn, the constant reminders of everything she's lost."

"Regular social interaction is important to teenage girls, no matter what physical challenges they're dealing with."

"I can see that. Before the accident, she always had a friend or two around the house. If you think it's all right, I'll call Hannah's mother and let her know the girl can visit."

"Maybe we can incorporate social interaction into her therapy plan somehow. I'll speak with the speech therapist when she comes tomorrow."

"Thank you." He paused, looking uncomfortable. "I'm afraid I didn't say that the other day when you were here. I know helping my daughter isn't something you want to do. My mother wouldn't tell me why, only said you have your reasons but…thank you for helping us anyway."

Discomfort crawled up her spine when she thought of how pissy and pouty she'd been inside her own head since Sunday when he'd first approached her. If circumstances had been different, if she had been stronger, she should have been eager to take on the challenge. Any decent person would have jumped at the chance to help a girl who had already endured so much. It shamed her that she had been dragging her feet all week and manufacturing a hundred different excuses to wriggle out of the obligation.

She supposed even the Swiss sometimes wondered if they ought to occasionally step up and take a stand.

"You're welcome," she finally said, feeling her face heat.

He gazed at her out of those dark-fringed, impossibly blue eyes and for just an instant she was almost certain his gaze rested on her mouth. Her breath caught and she fought the sudden wild impulse to lick her lips.

"I'd better get in there and help your mother transfer Taryn," she said quickly.

He blinked a few times. "Right. Do you need my help? I've got some phone calls to make but they can wait awhile."

She shook her head. "We'll be fine. It will be good practice for all of us to use the lift system you've got in there."

"My home office is down at the end of the hall. If you need me, just yell."

She nodded and watched him walk away, his body tough and athletic. Oh, she definitely would have to be careful around this dangerous but infinitely appealing man. She had a feeling it was going to be very tough to remember she was freaking Switzerland, especially when she suddenly wanted to throw open every border to him.

Five

Less than a week later, Evie threw Switzerland out the window and decided she would far rather be Napoleon marching across Europe, cannons blazing, swallowing up borders and taking no prisoners.

Despite her best efforts, she wasn't aloof and detached anymore. Instead, she was frustrated, tired, achy and cross. Every minuscule shred of patience she might have once thought she could claim lay in ruins.

In nearly a decade of her private practice in Los Angeles she had known her share of stubborn patients. Kids who refused to do their exercises unless they were in the mood or insisted on working to a particular song or who had to have the lights just so before they would even consider doing as she asked.

They were nothing compared to the sheer unbreakable will of this fifteen-year-old girl. "Come on, Taryn. You can do this. I've read the notes from your therapists at the rehab center. According to them, you've been standing on your own for up to twenty seconds at a go for the last two weeks but you haven't done it one single, solitary time for me. Is everybody lying or have you forgotten how?"

Taryn managed a shrug and Evie wanted to scream.

Every time they worked on standing, Taryn's legs would collapse as if they were filled with mascarpone. "I just want you to show me. One time. Come on, honey. How are we going to work on walking up those stairs to your bedroom if you won't even show me how well you can stand?"

Taryn sent her a sidelong look then glanced away as if she didn't understand a word. Evie wasn't fooled. Taryn understood everything, even if she couldn't always communicate her needs. She knew just what Evie wanted of her, she simply didn't want to cooperate.

"I want…to watch TV," she said.

Taryn inclined her head toward the big flat-screen TV set in a niche of the wall, and Evie was by turns frustrated and heartened. Already, Taryn was doing a better job of stringing together words, which forced Evie to wonder what she was doing wrong and why she was meeting roadblocks at every turn.

"Fine," she said. "You stand for thirty seconds to show me you can do it and then you can watch whatever you want for fifteen minutes. Deal?" Taryn favored reality-TV shows with no redeeming value but if that's what it took to get the job accomplished, Evie was willing to try anything.

The side of the girl's mouth lifted in her half smile. "Deal."

Evie pulled her from the chair, feeling the strain in her back as she took most of the girl's weight. Taryn was still thin, her wrists spindly as twigs. Before the accident, she had been vivacious and fit, always surrounded by other teenagers. When she used to come into the bead store, she seemed to bring a glow with her that lit up everyone else with her smile.

Brain injuries sucked, Evie thought as she supported Taryn's weight. Two people could suffer the exact same

injury—same location, same intensity, same everything—
and manifest completely different outcomes.

She completely understood now why the staff at the
rehab facility had thrown up their hands and suggested giving in to Taryn's wish to be home. The only trouble was,
now that she was back in Hope's Crossing, Taryn didn't
seem any more motivated to do the exercises necessary
to regain as much function as possible than she had when
she'd been in rehab.

Evie had to figure out a way to reach her, but she didn't
have the first idea how to accomplish that. Every technique
she'd tried thus far had been a big bust. If Taryn would
work in exchange for the dubious privilege of watching a
few minutes of some reality-TV crapfest, Evie wouldn't
quibble.

"I've got the walker right here for you to hold on to if
you need it. Are you ready for me to let go?"

At Taryn's nod, Evie released her grip on the girl,
though she didn't move her hands away far. Much to Evie's
pleasure, Taryn actually took her own weight and stood,
though she kept her hands on the walker.

Evie had only counted to fifteen when she noticed
movement out of the corner of her gaze and saw that Brodie had come into the room.

"Dad," Taryn exclaimed, sagging backward.

Evie caught her before she could fall. "That wasn't
thirty seconds. You stopped about ten seconds short. I
guess no Snooki for you then."

Taryn made a face but she straightened again. Exactly
ten seconds later, she collapsed into her chair again.

Evie laughed. "Look at you, counting in your head. All
right. I guess you've earned it. Fifteen minutes, okay?" She
pushed the girl over toward the big screen and handed her

the adapted remote pad with the large buttons that Taryn could easily press.

"Interesting choice of motivator," Brodie murmured from beside her. She couldn't tell by his tone whether he approved or not.

"Hey, if I find something that works, I'm going to use it. Even if it's ridiculous trash."

As her solitary patient would be occupied for a few moments, Evie began to clean the exercise ball and the walker and the rest of the equipment they'd used that day—anything to distract her from the ridiculous simmer of awareness that bloomed whenever Brodie came in to check on things.

"You don't have to do that. Mrs. O. could probably take care of it for you."

"It's an old habit. When I was in private practice, most of my clients were medically fragile. We had to sanitize everything between patients for their safety. I just figure it can't hurt, even when only Taryn is using the equipment."

"Is she? Using the equipment, I mean? Has today been any better?"

Since she'd started the week before, Brodie had checked in with her every afternoon. She didn't want to admit that some silly part of her actually waited in anticipation of these visits.

"The last few minutes have been her best in several days, even if I had to use MTV to motivate her. I'm earning every penny of the exorbitant fee you're paying to the Layla Parker scholarship fund. How is the search for my replacement coming?"

"I'm interviewing another possible applicant tomorrow. Would you be willing to sit in again and give your opinion?"

So far the applicants for the position either had been

underqualified or looking for something a little less neb-ulous and a little more permanent. She was flattered that Brodie apparently was willing to trust her judgment on a couple of them. When she'd voiced concerns after the re-spective interviews, he had agreed to continue looking.

"What time?"

"Nine."

"That's fine. I should be able to come a little earlier than I'd planned in the morning."

Taryn suddenly laughed at something on the screen and her laugh sounded exactly as Evie remembered—full and rich and brimming with life.

When Evie turned back to Brodie, she found him watch-ing his daughter with a look of stark emotion.

"I've missed that laugh. Stupid, isn't it?"

"Not at all," she murmured.

His fingers drummed on the countertop. "The last few years have been rough. Teen growing pains. We fought all the time, you know? It seems like I wasted so much time with her before the accident being frustrated and impa-tient about dumb little things and my own unreasonable expectations that I rarely took a chance just to listen to her and remember to savor these moments."

The orange scent of the disinfecting wipe grew stron-ger as she clenched her fingers more tightly around it to keep from touching his arm. "Here's your chance. Maybe you ought to go numb your brain for a few minutes and watch with her."

He made a face. "Ugh. Bonding over *Jersey Shore*. Just shoot me now."

She laughed, entirely too drawn to the blasted man. His glance flickered to her mouth and Evie caught her breath as heat sizzled and tugged between them. The sounds of the silly television show faded away and she forgot Taryn was even in the same room, mesmerized by those blue eyes.

Evie was painfully aware of him, of the low, fluttery curl in her belly and the insane urge to step forward, dig her fingers into the cotton of his shirt and tug him toward her.

Whoa. Slow down, she told her errant hormones. Stupid idea, letting him stir her up like this with just a casual look. Okay, he might not be the arrogant jerk she had taken him for since she'd arrived in Hope's Crossing, but that didn't mean she needed to go all soft and gooey over him.

He was still not her type. That hadn't changed simply because she was discovering these different facets of the man. He might be a good parent. But he was also motivated by the almighty dollar, just as her own father had been.

He was the first one to blink in the sensual game of chicken they were apparently playing. He jerked his gaze away and looked down at his watch. "I only have fifteen minutes to spare. I've got a conference call I can't miss."

"That should give you just enough time to watch the ending," she said.

"Lucky me," he muttered and headed over to his daughter's side. He pulled one of the chairs over from the table-and-chair set he had, indeed, carted into the room for their use, and set it beside the wheelchair.

Evie wasn't about to let herself be dragged into the show and she decided this would be the perfect time for her to catch up on paperwork. She had been trying to take copious treatment notes about each day for her successor. After breaking out her laptop, she sat at the table and tried to focus on recording their activities of the day, from their frustrating time in the pool that morning when Taryn had refused to use the kickboard, to the equally frustrating work at the table, where Taryn refused to practice using silverware.

The litany of her defeats left a sour taste in her mouth. She didn't remember ever feeling like such a failure during the time she was actively practicing P.T. Maybe she needed to throw in the towel and let Brodie find someone else who might be better at reaching the girl. Heaven knew, she certainly didn't seem to be up to the job.

"It's over." Taryn's petulant words interrupted Evie's self-flagellation.

"Darn. Just when it was getting good," Brodie said drily.

"You'll just have to watch again next week with Taryn so you can keep track of what's happening," Evie teased.

He gave her dark look. "Isn't there a good PBS special or something we could watch instead?"

"Boring," Taryn declared.

Brodie shook his head but leaned over to kiss the top of her elfin curls. "Remind me to do something about your pitiful taste in entertainment, kiddo. But not right now. I've got to take a conference call. Give Evie your best effort, okay? Remember that ski trip to Chamonix we've been talking about? You've got a fair bit of work ahead of you if we're finally going to make it this winter."

Taryn's smile faded and she looked down at her legs. "I...can't...ski."

"Keep at it, sweetheart," Brodie said firmly. "You can do anything you set your mind to. And Evie is here to help you."

He waved to them both and headed out of the room. Evie watched him go for about thirty seconds longer than she should have before she forced her attention back to Taryn.

Yeah. Stupid idea, entertaining those crazy thoughts about him for even a minute. In her experience, letting herself go soft and gooey usually only led to one big, sticky mess.

* * *

Taryn lay on the stupid padded table, hating her life. This dumb room, her weak legs, that big mirror that showed how ugly she was now.

And Evie. Especially Evie.

Evie was pretty, with blue eyes and that long blond hair, like some kind of angel.

A bitchy angel.

"Come on. Four more. You can do this."

"I…don't like…leg lifts." The words sounded stupid, too. They were mushy, like eating peanut butter, and she hated that she had to work so hard to squeeze the right ones out when they were right there in her head. It was easier not to say much of anything. "Leg lifts…hurt."

"We're almost done. Hang in there."

"I want…to rest now."

"In a minute. Four more."

No. She wanted to be done. To watch more TV and be quiet and forget her stupid life.

"Excuse me. Sorry to interrupt."

Mrs. O. peeked her head into the room. Taryn lowered her leg. *Interrupt. Please. Go ahead.*

"No worries." Evie smiled. "What can we do for you?"

"A young lady is here to visit Taryn. One of her friends. I didn't know if she might be up to visitors."

Taryn looked in the mirror she hated. She was gross. Short hair now, scars on her cheek. Worst of all, Evie made her put on her own makeup earlier and she couldn't do it and now she looked like a clown.

"You look beautiful," Evie had said when Taryn had tried to take it right off. "It will get easier. Believe it or not, this is good practice and will help you regain your fine-motor skills."

She didn't want to do that. She just wanted everyone to leave her alone.

"What do you say, Taryn?" she asked. "Are you in the mood for a visitor? It's really up to you."

It was better than therapy. Evie could talk for her. "Wash…this…off first," she mumbled, with a gesture to her face with the hand that still worked okay.

Evie rolled her eyes. "You look perfectly fine, but whatever." To Mrs. O., she said, "Give us five minutes, will you, so we can primp a bit."

Mrs. O. smiled. "Of course. I can chat with her out in the foyer for a few minutes."

Evie helped her stand to transfer to the chair and then wiped off the ugly makeup. "Want me to put more makeup on?"

"Eye…shadow," she muttered in her stupid mushy voice.

Who was here? she wondered. Probably Brittni or Lyndsey. School was starting soon. Maybe they had new cheerleader uniforms to show.

Evie put on Taryn's makeup and it looked okay. Better than what she'd done before.

"Are you ready?" Evie asked.

"Yeah."

Evie opened the door to let Mrs. O. know she could let the visitor in. Not Brittni or Lyndsey, she saw, surprised. Hannah Kirk. Her old best friend. She looked big and kind of sweaty.

"Hannah. Hi!" Evie smiled, happy to see Hannah.

"Hi, Ms. Blanchard. I didn't know you would be here."

"I'm helping Taryn for a few days while she settles in at home."

"That's nice of you."

"I'm glad to do it," Evie said. "It's been fun."

Lie, Taryn thought. She wasn't glad and it wasn't fun. Evie didn't want to be there at all, Taryn could tell.

"I'm sorry I haven't been at String Fever to help you with your mother's earrings," Evie said. "I'm afraid I've been a little distracted the last few days."

"No problem. I haven't had time anyway. I've been working pretty long hours at the Snow Chalet. That reminds me," she said suddenly, pulling her hand out from behind her back. "I brought Taryn a blue raspberry. That's the kind her dad ordered for her the other day. I thought she might like another one. It's so hot!"

"That's really thoughtful of you," Evie said, smiling.

Taryn stared at it, wishing she could think of something to say.

"It melted a little while I was riding my bike up the hill but I put it in an insulated coffee go-cup I brought from home. It should be okay."

"Aren't you clever? Taryn, look what Hannah brought you? Isn't that nice?"

She looked at Hannah. At the cup. At her hands. She couldn't hold it, drink it, without help. Like a baby.

"That is the perfect thing on a hot August afternoon. Here, honey, would you like some?"

She frowned. "No."

Evie blinked. "No?"

"I don't want it."

Hannah turned pink, like watermelon ice. Taryn felt bad but her words were slippery. She looked at Evie, pleading.

"Later."

"You're probably full from lunch, right? We can put it in the freezer and then see if you're more in the mood in an hour or so."

"Good. Yeah."

"I'm just going to put this in one of the cups from the

kitchen and rinse yours out so you can take it home. Will that work?" Evie asked Hannah.

"That would be good. My mom takes that one to work at the grocery store. She might be mad if she can't find it."

"Why don't you two have a visit for a minute and I'll run to the kitchen to take care of this?" Evie said.

Taryn wanted to yell at her, tell her to stay so someone would talk to Hannah but Evie left too soon.

Hannah looked down at her legs. They were chubby but tan. At least *her* brain could make them work. Finally she looked up. "Your dad said it was okay if I came to visit you, but you don't really want much company, do you?"

No. Go away. She shrugged.

"I know we haven't really been friends since about sixth grade. I understand. You're smart and pretty and popular and all that stuff. I'm, well, not. But even though we haven't been best friends in a long time, I'm superglad you didn't die in the accident. Everyone is."

She wasn't. She should have died.

Taryn frowned. Lots of words crowded her throat but she couldn't say them. Hannah was still pink. She looked at the door but Evie didn't come in.

"This is a really nice room," she said after a minute. "I love the view. You can see all of Hope's Crossing from here."

Taryn didn't pay it much attention most of the time, except at night when she saw the lights.

"I've never been up here to your house before. It's a lot bigger than the house you lived in by us on Glacier Lily Drive, isn't it? It's nice."

Taryn remembered her old house. Her little bedroom, the swing set in the backyard, Hannah just across the street. They'd played Barbies and listened to music all summer long.

Fun. Hannah was always fun.

"Do you remember how you used to stay over at our house and we would dress up in my mom's clothes and make up dance routines to old songs? And we were going to have our own band, remember? You were going to be the lead singer and I was going to play the drums. We called ourselves the Danger Girls and we even painted a sign to put on the bass drum of the set I planned to learn how to play. I found it the other day in the back of my closet. I should bring it over sometime for you to see. It was *really* terrible."

Taryn laughed out loud, even though her heart hurt a little. She missed that time when she could dance and sing and be silly. She missed it so much.

Hannah laughed with her but then her smile died. "I guess you probably heard my dad moved out earlier in the summer. He's living in Steamboat Springs now."

"Sorry." She wanted to say more but the words weren't there.

"I know. It sucks." Hannah's chubby chin quivered a bit and Taryn wished she could help. "I'm doing okay but it's been hard on my brothers. My little brother, Jake—remember what a cute baby he was and how we used to push him up and down the street in his stroller so my mom could have a rest—he's six now and he cries a lot more than he used to. It really gets on everyone's nerves. Caleb is even more of a pill than ever. He's nine. Daniel thinks he's too cool to be upset but he's grouchy all the time."

Even though she was talking about sad stuff, Taryn thought it was nice to have Hannah here.

"My mom. She cries a lot. She had to get a job and it's been pretty hard. I have to watch my brothers a lot more and cook dinner and stuff. That's why I've been working so much at the Snow Chalet, so I can help out a little."

She was quiet for a long time and Taryn wanted to say something. "It will improve, right? Remember how we used to dance to that old Howard Jones song, 'Things Can Only Get Better'? I heard that on the radio the other day and it made me think of all the fun we used to have together. I felt good, you know?"

Tears burned Taryn's throat, remembering. Hannah had been her best friend once. What had happened?

"Working at the shave-ice stand isn't that bad. It's only for another week, until school starts. Just about everybody in town stops in sometimes. Lots of tourists come there, too." She smiled, pretty. "Cute boys, too. Yesterday a couple of guys came in from California. I didn't have any other customers so they stayed and talked to me for a while, asked me about hiking trails and stuff like that."

Hannah laughed a little. "If you'd been there, you would have known how to flirt with them. You've always been so much better at that than I could ever be. I just gave them their tiger's blood shave ices and took their money and mumbled something stupid about how they should take the Woodrose Mountain trail for the best view of town."

"It's...nice." Taryn meant the trail but all of this, too. Having Hannah here, that she remembered to bring her a shave ice, that she brought back memories of fun and being a kid.

"I'm really sorry about what you've been through, Taryn. You didn't deserve to have such a terrible thing happen to you."

She did. She deserved all of it. Her fault. Layla was dead and it was her fault.

"And I'm sorry I'm babbling on. I mean, why would you ever be interested in my boring life?"

"I am." She was. She *was*. Struggling, straining, she lifted her hand to touch Hannah's hand. "Sorry." For everything. Especially for dropping a friend because she wasn't as popular and probably would never be. It hadn't been nice. Or right.

Hannah laughed. It was a good, big laugh. She'd forgotten. "You're sorry my life is so boring? I don't blame you for that. No one is more sorry about it than I am, believe me."

The door opened and Evie came back, pretty and smiling.

"It took me longer than I'd expected. I got talking with Mrs. Olafson and lost track of time. Are you having a nice visit?"

Hannah stood. "You know, we really are. But I'd better go. My mom is working late and I have to go fix pizza for my brothers." She paused. "Would it be okay if I came back, Ms. Blanchard?"

Evie looked at Taryn, the question in Evie's eyes.

Taryn formed the word carefully, so there could be no mistake. "Yeess."

Hannah had been her best friend. Maybe they could be friends again.

"I just had a great idea," Evie exclaimed. "Are you working tomorrow?"

"My shift doesn't start until two."

"Are you free in the morning?"

"I think so. Friday is my mom's day off."

"Great! I still want to help you make the earrings for your mom's birthday. I've got a few other things I need to do at the store and I've been trying to juggle everything. Why don't I take Taryn down to String Fever tomorrow and we can all work on them together?"

"That would be terrific!" Hannah was happy.

Taryn wasn't. She was scared. She was too different and too many people she knew came to the bead store.

Evie saw her frown. "Are you okay with that? We can go early enough in the day that the only people there will probably be your grandmother and Claire. Won't it be good to spend some time somewhere besides a hospital room and your house?"

Not really. Not when people might stare. But Hannah looked happy and Taryn didn't want to ruin it. She shrugged.

"We'll see you at nine-thirty then. Does that work for your schedule?"

"I think so. I'll call you if it doesn't. Thank you. Thank you so much, Ms. Blanchard. I'll see you both then."

Taryn watched her go, mad at herself that she hadn't said no. She didn't really deserve friends. She didn't deserve to be happy, to get better. She should tell Hannah to stay away. She would only hurt her again, like she hurt everybody.

Slow progress was still forward momentum. Evie refused to believe it was anything else. She had listened outside the door as Hannah had spoken so kindly and warmly to Taryn. Through the crack in the doorway, she had seen the excitement in Taryn's features at having her friend there to talk to her. Though she hadn't spoken much, Taryn had seemed brighter and far more interactive than usual. Evie was certain she had genuinely enjoyed having her friend over for a visit, just like any other teenage girl.

The whole one-step-forward, two-steps-back thing had her ready to tear out her hair, though. If Evie had expected Taryn to be cooperative after Hannah left, she would have been doomed to disappointment. For the rest of the afternoon, Taryn fought her at every turn. She was sullen and distracted and didn't seem to want to do anything, no matter what Evie tried.

For the first time, she even refused to cooperate with the speech therapist Brodie had hired, a very nice middle-aged woman who, like the O.T., drove from Denver three times a week to work with Taryn.

All in all, what had started as so promising with Hannah's visit deteriorated into a long, frustrating afternoon. By the time the home-care nurse arrived for the evening to help Taryn shower and administer her evening medications, Evie wasn't sure whether she or Taryn was more exhausted. Every joint and muscle ached. She'd forgotten the sheer physical toll this kind of work could take on the therapist, twisting and stretching and lifting.

"I'm coming back tomorrow," she told Taryn. "You can keep trying, but you're not getting rid of me this easily. What will it take for us to have a better day?"

"Maybe...I should...put makeup on you."

She stared at Taryn. "You made a joke! Wow! And it was a great one."

Taryn's smile was tired but mischievous. "No joke. I want to."

The laugh bubbling up inside Evie was probably just a by-product of her emotional and physical fatigue but she didn't care. It still felt great, especially when Taryn laughed along with her.

Warmth seeped through her like water trickling under the gate of an irrigation canal. Yes, Taryn might be sullen and uncooperative. Who wouldn't be, given the lousy hand of cards she'd been dealt? She was a teenage girl whose world had been completely rocked. Despite it, she had these flashes of humor and grace that made her very, very tough to resist—even for someone determined not to care about her.

"All right. It's a deal. Tomorrow before we go to the bead store, you can put makeup on me when I get here."

"Even...lipstick?"

The way Taryn still struggled with fine-motor command, Evie shuddered to imagine what she might end up looking like but she vowed not to complain. A surreptitious tissue would take care of the worst of it, if matters came to that. "If you swear to work harder tomorrow, I'll even let you put lipstick on me."

"That should be interesting."

The unexpected male voice in the room jerked her attention away from Taryn. She whirled and found Brodie leaning against the doorway, a warm, amused light in his eyes.

"Dad! Hi."

For some ridiculous reason, Evie's face heated. How did he keep *doing* that? The man had a very frustrating habit of turning up when she was most ill-prepared. To be fair, it *was* his house, but she'd still like to ask him to knock so she could have a little warning. Even a few seconds might give her time to brace herself against the ridiculous reaction she couldn't seem to control.

"Hey."

"Must have been a rough day if we're bribing with extreme makeovers."

"Nothing we can't improve on tomorrow, right, Taryn?"

"I guess," Taryn said.

"Hannah Kirk came by and we had a really nice visit earlier this afternoon," Evie informed him. "And we've spent the rest of the day working on stretches and a few exercises to work tone and strength."

"How has it been going?"

Like wrestling a very uncooperative alligator in a vat full of vegetable oil. "Great," she lied through her teeth. "Taryn is working very hard."

Taryn ducked her head, refusing to look at either of them. Brodie didn't answer for a moment and when Evie met his gaze, she saw just a hint of sympathetic apology there. "As long as you're trying your best, kiddo. That's the important thing. Are you guys done for the day?"

"Yes. I'm actually on my way out," Evie said.

She suddenly was in desperate need of a little time and distance, space to remind herself of the hundreds of reasons she couldn't afford to fall for Taryn—or Brodie, for that matter.

"I'll walk you out."

She eyed his fingers on the door—strong and blunt-tipped and drumming slightly on the wood, as was his habit, she'd noticed.

If she were clever and smart, she would come up with some way to tell him she didn't need pretty manners from him. She could find her own way out the door. *Excuse me, but you make me nervous. I'd rather you stayed far, far away* didn't seem like a very mature, intelligent response. Instead, she forced a smile. "Right. I just need to grab my bag."

She found it and said goodbye to the home-care nurse and then again to Taryn, promising to bring her makeup kit with her in the morning.

Nerves skittered through her as they walked outside and she was aware of him with almost painful intensity. Like a toothache, she told herself.

As they walked outside, she inhaled deeply of the evening air, cool and sweet with the scent of pine and sage. Though still an hour or so from full dark, an owl hooted from the forest that surrounded Aspen Ridge. Summer evenings in Hope's Crossing were nothing short of spectacular—late-summer evenings perhaps even more so since there was an edge of desperation.

Mother Nature seemed to be urging everyone to enjoy

what they had now because in a few short weeks she would start hurling wind and snow and cold at them all.

When they approached Evie's little SUV, Brodie reached to open the door for her. "I've got another interview tomorrow," he said. "Want to sit in? I'm sorry this morning's was another dud. If you hadn't been there and at the others, I could have made some hiring disasters."

She thought of the arrangements she had made with Hannah earlier. "Um, what time?"

"Early. Eight-thirty. How does that affect your make-over plans?"

They might just barely make it. "We can adjust. Afterward, if it's all right with you, I'd like to take Taryn on a little field trip into town."

The blue of his eyes looked murky in the gathering twilight. "You really think that's a good idea?"

"Why, don't you think it is?"

"I don't know. She still seems vulnerable right now, emotionally *and* physically. Everyone in town is so invested in her recovery. I'm not sure she's ready to be shoved on display like that when she still has a long road ahead of her."

The fire of her temper began to simmer and she worked hard to tamp it down. "She wouldn't be on display. I only wanted to get her out of the house."

"And I think that's a great idea. Don't get me wrong. I just know how people can be in Hope's Crossing. The minute she walks into town, everybody is going to be staring and whispering. *There goes the girl who was in the coma for six weeks. Look at her now. She used to be so pretty.*"

"She's still pretty," Evie said stiffly.

He seemed a little taken aback by her tone. "I couldn't agree more. My daughter is beautiful. More beautiful than ever to me, because I see just how courageous she's been in the face of some pretty terrible stuff. But not everyone is going to see her situation the same way you or I do. People can be idiots. I just don't want someone to say something hurtful to her."

She ratcheted back her anger. Brodie was only a father trying to do the best he could for his child under the circumstances. She needed to give him more credit—at the same time, she felt obliged to point out the hard truth.

"You can't protect her from the inevitable, Brodie," she murmured. "Eventually somebody's going to say something stupid or thoughtless or both."

"I know. Can you blame me for trying to protect her as best I can?"

"How could I blame you for that? Listen, my plan is to take her to String Fever for no longer than an hour. Most of that will be before the store even opens. The only people we'll probably see will be Claire Bradford and perhaps your mother. She'll be fine, Brodie. I promise. I'll watch out for her."

He couldn't doubt her sincerity.

Evie's blue eyes glowed with passion and resolve. She even reached out to touch his hand in that intriguing way she had of using touch to emphasize a point. Heat from her fingers radiated on the back of his hand and for an instant, he completely lost his slippery grip on the thread of their conversation.

"If we see anyone else, it will only be perhaps a few bead store customers. I don't know how much you interacted with your mother's customers when she owned String Fever, but I can promise you most of the women who come into the store are bubbling over with kindness and compassion. No one will hurt Taryn."

"You really think she's ready?"

"It's only a quick trip to a bead store, Brodie. I think she'll be just fine. At this stage in her rehab, I promise I would never ask her to ride on a float in the Independence Day parade. But I think a small outing among caring friends will be very helpful."

The breeze coming down from the mountains played with a few wispy blond strands of hair that had slipped free of the twisty thing holding the rest of those luscious curls at bay. He was vaguely appalled by his sudden urge to reach out and slide it between his fingertips just to feel if her hair was as soft as it looked.

"You probably think I'm crazy to worry so much about her."

"I think you're a concerned father watching out for his child. Nothing wrong with that."

"I suppose she might benefit from returning to some of her familiar places. It might give her the motivation to work on her goals. Crap television apparently can only take you so far. Who knew?"

She laughed again and it slid down his spine, low and sultry. He really had to get control of himself. Every time he was around her, he felt this wild attraction seethe between them. At first, he thought it must be completely one-sided and he felt like an idiot for being so drawn to her, but lately he was beginning to wonder.

The last few times he'd come into Taryn's room while Evie was working with her, he was almost certain she had blushed a bit—a hint of color, just a pale pink wash over her healthy tan. She invariably tried to hide it behind bold confidence, but he sensed something in the way she looked at him that wasn't completely immune to that same simmer of awareness.

He had to remember that, mutual attraction or not, she was here only because his mother had forced her through

emotional blackmail to help them with Taryn. She didn't
want to be here and the first chance she had, Evie would be
returning to her job at String Fever. When that happened,
no doubt they would once more find themselves on opposite sides of any issue that came along affecting their town.

"I guess it should be fine tomorrow," he finally said,
firmly reminding himself his responsibility right now was
to Taryn, not to his long-neglected love life. "You'll have
to take her in the wheelchair van. I can give you a quick
lesson on the ramp and tie-downs in the morning, after
the interview."

"No need. I'm sure I'll figure it out. Most of them work
the same and... I used to have one myself."

She said the words in such a rush, he thought at first
he'd misunderstood. "You had a wheelchair van?"

Those delicate strands of hair danced across her face
and in the fading light she suddenly looked vulnerable
and remote as she looked out at the valley below them. "A
few years ago I adopted a young girl with special needs,"
she finally said.

Shock held him silent for just a few beats. He couldn't
imagine anybody stepping up to volunteer for the misery
of uncertainty and struggle his family had lived through
the last few months. "Seriously?"

Evie sighed. "It's kind of a long story. She was a client
of mine at my physical therapy practice. Her mother and
I became friends over the years. When Meredith, Cassie's
mother, found out she was dying of cancer, she didn't have
anyone else to turn to. Her family was all gone and Cassie's
father had never been in the picture. She asked if I would
consider guardianship. I had worked with Cassie for several years by that point and I loved her. I couldn't bear the
idea of foster care for her so I agreed."

Somehow he didn't imagine the story was as simple as

she made it sound in that no-nonsense tone. What sort of sacrifices had she been forced to make to provide a home for someone else's child?

"Cassie's disabilities required her to use a wheelchair, like Taryn, so we also had a ramp-equipped minivan. I'm sure I'll remember how to work the ramp and the tie-downs on yours. If not, I'll figure it out."

Of all the life journeys he might have expected Evie Blanchard to have traveled, this one wouldn't even have made the list. With those hippie clothes she favored and her bleeding-heart politics, he could easily picture her volunteering at some orphanage in Latin America or driving food-aid vehicles into distant African villages or joining the Peace Corps to teach school in New Guinea.

So why did adopting a child with disabilities seem such a startling concept?

"What happened to her?" He had to ask the obvious question, even though part of him was quite certain he didn't want to know the answer.

She gazed down at the lights of town, beginning to flicker on with the sunset. "She died two years ago. Before I came to Hope's Crossing, obviously."

He had known, without her even saying the words. He'd seen the truth in the shadows in her eyes.

"I'm sorry." The words seemed pitifully inadequate, especially from his own recent perspective of coming so close to losing Taryn. Right after the accident, doctors had tried to prepare him that the outcome was likely grim because of the extent of her injuries. During those long weeks of her coma, he had lived through a wide gamut of emotions. Fear and guilt, sorrow and sheer pain.

In the end, they'd been given a miracle. Taryn had come out of the coma on her own and she was, step by arduous step, rebuilding herself.

"I'm very sorry," he repeated.

"I had two years of her love. I have to consider that a blessed gift."

He gazed at her—delicate and lovely, yet with this core of strength he was still discovering. "This is the real reason you left physical therapy. Why you didn't want to help with Taryn's care."

She didn't answer, only shrugged.

"Good to know it wasn't simply because you dislike me so intensely, then."

He was grateful for his attempt at levity when amusement flickered briefly on her features. "Well, that was certainly a factor."

Her small smile faded quickly. "Actually, Brodie, my reluctance to help Taryn didn't really have anything to do with either of you. After Cassie died, I just…lost my heart. I couldn't do the job anymore. Everything was too painful. I would be working with a patient and suddenly burst into tears for no reason. I would have to reschedule an entire day's calendar of patients because I was huddled in my office, trying to muster the energy and strength to face the treatment room. I couldn't help them. If I couldn't save my own child, how could I help anyone else's? And why should I bother to try?"

His heart seemed to squeeze in his chest. How had she come through that kind of pain?

"Since I couldn't give my patients what they needed anymore, I knew I had to get out. What to do with the rest of my life, though? That was the dilemma. Your mother came along at just the right time, convincing me to come to Hope's Crossing for a visit."

"And you stayed."

The gleaming lights of town below reflected in the intensely blue depths of her eyes. "I stayed. I can't explain it but Hope's Crossing soothed all those angry, wailing voices inside me. I found peace here working at the bead store, hiking in the mountains, creating my own bead pieces."

"That's what my mother meant when she said she knew the steep price of what we were asking of you."

"I could have said no."

"But you didn't." He was struck again by how lovely she was, that silky mass of blond hair slipping free of its pins, the delicate planes and curves of her features. "We dragged you out of that serenity you fought so hard to find and shoved you back into doing all this again. I wish I'd known."

"Would knowing have prevented you from pushing me so hard to take on Taryn's case?"

She looked genuinely curious, not accusatory and he wasn't sure how to answer. He wanted to think he would have been compassionate to her pain over losing a child. But his daughter had survived, against all improbable odds, and he was fiercely determined to provide her the best chance at a normal life.

"I don't know," he finally answered. "But I *am* sorry if we've added to your pain."

She seemed surprised that he could apologize and he wondered just how big an ass she thought him.

"I've reconciled to it. I'm doing my best to be Switzerland. Staying detached and uninvolved."

"Is it working?"

"No," she murmured, her voice rueful. Over her shoulder, he could see Woodrose Mountain, sure and solid in the murky light.

"I can't say Taryn is an easy patient but despite her stubbornness, she's tough," Evie went on. "And there are definitely glimmers of who she really is. You have to watch for them but they peek out every once in a while. All in all, she's pretty irresistible. But I guess you know that, too."

Brodie was more than a little shocked to realize Taryn wasn't the only irresistible female in his life. Invisible threads seemed to tug him toward Evie. The harder he tried to break free of them, the tighter they pulled. Every time he was with her, they tightened another notch.

"Thank you for not telling us to go straight to hell." His voice sounded low, slightly husky, and he really hoped she didn't notice.

"Let's just leave that option on the table, shall we?"

He had to laugh, even though her smile tempered the words. She blinked a little at the sound and her gaze danced to his mouth. Just like that, those silken threads coiled and strained.

He wanted to kiss her. The urge was a physical ache inside him. He wanted to pull her against him, to cover that soft mouth with his, to touch and taste and explore.

Not smart. What was it about cool and lovely summer nights that seemed made for just that sort of thing? Best not to dwell on it. He would be far more wise to simply send her on her way.

"Good night, Evie. Thank you for everything today." He held the vehicle door open for her.

"You're welcome. I'll see you in the morning."

She moved past him. Just before she slid into the SUV, she paused for a long moment, her eyes huge in the darkness. She seemed to want to say something else but instead, much to his astonishment, she leaned up and gently pressed her mouth against the corner of his. "Good night, Brodie," she murmured.

Shock held him still for just an instant, but he managed to catch her before she could slide into her vehicle. He had just an instant to think that this moment was pivotal, like that moment on a jump when, against all reason and sense, his skis left the snow and he was supported only by physics and aerodynamics. He had loved that moment, the clutch in his gut. He had craved it like a junkie jonesing for his next fix.

But nothing in his life experience—not winning his first ski-jump competition or opening his first restaurant—compared to this perfect moment, when he lowered his head, drew in a ragged breath and kissed Evaline Blanchard.

Six

Her mouth was silky soft and she tasted cool and sweet, like the evening. At the first connection of their mouths, she froze, her muscles taut against him. No doubt she was probably as shocked as he was by this crazy impulse.

His mind scrambled to come up with some casual off-hand remark about summer nights and beautiful women and irresistible temptations. He was trying to work up the resolve to pull away when he felt the tentative touch of her arms at his waist, felt her muscles relax as she leaned closer and eased into the kiss like a child testing the stream with a toe before diving in.

This soft, wary surrender aroused him more than if she had suddenly stripped off her clothes and thrown him back onto the seat of her vehicle. Everything inside him was urging him to deepen the kiss, to press his body to hers and seize everything he suddenly wanted with fierce heat, but he forced himself to keep the kiss slow and easy. Gentle as the breeze.

This felt too perfect, standing out here on a summer evening with her mouth tasting his while the cool air eddied around them and that owl hooted softly in the trees.

She smelled of flowers dusted with a hint of spice and

he wanted to bury his face in that delectable curve where her neck met her shoulder and just inhale.

This was Evie. Frustrating, bossy, argumentative Evie. How could he feel this fragile tenderness—mingled with sheer mind-stealing lust—toward a woman he wasn't even sure he liked?

The sound of tires humming on asphalt finally pierced the fog around his brain. Move. Now. The message slowly seeped through and he just barely managed to ease away from Evie before his mother's silver BMW SUV pulled into the driveway.

Evie seemed to be struggling to catch her breath—an endeavor to which he could completely relate. He couldn't seem to suck enough oxygen into his brain, and could only stand and stare at her, his thoughts a muddle of shock and a sort of numbed dismay—and above all the urge to grab her close and taste her all over again.

Katherine parked beside Evie's vehicle and he could see Evie weighing whether to drive away or wait to speak with his mother. She ended up staying, though he had the feeling that particular state of affairs was mainly an effort for her to catch her breath after that stunning kiss.

"I'm sorry I'm so late," his mother said with a cheery smile. "Wouldn't you know, my hair color went long—I'm afraid Chet isn't happy with me for ignoring my roots. And then I stopped off at the store for a few things. At least I had the chance to see you for a moment before you leave for the evening."

She pressed her cheek to Evie's and then stepped back. He knew precisely when his mother picked up on the currents zinging between him and Evie—a little pucker suddenly appeared between Katherine's eyes and she cast a quick, sharp look in his direction.

"Sorry. Am I interrupting something?"

He glanced at Evie, whose features had turned a quite delectable pink.

"Not at all," she said quickly. "I was just leaving for the day. We were, um, talking about my treatment notes for the day."

He was quite certain his mother wouldn't fall for that, especially when Evie refused to even look at him—a conviction that was reinforced when Katherine sent him a swift, censorious look.

"Is that right?" she asked blandly.

"Yes," Evie said. Her voice sounded a little thready and she cleared it before continuing. "I also needed to check with Brodie about taking Taryn into town to the bead store tomorrow. I told Hannah Kirk I would finally help make those earrings I've been promising for her mother's birthday. I thought the outing might be good for Taryn."

"Oh, Taryn will probably adore that. She always loved coming to visit me at the bead store."

"I hope it will remind her of some of the things she once enjoyed."

"Great idea." His mother beamed, though there was still suspicion in her eyes. "Whatever you need my help with, make sure you let me know."

"I will." Evie looked desperate to leave suddenly, her gaze darting between Katherine and the road and her vehicle.

While he didn't necessarily want her to leave—after that kiss, he would be more than happy to drag her into the bushes right now—he also didn't want his mother asking her probing, uncomfortable questions.

"I'll see you tomorrow for the interview then," he said.

He really wished he could read her expression but it was difficult in the dusky light, especially when she wouldn't look at him. "Right. I'll be here. Eight-thirty sharp."

"Oh, and don't forget your lederhosen."

"My…oh."

She shook her head at his reference to Switzerland and her intentions to remain neutral. "I think it's way too late for that, don't you?" she muttered, then climbed into her car and turned the key.

A moment later, she backed out and then headed down the winding road. He watched her for a moment, then turned reluctantly back to his mother—only to find Katherine wasn't watching after Evie. She was gazing at *him,* her mouth a stern line.

"Don't even go there," Katherine spoke firmly.

The phrase might have sounded more appropriate coming from Taryn and her friends than his sixty-year-old mother.

"Go where?"

"Evie is my dear friend. I love her like a daughter. I won't let you hurt her."

He frowned, more than a little annoyed at the assumption. Yeah, he might have been a little wild when he'd been on the ski-jump circuit and had gone through a healthy line of women. He'd been young, athletic, moderately good at what he did. Ski bunnies had been an inevitable part of the life.

Compared to the other guys on the team, he'd been a freaking monk but, okay, he still had liked to party. Those days were long gone. A wife and a kid on the way tended to settle a guy down in a hurry—or at least they did when said wife—and mother of said kid—was a wild party-girl herself who would have rather been out making the rounds of après-ski events than taking care of their child.

Marcy had been irresponsible and selfish and spoiled. When he'd dated her, he had not been interested in her character, only in her wild reputation. It seemed the height of childishness now but he'd dated her at the time mostly as one more way to piss off his father—and then she'd gotten pregnant and his world had changed. One of them had to be the grown-up after Taryn came along and the job title had gone to him by default.

He turned his attention back to his mother. "Why would I hurt Evie?"

"I'm not saying you would be deliberately cruel."

"Aren't you? Do go on. This is fascinating."

She sighed. "Don't be mad, Brodie. You know I love you. It's just that… Evie needs heat and passion. A man who adores her with every breath."

Instead of someone cold and unfeeling, like his bastard of a father. Katherine didn't say the words—she probably didn't even think them—but that's how Brodie interpreted her meaning.

Did she really see him that way? Cold and unfeeling? Okay, maybe the disaster of his marriage had sobered him, literally and figuratively. He hadn't wanted to become a father, but once Marcy declared she was keeping the baby Brodie had channeled his competitive drive from the slopes into making the best living he could for his family.

He'd done a pretty damn good job, too, he thought as he looked at the sprawling house here in the foothills. Nobody could argue that point.

He wasn't looking for heat or passion. Marcy had been one big, messed-up bundle of emotions, and just look how delightfully that had turned out for all parties involved. Of course, she had also been childish and irresponsible and addicted to drama. By the time she'd left for good, when Taryn was three, he'd been mostly relieved.

"You're imagining things." He reached into the car for the shopping bags Katherine had been grabbing. "In case you haven't noticed, I've kind of got my hands full here right now, Mom. I'm not exactly in the market for the complicated mess of a relationship right now. Even if I were, Evie isn't really my type."

He needed to keep reminding himself of that, he thought as he headed into the house. Despite that delicious kiss and that silky tug of desire between them, they were complete opposites.

"What's wrong with her?" Katherine asked from behind him. "She's a wonderful girl, better by far than any of those cool customers you tend to date with such careful discretion. The ones you don't think I know about."

Brodie laughed in disbelief. No wonder he had absolutely no understanding of how the female brain worked. His mother first told him to stay away from her friend and then she acted out-of-sorts when he made it clear he intended to do just that.

"Nothing's wrong with Evie. Absolutely nothing."

Other than her bleeding heart, her zeal for fighting injustice, the way he completely lost his head when he was within ten feet of her. "We just don't have much in common. Not that it matters, because she's only working with Taryn for a few more days and then she and I will go back to politely ignoring each other when we cross paths in town, and sitting on opposite sides of the city council meetings whenever you and your cronies are debating anything remotely controversial."

"Be kind to her, okay?" Katherine said after a pause. "You have no idea what we've asked of her by bringing her here to help us with Taryn."

He shifted, suddenly angry with his mother for reasons he couldn't fully explain. "Yes, I do. She told me tonight about losing her adopted daughter. I'll remind you that I didn't have any idea about it when we asked her. You, on the other hand, knew full well the cost to her and you asked her anyway."

Katherine looked guilty and shocked at the same time. "She told you about Cassie? I can't believe that. Evie is an intensely private person. She never talks about her daughter. I don't think Claire or Alex or Maura even know, as dear friends as they have all become."

He shifted uneasily. So why would she have confided in him? Brodie wasn't sure how he was supposed to feel about that. She didn't tell her long-term friends something so personal and painful but she had spilled it to him. Why?

Suddenly he almost wished she *hadn't* told him. He wanted to turn back the clock about twenty minutes, to that moment when he'd been standing in Taryn's doorway watching Evie tease and cajole and make his daughter laugh.

He didn't want this soft tenderness somewhere in the vicinity of his chest when he thought of the courage it must have taken her, agreeing to help Taryn when it obviously caused her pain.

And he certainly didn't want this urge to tuck her away and keep her safe from any further harm. "The point is, now I know. Since we've had such a devil of a time finding someone else competent enough to take over Taryn's home therapy, I was thinking about trying to persuade Evie to continue on with the great job she's doing. Obviously I can't do that now, so I guess it's back to the candidate search."

In the meantime, he owed her the courtesy of ensuring he did everything he could to make sure she didn't regret helping them. If that meant resisting any inconvenient, overwhelming urges to kiss her again, he would just have to make that sacrifice. No matter the cost.

* * *

"You're going to have to give me a break here, kiddo, and slow down."

Jacques didn't listen to her, only continued bounding up the Woodrose Mountain trail with his tail wagging like crazy and his long retriever nose sniffing the trail for possible enemy combatants. He would have made an excellent trainer on *The Biggest Loser,* since he seemed to have no pity whatsoever and no patience with normal things like sore muscles and general exhaustion.

She would have loved to skip the run this morning, for once. Turning off the snooze on her alarm clock just before the sunrise had been harder than walking out of a bead store without buying anything. But Jacques needed exercise. So did she, come to think of it—not only for the obvious physical benefits, but for the energy and stamina it gave her to face another day with Taryn.

Though she hadn't wanted to get out of bed, she had been surprised by the little burst of anticipation tingling through her for the day. She couldn't wait for the outing to String Fever with Taryn. Time spent in the bead store was never wasted, even if Taryn proved as reluctant to cooperate there as she did at home.

For all her frustration at not finding the right combination of things to motivate Taryn, Evie wasn't completely hating her work with the girl. This seemed different somehow from the professional paralysis she'd slipped into right after Cassie's death. She found a definite challenge in trying to come up with creative ways to help Taryn and in the knowledge that she just might be making a difference.

Friends back in L.A. used to ask why she'd chosen to specialize in pediatric rehab physical therapy instead of the sometimes more lucrative fields of geriatrics or sports physical therapy—and why she had chosen to work with those who had the most severe disabilities or acute injuries requiring extensive care.

Her answer had always sounded trite but it was the truth. Knowing she was helping children in real, quantifiable ways had been a powerful motivator. She still loved knowing there were former patients of hers in California who could do things now they hadn't done before, in part because of her help. She wasn't arrogant enough to think no one else could have helped them, but *she* had been the one to do it.

Maybe she *had* let herself get a little too close to her clients. Cassie hadn't been the only one, though her situation had been most obvious. Evie had genuinely cared about all of them. She had rejoiced in their successes, she had visited them when they were hospitalized, had comforted confused and frightened parents dealing with a new diagnosis—and had wept after a session more than a few times when she'd known she had to cause pain in a child suffering already in order to help him or her heal correctly.

Never had she pushed that personal/professional boundary as far as with Cassie. She and Cassie's mother had become friends over the years, mostly because of their shared passion for beading.

Meredith was a schoolteacher, but she supplemented her earnings by making jewelry and selling it at a few boutiques around town, all so she could buy a few necessary extras for her child that insurance wouldn't cover.

Evie had admired Meredith Rentera's strength of will, her determination to provide the best for her special-needs child, no matter the cost.

Much like Brodie, Evie thought now as she followed Jacques farther up the trail, where tendrils of morning mist curled and twisted through the aspens and pines. Meredith would have done anything for Cassie. But she couldn't hold back her own deadly disease.

When Meredith was first diagnosed with breast cancer, Evie had done her best to help where she could, especially by providing respite service for Cassie when Meredith was too sick from the chemotherapy to meet the demands of caring for her child.

After a year, the breast cancer had begun to spread through her lymphatic system to her other organs. Evie's friend had been terrified, her first and only thought, who would take care of Cassie. Like Evie, she hadn't had any family left she could count on—in Meredith's case, no one except a drug addict of a brother. She hadn't been able to bear the idea of this fragile, needy child going into foster care after her death.

One night a few months later, Evie had invited Meredith and Cassie to dinner. She could picture it clearly even now as she walked behind Jacques. They had enjoyed chicken salad and fresh rolls out on the deck of her house while the canyon winds rustled the trailing branches of the pepper trees around her property.

"I can't escape the truth any longer," Meredith had said, her face gaunt and pale beneath her kerchief, while Cassie stroked Evie's plump cat on the other side of the deck, out of earshot. "None of this is working. I'm dying."

At first, Evie had tried to protest, to assure her friend they would find other options, but Mere had remained firm. "I appreciate your optimism. It's one of the things I admire most about you, Evie. But I have to be realistic. I'm going to die. Maybe in a few months, maybe a little longer, but it's foolish to continue to ignore reality. I have to make arrangements for Cassie before I'm no longer capable."

Her heart leaden and achy, Evie had held her friend's

hands, marveling at her strength to speak in this dispassionate tone.

"What can I do to help?" she had asked.

"Funny you should ask." Meredith had given her a lopsided smile. "I want you to know, I have other options. Let's just get that out of the way up front. I know exactly what I'm asking you and I don't want you to feel obligated in any way."

"Mere—" She remembered being terrified suddenly, wishing she could stop the words.

"I'd like you to consider adopting Cassie after I'm gone."

And just like that, in a single instant while the canyon winds blew and the sun set over the ocean and a couple of robins twittered in the trees, her world had changed.

Meredith had insisted she think about it; she wouldn't even consider hearing Evie's answer until another week had passed. In that week, Evie had fretted and stewed and waffled. She knew exactly what the demands on her life would be. Hadn't she spent years as a physical therapist watching other parents?

But she had also known in her heart it was absolutely the right thing.

She would never regret taking guardianship of Cassie, she thought now as she watched Jacques nose the roots of a columbine. She had loved the girl dearly—her laughter, her joy at life, the love she freely gave. Even if Evie had known how things would end, she would never have surrendered those two years she had with her.

She stopped to take a rest and pressed her fingers to the pain in her chest that—despite the altitude and the exertion—had nothing to do with her workout.

She could see Hope's Crossing below, soft and lovely

in the early-morning light. It looked to be another beautiful August day, perfect for taking Taryn to the bead store.

"Come on, Jacques," she called after a moment and started back down the trail. She would barely have time to shower and change before she was supposed to meet Brodie for the job interview. Time to pick up her speed. She sighed and carefully jogged downhill. A few wildflowers still bloomed, Indian paintbrush and purple beeweed and the ever-present columbines, though she knew the approaching cold would wither them soon enough.

She would just have to enjoy them while she could. For some reason, their jewel-bright colors brought back a memory of the cheery houses on the island of Burano, near Venice, that had gleamed just that way in the early-morning light.

After Cassie had died and Evie realized she could no longer function as a therapist, she had closed her practice and decided to travel around the world for a while to lose herself in other cultures.

Venice had been her first stop on this grand world tour. On a random day-trip to Murano, another island in the lagoon, she had stopped to watch the glassblowers in the factories that had been forced to relocate there centuries ago after their glassworks were deemed a fire hazard for careful Venetians.

She had ended up filling a small bag with art-glass beads, perhaps as an impulse, perhaps as some kind of homage to that hobby she and Meredith had shared. She had continued buying beads during all her travels: old costume jewelry from secondhand charity shops across the U.K., shells and small stones from Africa, silver filigree beads from Bali. By the time she'd returned to the States she knew beading was her new passion.

Walking away from her career had been the right

choice, though she still missed it sometimes. Despite her best efforts, though, here she was, full circle, trying hard not to let another girl into her heart.

As she approached an area of the trail cutting across a rocky talus that dropped treacherously, Evie slowed her pace. She was always cautious here. One wrong step, a twisted ankle on one of the zillions of fist-size rocks that spilled down the mountainside, and the unwary hiker could tumble over the side. She was nearly to the end when Jacques gave one of his rare polite barks of greeting and stood looking below the trail.

Hoping it wasn't a skunk—wouldn't that be a lovely start to the day?—she approached warily. She saw a mountain bike on its side next to the trail and she glimpsed a flash of yellow on a rocky outcropping about ten feet below the trail. A boy, she realized. He stood on the wide ledge gazing down at the town below, heedless of the three-hundred-foot drop just inches below him.

This steep, rocky overlook would be an easy place to die. A missed step, a little stumble—accidentally or on purpose—and someone could check out in a heartbeat.

She thought of her mother, overdosing on pills to finally silence her physical and emotional pain, and stepped quickly forward. "Good morning."

The boy must have heard Jacques bark but he still seemed shocked to find a human associated with the dog— and she was equally shocked when she recognized his identity.

"Hey," he muttered.

Charlie Beaumont was dressed in bike shorts and a bright yellow jersey, its cheerful color a vivid contrast to the tight, sullen look he always seemed to wear.

She didn't like this boy. How could she, when his recklessness had killed the child of a dear friend and severely injured the grandchild of another? But something about his posture, the defeated slump of his shoulders, the hint of desperation in his eyes, prevented her from just continuing down the trail.

"It looks like a perfect day for a bike ride."

He gave her a stony look. "Is it?"

"Are you heading up to Crystal Lake?" The glacier-fed lake filled a small alpine valley another two miles up the trail and was a favorite with mountain bikers for the vast network of trails surrounding it.

"Haven't decided." His words were clipped but she had the impression he was not necessarily being surly. There was a sadness about him, almost despair.

"You're Charlie Beaumont, right? I'm Evie Blanchard. I work at String Fever, the bead store in town. I know your mother and your sister."

"Lucky you," he muttered.

She should just keep going. Brodie would be waiting for her to arrive at the interview and she had a very strong suspicion he wouldn't be thrilled if he knew the delay was because of this kid, who had ruined his daughter's life.

On the other hand, she wouldn't be able to live with herself if she ignored her instincts and left him alone up here if he were indeed suicidal.

She shouldn't have any sympathy for the kid after what he had done, recklessly drinking and driving with a pickup truckload of teens, after driving the getaway car for several burglaries in the area. He was a punk with an attitude born from parents who by turns ignored him and indulged him.

But it was also obvious the kid was hurting.

She stepped closer and Jacques decided this was tacit permission for him to do the same, and more. He picked his way around boulders and young saplings toward the boy, planting his haunches on the ledge right next to him.

"That rude creature is my dog, Jacques. Don't worry, he's friendly. To a fault, actually. Jacques, this is Charlie."

The Labradoodle wagged his tail quite violently in his usual bid for attention. After a surprised moment, Charlie gave Jacques a tentative pat or two as if he hadn't been around animals very often. Too bad, she thought. In her experience, kids were generally a little more responsible and a little less self-absorbed if they had another creature depending on them.

"You're out early." She perched on a rock close enough that she hoped he wouldn't feel threatened.

"It's a good time to ride. Not as many idiots on the trail to get in the way."

Either he very much liked his privacy or right now Charlie Beaumont was having a tough time dealing with other people. She was willing to bet it was the latter.

He cut his gaze down the cliffside and her instincts flared again. "Sometimes it must feel easier to be on your own," she said calmly.

"What's that supposed to mean?"

She thought about dissembling but he struck her as a boy who needed a little more than he needed some-one else in his life being careful not to hurt his feelings. "Only that you can't be the most popular guy around town right now."

His expression darkened with anger—but she was al-most certain she saw a shadow of despair in his eyes. "You think I care about the opinions of a bunch of stupid-ass little people in a stupid-ass little town?"

"You tell me."

"Hope's Crossing can go to hell. I don't give a shit about anybody." His color was high and his hands shook a little where he gripped Jacques's curly fur.

She pushed away a deerfly from her arm. "See, funny thing. I think you do."

"Why do you say that?"

"It has to bother you, doesn't it? What people are saying about you?"

He didn't look at her, just gazed down the mountainside again. "Why would it bother me? It's the truth, isn't it? I killed Layla and turned Taryn into a vegetable."

A huge weight for any seventeen-year-old to carry, even if he had earned it. She must be the bleeding heart Brodie seemed to think if she could feel this pang of sympathy for this defiant young man, even knowing his stupid decisions were to blame for the pain and loss that affected an entire town.

"She's not. A vegetable, I mean."

He frowned. "She's in a wheelchair. She can't talk. Brittni Jones, one of her stupid friends from the cheerleading squad, says she can't even feed herself."

"She's working on all those things."

It wasn't exactly a lie, she told herself, even though right now Taryn didn't seem to want to work on much of anything. A tiny niggle of an idea sprouted in Evie's head, completely, fantastically inappropriate. She tried to dismiss it but it didn't seem to want to wither away.

"Before I came to Hope's Crossing, I was a physical therapist. Right now I'm helping to set up a program of rehab exercises that will help Taryn continue to improve at home." If the girl actually could be bothered to *do* them, but Evie decided not to mention that to Charlie.

At least he was looking at her now and not the steep drop-off. "How is she?" He hesitated. "Is she making progress?"

"It's slow, certainly, but yes. She's improving."

That germ of an idea refused to die. It was completely

crazy but some of her best ideas were. "Why don't you come visit her and see for yourself?"

He gaped at her. "I couldn't!"

"Why not? I think Taryn would enjoy the company. She spends all day surrounded by therapists and nurses and home-health aides. I imagine she's desperate for a little conversation that doesn't revolve around exercises or medications."

"Her dad would never let me in the door. He'd string me up by my b—um, arms if I tried it."

He was probably right about that. Brodie would be furious if he knew she was even suggesting it to the kid. Somehow this seemed just the way to take care of two problems at once—give Taryn someone else her own age to interact with besides Hannah and give Charlie something else to focus on besides that steep drop-off and the people below who now treated him like a pariah.

"We're going to String Fever this morning. If you wanted to see Taryn, you could come there. That way her father wouldn't have to be involved."

It was a huge risk but somehow this felt right.

"She wouldn't want to see me."

"Maybe not. But we won't know if you don't try. Stop in for a minute and say hi. That's all. I think it would mean a lot to Taryn to know you cared."

She paused, giving him a careful look. "You owe her that, at least, don't you?"

Charlie closed his eyes for an instant and inhaled sharply as if she'd just chucked a rock at his gut. His fingers dug into Jacques's fur and he let out his breath slowly.

"I don't know."

"We'll be there for about an hour this morning, around nine-thirty." She whistled to Jacques. "Come on, boy."

The dog seemed reluctant to leave the boy but he finally bounded up to her.

For an instant, she experienced a pang of misgiving. If the boy was really suicidal, wasn't she taking a huge chance to leave him here in the mountains by himself? She wouldn't be able to bear it if she found out later he had harmed himself and she might have prevented it by staying a little longer or walking with him down the hill or something.

No. He was still looking down at the town below but she sensed something else in his posture now. Some of that desperate edge seemed to have seeped out of him and now he looked almost pensive.

She couldn't really have explained it, no more than she understood what impulse had led her to invite him to the bead store that morning, but her instincts were telling her any threat of suicide, real or imagined, had passed.

She whistled to Jacques and the two of them headed down the trail, leaving the boy alone.

Seven

"No. No, no, no."

Taryn hadn't quite resorted to splaying her arms out to keep Evie from pushing the wheelchair through the doorway of the van and down the ramp but it was a near thing. She had been chanting *no* ever since the moment Evie had pulled the van into a parking space behind the bead store.

Evie ground her back teeth. "I promised Hannah I would help her with her mom's earrings, Taryn. I gave my word. You said it would be okay."

"I…changed…my mind. Don't want to now."

That was as many words as Taryn had strung together at one time in her presence. While she knew the girl's growing verbal skills ought to please her, she had to fight down frustration. This frustration was all her fault. That's what made it all the more aggravating.

She'd been running late all morning. Those moments she had spent talking to Charlie on Woodrose Mountain had thrown off her entire schedule and she had barely made it to the house for the last few minutes of Brodie's interview with the latest uninspiring candidate.

It was all a ripple effect. Now they were late to the bead

store as well. She only hoped Hannah wasn't already waiting for them inside.

"Why don't you want to come here anymore? You used to love going into String Fever and playing around with bead designs."

"Not the same...now."

Evie knelt beside the wheelchair, her heart aching for Taryn and everything the girl had been forced to give up. What did her own schedule matter? The girl's discomfort was the important issue here.

"No. It's not the same. But some things haven't changed. I think you will still like making things. What girl doesn't like jewelry, am I right?"

Taryn cast her a sidelong look under her lashes and shrugged.

"I promise, it's going to be okay. It's early and the store hasn't even opened yet. Your grandmother is there and Claire Bradford and Hannah. That's all. People who love you and want to help you."

She decided not to mention Charlie and her spontaneous invitation for him to join them that morning. What would be the point? He probably wouldn't come anyway.

"It will be fun, I promise," she said. "And isn't it nice to be somewhere beside your house for a change? I don't know about you, but I was getting sick of Mrs. Olafson's terrible cooking all the time. If I had to eat another dozen of those sugar cookies of hers, I just might have to be sick or something."

Taryn giggled, fully aware that Mrs. O. was a fantastic cook. Evie was going to gain ten pounds before she was done with this temporary job.

"Look at you, out on the town. We'll go into the store, help Hannah make a couple sets of earrings and be back home in an hour. While we're there, you decide what kind of project you want to make. Maybe a simple charm necklace or a bracelet or something. Whatever you want and we'll make it together."

Taryn lifted her hands. Though the function in the right hand was coming along nicely, the left one was still difficult for her to use. "I…can't…bead."

"Sure you can. We'll start slowly. Trust me, if the old ladies with arthritis who come to the Bead Babes class at the senior center can do it, you certainly can. I bet you can bead rings around those old biddies."

"Not rings. Just…a bracelet," Taryn said slowly and Evie laughed and hugged her. Another joke! She loved when Taryn allowed her sense of humor to shine through her challenges. Those little moments gave her hope.

Right now, Taryn's biggest issue besides her attitude was the muscle tone that had been weakened by six weeks in a coma, but the fact that she was alive and here cracking jokes was nothing short of a miracle.

"A bracelet it is. Are you ready, then?"

Taryn sighed, apprehension still twisting her features, but she nodded. Overwhelmed by the girl's courage, Evie bent down to unfasten the tie-downs lashing the wheelchair in place in the van and then rolled her down the ramp toward the back door.

Their path took them through the gate and the small fenced garden, lush and fragrant from the madly blooming lavender and lemon balm. When she'd left String Fever an hour before, she had put Jacques outside in the garden so he could play with his best friend, Claire's old basset hound, Chester. Apparently Claire was already there, because both dogs seemed to be waiting for them. They immediately headed over, Chester's sturdy little body waddling and Jacques loping in his elegant stride.

"Oh!" Taryn drew back a little in her chair.

"Nothing to worry about, sweetheart. You know Chester, Claire's dog, right? He's been around the store forever. This other gorgeous dude is my Labradoodle, Jacques."

To Evie's delight, Jacques padded to Taryn and rested his chin on her leg, gazing up into her eyes with that soulful look he had perfected.

If this had been a cartoon version of life, a spangled flurry of pink, glittery hearts and flowers would have erupted between girl and dog as the two of them quite obviously fell hard for each other. Evie saw instant adoration in her dog's eyes and a similar glint in Taryn's.

Evie held her breath as Taryn lifted her left hand, the one she tended to avoid using, and patted the dog's curly woollike fur.

"So cute," she exclaimed.

"Careful there." Evie smiled, delighted and feeling almost a little weepy, for some ridiculous reason she couldn't explain. "He's very much a manly male and doesn't like to be called cute."

Her reluctance to be at the bead store apparently forgotten in the excitement of new friends, Taryn giggled and petted the dog a little more, moving her arm more than she had through all the exercises combined the occupational therapist had tried on her.

Though she was still aware Hannah might be inside waiting for them, Evie didn't want to ruin the sweetness of the moment—or Taryn's impromptu occupational therapy—so they stayed for a few moments in the little garden while birds chirped in the branches of the butterfly bush and red-osier dogwood against the fence, and the summer air drifted around them, sweet and cool.

Finally she decided they should probably head inside. "If you'd like, Jacques can come inside and help us bead.

He's not so great at working with the pliers but he can be pretty good company."

Taryn giggled again, a genuine sound that sounded lovely and pure in the morning air.

"He'll behave," Evie assured her. "If he doesn't, Chester can keep him in line, right, buddy?"

Claire's dog gave his morose grin and waddled to the door. Evie was relieved to see all of Taryn's unease seemed to have drifted away like seed puffs on the morning breeze. The girl was even smiling as Evie propped open the back door and pushed her through.

"There you are," Katherine exclaimed. "We were beginning to worry you wouldn't come."

"Oh, yay! We've been waiting *forever!*" Claire exclaimed. She was so genuinely sweet it was hard not to like Claire, though in her smaller moments Evie had to admit all that warmth and kindness sometimes exhausted Evie, who would definitely win any snarky contest between the two of them.

"Sorry we're late," she said. "It's been a crazy morning."

"No worries. You're here now. Hi, Taryn." Alex McKnight, Claire's best friend since childhood, smiled at the girl and Evie hoped the addition of one more person to their little party wouldn't throw Taryn for a curve.

The girl maintained a hold on Jacques as if she didn't dare release him. The dog remained motionless, apparently content. Evie blinked a little. Jacques was usually a calm creature but this was unusual serenity, even for him.

"Roll up to the table here, darling," Katherine said to her granddaughter. Evie pushed Taryn forward and was amused when Jacques trotted right along with her.

"Hannah's not here yet?"

Claire shook her head. "It's probably not that easy for

her to get away from home. If she said she would be here, I'm sure she will show up."

Sometimes Evie wondered how Claire could have such unshakable faith in the goodness of everyone around her, especially when she had seen ample evidence to the contrary.

"What are you three working on?" Evie asked.

"Katherine has decided to teach another class on wire wrapping. We're trying to come up with a pattern for her."

"Ooh. Fun. My favorite thing. While you're busy with that and while we wait for Hannah, Taryn and I are going to work on a bracelet. I thought we should use some beads that aren't too heavy but big enough for her to handle easily. I'm also thinking smooth and soft so they feel good when she wears them. Maybe polymer clay? What do you think?"

Claire's expression brightened. "I've got the perfect beads! They just came in yesterday and I haven't even had time to unpack them."

She jumped up from the table and headed toward her office, where deliveries were sometimes stacked until they could be dealt with later.

"While she's looking for that, I'll find some cord," Evie said. "I'm thinking elastic to make it easier for you to put on and take off. Does that work for you?"

"Yes," Taryn said, enunciating carefully. "Thank…you."

Katherine's mouth trembled a little and Evie was afraid she would cry. The older woman gazed at her granddaughter with a mix of love and pride. On her way to the rolls of cording, Evie pressed a hand to Katherine's shoulder as she passed and her friend reached up to squeeze her fingers.

"Thank you," she murmured.

She smiled. "Anybody else need anything while I'm up?"

"How about something tall, dark and gorgeous?" Alex

asked. Immediately, an image of Brodie flashed in Evie's mind and that stunning kiss of the night before that she hadn't been able to get out of her head. Her stomach fluttered and she could feel hot color crawl up her cheeks.

"Can't help you there, unless Claire got a delivery of those too yesterday."

"Why would I?" Claire called from the office. "Riley is all the tall, dark and gorgeous I can handle."

"Ew. Stop. Don't want to hear about it," Alex said, rolling her eyes at Taryn, who giggled.

Evie smiled as she headed toward the rolled cord. Alex might protest that the idea of her best friend and her younger brother together was just too weird for her but Evie didn't doubt for a minute that she was secretly thrilled for both of them.

She quickly selected the right cord weight and was looking over spacers when the chimes on the door gave a slow peal, as if whoever was pushing the door open wasn't quite sure whether to come in.

A moment later, it opened farther and Charlie Beaumont stepped through. He had changed from his biking clothes into khaki shorts and a polo shirt and looked as if he'd rather be anywhere else on earth.

Nerves fluttered in Evie's stomach. Okay, this had been a really stupid idea. What had she been thinking? Right now she wished she could send him right back out the door but she had no idea how to go about doing that.

"Hi," she said calmly. "I wasn't sure you'd come."

"I shouldn't have. This is stupid." He glanced at the front door again, then back at her. Though outwardly he looked defiant, his eyes looked haunted. She knew she had no business feeling that dratted compassion for him again but she couldn't seem to help herself.

"I should go," he muttered.

"Running away is what's stupid. But I don't have to tell you that, do I?"

His mouth tightened—Charlie had been trying to escape a police pursuit when he'd spun out of control on a snow-slicked roadway—but he said nothing. Nor did he whirl around and head back out the door. She supposed that was an encouraging sign.

"Taryn is back in the workroom. Come with me."

She had to give him credit for guts. He released a long breath but followed her toward the back of the store and the worktable.

Oops. Perhaps she should have warned the others he was coming. Evie winced. Too late for that now. If she *had* thought of it, Charlie's sudden appearance in the workroom of String Fever might not have reverberated around the room as if she'd just sprayed everybody down with a fire hose.

Claire was just coming out of her office, holding a package. Her mouth sagged open and she nearly stumbled. Alex knocked over a cup of seed beads she'd been working with, while Katherine just stared.

"Look who's here, everyone." Evie tried for a cheery tone. "I ran into Charlie this morning on the Woodrose Mountain trail above town. He was asking about Taryn and I happened to mention we were coming to the bead store this morning. He wanted to stop by and say hello."

Alex's green eyes sizzled with sudden anger and Katherine's features were set in the same stony, hard look Evie was beginning to recognize in her son.

Okay. This had been a monumentally crazy idea. Sometimes Evie let her compassion and good intentions override common sense. It was a fatal flaw, really, probably stemming from her innate desire to fix everything.

She had always been that way, from the time she was a

little girl always charged with watching over her sister, two years younger. *Keep an eye on Elizabeth, Evaline. You're the oldest. Don't let her go too far out in the water. She's your responsibility.*

In the end, she had failed. She hadn't been around to watch out for Lizzie and hadn't been able to do anything but watch helplessly from beside her sister's hospital bed while Lizzie suffered excruciating pain from her second- and third-degree burns—nor could Evie hold back the infection that had eventually killed her sister.

And Cassie. Despite all the love and care she had given her child, she hadn't been able to save her either.

Maybe someday she would finally learn the lesson to just stop trying.

Now what, though? She had to muddle through this latest mess she had created somehow. She was trying to figure out how to smooth over the tension of the moment when help arrived from an unexpected source.

"Char—lie. Hi." Taryn spoke the words slowly but clearly. To Evie's shock, Taryn raised her hand from Jacques's fur and held it out for the boy. Her smile was wide, genuine.

The teenager looked at Taryn's hand and then back at Evie as if seeking direction. Not knowing what else to do, she gestured him forward. After an awkward pause, Charlie reached out for Taryn's hand.

"Hey, Tare. Um, how are things?"

"Been better," Taryn said.

Charlie tensed and looked ready to flee again until Taryn's mouth lifted in a teasing grin. "You?" she asked.

"Um, okay."

Okay. So far, so good. Nobody was throwing things at him, even if Alex did look ready to poke out his eyes with her split-ring pliers.

"I found the elastic cord," Evie said when the silence dragged on a little too long. "Claire, where are those gorgeous polymer beads you were talking about?"

That seemed to ease the tension a little more. Beading had a way of doing that, she had discovered.

"Here you go," Claire said, rather stiffly. "Just in from that supplier we like in Oregon."

Evie admired the boxful of beads in a variety of shapes, from rounds to ovals to flowers in all different colors. "Wow. You're right. They are beautiful. I think they'll go well with these new spacers."

The beads clacked softly as Claire shifted the box and set it down rather abruptly on the table.

"Which ones do you like, Taryn?"

Evie poured a handful onto the table, Taryn began to sift through them. After a minute, she laboriously separated a colorful pink-daisy bead from the pile and then a green tube-shaped bead with pink polka dots.

"Oh, perfect," Evie said. On impulse, she pulled a chair from the perimeter of the room and set it next to Taryn. "Here, Charlie. Maybe you could help Taryn make a bracelet."

"Wha—at?" He jolted as if she'd instructed him to go outside and stomp on a couple of baby bunnies. "I don't know anything about beads."

"I'll show you what to do. First you need to sort through this box and find more just like those two. Start with about ten each, though we might not need that many. I think a basic A-B-C-B pattern here, don't you, Taryn? Daisy, spacer, green-tube bead, spacer, daisy, spacer and so on. Here, I'll get you started."

She knotted the cord and quickly strung enough beads to show the pattern twice before she handed it over to him. "Your turn. Taryn, your job is to pick up the bead or the spacer you want—with your left hand—and hold it steady so Charlie can thread the cord through. Got it?"

"Yes," Taryn said. She actually looked excited about it, something Evie would never have anticipated.

After an awkward moment, everyone returned to her own project at the table, though Evie didn't miss the frequent narrowed gazes as Charlie and Taryn worked together on her bracelet. The boy didn't say anything for several moments but soon he was telling Taryn about a movie he had seen the weekend before and about a waterfall he had discovered back on one of the mountain-bike trails surrounding Silver Strike Reservoir.

Taryn floundered with the fine-motor skills necessary to pick up just the correct bead but she didn't give up. With her brow furrowed in concentration, she would painstakingly struggle until she was able to clasp the requisite bead between her thumb and forefinger and then she and Charlie would work in tandem to thread it on the cord.

It was actually a little sweet, but Evie was quite certain she was the only one at the table who thought so.

"I left a project upstairs last night, that crimped crystal necklace I've been working on. I'm going to run up to my apartment and grab it, since Hannah's not here yet."

No one answered her, everyone either ignoring her or concentrating on what she was doing. Evie really hoped it was the latter, that she hadn't just destroyed these cherished friendships. She headed for the back door and had just started to close it behind her when Claire pushed it from the other side.

"What are you doing, Evie?" Claire murmured after she closed the door behind her.

"Grabbing my project."

"You know what I mean. With Charlie Beaumont."

Claire gestured through the back window and from here Evie could see the two young dark heads bent together.

She sighed. "He's just a kid himself, Claire. Everyone in town has turned him into the Antichrist."

"Have you forgotten Layla? She's dead because of him. My children *nearly* were!"

Claire was moving around so well these days it was sometimes hard to remember she had also been involved in the accident that night and had spent months in multiple casts from her injuries.

In his rush to escape police pursuit, Charlie had forced Claire's vehicle off the road during a late-spring snowstorm and she had ended up driving into the icy reservoir. If not for Riley's heroic efforts, she and her children might have died from exposure to the bitterly cold water.

"Of course I haven't forgotten Layla or anything else about that terrible night! Charlie Beaumont made some really stupid choices, especially to drink and drive. As a result, people's lives have been altered forever. I understand that."

"So why encourage him? He should be in jail, not out walking around as if nothing has happened."

"He's not untouched by this, Claire."

"Big deal. So he might have to spend some time in juvenile detention."

Apparently Claire didn't always see the good in people. Evie supposed it was refreshing to know her friend was capable of anger against someone who deserved it.

How could she argue with Claire's distress? She had been physically and emotionally injured because of Charlie's actions. Beading was still difficult for her because of her injured wrist but she managed to work through the pain to create beautiful work.

"I'm sorry," Evie said quietly. "I shouldn't have invited

him. I thought it might be good for Taryn. I get the feeling she misses her social life more than she misses all the other things she can't do yet."

Claire looked slightly mollified by that. She looked back inside the store, where Taryn was now smiling at something Charlie had said to her.

"I can see how hard it must be for a fifteen-year-old girl to lose her social network along with everything else."

"It's my fault he's here. Do you want me to ask him to leave?"

Claire seemed to consider. After a moment, she sighed. "If he's really helping Taryn, I suppose it's okay, for now."

"I should have asked permission from you first. I'm sorry for that."

To her vast relief, Claire stepped forward and hugged her. Tears swelled in Evie's throat and the tension she hadn't realized had a tight grip on her shoulders seemed to ease. "You don't have to ask me for permission to invite people to the store. Good grief, am I that much of a tyrant?"

"Yes. Working for you is worse than a highway chain gang. I go home every night wondering how I'll possibly make it through another day."

Claire laughed and hugged her again. "You have a soft heart, Evie. If you're not careful, one of these days it might lead you into trouble."

Like compelling her to take on a job she didn't want so she didn't hurt Katherine? "Thanks for the warning." Somehow she managed to hide her dry tone.

"That's what friends are for, right?" Claire smiled, then gave her a careful look. "Are you doing something different with your makeup these days?"

Evie grimaced. In the chaos of her morning, she had completely forgotten what she must look like. "I let Taryn go all Mary Kay on me. We made a deal and I had to keep my end. It was occupational therapy, right?"

Claire's features softened and she hugged Evie again. "You're going to make me cry now. You're a wonderful person, Evie, and I'm honored to call you my friend."

Evie rolled her eyes. "You know better than that, honey. But thank you."

She hurried up the stairs to her apartment and quickly found the box containing the project she'd been working on the night before, mostly as therapy to help her calm her troubled mind after that kiss with Brodie.

A quick side trip took her into the bathroom with its old-fashioned fixtures for a good look in the round, slightly wavy mirror that she liked to think was original to the old building.

Really, it wasn't as bad as she'd feared, just a few eye shadow smears around the corners of her eyes and a little bright on the blush, something she rarely used anyway. She did her best to fix it as best she could, then grabbed her project box and hurried back down the stairs to the store.

To her vast relief, the mood seemed a little warmer when she returned—maybe just a degree or two above freezing. It was still uncomfortably nippy but at least seemed out of the frostbite zone.

Katherine and Alex were even laughing about a story Claire was telling about how Riley and her son Owen were trying to build a tree house behind her graceful old brick house on Blackberry Lane.

Charlie stayed about ten minutes longer, until he and Taryn had finished stringing enough beads to make a bracelet.

"I can finish it," Evie said, when Charlie looked to her for guidance. She took the bracelet and quickly knotted the ends together.

"Great job, you two. It's wonderful." She snipped the ends and helped Taryn slide her wrist through the loop.

"I'd better go," Charlie said abruptly.

"Thank…you," Taryn said, holding up the arm adorned with the flirty new bracelet.

"You're welcome. It was, uh, fun. See you around."

He hurried out of the store, his face tight and set, before Evie could even say anything. Sludge-thick silence filled the room after his hasty exit.

"Don't start on me yet, before I can even apologize," Evie said to Katherine and Alex, when they turned toward her in tandem. "I invited him completely on impulse. I never really expected him to stop by, I swear."

"Why…not?"

She blinked at Taryn's question, unsure how to answer.

Katherine grabbed her granddaughter's hand. "Because he hurt you, darling."

Taryn frowned. "How?"

The four women looked at each other. Evie was finally the one who spoke. "He was driving the pickup when you were injured. You remember that, don't you?"

The girl's frown deepened. "It wasn't…his fault."

Evie didn't quite know how to answer her. No one—not even Charlie's father or any of the other attorneys in his firm—disputed that Charlie had been driving the pickup that fateful night. Riley McKnight had seen him behind the wheel when he'd tried to pull over the truck on suspicion that the teens inside had been involved in a series of robberies in town and at vacation homes in Silver Strike Canyon.

"Why do you say that?" Katherine asked, but before Taryn could answer, the door burst open and Hannah Kirk rushed in.

"I'm sorry I'm late. I'm so sorry. My mom had a meeting with the divorce lawyer and she needed me to watch my little brothers. I thought I would be done in time but her meeting went longer. I've been going crazy. I would have called but I couldn't find the number. I'm so sorry."

"No worries," Evie assured her. "You needed to be helping your mother. We had plenty to do this morning. Taryn, show her your bracelet."

Taryn gingerly held her arm out again for Hannah to admire. "Nice. Really nice! Is it too late to do my mom's earrings? It's okay, if it is. I can come back another time."

"Taryn, what do you think? Can we stick around a little longer?"

Taryn smiled. "It's...better...than therapy."

They stayed and beaded with Hannah for another hour. In that time, a few other customers wandered into the store, mostly tourists. Though Hannah, Evie and Taryn attracted a few curious looks, they were removed from the main sales floor slightly and most of the shoppers seemed to barely notice them.

By the time they'd finished, Hannah had created a half dozen pairs of earrings with Evie's help, using both wire wrap and basic earring headpins.

"Thank you so much for this. Um, I only paid for the fittings. How much do I owe for the beads?"

"Nothing," Evie assured her firmly. "These were old beads I've had lying around for a long time. I had no plans for them. Really, I'm just happy to see you making good use of them."

"Are you sure? It doesn't seem right, somehow."

"I promise. I hope your mother enjoys them."

"She will. I'm sure of it. Thank you. All of you. It was the best day I've had in a long time."

Evie smiled. "We enjoyed it too, didn't we, Taryn?"

The girl nodded, but her eyes were a little glazed over

and Evie wondered if the morning had been too much for her. "We'd better go, too," she said to Katherine and Claire. "Thanks for the help."

"Do you have to?" Katherine asked.

Evie gestured to Taryn, who had a distant, tired look. "We'd better."

Despite the shortness of the drive through town and then up the hill toward Brodie's house, Taryn dozed off against the head support of her wheelchair before they reached the summit.

Even after they pulled into the driveway, she didn't open her eyes. Evie sat behind the wheel, pondering her options: Should she let the girl remain sleeping in that uncomfortable position or wake her up and take her inside for a real rest?

She was still trying to make up her mind a few moments later when the front door of the house opened and Brodie walked out toward her. He wore tan slacks and another of those ubiquitous cotton oxford shirts, this one a soft pale blue that made him look more dangerously masculine in contrast.

Her insides did a long, slow roll and she wanted to smack herself. This ridiculous reaction to him had to stop. She was acting like some kind of girl Hannah and Taryn's age with a crush on the captain of the football team, turning giddy every time he was near.

"What's wrong?" he asked. "I was working in my office and saw you pull up a few minutes ago. When you didn't leave the van immediately, I thought maybe you were having trouble with the ramp or something."

"No trouble." She pitched her voice low and gestured toward Taryn, who still hadn't stirred. "She fell asleep on the way home. I thought she could use a few moments to rest before I take her inside for lunch and our afternoon exercises."

"Ah. How did things go at the bead store?"

She debated telling him about Charlie coming into String Fever at her invitation and helping Taryn make a bracelet, then decided against it.

Okay, maybe she was a blatant coward but she chose to avoid the inevitable confrontation and opted to keep that information to herself for now. Katherine—or Taryn herself—would probably tell him anyway.

Besides, she hadn't done anything wrong. Not really. And her crazy impulse had paid off. Taryn had been attentive and involved, had even participated a little in the conversation, and had utilized more fine-motor skills in the half hour she and Charlie had cooperated together on the bracelet than during the entire week Evie had been working with her.

"The visit went well," she finally answered, then decided she didn't want to continue talking in whispers through the window.

A quick glance in the rearview mirror revealed that Taryn hadn't awakened yet, so Evie climbed out the driver's-side door and closed it gently behind her.

"I think she had a good time," she continued. "She seemed to be enjoying herself, anyway. She made a very pretty bracelet, which I'm sure she'll love showing off."

He studied her, head canted to one side. "I guess you probably want me to admit I was wrong."

She laughed. "No. I think we can both agree it's more important that you admit I was right."

His smile lit up his features, making him look far less austere and forbidding. "You were right. There. I said it. And the words only burned a little." He studied her, a soft light in his eyes. "Seriously, thank you, Evie. For pushing both of us outside our comfort zones. You're making a huge difference in her life."

"I hope I can help for the short time I'm here," she said.

He looked briefly annoyed at the reminder that her involvement in their lives was fleeting and conditional but he concealed it quickly. "So you rushed off this morning before we could talk after the interview. What did you think about Ms. Martin?" he asked.

"She certainly seems to know what she's doing," she said, picking her words with care.

He picked up on her hesitation. "But?"

"I know it was a job interview and those can certainly be stressful, but she didn't seem particularly warm, did she?"

"In what way?" He looked genuinely confused and she wondered just where his attention had been focused during that interview if he hadn't picked up the same vibe.

"Didn't you notice? She didn't smile or laugh one single time for that entire half hour, not even when we were just making small talk at the beginning of the interview, talking about her family and college and friends."

He frowned. "Are you sure?"

"Yes. I was watching for it. She answered every question as if she were in the middle of a congressional hearing."

"Maybe she's just a serious person. There's nothing wrong with that. Not everyone can be the life of the party all the time."

Ah. *That's* why he hadn't noticed. Because Brodie himself was one of the most measured, careful people she'd ever met—most of the time, anyway. She decided not to count that heated kiss that she was really, *really* trying not to dwell on more than, oh, once or twice every five minutes.

"I agree. There's nothing wrong with being serious all

the time. I'm sure it's a very good trait if you're a funeral director."

Or a sexy entrepreneur whose seriousness tended to make a woman's mind race with various ways she could help him lighten up...

She dragged her mind away from that dangerous plan. "I'm just not sure she would be the best one to encourage and motivate a somewhat stubborn fifteen-year-old girl."

"Warmth can only take you so far. Look at my parents. My mother is probably the most kind, encouraging soul in town. But when it came to motivation, I invariably worked harder for my father, whom anyone in town can tell you was one serious son of a bitch."

She had heard a few murmurs about Katherine's husband and had picked up the impression that he had been stern and uncompromising. She was sad for Brodie, suddenly. Her own father had been mostly a distant figure in her life, busy with work and his civic involvement, moving in Santa Barbara political circles.

He had died of a massive heart attack when she was a teenager, probably in part because he'd also been one of those serious, solemn people who didn't take nearly enough time to laugh at the inevitable craziness of life.

"Is that what you think Taryn will respond to?" she asked him.

"I'm guessing you don't think I should hire the woman."

"I can't make that decision for you, Brodie. You're Taryn's father. You have to do what you think is best for her."

"What if I think the best thing in the world for Taryn would be for you to continue working with her until she no longer needs help?" As soon as he said the words, he looked as if he regretted them.

Her mouth firmed into a tight line. She'd already told him she couldn't do it. He *knew* why this was hard for her.

Every day she spent with Taryn—and Brodie—was another gouge in her heart.

"Two weeks. That's what I told you. I can't give more than that."

She hated that disappointment in his eyes but she couldn't bend on this. If she caved, before she knew it, she would be wrapped so tightly around their lives she wouldn't be able to pry herself loose.

"I'll keep looking then. But if I can't find anyone we both deem suitable, I may end up having to hire Ms. Martin anyway."

"Understood. Let me know if you would like me to sit in on any other interviews."

"I'll do that."

They lapsed into silence and she was again aware of him with that almost painful intensity. Though they were standing a few feet apart, she could smell him above the late-summer scents of sunshine and flowers. She'd noticed his aftershave before, something masculine and undoubtedly expensive that called to mind long walks in a mountain forest after a rain shower.

That silly schoolgirl wanted to just stand here for a few minutes and inhale. She swallowed and met his gaze and found it resting on her mouth again. Her insides tumbled, tumbled, tumbled.

Oh, drat the man. Just when she'd convinced herself she could keep things on a casual, professional level with him, he had to go staring at her mouth again, conjuring up all sorts of crazy, wholly inappropriate impulses—like stepping forward, grasping him by the front of that crisp, sexy shirt and indulging in another of those incredible kisses.

He had to stop this. Right now. He was spending entirely too much time fantasizing about Evie, all that luscious blond hair and her soft mouth and those soft, thick-lashed exotically shaped blue eyes. It was ridiculous, especially when he planned to do absolutely nothing about this attraction except take more cold swims in the pool out back and fight to keep his hands to himself.

"It looks like Taryn's still sleeping. I guess I should wake her up," Evie said after a pause, looking at the van and not at him, and he wondered if he'd imagined that tiny flare of heat he'd seen in her eyes.

No. Probably not. He was almost sure he wasn't imagining the sudden sexual tension seething and tugging between them.

"Do you need me to help you take her inside the house?"

"No. I think I can handle it." She brushed an errant strand of hair away from her face and he ached to reach out and feel it.

She swallowed, still avoiding his gaze. "Oh, I almost forgot. I needed to talk to you about something. I want to incorporate more social interaction with Taryn's therapy as motivation, but also to help her work on regaining those skills. She seemed to really respond to the interaction with her peers at the bead store."

He didn't want to talk about this. What he really wanted to do was press her up against the nearest sun-warmed tree trunk and kiss her again until both of them dissolved into the grass.

"Would her friends actually help with the therapy?"

"A little, maybe. We could invite a few over to play around in the pool or maybe come over to do hair or something. Or more beading. That always works."

"You and my mother both think beads can solve the world's problems."

"It's a start, anyway."

He shook his head. "I suppose incorporating friends

into her therapy makes sense. As long as you're not talking wild parties long into the night every weekend."

Her smile was lovelier than the native wildflowers his gardening service so carefully cultivated. "Not yet. We build to that. I thought maybe we could start out with having Hannah and some other friends help with her therapy. She might be more motivated to work if someone is here making it more fun."

How was he supposed to focus on these important questions when his stupid one-track male brain was thinking about that smile and the little sound of surprised desire she made when he kissed her? He forced himself to do his best to pay attention.

"Friends. Uh, that makes sense. She's been a social butterfly all her life. I believe she first started gabbing to her neighbor while she was still in the incubator in the hospital nursery."

"Oh. And one more thing." Evie's tone was suddenly rueful. "She and my dog hit it off. Would you have any objection to me bringing Jacques with me tomorrow? He's very well behaved and certainly housebroken, I promise."

"Give you an inch." He shook his head.

"I know. I take a mile. But if you give me lemons, I make lemonade. I'm what you call multitalented."

He laughed, thinking how perfect it was to be standing outside in the afternoon sunshine with the hum of bees in the flowers and the air sweet and clear and a beautiful woman beside him who, despite all his common sense, somehow made him laugh.

"Speaking of lemonade," she said, "I'm dying for some of that peach lemonade Mrs. O. makes. And lunch, of course. Guess it's time to wake up Taryn."

She opened the sliding door of the van at the same moment he heard the sound of a vehicle turning into the driveway. Probably his mother coming home for lunch. Brodie turned to look but instead of his mother's vehicle, he saw a delivery truck pulling in.

Weird. He wasn't expecting anything and he typically had most deliveries sent to his office for his assistant to handle. Maybe Katherine had ordered something.

"Is this the Thorne residence?" the driver asked after he climbed out with alacrity.

Brodie stepped forward. "Yes. I'm Brodie Thorne."

"I need your signature for this one, please."

Brodie quickly signed the electronic pad and took the bed-pillow-size package from the man, who then hurried away in that quick way delivery drivers had that made you feel they had less than a microsecond to spare for you.

"Looks like Taryn is waking up," Evie observed. Brodie supposed that wasn't a big surprise, with the big truck rumbling behind her.

"Let me set this inside and I'll help you take her into the house." He took a look at the label. "Hey, it's for her!"

"For Taryn? Are you expecting medical supplies for her?"

"Not that I'm aware of. Those usually come through our home-health company anyway. This doesn't have a return address so I can't tell who sent it."

"Now I'm curious. Since she's awake anyway, I say we let her open it."

Evie hit the remote on the keychain that extended the automatic ramp on the passenger side of the vehicle. She reached in to release the tie-downs, speaking quietly to Taryn as she did. He couldn't hear what they said but he saw Taryn's sleepy smile in response, saw Evie rest a hand on his daughter's hair, and something tender and fragile shivered in his chest.

"Hi...Dad." Taryn smiled at him, still half-asleep, reminding him of long-ago snowboard trips when they would wake up early to drive to one of the other ski resorts in Colorado for the day.

"Hi, bug." He had let too much distance come between them over the years, had allowed himself to become too immersed in building his business and too focused on his own expectations for Taryn. Shame on him that it had taken his daughter nearly dying before he finally realized it.

"Look," she said, holding out her arm, just as Evie had predicted she would. He saw a bracelet of pretty, colorful pink-and-green beads.

"Nice," he said.

"Made it with Char…"

"Let's get you inside," Evie said quickly, pushing Taryn toward the house and making him curious about her haste.

"You've got a package," he said. "Want to open it?"

"Really? For…me?"

She had always loved opening presents on Christmas, he remembered—until the last few years, anyway, when she had started asking for money to buy her own gifts.

"Why don't I tell Mrs. O. to bring lunch out back by the pool? You can open your package there."

"Okay. Bathroom…first."

"I'm on it." Evie helped Taryn to her room and the en suite bathroom while he went in search of his housekeeper to ask if she would mind serving lunch outside. He didn't really have time to stop for lunch since he had only come home for a moment to take care of some loose ends, but he supposed he could find a few minutes to spare for his daughter, especially when he'd nearly lost everything with her.

Ten minutes later, the three of them converged outside at

the covered table near the pool. The waterfall built into the landscape gurgled, reflecting flashes of afternoon sunlight.

"Mrs. O. made chicken-salad sandwiches. My favorite," Brodie said.

"She...loves...you," Taryn said with a teasing grin.

His eyes met Evie's and he was embarrassed to feel himself blush. Mrs. O. was nearly sixty years old, for heaven's sake.

"She appreciates that I pay her a decent wage and that I don't make her work on weekends."

"That's...not all."

"Why don't you open your package?" he said quickly. "I'm dying to know who's sending you things and what it might be."

"I brought some scissors out to help us," Evie said. For all her free-spirited ways, she was hyperorganized about things like that, he was discovering. Because of his ADD, he had trouble focusing beyond right this moment and had always greatly admired others who could think ahead three or four steps beyond the now.

With help from Evie and the scissors, Taryn laboriously worked to open the package. Where he wanted to jump in and take care of the situation, Evie helped a little but mostly made his daughter do the work herself. He let her, appreciating her wisdom. Taryn would let everyone fuss and fret over her as long as she could. Evie instinctively seemed to understand that.

Finally it was open and Taryn and Evie both stared inside.

"What is it?" he asked, since the flaps of the box prevented him from seeing the contents.

"It's a game system," Evie said. "The kind where you don't need a remote, just your own motion."

"And some games," Taryn said, looking baffled at the

gift. He didn't blame her. She'd never been much of a gamer.

"This is fantastic," Evie exclaimed. "Think of how much fun we can have with this."

"Really?" Taryn asked.

"Yeah! We'll figure out some ways to incorporate beach volleyball or soccer or the dancing one into your therapies. And you won't even have to hold a remote!"

"Okay." Taryn didn't look convinced.

"Who sent it?" he asked. He assumed maybe his mother had ordered the game system and just forgotten to let him know.

"There's a card," Evie said, pulling it out of the box and handing it to him. As he reached for it, his skin just brushed hers. A spark leaped between them and she quickly drew her hand away.

"Sorry," she murmured.

He decided not to mention that, whatever she might think of him, he was as susceptible as the next guy to sparks flying at him from a beautiful woman.

"Welcome home," he read. At the bottom of the note was a stylized line drawing of a little angel.

Evie looked over his shoulder to read the note and he was fascinated to watch her expressive face light up with excitement.

"Wow, Taryn. You received a gift from the Angel of Hope!" Evie said.

"I did?"

"Looks like it," Brodie said. "There's an angel on here."

"Like…my…flowers."

"Flowers?" Evie asked.

"While she was in the hospital after the accident, Taryn received fresh flowers once a week, with no name on them—only a little angel on the card," he answered. "The whole time, without fail."

He had wanted to seek out the florist and find out who the hell was sending the flowers but Katherine had talked him out of it. She thought the mystery identity of the town's Angel of Hope added to the fun of the gift.

"Very cool," Evie exclaimed. "I've never had something from the Angel. Claire got a care package after the accident but that's as close as I've come."

He didn't understand the whole Angel of Hope phenomenon that had swept through Hope's Crossing for the last year. Someone had been going around town anonymously doing good deeds for people. An envelope full of money on a doorstep, paying outstanding medical bills, a basket of goodies just when someone was in the middle of a crisis.

Speculation was still running rampant around town about who might be instigating the acts of kindness— and the Angel had even been the inspiration for the town sponsoring an entire day of service, organized by Claire Bradford, his mother and the other women who hung out at String Fever.

To him, it all seemed an exercise in futility. People either helped themselves or they tended to wallow in their misery. "I would have thought the Angel would have given up by now. He—or she—can't help everyone."

Evie made a face at his cynicism. "Probably not. But sometimes a single kind gesture can be exactly the handhold someone needs to climb out of a dark hole."

"That sounds like the voice of experience," he said, even though it was none of his business.

"Your mom was my angel," she said simply. "She invited me to visit Hope's Crossing at exactly the perfect time, when I most needed a lift. I think the Angel is like your mom. I've often thought it might *be* your mom. Who-

ever it is has an uncanny knack for knowing just the perfect thing to help someone when he or she is in need.
Frankly, I don't know how one person could possibly know
all that. Claire believes the Angel might be a group of people, working in unison. If that's true, I think your mother
is at least in on it."

"My mother? Really?"

"Sure. Why not?"

"I don't know. It might have escaped your notice but
my mother has been a little distracted the last few months,
helping me with Taryn. She really hasn't had a lot of time
to go around throwing out good deeds hither and yon."

"Well, whoever it is, I think the Angel is wonderful."

"This…could be fun," Taryn declared, inclining her
head to the game system, still in the box. "Maybe…my…
friends could play."

Evie touched her hand to Taryn's fingers, which lay
mostly useless on the table. "That's a great idea. We'll invite some over first thing, okay?"

Taryn smiled at her and as he watched the two of them
together, something soft and terrifying bloomed inside
him. He didn't want this. He had enough to worry about
right now without having to wonder if he was falling for
someone as completely unsuitable as Evaline Blanchard.

Disconcerted, he pushed his chair away from the table
just as Mrs. O. came bustling out with the tray of sandwiches.

"I'm sorry," he said abruptly, "but I hadn't realized the
time. I've got a meeting this afternoon and I told my assistant I'd be back shortly to sign some papers at the office first. Mrs. O., do you mind wrapping my sandwich
up? I'll eat on my way."

"Of course," his housekeeper said.

"Do you...have to?" Taryn's mouth drooped with disappointment.

"I'd better. Practice hard on your new game system and maybe when I come home I'll let you whip my butt at something."

"Dancing," Taryn said firmly and he groaned, even as it warmed him that she was willing to try.

Maybe the Angel was onto something after all.

Eight

Oh, she was tired.

After a full day with Taryn, all Evie wanted to do was head up to her apartment and soak in the big claw-foot tub, the one she had always suspected was original to the building when it had been a brothel.

Downtown Hope's Crossing was hopping, for a Thursday night. As she drove down Main Street, she could see crowds in the few stores that stayed open later and a line of tourists waiting outside Sugar Rush, probably for some of the sweetshop's ice cream flavors or famous blackberry fudge.

Why did people on vacation always glom onto fudge and pulled taffy? she wondered idly. They didn't touch the stuff three-hundred-sixty-four days out of the year, but suddenly on vacation people couldn't seem to get enough. Go figure.

Though Hope's Crossing catered mostly to winter recreationists with its immaculate slopes and après skiing, the town had been making a push the last few years to draw visitors for the summer months to enjoy mountain biking, fishing, hiking and ATV riding.

The town needed the tourists to survive. She understood

that. Without any other major industries, Hope's Crossing would die without those who came to appreciate the town's charm and spectacular surroundings. Without a doubt, though, the influx of visitors sometimes complicated life for year-round residents—like the endless quest for a decent parking place and having to pay jacked-up tourist prices at the supermarket for a gallon of milk.

Unfortunately, such was the price the year-rounders had agreed to pay in exchange for the chance to live surrounded by gorgeous mountains and endless recreational opportunities.

As she drove down Main Street, she saw quite a few people inside Maura's bookstore, Dog-Eared Books & Brew. Book-club night, she remembered somewhat guiltily. Traveling the summer art-fair circuit had contributed to her missing the regular book club most of the summer. She would do better in the fall, she promised herself.

And Maura. She needed to be a better friend there as well. Maura seemed to be coping since her daughter's death. At least she'd returned to work—Evie had spoken with her several times when she had stopped into the bookstore and coffeehouse to grab a latte.

Returning to a regular routine had probably helped with the overwhelming guilt. And really, what else was a grieving mother supposed to do? Life had to go on. Bills had to be paid, obligations met, friendships maintained to the best of one's ability.

Evie remembered those efforts all too well, erecting that facade to the world, as if she were like some old building in a frontier ghost town somewhere—an elaborate face that concealed emptiness behind it.

As she headed toward her usual parking spot behind String Fever and found it blessedly empty despite the crowds, she made a mental note to take Maura to lunch as soon as she had the chance, perhaps when her time with Taryn was done. Like it or not, she and Maura shared a bitter legacy, mothers who had both lost children. The circumstances of those respective losses were very different but she had some small understanding of the deep and abiding sorrow that would never quite leave Maura.

She headed toward the small walled garden in back of the store, not surprised when Jacques didn't greet her there. Claire's adorable eight-year-old, Owen, had agreed to walk him a couple times a day while Evie was working at the Thornes'. Owen had probably let him back into her apartment after they'd walked around Miners' Park a few times.

Jacques would enjoy the next day at the Thorne house, playing with Taryn under the guise of therapy. She was already coming up with a variety of ways to incorporate him into their routine. How would Brodie feel about a nonshedding dog swimming around in his pool, chasing after whatever she could convince Taryn to throw at him? she wondered.

In the garden, she paused to enjoy the quiet calm there, the mingled scent of flowers and soil and sun-warmed brick and the vast spill of stars overhead that seemed so much closer here in the Colorado mountains than they ever had in California.

Her muscles ached from several days spent working with Taryn and she reached her arms high overhead and behind her back in one of the sun-salutation poses. She held it for a few moments and felt the healing energy flow through her.

Beading sometimes worked just as well to soothe her mind and calm her spirit, but she wasn't sure she had the energy or focus for anything right now but that long soak and the very pleasant mystery she was supposed to have finished for the book-club meeting that night.

"Excuse me."

The voice behind her startled her so much she lost the pose and nearly tipped over backward into the garden. She whirled around and in the pale streetlight, she saw Charlie Beaumont standing just outside the gate.

"Sorry. I didn't mean to startle you. I was just, um, riding by and saw you pull up."

Did the kid do nothing from sunup to sundown but ride his mountain bike around town? she wondered. Charlie was seventeen, beginning his senior year of high school, certainly old enough for a little autonomy, but she had to wonder if his home life was so very unpleasant he had to spend all day trying to escape it.

She ought to tell him to go away. She still felt more than a little guilt at not telling Brodie the truth about who had been helping Taryn that morning at the bead store, and for deflecting the girl's attention when she would have told her father herself.

The moment hadn't seemed right, not when Evie and Brodie seemed to have developed this fragile and rather lovely sort of truce between them.

"It's okay," she answered, and walked back toward the gate that he was leaning against. He could easily have opened the latch and come inside but for some strange reason, perhaps the fine tension she sensed in the boy, she had the feeling he needed that physical barrier to keep anyone from getting too close.

"Thanks for your help today," she said. "I think Taryn had a good time. She was showing her bracelet to everyone all afternoon."

"Yeah. Well. That's what I, um, wanted to ask you. I was wondering, um, can you, that is, is there anything I can do to help you with Taryn? I was thinking I'd like to visit again, if you thought that would be okay and everything. I could maybe take her for a walk or...or help her catch up with homework or something. Or we could make another bracelet. That was okay."

She narrowed her gaze at something in his tone. "That depends. Why the sudden offer?"

"I just want to help her. That's all."

"It has nothing to do with your trial coming up?"

He looked away. "I told my dad about going to the bead store today and he thought it would be a good idea if I tried to help Taryn some more. Show the judge I have, you know, genuine remorse and stuff."

"Do you?"

He didn't answer for a long moment, just turned his gaze to the dark, craggy silhouette of the mountains looming over them and that glittery spread of stars. When he looked back at her, his eyes were as shadowed as those mountains. "Have you ever wanted to start your life over again?"

"Yes," she answered quietly. "I think everybody probably has at some point. But I've learned after three decades on this earth that while you can't start over, you *can* change direction. It's not always easy, but it's possible."

"I don't know about that. I just want to come see Taryn again. Do you think it would be okay?"

Evie mulled how to answer him. On the one hand, Taryn had responded to Charlie that morning with amazing enthusiasm. In a week of working with her full-time, Evie hadn't seen the girl light up like that for anything else, not even the crappy MTV reality shows.

On the other hand, only one word. Brodie.

He would be furious if he knew she was even considering this. He hated Charlie. Really, how could anyone blame him? Charlie had been drinking and driving recklessly and lives had been changed forever because of it.

She understood Brodie's perspective. If someone had caused any injury to her child, she would be ready to climb up into their faces like Smokey Bear's vicious mama.

She weighed the decision for a moment longer, then sighed. Bottom line, Brodie trusted her to make the right choices for his daughter. He had given her full authority to oversee Taryn's care plan while she was directly working with the girl and to organize the treatment for whomever succeeded her. Yes, she had demanded it but he hadn't been grudging in his agreement.

She could make the argument that by allowing Charlie to visit, she was only doing what she deemed best for the girl. How could he argue with her if Evie told him she had determined the most effective way for Taryn to achieve her goals was through peer interaction with the very person Brodie blamed for causing her injuries in the first place?

Anyway, what was the worst he could do? Fire her? She hadn't wanted the job in the first place and was only doing it as a favor to Katherine. If he threw her out, she would be right back where she wanted to be, working at String Fever and fighting to reclaim her hard-fought peace and serenity.

The assurance didn't ring quite as true now as it might have a week ago but she decided she was too tired to dwell on that right now.

"Let's make one thing clear."

"Okay," Charlie said warily.

"If I agree to let you visit Taryn, I'll insist on one supreme condition. You need to be perfectly clear in your head about this, got it?"

"That depends."

"You need to decide right now what your motives are in doing this. Are you wanting to help Taryn in order to influence a judge and jury about how remorseful you are, or do you want to help her because in your heart you know it's the right thing to do and that you owe it to her? Let this be your moment to change direction, Charlie."

She expected him to say no. The surly, petulant kid she'd seen around town likely would tell her to go straight to hell.

Instead, he looked up at the stars again and the dark mountains and this quiet garden that seemed far from the bustling nighttime activity of the town around them, then turned back to her, his face still in shadows. "Yeah. Okay. I guess that's fair."

Her stomach swooped somewhere in the vicinity of her knees. Crap. Now what was she supposed to do? She couldn't very well tell him she'd changed her mind in the last twenty seconds.

She would just have to let him come to the house, and she would figure out how to deal with Brodie's wrath later.

"All right. How does ten tomorrow morning work?"

"Okay. What else would I be doing?"

"Not my problem. We'll see you at ten, then. Plan on about forty-five minutes the first day and we'll see where things go."

He nodded and started to go, then turned back. "Thanks, Ms. Blanchard."

"Don't thank me yet. Taryn's not exactly easy to work with right now." She debated adding the harsh truth, and decided Charlie needed to hear it. If Brodie could hear her right now, even he would have to admit her heart wasn't always soft and bleeding with compassion.

"You need to prepare yourself, Charlie," she warned, her voice colder than she intended. "Today at the bead store was a breeze compared to most of our therapy. It's grueling, painful, frustrating work reteaching someone how to do virtually everything. I haven't spent one day working with Taryn when she didn't end up in tears at some point."

Angry tears, usually, but she didn't tell him that, especially since his face was ghost-white in the shifting moonlight.

"If you go through with this," she went on, her tone slightly softer, "you need to be ready to confront, up close and personal, exactly what challenges she's facing now. You won't be able to hide from it, Charlie. You will know that every frustration, every single exercise she has to do, every painful muscle spasm I have to put her through, is because of you."

He looked stricken and she felt a little as if she'd kicked Jacques and Chester and every other innocent dog she'd ever known. Except Charlie wasn't innocent, she reminded herself. He had made stupid, terrible choices and Brodie was right about one thing, at least. His family was doing him no good trying to protect him from the consequences of those choices.

"I'll be ready," he said, his voice low but resolute, and she had to fight the totally irrational impulse to reach across the gate and hug him. "See you tomorrow."

She watched as he climbed back on his mountain bike and pedaled quickly away. At the end of the street, he turned and rode hard up the hill toward the Woodrose Mountain trail and she whispered a little prayer there in the garden for him—and for Maura and Taryn and Brodie and everyone else who had been affected by that fateful night.

"Come on, Taryn. Stop complaining."

Evie was frowning. She was disappointed in her, Taryn could tell.

"You can do this. I know you're playing games with me. I've seen you do this before. I only need you to take five little steps and you can hold on to the bars the whole time. Work with me here."

Everything ached. Her legs. Her back. Her head. It took too much work, and for what? She would never be right again. It was easier to stay in the chair, where people didn't expect her to be normal.

Once Evie knew she could do it, she would make her walk again and again and she hated walking. She looked like a dork and she had to fight for her balance like a big, stupid baby. "I can't."

"I know you *can*. It's only five little steps. If you can bead that bracelet you're wearing, you can take five measly little steps."

"It's…boring." That was a lie but she didn't want to say the truth.

Evie snorted. "You think it's boring for *you*, try being the one nagging at you all the time. It's not exactly a thrill a minute, sweetheart."

She smiled, even though she hurt. She couldn't help it. She liked Evie. She was pretty and funny. Sad, sometimes, though Taryn didn't understand why.

She liked Evie—but that didn't mean she wanted to work so hard.

"How about another deal?" Evie asked. "You finish the walking you need to do, then we'll do your stretches. If you quit complaining about it, we can work on another bracelet if you want or maybe a pair of earrings. I've got bead stuff in my car."

Taryn saw the mountain through the window and the sunshine. She had missed sunshine in the hospital, so much. "Outside? With Jock?" She never could speak French. *Jacques* was too hard for her mush-mouth. She would keep trying. She might hate walking but she *loved* Evie's darling dog.

"Sure. It's a lovely morning. When we're done, we can sit on the deck and work on your manual dexterity."

"I don't…want to work on m-manu…that." Some words were still so hard for her dumb mouth. She could think it just fine but when she tried to speak, it was like her mouth froze up, like Stacy Jacobs did last year at cheerleading tryouts. "No work. I only want…to bead."

"Too bad for you. You can't have one without the other. Come on, let's try one more time."

With a sigh, she stood up. Evie wouldn't stop nagging until she did it, so she should just give in. She managed to move one foot forward, then the other. The third time, Mrs. O. came to the door. Her face looked funny.

"Ms. Blanchard, we have a problem."

What problem? Taryn froze, holding on to the rails, wanting to hear.

"What's wrong?" Evie asked.

"Someone's at the door and… I'm not sure what to do about it." Mrs. O.'s round face was pink, her mouth tight as if she had eaten something bad.

"Oh." Evie looked weird, too. Kind of nervous. "Er, who is it?"

"That boy is here. He wants to see Taryn."

A boy? She looked in the mirror at her ugly, curly hair, at her workout sweats, at her dumb, twisted legs.

"What…boy?" she asked.

Mrs. O. looked more upset. "*That* boy. The Beaumont boy."

Oh. Taryn let out her breath. Just Charlie. No big deal.

Evie still was nervous and maybe a little guilty. "It's all right, Mrs. Olafson. I told him he could come to visit."

Mrs. O. was quiet for a long time. "Mr. Thorne won't like this. Not at all."

Evie's cheeks turned kind of pink. "I'm fully aware of that."

"It's not right, after what he's done, having him here. Not right!"

Taryn frowned. Why was everyone mad at Charlie? She didn't understand it at all.

"It's tricky, I agree." Evie sighed. "Look, he met us at the bead store yesterday and Taryn very much enjoyed talking to him. He stopped by my place last night to ask if he could visit again and I couldn't see the harm in it."

"No harm in it? How can you say that?"

"Charlie is my...friend." The words were a struggle, especially the *F* but she kept going until it sounded right. "Please, Mrs. O. Can he come in?"

The housekeeper frowned even more than Evie. "Mr. Thorne won't be happy about this. Not happy at all."

"I'll talk to him about it," Evie told her. "You don't have to get involved, I promise. I'll take full responsibility. I'll be certain to tell him you objected but I insisted and you didn't have a choice."

"It's not right," she grumbled, but after a minute she left the room and soon came back with Charlie.

Taryn had seen yesterday that he was growing his hair a little. She liked it better short and a little in his face.

"Hey." His shoulders were slumped as if he was in the school counselor's office. Maybe he didn't really want to be here.

"Hi, Charlie. Thanks for coming." Evie smiled a little. "We were just working on walking. Taryn, why don't you show Charlie how far you can go?"

She gave Evie a secret glare where Charlie couldn't see. Evie knew she couldn't piss and moan about it now, in front of him.

"Not f-fair," she muttered.

Evie grinned at her. "I'm a sneaky thing, aren't I?"

"Yes," Taryn said but she laughed, too. She felt better with Charlie here. He was her friend and he'd come to see her and she suddenly didn't mind that Evie made her work so hard.

"Come on over, Charlie," Evie said. "You can stand on her other side and hold her arm. You'll have to catch her if she decides not to work anymore."

"I won't," Taryn said.

Evie grinned. "That's what I'm counting on."

She didn't want to look stupid with Charlie here. When he grabbed her elbow, she took a deep breath and thought as hard as she could to make her leg move right. Yay! It did. She moved the other one. Double yay! She went seven steps, more than she ever had. At the end of the room she stopped, tired.

"Now back," Evie said.

She glared at Evie, who just smiled at her.

"This is awesome," Charlie said. "I had no idea you could walk so far. Way to go, T!"

What else could she do but turn around and walk back the other way? By the time she had walked back to her wheelchair, she knew she was sweaty and gross. Charlie wouldn't care. He was her friend and he didn't like her *that* way. He had liked Layla. But Layla was dead now. Taryn tried not to think about that, since it made her knees shake.

"Here's your chair. Take a breather for a minute and we'll try one more time, maybe not as far next time."

She was such a wuss now. So tired all the time. She was glad for the chair and sagged into it. "Can I...have a drink?"

"Of course!" Evie exclaimed. "I'll run into the kitchen and grab us all water bottles."

When she left, Charlie pulled a chair up beside her. "Seriously, Taryn, that was amazing!"

"Not...really." She couldn't go far at all on her own,

only a few steps. Maybe she'd have to go back to school with a walker. If she ever went back to school, anyway. Her dad didn't want her to. Maybe she'd have to go in the special-ed classes now.

"Trust me. You're rockin' it. I had no idea, Taryn."

What he said made her feel warm and happy inside, not so tired, and she was superglad he'd come.

"How long have you been able to walk?"

"A few…weeks."

"You're going to be hiking up the Woodrose trail before you know it."

"Evie says…that."

"She's right. I thought, you know, that you'd never be able to walk again. That's what everybody said. I know how much you used to like to ski and mountain bike and the cheerleader stuff and I…that's been really horrible, you know? Thinking you'd be in a wheelchair your whole life."

She looked away from him, toward the weights and stuff in the room. She still thought maybe she would be in the wheelchair, at least if she didn't start working harder. It hurt to work and she was tired of hurting. Hurting meant she was getting better and she wasn't sure she was supposed to get better.

"Hey. I didn't mean to upset you. I'm sorry."

She shook her head. "It's okay."

He looked upset. Sad and mad and kind of scared at the same time. "It's not okay. What I did. I mean, Layla. Jeez. And you."

"Don't talk…about Layla."

He slid back in his chair, more upset. "I know. I know."

She wanted to cry, but not in front of Charlie. Evie came back with a tray just in time.

"Mrs. Olafson reluctantly made some lemonade. I don't think she poisoned it but maybe I ought to taste it first. If I keel over, you can call the paramedics. Make sure that cute Dougie Van Duran comes to give me mouth-to-mouth."

Taryn smiled a little. She was glad Evie came in then. She couldn't think about Layla. It hurt more than walking a mile.

My fault, Taryn thought. *All my fault.*

Once in a while her harebrained ideas seemed to work. Charlie stayed for forty-five minutes, just as he had agreed the day before. It was the perfect length for a visit. Long enough to be fun and encouraging but not so long that Taryn grew bored.

Between Charlie and Jacques, Taryn didn't have time to show fatigue or petulance. When she started to show signs of wanting to stop, Jacques would come up beside her and nudge her hand or Charlie would say something funny or snarky and she would laugh, take a breath, and try again.

The petulance and general grouchiness Evie had been dealing with since Taryn's release from the care center was nowhere in evidence. It seemed to have magically floated away on the summer breeze. Taryn was laughing and talking in her hesitant way and, best of all, doing exactly what Evie asked of her. By the time Charlie glanced at his watch and announced he had to leave, Taryn was even taking three or four shuffling steps with only the walker to support her, quite miraculous progress.

"Come back," Taryn ordered Charlie before he left.

The kid had stared at her with a range of emotions on his pretty, preppy-boy face and then he nodded. "I'll be back in a couple days, if it's okay with Ms. Blanchard."

What else could she say? Despite her misgivings about Brodie's reaction when he found out, she couldn't overlook Taryn's astonishing attitude shift, nor could she afford to lose this momentum.

She only hoped Charlie wouldn't flake out and decide he'd done his part and no longer needed to hang out with a girl who had serious limitations on her ability to make witty banter.

Evie decided she would just have trust that the boy would keep his word and come again. She had a strong feeling Taryn would be heartbroken if he dropped off the face of the earth again.

Brodie still wouldn't approve of the boy visiting and Evie felt more than a little squeamish about allowing it when she knew perfectly well he would object. She ought to tell him tonight just what she had done, but somehow she knew that would ruin everything.

She usually tried to be a scrupulously honest person but she couldn't risk his forbidding the boy to come again before Evie even had a chance to see if today's incredible progress with Taryn was simply a fluke.

Besides, what he didn't know, and all that, right?

"That was f-fun," Taryn declared, after Charlie had left. Evie doubted she even noticed she was using her left hand to pet Jacques's head. The bones in that hand had been crushed in the accident and she usually complained when Evie tried to make her use it.

"See. I told you therapy wasn't so terrible."

"With Charlie, maybe."

Evie shook her head, refusing to be goaded into a response, despite Taryn's implication that regular therapy *wasn't* a barrel of laughs.

"It's too nice to be indoors today," she declared. "We don't have many of these nice late-summer afternoons left. Let's see if we can have lunch outside again today and maybe we can make something with those beads I told you I had in the car. I was looking on my calendar this morning and remembered someone has a birthday next week. Any guesses?"

Taryn screwed up her features, thinking, then she smiled. "Grandma!"

"Right. And I brought some beading supplies as well as a collection of some of my favorite glass beads. You can pick the colors you think your grandmother will like."

Brodie's landscaper had created a lovely spot, she thought a few moments later, after they were settled out on the big, multilevel deck that terraced up from the swimming pool. Brodie had added temporary ramps so that she could move Taryn from level to level.

She couldn't imagine a more perfect afternoon than sitting here on Brodie Thorne's lovely deck while a warm breeze, sweet with sage and pine and mule-ear daisies, rustled the leaves of the aspens around his landscaping.

A mountain bluebird flitted in the trees. A sign of luck. She watched its color amid the green, aware that in a few short weeks all the leaves would be turning and the bluebirds would be flying someplace else to spend their winters where they could find food.

Taryn seemed to be enjoying herself. She hummed some nameless tune Evie couldn't identify, as she sifted through the soft, smooth glass beads in the tray.

"What's...this one?"

"I bought that one from a tiny little lady with a face like a garden gnome on the island of Capri."

"I like it."

"You can keep it if you'd like. After we're done with your grandmother's necklace, we can make a simple one for you out of cord with just that charm if you want."

"Thank...you!"

Taryn smiled her lopsided little smile at her and something gentle and warm stirred in her chest. Not good.

Not good at all. She shifted, uneasy. This soft affection for Taryn scared her. She was becoming far too fond of the girl, sour moods and all. This was exactly what she'd feared, that her life would become tangled with the Thornes, Taryn and Brodie both.

She was already invested in Taryn's recovery. She wanted the girl to overcome the roadblocks, both mental and physical, that seemed to stand in the way of her regaining many of her old skills. The last week had been challenging, yes, but also infinitely rewarding. Taryn was eating better on her own now. Her tolerance for their activities had increased, even while she grumbled and moaned about doing them.

And with increasing frequency, she was beginning to show these glimpses of her personality that Evie loved.

How would she ever find the strength to walk away?

"This looks likes the place to be on a lovely summer afternoon."

She jerked her head to the doorway and found Brodie watching them, arms crossed and hip angled against the doorframe, his toe tapping a little in that restless way of his.

He looked quite comfortable, as if he'd been there for some time, and she flushed a little, wondering how long he'd been watching them.

She was angry, suddenly. Furious with him. This was his fault. If not for Brodie, she wouldn't be sitting here while the carefully nurtured ice around her heart, cracked apart as if someone had taken a sledgehammer to it.

"It's...nice," Taryn said, hesitating only an instant between the words. Her speech was coming along so much better than her physical skills but that wasn't uncommon in Evie's experience.

"Mind if I join you two? Mrs. Olafson was just telling

me that lunch is nearly ready. She's the one who told me where to find you."

What else had Mrs. O. told him? He didn't seem furious with her, so Evie had to assume the housekeeper had decided to keep her mouth shut about Charlie's visit. She ought to be making Mrs. Olafson a bracelet, too.

"Yes!" Taryn said. "You can help bead."

"Hey, I signed up for lunch, not work."

"Beading isn't work. Only...fun," Taryn declared.

He aimed a questioning look toward Evie, who shrugged. "Apparently I've brought her over to the dark side. I guess my work here is done."

"Not yet," he teased. "You still promised me another week."

Just how was she going to make it through another week with her defenses intact when she was already beginning to care for both of them entirely too much?

"What are we doing here?"

"It's for Grandma's...birthday."

He blinked, apparently taken aback. "Is that coming up? Shoot. I guess I'd better hurry to get her something. I completely forgot."

"I thought I was...the one with the...brain injury."

He stared at Taryn for a full ten seconds before he busted up laughing. Evie couldn't help laughing along, charmed that Taryn would joke about her condition. Her gaze met Brodie's and she could feel her smile die away. That sizzle of attraction sparked between them and she was once more standing in the moonlight, pressed against the door of her SUV with his mouth dancing over hers, wanting to wrap her arms around him and hold on forever.

Oh, this was *so* not good.

"Will you help?" Taryn asked her father.

"Sure, kid. Just tell me what to do."

In her halting sentences, she explained the simple pattern they were using on the beads and for the next few moments of the two of them worked, dark heads bent together, leaving Evie's mind entirely too free to fret while she worked on her own project.

She was relieved when Mrs. Olafson brought their lunch in, perhaps fifteen minutes later—until she saw the other woman's expression. Mrs. O. looked as if she'd sprinkled alum on her tongue just before walking out of the house and Evie winced, knowing all that disapproval was intended for her, for allowing Charlie into the hallowed Thorne halls.

She owed the housekeeper a huge apology for placing her in the position of being deceitful to her employer.

Despite Mrs. O.'s mood, lunch was delicious, as always—a salad of mountain greens, Gorgonzola cheese and sliced strawberries, along with cold salmon sandwiches and a scrumptious dill sauce.

"How do you keep so fit while you're eating Mrs. O.'s delicious food?"

Brodie smiled. "Why do you think I had to put in a swimming pool? If I slack off on the laps in the morning, I pay for it."

Taryn, she was happy to see, only needed minimal help cutting her sandwich into small, more easily handled portions. She struggled a little with the salad greens but managed to maneuver more into her mouth than on the plate. She didn't even spill her drink, something they'd been battling all week.

This was the addictive part of being a therapist: charting real, practical progress in everyday ways that helped someone live better.

Their conversation over lunch drifted between topics, from the bead project she was working on, to a new Asianfusion restaurant he was opening in a new development in town, to his time as a ski jumper.

"Are you okay, sweetheart?" Brodie asked after a half hour or so and Evie realized the girl had set down her half-eaten sandwich and hadn't contributed to the conversation in some time.

Taryn gave her lopsided smile. "Tired."

"We have had a full morning," Evie said. "You worked hard today. Do you want to take a little rest in your room before we start the plan for the afternoon? We can put the beading away until later."

Taryn nodded and Brodie pushed away from the table. "I'm finished here. I can take her inside and help her to transfer."

Evie was finished as well. "I'll clean up out here."

"Mrs. Olafson can take care of that."

"So can I," she returned. Though her family had always employed a cook and a housekeeper, her mother had insisted Evie and her sister clean up after themselves—and besides, right now she needed to do all she could to stay in the housekeeper's good graces.

When she carried the tray of dishes into the kitchen, Mrs. Olafson was rolling pastry dough out on the counter.

"You can set those by the sink. I'll take care of them when I'm finished here."

Evie thought about loading them into the dishwasher but decided heeding the other woman's wishes would be the wiser course, given the circumstances.

"Thank you for lunch. It was delicious, as always. You have a gift."

Mrs. O. didn't answer, only continued wielding the rolling pin with rather jerky, abrupt motions. Evie released a heavy breath.

"I know you think I overstepped by inviting Charlie

Beaumont to visit Taryn. But you should have seen her walking today, Mrs. Olafson. She has never gone that far just for me alone."

"It's not right. I don't like being deceitful."

"I'm not asking you to deceive anyone. Go ahead and tell Brodie right now if you feel it's the right thing to do. He's in Taryn's room."

The other woman looked at her. "He won't allow the boy back in the house."

"I know that."

Mrs. O. paused. "You say she was walking more when he was here?"

"She walked the entire length of her rooms three times without a single complaint."

"That's something."

"I agree." Evie held her breath as the woman seemed to be considering.

"I won't say anything for now. But I still don't like it."

"Thank you, Mrs. Olafson. And thank you again for lunch. You do a marvelous job taking care of the Thornes. They're very lucky to have you."

The housekeeper seemed slightly mollified by that, but Evie felt uneasy about placing the other woman in such a difficult position.

When she returned to Taryn's rooms, she found Brodie backing out, moving with extraordinary stealth for such a large man.

"Is she already asleep?"

"Close enough. Your dog definitely was. He curled right up beside her bed. You must have exhausted both of them today."

This was the perfect time to mention Charlie. The words hovered there but she couldn't quite do it. "Taryn worked hard," she said instead, feeling like an abject coward. "She deserves to rest for a few minutes."

"So do you."

"I just had a lovely lunch break, and before that I was beading for an hour. Not exactly hard physical labor."

"I know Taryn's not an easy patient."

"She hasn't been that bad," Evie said.

"Yet you still don't want to keep working with her?"

She gave a rueful laugh. "Nice try, Brodie."

"I promised myself I wasn't going to keep asking after what you told me the other night about your daughter, but I can't seem to help it. Sorry."

"You can keep asking and I'll keep turning you down," she said. Better not to think about what else had happened that night.

"Every business owner knows he needs a contingency plan. I've got a few more résumés in my office. Since Taryn is resting, do you have a moment to look over them with me and help me vet the potential candidates?"

"Sure. Of course."

Much to her dismay, the memory of that kiss haunted her as they walked down the hall toward his office. She could still feel the heat of his mouth on hers, feel the leashed strength in his muscles as she had foolishly wrapped her arms around him.

Perhaps being alone with him wasn't the smartest idea. She wondered how he would respond if she suggested calling Mrs. Olafson in to chaperone—not that he had indicated any interest in kissing her again.

That was a good thing. Or so she tried to convince herself.

His office was a masculine space near the front door, painted in rich, earthy brick tones, with wide French doors leading into it and expansive views over the valley. She hadn't been inside before, as he had chosen to conduct the two job interviews she'd attended in the more formal setting of the living room.

As he shuffled through a folder of papers on his desk, Evie happened to notice a collection of framed photographs on a shelf above the console table adjacent to his desk. She moved closer for a better look. Most of them were of Taryn through various stages of life and she found this evidence of unexpected sentimentality from him rather endearing.

One in particular caught her attention. It had been shot on what looked like a sunny, wintry day and showed a little girl who looked about three years old with big blue eyes and long dark curls. She was dressed in a pink ski suit, perched on a snowboard and grinning from ear to ear. Bent over her and holding her hands out to the side as if helping her with technique was a lovely petite woman, her auburn hair in pigtail braids under a beanie and her own snowboard propped at the edge of the frame.

"Is this Taryn's mother?" she guessed.

He looked up from the file folder with a slightly unfocused look in his eyes. It took a moment for his gaze to sharpen.

"Right. That's Marcy." He made a rueful sort of face. "And before you think I keep the picture around with the rest of those as some physical token of my undying love, let me assure you that's definitely *not* the case. I keep the picture partly for Taryn's sake, to help her remember her mother. But also because it reminds me that life can change in an instant."

Why did he think he needed a constant reminder of that delightful little fact of life? she wondered.

He took the frame and held it for a moment, then shook his head and set it back on the shelf. "Marcy took off not long after that was taken. I was out of town meeting with investors for my first restaurant, which is probably why she picked that particular day to leave. At least she stopped long enough to drop Taryn off with my mother before she skipped town with a guy she had just met on the slopes."

"Wow. You had no advance warning?"

"Technically, no, but I should have known. We were broken long before she left. I ignored plenty of signs that she had been trying to edge out of our lives for a while. She kept dropping all these hints and I ignored them, too busy trying to provide for her and Taryn. In case you haven't figured it out yet, I'll tell you. We weren't exactly what you'd call a match made in heaven. If you want the truth, I married her mostly to piss off my father."

She gave a rough laugh at his matter-of-fact tone, though it wasn't amusing in the least. "Quite a reason to bind your life to someone."

"Well, that's the reason we dated, anyway. Marcy was a party girl. She skied hard and she played hard, just like I did. My father hated her and I hated my father so it seemed a perfect scenario. I wasn't the most mature twenty-one-year-old guy around, I'll freely admit it."

"Most aren't," she murmured.

"Marcy and I were just messing around, you know? Neither one of us was serious—and then we found out she was pregnant."

"A shock for both of you, I'm sure." She had to admit, she had a tough time picturing Brodie as a wild young man, though she had heard the stories. She knew he'd been a rising star in the heavily competitive ski-jump world and that he'd trained for the Olympics. She found it tough to gel that image with the driven entrepreneur he'd become, though she wasn't sure why. She could imagine he had to use some of that same dedication and drive in any competitive athletics that he used in the business world.

"I didn't want to keep her. Taryn, I mean. Deep down, despite her party-girl ways, Marcy was Catholic and would never consider terminating the pregnancy. At first, I pushed her to give the baby up for adoption. The last thing I wanted at the time was to be tied down with a kid."

Guilt flickered in his gaze and he sighed heavily. "I sometimes think Taryn would have been better off if I had continued to push for that. If Marcy and I had decided not to get married instead."

"How can you say that? You love Taryn."

"I love her but I haven't been the best father."

He spoke in a low voice, his mouth tight and those shadows of guilt in his blue eyes, and her heart ached for him. She felt extraordinarily touched that he would confide this in her, something she very much doubted he had ever shared with anyone else. At the same time, it terrified her. In only a matter of days, their relationship had shifted from tension and dislike to something far different. Something intense and rich and sweetly profound.

She touched his arm. "All parents wish they had done something better. It's part of the universal code of parenting, I think. Don't beat yourself up, Brodie."

The muscles beneath her fingers flexed. "I pushed her too hard. The last few years, it seems like I rode her all the time. About grades, about boys, about her clothes, about wasting so much time online and texting."

"You mean like any concerned father would?"

"Between my work schedule and her hectic school and social life, it seems like the few moments I did spend with her at dinnertime or whatever were always strained and tense. She wanted something from me and I couldn't for the life of me figure out what the hell it was."

Your love. Just your love. She bit her lip and remained silent, not wanting to add to his guilt.

"Even though we had my mom to pick up the slack, losing Marcy when Taryn was just a little kid was tough on her," he went on after a pause. "I think it was harder because for those first few years Marcy would flit in and out on a whim, make all kinds of promises, then never keep any of them. You want to know what a terrible, self-ish person I am? It was almost a relief to me when Marcy was killed in an avalanche heli-skiing in Chile somewhere. Yeah, I grieved for all those missed chances and for the woman I'd tried to convince myself I loved years ago, but at least after she died, I knew she couldn't break Taryn's heart anymore."

"You're not a terrible person, Brodie." It would be far, far easier for her if he were. She could feel those cracks in the ice around her heart cut deeper, almost hear the thunder in her ears as pieces of it fell away like glaciers calving in the Arctic sea.

"I should have tried harder to keep my marriage to-gether so Taryn could have had a chance at a regular life, with a mother who wasn't always looking for the next thrill until it killed her."

Evie didn't want this, the sweet, seductive tenderness that curled around and between them. She wanted to run as far and as fast as she could away from this soft warmth.

"I didn't know you then but I have a little experience with who you are now. I have no doubt whatsoever that you did all within your power to make things work. Trust me when I say you're the most determined man I've ever met."

"Is that a compliment or an insult?"

A few weeks earlier, her words might have been edged with derision. She had viewed Brodie as a man who took what he wanted, regardless of the consequences. She had seen firsthand the power he wielded in Hope's Crossing, the way he could sway a roomful of civic leaders to his way of thinking.

What she had once considered arrogance, now she recognized as vision and sheer strength of will. He knew what he wanted—and unlike most of the world, he had no problem doing what was necessary to make it happen, whether that was developing a neighborhood or healing his daughter.

"A compliment," she murmured. "Definitely a compliment."

"I'll take it as such, then."

Their gazes met and the air between them suddenly seemed to crackle and spark with electricity. She knew he was thinking about that kiss. She could see it in the way he swallowed and the expansion of his pupils, until the dark almost overtook the blue of his irises.

He wanted to kiss her again. And she wanted to let him.

"Taryn is probably awake by now," she said, then was embarrassed by the huskiness of her voice.

"I doubt it," he said. "She can be a pretty sound sleeper."

She needed to go now, while she could. *Move.* The warning registered in her mind but she couldn't seem to make her feet cooperate. With a funny sense of inevitability, she saw Brodie walk around his desk to stand in front of her.

"Evaline," he murmured. Just that, only her name, and she was lost. She didn't resist when he pulled her to her feet or when he curved one hand around her cheek, his fingers warm on her skin, or when he lowered his head and his mouth found hers.

He tasted delicious, of cherries and a hint of chocolate, probably from that thin slice of cake he'd had for dessert after lunch. Somehow she had always known chocolate would eventually be her downfall but this wasn't quite what she'd expected.

Where their first kiss had been slow and easy, this one was...*more*. More sensual, more intense, more demanding. More...*wow*.

His tongue licked at the seam of her mouth and she couldn't resist parting her lips, drawing him closer, pressing her body to his as he deepened the kiss.

Oh. My. He was an extraordinary kisser. Who would have thought serious Brodie Thorne would kiss a woman with this knee-weakening intensity that made her want to throw every shred of common sense down the mountainside, crawl right into his lap and stay for a week or so, just learning the mysteries of his clever mouth?

Somehow—she was only vaguely aware of the logistics of it—he shifted their position until she was perched on the edge of the desk and he was standing between her legs. The heat of him was intoxicating. It seeped through her skin, warming all those cold and empty places inside her.

They kissed for a long time and might have continued indefinitely, heedless of Taryn or Mrs. O. or anything else, except a phone suddenly bleated softly between them.

He drew back a little, his eyes murky and aroused and filled with regret. The phone rang again and she scrambled back a little way on the desk. "Aren't you going to answer that?"

"I don't think so. Who knows what I might say? I'm not sure I have a functioning brain cell in my head right now." He paused and gave her a long look. "This is going to be a problem, isn't it?"

She swallowed hard, wanting nothing more than to sink back into him. She had a job to do here, she reminded herself, and it didn't include kissing her employer until she forgot everything, including her patient.

"Depends how you define *problem*."

He sighed and moved away from her, much to her regret.

"I know how much I owe you. What you're doing with Taryn is amazing. She's showing real progress and I don't want to do anything to screw that up."

"It was only a kiss, Brodie."

"A pretty spectacular one, as far as kisses go."

She refused to feel flattered by that. Or so she told herself. "Don't worry about it. For some reason I don't quite understand, we happen to have this…vibe…between us. It's completely insane. I get it."

"Not *completely* insane," he murmured.

"Sorry?"

"You're a beautiful woman, Evie. I've been attracted to you since the day you showed up in Hope's Crossing."

"You have not. You hated me when I came to visit your mother the first time!"

"*Hate* is a strong word. *Distrust* fits better. I tend to be protective of the people I care about. I was looking out for my mother, wondering at your motives for befriending her. I won't deny that, but even when I was suspicious of you, that didn't stop me from having, uh, completely inappropriate thoughts about you. For one thing, I've been wondering for months how all that wondrous hair would feel if I ever had the chance to slide my fingers through it."

She shivered, enthralled by his words even as she knew she ought to tell him to shut up now, while she still had half a chance of walking out of this room without kissing him again. She didn't, though, and her penance was that he continued to seduce her with those low, murmured words.

"Having you here in my house has only intensified my attraction to you. Not only that, but I'm beginning to see someone even more amazing on the inside. Strong and kind, clever, compassionate, funny. How could any man in his right mind not be dying to kiss you?"

She hitched in a ragged little breath, wanting desperately to jump back into his arms again.

She couldn't. If he knew she had allowed Charlie in his house, he wouldn't see her as any of those things. More like manipulative, devious, seditious.

The reminder compelled her to ease away from him. What was the word he'd used? *Inappropriate.* This whole tangling of tongues thing was completely inappropriate, especially given her deception.

With a great deal of effort—and no small amount of regret—she eased away from him, scooting to the side of the desk and standing again. "I'd better go check on Taryn."

His expression was rueful. "Yeah. It's going to be a problem."

"Not if we don't let it be. Let's just pretend this kiss and the one the other day never happened. Whatever the catalyst—stress, proximity, whatever—they were both mistakes. Yes, I'm attracted to you. I'm sure if I stood on Main Street and took a poll, half the women in town would be able to say the same thing. But I can't afford this kind of…distraction…right now. I'm here to help Taryn transition to her home-based program. That's all. This is a critical time in her therapy and we would both do better to focus on our objective here."

"Our objective. Right."

"Taryn needs my attention right now. Her occupational therapist is coming this afternoon so I need to go make sure she's ready."

They never *had* discussed possible candidates to replace her, Evie realized as she left his office and walked down the hall toward Taryn's rooms. Let him figure it out himself. She wasn't about to head back into his office right now—not when it was taking all her strength to walk away.

Nine

It was only a kiss. A simple merging of mouth against mouth, with a jumble of highly compatible pheromones thrown in to make things interesting. More than a week later, Brodie was still trying to convince himself of that—and still trying to talk himself down from trying it again.

Evie had made it abundantly clear she wasn't interested, despite the tension that seemed to shiver in the air whenever they were in the same room. Her priority was Taryn and she considered this attraction between them merely a distraction.

Under other circumstances, he might have appreciated the irony that Evie Blanchard—of the bleeding heart and the hippie-chick clothes and the zeal for beading—was the one being brisk and businesslike here.

He knew she was right. Beyond that, while they might share an attraction and he was coming to see her in a much more favorable light as he watched her care for his daughter, on the most basic of issues they were highly incompatible. He craved structure and order and calm. Evie was the complete opposite of all those things. She was color and chaos, passion and heat.

And yet. There was a softness about her, a fragile vulnerability, that called to him even though he knew it was, in her words, completely crazy.

He hadn't been able to stop thinking about her for more than a week. In the middle of a business meeting, he would remember the particular curve of her mouth, that sexy little hitch in her breath, the sweet, wildflower scent of her, and his thoughts would scatter like the aspen leaves that were turning gold now as August faded towards September.

The smartest thing, the only thing, had been to avoid her—and he'd done his best for more than a week. He had mostly stayed away from the house during the time he knew Evie was likely to be there, choosing to move more of his work responsibilities to his office in downtown Hope's Crossing.

The only time he'd spent more than a brief moment with her had been a week earlier, Wednesday, when Evie had agreed to sit in on another interview for Taryn's rehab therapist. This candidate had been perfect—fresh out of physical-therapy training, enthusiastic, energetic. Evie had approved of her right away. He wondered if her alacrity was indeed due to Stephanie Kramer's credentials or if Evie was that anxious to return to her job at the bead store.

Stephanie had been excited to take the job but because of other commitments she couldn't start until the following week. With obvious reluctance, Evie had agreed to stay on another week, until after Labor Day.

For Taryn's sake, he was relieved since his daughter's progress the last ten days had been nothing short of miraculous. She was taking several steps at a time unassisted and her vocabulary and sentence structures—while still a little hesitant—were head and shoulders above where she'd been before she'd come home.

He was deeply grateful for Evie, though her continued

presence at his home also meant another week of his keeping as healthy a distance as he could manage.

Even when he stayed away, he wasn't doing a very good job of maintaining focus in the rest of his life.

Right now, for instance, he was supposed to be in a meeting with his attorneys for a rehab project he was considering in a section of tiny crumbling houses in the Old Town area of Hope's Crossing. Instead, he had been forced to leave them all waiting so he could run home like a kid who'd left his homework on the kitchen table instead of stuffing it in his backpack to take to school.

Evie's arrival that morning, along with her gangly yellow-haired Labradoodle, had distracted him so much as he'd been on his way out the door that he'd completely forgotten a pile of vital contracts he needed for the meeting.

His plan was to slip into his office, grab the contracts and leave again without anybody being the wiser. No witty banter with Evie, no soft exchange of confidences, and definitely no more of those delicious kisses.

Too damn bad for him.

The house was quiet. He knew this was the morning Mrs. Olafson usually went to the grocery store but he might have expected to hear Taryn and Evie rocking out in the therapy room to the music Taryn liked to work to, or playing the game system the Angel of Hope had sent, or at least laughing and talking about something, as they tended to do.

Nothing. Just silence.

The van had still been parked out front so he knew they hadn't gone anywhere. Curious, he couldn't resist peeking his head into her suite of rooms, and found them empty. Maybe they were out in the pool, though late-August mornings in the mountains were cool enough for sweatshirts, at least until the sun burned off the mist. He kept the water comfortable for his own laps and could usually swim until the first snowfall. Since the all-season cover for the pool was set to be installed in a few weeks, he could swim all winter if he wanted.

Once Evie was out of his house and his mind, he probably wouldn't need the relentless distraction of laps.

If they weren't swimming, they could have gone for a walk. Evie liked being outside. He wouldn't exactly call her a nature girl but she definitely thrived on sunshine and fresh air. He could understand that. Being outside helped him think more clearly, probably because of the ADD.

Forgetting these contracts seemed an entirely too familiar habit, one he had worked hard as an adult to overcome. School had been a nightmare for him of missed homework and forgotten assignments, notes from teachers, frustration all the way around. His father had despised that weakness in his son and couldn't understand why Brodie couldn't just put his mind to it and succeed.

He'd tried. The only saving grace for him had been sports. When he was swimming or skiing or running, all the connections in his brain seemed to click along just fine.

Now that he was an adult, he'd managed to come up with techniques to block out the chaos in his head but sometimes when he pushed himself too hard or worked outside his comfort zone, he could still stumble. These contracts were a perfect example. He should have remembered them. The meeting was his main priority for the day and he'd known he needed the contracts. He had even set them on the corner of his desk, after vetting them the night before, in plain view so he wouldn't forget them.

By now, he should have known his own weaknesses well enough to have had the foresight to slide the contracts into his laptop case when he'd finished with them. Since he hadn't, here he was, burdened with the complication of having to run home for them.

He located them quickly and stuck them under his arm, then decided to run into the kitchen for a slice of the banana bread Mrs. O. had made earlier. Though it had filled the house with the delicious nutty scent, he'd left in too much of a rush to enjoy it then.

The window was open above the sink in the kitchen and he heard a muffled bark from outside, saw a shadow of movement. Ah. There they were. He should have known. The backyard, with its sweeping views of Hope's Crossing, had become a favored spot for Evie and Taryn.

He had twenty minutes before his rescheduled meeting, which left him just the right amount of time to say a polite hello and then leave before he could cross any more boundaries with Evie, he decided.

The morning was cool but pleasant as he opened the door leading to the deck. He closed it behind him with a snick, then turned back around. "Good morning," he started to say, but the words and everything else inside him seemed to stutter to a grinding halt and he only got out the first consonant.

For a full thirty seconds, he could do nothing but stare, shock paralyzing his thoughts, and then fury washed over him, fierce and hot.

"What the hell is this?"

Evie whirled around at his voice and he saw guilt and panic bloom in her blue eyes. Her mouth opened slightly but she didn't say anything. Instead, she turned her attention quickly back to Taryn until the girl, standing unassisted, threw a ball for Jacques.

The dog caught the ball easily but even he seemed to sense something wrong. He padded toward Taryn and planted his haunches in front of her.

On some peripheral level, Brodie was aware of the others. Evie. Taryn. The dog. But the bulk of his attention was focused on one person, the young man standing on Taryn's other side, whose features had gone as white as Woodrose Mountain in January.

Brodie was vaguely aware he was crumpling the contracts but he couldn't seem to make his fists unclench. Charlie Beaumont looked as if he'd like nothing more than to take a step backward, out of his reach, but he stayed frozen in place.

"Get away from my daughter, you little son of a bitch."

"If he moves, she might fall." Evie's voice was calm, which somehow seemed to infuriate him even more. He threw the contracts down on the deck table, wedging them under the centerpiece vase filled with flowers from the garden, to keep the papers from fluttering away in the breeze.

Charlie Beaumont. The kid who had decided it would be a barrel of laughs to drive drunk with a bunch of teenagers in his car, rob a bunch of businesses, including several of Brodie's own, and destroy dozens of lives.

If not for him, Taryn would be starting school again this week. She would be going to cheerleader camp and texting her friends nonstop and beginning to think about college applications.

Instead, here she was having to relearn even the most basic functions—while Charlie Beaumont stood by, probably to mock and laugh at her.

It was taking every ounce of his self-control to keep from stalking forward, scooping Taryn up and carrying her far, far away from this punk who had hurt his baby girl.

He turned his rage on Evie, the obvious accomplice in the whole thing. She stood there looking perfectly calm, perfectly serene, while he wanted to yell and curse and break something. Preferably something attached to Charlie Beaumont.

"This is completely messed up. What the hell is he doing here?"

"Right now we're working on multitasking. Taryn is throwing the ball to Jacques while balancing at the same time, which works multiple gross-motor skills as well as focus and concentration. Charlie is spotting if she needs help."

"You know that's not what I meant."

She sighed, looking slightly apprehensive. Good. She should be.

"If you're going to yell at me, let's get Taryn to the deck. She can't stand this long."

Much to his astonishment, Taryn turned with Evie and Charlie's help and made her painstaking way to the steps. Charlie grabbed her walker when Evie asked him to and carried it over to Taryn, who used it without help to make her way up the four wide, low steps leading to the terraced deck. How long had she been tackling stairs? he wondered. He'd had no idea she had progressed so far.

Pride warred with his anger and confusion as he watched Charlie smoothly take the walker from her and grab her elbow to lower her to one of the teak chairs, as if he'd done it dozens of times.

When Taryn was settled with the dog at her feet, Charlie shoved his hands in the pockets of his cargo shorts. Brodie had to give the kid credit for looking him in the eyes, though he looked scared to death.

"I'll go," he said quietly.

"Good idea." He knew he sounded like an ass but he was so furious he didn't trust himself to be around Charlie Beaumont right now. "On second thought, you can stay until somebody tells me what's going on and why I shouldn't have you arrested right now for trespassing."

"Dad, stop." Taryn gave him a disgusted, eye-rolling look that was so painfully familiar from the time before her accident that he almost had to stare. "Chill. It's f-fine."

"Not with me."

"Charlie…is my f-friend. Therapy is…f-fun…with him."

"How long has he been coming here?"

Evie looked as if she didn't want to answer but she finally sighed. "Over a week. Since the day after we went to String Fever that first time. He's been coming just about every morning for an hour or two, then Hannah Kirk comes for another hour or two. I should have told you. I just…knew this is how you'd react."

"How am I supposed to react when somebody I trusted with my daughter's *life* betrays me in my own home?" He thought of the soft tenderness of their kiss, of the growing feelings he had been doing his best to ignore.

He was not a man who trusted easily. Growing up with a father who treated him like a failure had left him wary and prickly. Marrying a wild, immature woman and then having to stand by and watch his child suffer because of it hadn't helped alleviate his unwillingness to let someone else into his life.

But he had trusted Evie, more than any woman except his mother. How could she have brought Charlie into his house, into his daughter's life, knowing Brodie's animosity toward the kid who had destroyed everything?

"I should have told you. That was certainly wrong and I'm sorry. But everything I did was for Taryn's sake."

He opened his mouth to argue but closed it again. He had no desire to leave Charlie alone with his daughter out here but he also didn't want to fight this out in front of a couple of teenagers and a very curious-looking dog—not when this duplicity seemed so very personal.

"Ms. Blanchard. May I have a word with you inside?"

At his icy tone, her eyes turned cool as well, a far cry from the soft warmth in them when he'd kissed her. Even then, she had been keeping this from him, he realized with disgust.

"Of course. You can still throw the ball to Jacques from the chair," she instructed Taryn. "Try an underhand throw with your left arm. Like you're lobbing a softball pitch. That's it. Good."

She led the way back into the kitchen, which now seemed stuffy and close compared to the cool mountain air outside.

"All this time. You've been letting him into my house for nearly two weeks!"

"He's helping her. You should see her, Brodie. When Charlie is here, her motivation is enhanced a hundredfold. He can help her master things in half an hour that it takes me days of pushing to even persuade her to try."

"You had to have known I would never permit it. You had no right to allow him here."

"Wrong. You gave me the right!"

He had seen her annoyed before but not angry. Now she was glaring at him and hot color climbed her cheekbones. He refused to notice how lovely she looked. "I didn't want to do any of this, remember?" she went on. "But you promised me I had full authority to do whatever necessary to help Taryn."

"Is that the reason you pushed so hard to get me to promise you that? Were you planning this from the very beginning?"

"Of course not," she said. "I never even talked to Charlie until a week after I started working with her."

"This isn't what I meant by full authority."

"Next time you should clarify, then. You give me full authority to try anything—except the one thing that seems to be working!"

He glared. How was he supposed to argue this point without sounding, again, like the world's biggest ass. "You should have told me."

"Yes. Absolutely. You had every right to know. I should have mentioned it the first time Charlie came to the house. I'll be completely honest with you, Brodie. Keeping it from you was sheer cowardice on my part. That is the one thing in all of this that I feel like I owe you an apology about. But I could see, even that first day, that Charlie was making all the difference in Taryn's motivation and I was afraid you wouldn't allow him to come anymore. I justified it by telling myself you would be more interested in outcomes than the methodology used to achieve those outcomes. It was wrong and I'm sorry."

Damn it. He didn't want her to go belly-up here. He just wanted the kid gone from his house.

"I can't even look at him without wanting to pound something."

"I know." With sympathy-drenched eyes, she rested her fingers on his arm in that physical way she had of communicating. The heat of her and the brush of skin against skin comforted him in ways he couldn't have explained, and he could feel some of his anger trickle away. How did she manage that so easily? She only had to touch him and his brain turned to pudding. He found it more than a little bewildering.

"I completely understand your anger toward him, Brodie, and I don't blame you for it. But like it or not, the day he came to the bead store, it was as if he flipped some kind of switch in Taryn. I can't argue with the results. You've said it yourself—look at how far she's come, especially this past week."

"Because of you and your hard work."

To his regret, she slid her fingers away as she shook her head. "I would love to take all the credit, but it's not me. Oh, I was making slow, steady progress but she fought me every step of the way. When Charlie is here, she works three times as hard. With Hannah, it's maybe twice as hard—Charlie seems to have the magic touch—but either of them can still cajole her into doing more than I can alone."

More than anything, he wanted to go back to those few moments before he'd walked into the house, when he had been in blissful ignorance that all this was going on behind his back. He didn't want to deal with it. If Evie was right and Charlie was helping Taryn, how could he bar the kid from his house?

Through the kitchen window, he could see them on the deck. Taryn was laughing at something Charlie said and she looked carefree and lighthearted. As she laughed, she must have drooled a little—something she didn't completely have under control yet—because Charlie picked up a cloth from the back of the chair and dabbed at the corner of her mouth in such a matter-of-fact way that he doubted Taryn even registered it.

His chest felt tight, fragile, as if a breeze might shatter something deep inside.

"What about Beaumont? Why is he doing this?" Brodie's voice sounded strangled and he cleared his throat, thinking of all the dreams he'd once had for his daughter and how that kid out there had destroyed them all in one night.

Evie didn't respond at first. She was silent for so long,

he finally had to shift his attention from the scene out the window to her.

"I don't know, if you want the truth," she finally answered. "I think he enjoys it, actually. At first I think he came out of guilt and…" She paused. "Okay, you won't like this either but Charlie has said something about his father encouraging the visits in the hopes it might reflect well on him during his judicial proceedings."

His anger, which had begun to cool, hit boiling point all over again. "That sleazy bastard. And you went along with this, knowing Mayor Beaumont would like Charlie to wriggle out of these charges with less than a slap on the wrist?"

"I was looking at what was best for Taryn. You can throw any motivation at me that you want but she remains my primary concern."

"If Charlie uses this to help him walk on the charges against him, I am going to hold you personally responsible."

"That's fair."

"*Fair?* Do you know how much I hate that word? Nothing has been *fair* in our world for four damn months! Including that the one person I trusted would go behind my back like this."

"So fire me. If you think what I've done is so outrageously egregious, I'll quit right now. You've only got a few more days before the new aide is supposed to start anyway. I'm sure you can hobble along without me."

He raked a hand through his hair. "How can I fire you? Look at her. She's a different person than she was two weeks ago."

"Then trust me, Brodie," she pleaded. "Trust me that I would never do anything to hurt Taryn. I'm trying to help her here. I knew you wouldn't like Charlie helping with therapy but I was willing to do it because it was working for Taryn. I thought that was worth the risk of you being angry."

He couldn't argue with that. Evie hadn't wanted to help them at all because of her past pain yet she'd spent more than two weeks here, day after endless day, exercising extreme patience and calm. All for Taryn. She hadn't acted maliciously by having the kid here. Brodie accepted that.

Right after the accident, those terrible, bleak days when doctors couldn't say whether she would even survive her extensive injuries, Brodie had vowed to God that if He would spare Taryn, he would do anything within his power to give her the best chance at a normal life. But damn it. This wasn't what he'd meant at all.

"I hate this."

"I know." She touched his arm again. Just as before, he could feel the tension and frustration inside him begin to ease as if she'd rubbed the tight muscles in his shoulders instead of merely brushing her fingers against the skin between wrist and elbow.

She hesitated for just a moment and then, before he quite realized what she intended, she followed up that soft caress with a tentative hug, her arms warm around his waist.

He froze, not sure what to do. He never had been much of a hugger, probably because his father had discouraged such obvious shows of affection. Not that his disapproval had stopped Katherine. He might have received stiff and hard disapproval from his father but Katherine had compensated with her steady love.

Evie's simple, unexpected embrace sent comfort and calm seeping through him. Though he found it as dangerous as it was enticing, he couldn't seem to stop himself from wrapping his arms around her and holding her close.

They stood that way for a long time, not speaking and

neither seeming eager to break this fragile, tensile connection between them.

She was the first to slide away and he thought he saw the shadow of something tender and soft in her gaze before she lowered her lashes and wrapped her fingers together. "If you absolutely can't bear the thought of Charlie being here, I'll go out there right now and tell him to leave and not come back. I can guarantee Taryn won't be happy about it, but this is your home and you're her father. You get the final say."

He was tempted. So tempted. Taryn would get over it. He was almost sure of it. The new therapist was starting the following week and maybe that would provide enough distraction that Taryn wouldn't even remember that Charlie wasn't here.

And maybe his mother would get a tattoo of a skull and crossbones on her forehead.

"He can keep coming but I don't want to see him. Make sure he's only here when I'm not."

Her smile was more breathtaking than the sunrise breaking over the mountains after weeks of gray muck. He had the grim realization that he would be willing to do just about anything if only she would smile at him like that.

"You're a good father, Brodie. Taryn is lucky to have you in her corner."

He wasn't so sure about that right now. Letting Charlie Beaumont even within a mile of her seemed like a huge mistake.

As big a mistake as allowing this dangerous tenderness for Evie Blanchard to filter through him even though he knew damn well it would never go anywhere.

Had she ever so monumentally misjudged a person? Though she knew she needed to return to Taryn and

Charlie on the deck, Evie paused for a moment to watch Brodie slide into his luxury SUV out front. She had always prided herself on her natural instincts when it came to figuring most people out, but she had been completely off the mark when it came to Brodie Thorne.

The man she had come to know these last few weeks was a vastly different creature from the cold, humorless man she'd believed him to be when she'd first arrived in Hope's Crossing. She had despised him from the very first, had wondered how Katherine—warm, generous, loving— could have produced a man so disagreeable.

The man she mistakenly had believed he was would never have backed down from this particular fight. He would have railed and blustered, demanding his way and threatening anything in his path.

Brodie had certainly been furious, as he had every right to be. He could easily have forbidden Charlie to continue coming to the house and sent Evie packing at the same time. As far as she knew, he was right. He might even have been able to bring in the authorities—though she seriously doubted Riley McKnight would have moved forward with trespassing charges against the kid when she had allowed him to continue coming.

Despite Brodie's anger at the deception, he hadn't forbidden Charlie from coming again. He had been willing to swallow his own wishes for the sake of what she considered best for Taryn, and Evie didn't know quite what to think about that.

Nor did she know why she had followed through on that insane impulse to give him a hug. She was still reeling from the sheer intimacy, the soft, gentle tenderness, of those few moments as he had wrapped his arms around her and held on tightly.

She sighed. Better not to think about it. She would be

leaving in a short time and her path probably wouldn't cross with either of the Thornes much after that.

When she walked back out to the deck, Charlie gazed at her, his eyes solemn. "I should go," he said.

"You don't have to," she assured him.

"I do, actually. I've got a meeting I can't miss with my attorneys."

Despite the remarkably graceful way Brodie had handled Charlie's presence, she could only be grateful he wasn't here to hear that particular announcement. She was quite certain Brodie wouldn't want to hear anything about Charlie's defense team.

"Thanks. You were a big help today."

"You're welcome." His voice sounded funny and she searched his features. He was looking at Taryn, not at Evie, and she saw guilt and regret in his eyes.

"I'll see you later, T."

"See...you." She lifted her hand and waved at him.

Jacques followed him to the side gate leading to the circular drive out front and waited there as if making sure the boy got on his way safely.

"My dad was mad."

"Yes." She slid into the chair where Charlie had been sitting. "He had reason to be. We should have told him Charlie has been coming to visit. I was too much of a coward. Why didn't you ever mention it to him?"

Taryn shrugged. "He doesn't like Charlie. He never did. Can he come back?"

"For now."

"Whew!"

Evie was compelled to be honest with the girl, as she should have been with her father from the beginning. "You need to prepare yourself that Charlie might not be able to come around much longer, Taryn. I know it's been fun to work with him but I can't promise it will continue. After I go back to work at the bead store next week, the new therapist might have different ideas, or your father might change his mind and decide he doesn't want Charlie around anymore."

"That's so dumb."

"It's not dumb for your father to be upset about what happened to you. He loves you. All parents feel responsible for making sure their children are safe. Your dad feels like he failed you—and he blames Charlie for that."

"I keep telling you, it wasn't… Charlie's fault."

They had already talked about this and Evie wasn't in the mood to travel this particular road again. She opted to divert attention away. "Hey, here's an idea. Since it's your grandmother's birthday, why don't we go clean up and drive into town to surprise her for lunch?"

"To String Fever?"

"We'll stop there and see where Katherine wants to have lunch. How does that sound?"

"Okay, I guess."

To Evie's relief, Taryn allowed her attention to be side-tracked. Evie couldn't understand this dogged insistence that none of them blame Charlie for what had happened. Taryn had a definite blind spot when it came to the boy.

She wanted to warn the girl to be careful and guard her heart well but for some reason she didn't care to identify yet, the advice seemed hypocritical coming from her. Instead, she helped Taryn find the gift she'd carefully made for her grandmother and wrapped during her last session with the occupational therapist, then ushered her out the door.

Taryn was quiet throughout the complicated process of Evie helping her into the accessible bathroom before they left, washing her face and hands, fixing her hair and makeup.

The home-health aides were only coming twice daily now, once in the morning to help her shower and dress for the day and again in the evening to deliver meds and help her to bed. Now that she could transfer herself from her wheelchair to the commode and to other chairs around the house, Taryn was almost to the point where she was able to handle most of her needs by herself, which was huge progress in only the few months since she'd been in a coma.

Finally they were on their way. Their route took them past the high school and, as they went by, Evie glanced in the rearview mirror and found Taryn gazing out the window, her mouth tight and her eyes upset.

She had lost so much. They were all so focused on the big picture, on Taryn regaining her skills, they sometimes forgot all the little things she'd lost, like back-to-school excitement in the fall, football games on crisp autumn evenings, bonfires in the canyon with friends as fall began to brush vibrant color on the leaves.

Hope's Crossing High School planned to send a series of tutors to help Taryn try to catch up from what she'd missed the previous year. Perhaps Evie ought to talk to Brodie about the possibility of Taryn attending an hour or two of regular school, just for the interaction with her peers.

Evie could certainly do that but in another few days, none of this would be her concern. Her replacement would be starting the day after Labor Day, less than a week away, and Evie would be out of their lives not long after that.

The thought should have cheered her. She wanted things to return to normal, wanted to be able to put this brief return to her therapy roots to rest once and for all. She thought about no longer making that drive in the morning up the hill toward Aspen Ridge and Brodie's house,

no longer having Taryn greet her every day with a mock
groan and her regular "You're here again?" refrain, no
more of Mrs. O.'s delicious food and her occasional dour
but amusing company.

Evie should have been anticipating the idea of her life
returning to normal. But all she could see right now was
how empty her days would seem.

Oh, this was not right. She *loved* working at String
Fever. Interacting with customers, talking to Claire, taking the chaos of a hundred disparate beads and jumbling
them together to create beauty and order.

But she also loved this, helping Taryn. Every day posed
a new challenge, another surprise, and she would miss it
terribly. She might tell herself she needed to distance herself from her chosen career as a physical therapist but some
part of her still found immense satisfaction in it.

She was still mulling the shock of that realization as
she circled the block, trying to find a parking space near
the bead store with enough room on the right to allow
her to lower the wheelchair ramp. A handicapped parking
spot finally opened up behind the store on her second trip
around the block and Evie grabbed it.

"Grandma will be surprised," Taryn said when Evie
turned off the van.

She managed a smile at the girl, despite the tumult of
her emotions. Taryn's returning verbal skills far outpaced
her physical abilities. If nothing else, Evie was deeply
grateful for that. The ability to communicate wants and
needs could take a person much farther in life than being
able to toss a ball to a dog.

"She might already have made lunch plans, or be
too busy to get away from the store this afternoon," she
warned. "We probably should have called her."

"What's the fun…of that?" Taryn's still-lopsided smile was bright and a little mischievous.

Evie had to sigh. Who was she kidding? She was already crazy about Taryn.

They let Jacques into the back gate and found Chester already there as if he'd known they were coming. He waddled to her bigger dog and sniffed him with that enthusiastic way dogs acted, as if they were being reunited after months apart.

"Smells pretty back here," Taryn said.

"That's the lavender and the phlox and the lemon balm."

"Do you…take care of the flowers?"

"I water and weed and plant a few here and there. Your grandma started the garden when she owned the store, then Claire added to it."

"It's nice here."

"I love coming out in the morning and watching the sun come up. You should smell the flowers then," Evie said. "You ought to plant a garden next spring. I'm sure your dad would let you take over a patch of ground at your house."

In her experience, gardening could be fabulous therapy, both mental and physical. Maybe she would talk to Brodie about letting Taryn use the warm, south-facing window in her room for an indoor container garden. She could see tarragon and rosemary, perhaps a tomato plant or two.

She caught herself. In a few days, Taryn's therapy would be none of her business. She needed to get that straight in her head once and for all. The new therapist would be making those sorts of decisions and that was just the way she wanted it, right?

They enjoyed the peaceful garden for a few moments more, then Evie pushed the wheelchair toward the door. Inside, they found Katherine and Claire both seated at the worktable while a customer browsed through the chain selection.

Katherine looked delighted. "Hello, you two! What a lovely surprise," she exclaimed.

"Hi, Grandma. Happy birthday."

"Why, thank you! It's been a lovely day so far."

"Can you...have lunch?" Taryn asked.

Regret flashed in Katherine's eyes and she opened her mouth to answer but Claire cut her off. "Of course she can."

"But you were planning to leave early," Katherine protested.

"Don't worry about that for a minute. I've got plenty of time. The kids are with Jeff and Holly, busy cooing over their new baby sister, who is adorable, I have to admit."

Again, Evie wanted to roll her eyes at her friend. She knew very few women who would be enthusiastic about their ex-husband's new child with another woman. But that was Claire.

"Riley has to run to Denver to track down some information on a case he's working and I'm driving in with him to do some wedding shopping, but we're not leaving until later. I've got all the time in the world. It's your birthday and I can't think of a better way for you to celebrate than lunch with Taryn."

"Good," Taryn said happily.

"Shall we go to the café?" Katherine asked.

Evie hesitated. Taryn still grew nervous when people watched her eat, as it could be an awkward, messy process. She'd been thinking more along the lines of grabbing something and coming back to the store to eat in the garden or grabbing a picnic table over at Miners' Park, but she decided to leave it up to Katherine's granddaughter.

"Taryn?"

The teen briefly looked indecisive, but finally nodded. "Okay."

"Give me a minute to touch up my lipstick and grab my purse," Katherine said.

After she walked to the back room, Taryn indicated she wanted to look at a new bead magazine that had just come in. While she was leafing through it, Evie pulled Claire aside to talk about the outdoor arts-and-crafts festival she was attending over the weekend and the local beaders who had left projects on consignment for the show.

"Everybody has really appreciated your hard work this summer. It's not easy going by yourself to these shows. Setting up, sitting there the whole time, dealing with all the looky-loos."

"I've enjoyed it," Evie answered truthfully.

"How is everything going with Taryn?" Claire asked after checking to be sure the girl was busy with the magazine and not paying them any attention.

"Wrong question to ask me this afternoon," she said.

"What's happening?"

She sighed. "I screwed up. You remember that day Charlie came to the store and helped Taryn make a bracelet?"

Claire huffed. "How could I not remember it? I had to take about four ibuprofen and half a bottle of Tums that afternoon."

"I'm sorry," Evie said with a quick hug, guilty again that she'd put her friend through that ordeal. "The thing is, Taryn really thrived during that visit so, um, Charlie's been coming to the house to help with her therapy several times a week. I decided not to tell Brodie about it—yes, I was too chicken—but he unexpectedly came home for something this morning and found him there."

"Uh-oh. Busted." Claire looked sympathetic and horrified at the same time.

She sighed glumly. "Yeah, it wasn't the smartest thing I've ever done. But Taryn loved having him there and she worked so hard whenever Charlie helped out. I figured Brodie, of all people, would agree that the ends justified the means, you know?"

"Is he still talking to you?"

She thought of the sweetness of that spontaneous embrace in the kitchen, how after that first awkward moment of surprise, he had wrapped his arms around her and held on tightly for a long time.

"He said Charlie can continue to come as long as we schedule his visits for times when Brodie isn't home. For all I know, this might be a moot point anyway. Tuesday is my last day with Taryn and it will be up to the new therapist to decide if peers ought to be incorporated in her treatment plan. I'll do my best to encourage it and explain how helpful they have been with Taryn but it will really be up to her."

"Evie, if you need more time, you know you've got it."

"More time for what?" Katherine asked, emerging from the back room looking as elegant as ever. Evie hoped she could age half as well as Brodie's mother.

"More time to figure out how you possibly can be celebrating another birthday yet look younger and more beautiful every day," she said promptly.

Katherine rolled her eyes, but before she could respond the chimes on the door sang softly and a couple walked into the store.

Evie almost laughed as all three of them gave a low, collective groan, just as if they'd practiced it.

"Good afternoon, Genevieve," Claire greeted the female half of the couple. Tall and slender with artfully streaked blond hair and always-perfect makeup, Charlie's older sister smiled vaguely at all of them.

The Beaumonts were among the wealthiest year-round residents in Hope's Crossing and Genevieve had no problem flaunting her family's affluence.

For the last nine months, she'd been Bridezilla on steroids—bossy, self-absorbed and unreasonably demanding. Claire, unfortunately for her, had been sucked into the gravitational pull of the Beaumont/Danforth wedding when she'd agreed to design custom beadwork on the bodice of Gen's wedding dress.

This was actually her second time around doing the work, as Gen's first dress had been cut to shreds during the robbery of String Fever that had preceded the violent car accident four months earlier.

Despite everything, Evie actually liked Genevieve. She had picked up the impression more than once that the young woman was more than a little nervous about her upcoming wedding and she found that rather endearing despite all of Genevieve's sometimes unreasonable demands.

Those nerves were nowhere in evidence now as Gen swept into String Fever, towing along an extraordinarily striking young man in his late twenties with dark curly hair and laughing blue eyes.

"I know you told me the dress wouldn't be ready for a few more weeks, but Sawyer is in town for a few days and I would *love* for him to see it."

"That's bad luck," Taryn said, enunciating more clearly than she had all day.

Genevieve twisted around to look at the magazine corner where Taryn was seated in her wheelchair. When she recognized the girl, Gen's gaze flicked between Taryn and her fiancé uneasily.

It wasn't tough for Evie to interpret the look. To Genevieve, Taryn must appear a blatant reminder of the scandal she would likely prefer to forget. Gen's fiancé, Sawyer

Danforth, was the son of a powerful Colorado politician who was reputedly grooming his son to follow in his footsteps.

Rumors around town had it that Gen was worried the Danforths no longer considered her good enough for their precious son, now that Gen's younger brother was facing serious charges in the robberies and the death of Layla Parker in the car accident.

"I don't believe in those silly superstitions," Gen said after an awkward pause. "Neither does Sawyer. Do you, darling?"

Her fiancé held up his hands. "Don't drag me into this. You're the one who wants me to see the dress. I told you I think you'd be perfectly lovely if we got married with you wearing what you have on right now."

Since Genevieve was wearing a plain pearl-colored short-sleeve sweater set and a skirt that made her look rather like June Cleaver, Evie found Sawyer's sentiment quite sweet.

"Oh, stop." Genevieve tapped him playfully on the arm. "You're such a dork sometimes. You really need to see my dress. It's absolutely stunning. A bit like Kate Middleton's but with more sparkle."

"I'm afraid I don't have it here," Claire said with that endlessly patient smile. Evie didn't quite know how she pulled it off after all these months of dealing with Genevieve. By now, Evie would have wanted to shove a couple of healthy-sized *tagua*-nut beads in her ears to block out the nagging.

"After what happened to the last one, I've been keeping your wedding gown at home under lock and key."

Taryn made a funny sound, like a little moan. She shifted in the chair and Evie wondered if she'd had a muscle spasm or something.

"Your house isn't very far from here, right?" Gen said, a persuasive note to her voice. "We would be happy to wait here while you go get it."

Sawyer shook his head, his cheerful blue eyes suddenly rueful. Poor guy. Until Gen mellowed out a little and learned not to take life—and what she wanted out of it—so seriously, she was going to lead him on quite a wild ride.

"I'm afraid I can't leave the store right now," Claire said in that endlessly calm voice. "Evie and Taryn are here to take Katherine to a special birthday lunch."

"Happy birthday," Sawyer said, beaming at the older woman.

Evie, Katherine and Claire all gazed at that spectacular smile, hypnotized. Eventually Claire shook her head a little as if to clear it. "Yes, well, I need to stay here to help my customers and then I'm leaving town for a couple of days."

"But Sawyer is only going to be in town until Saturday!"

"No worries." Sawyer gave them all that charming smile again and even Katherine seemed to go all gooey. With that smile and those good looks, he only needed half a brain—if that—to be a very popular politician, Evie suspected.

"I'll be back in a few weeks," he went on. "By then maybe the dress will be done and I'll have the chance to see the finished product."

"But it's *almost* done now," Genevieve insisted. If she had her way, Evie imagined she would insist Claire close the store for an hour simply to run home on Gen's whim.

"I don't mind waiting to see it. Thank you, anyway," he said. He smiled at all of them and even winked at Taryn, which rather endeared him to Evie. "Come on, darling. We've got lunch reservations at Le Passe Montagne."

"That's one of my son's restaurants," Katherine said.

"Make sure you leave room for their crème brûlée. It's divine."

"Thanks for the tip. I'll be sure to do that." He gave them all another of those killer smiles, tucked Gen's arm into the crook of his elbow and led her out of the store.

"Wow." Katherine blinked. "Okay, I finally get why Genevieve is a little anxious to make it official."

"He's cute," Taryn said.

"Maybe we should go to Le Passe instead so we can all gawk at him over our crème brûlée," Evie said.

Katherine laughed. "I'm perfectly content with the café. All that sugar hurts your teeth after a while. And the crème brûlée's not that great for you either."

Evie and Claire both laughed, though Taryn still looked confused.

"Thanks again, Claire," Katherine said. "Would you like us to bring something back for you?"

"You know I love their chicken salad sandwiches. That would be just the thing today."

"I'll have Dermot wrap one up for you," Katherine said. "Shall we?"

People were staring.

The café in town used to be her favorite place in town to eat, except Le Passe and the steakhouse her father owned up at the resort. The food was good and cheap at the café and her friends liked to come here together and hang.

Now everything was different.

Taryn slumped in the wheelchair, her chin on her chest. She wanted to go home, where people weren't looking at her as if they were waiting for her to dribble food down her chin or something.

She should have tried to walk in, but since she looked

like Bride of Frankenstein when she walked, they would only stare more.

They hadn't even gone to a table yet. The café was busy and the sign said Wait to Be Seated, which meant everybody could stare and stare.

She wanted to go home, but she couldn't. It was her grandma's birthday. She could take the stares for her grandmother.

"Look at this! Three of my favorite girls!" Mr. Caine, owner of the café, beamed at them. Mr. Caine was nice. He had white hair and blue eyes and smiled as much as her grandma did. "How did I ever get so lucky to have you all here at once?"

"It's Katherine's birthday and we're celebrating with her," Evie said.

"Wonderful!" Mr. Caine grabbed her grandma's hands, which looked tiny and white in his bigger ones. Grandma turned a little pink. "I just took out a fresh blackberry pie. I'll save three slices all around for you. My gift to the birthday girl. What do you say?"

"Sounds perfect," Evie said. "Dermot, it looks like the back section is closed. Any chance you could make an exception and seat us back there, away from the crowd a little?"

Evie was asking because of her, Taryn thought. She should be embarrassed but she was happy when Mr. Caine beamed at them, cheery and nice. "Of course. Of course! That's our special reserved birthday section, just for my three favorite ladies. Come right this way."

Grandma led the way and Evie pushed Taryn behind them. The other area was around a corner from the rest of the café and Taryn relaxed a little. It was quiet here and cool. Best of all, no one else was around to stare.

"This is perfect," Evie said. "Thank you, Mr. Caine."

Mr. Caine handed them a menu. "I'll tell you a little secret. The turkey wraps are especially good today. I added a secret ingredient." He winked at Taryn. "Lemon dill from my own garden. But whatever you pick, I'll make it perfect for you."

Before he left, he picked up Grandma's hand. "And a very happy birthday to you, Katherine m'dear," he said, his voice more Irish than usual. Taryn's eyes widened when he kissed the back of her grandmother's hand.

Evie raised her eyebrows after he walked away. "I had no idea Dermot could be so…charming."

"Oh, hush," Grandma said, but she looked pink and Taryn saw her looking at where Mr. Caine had gone. Grandma and Mr. Caine? Too weird. Almost as weird as when she'd looked in the kitchen window that morning and seen her dad hugging Evie.

She still didn't know what to think about that. She liked Evie—most of the time, anyway. But her dad hadn't dated anybody since, well, since she could remember. Maybe they weren't really dating. Maybe they were just friends. She hugged her friends. Or she used to, anyway.

"Oh, look." Evie's voice was excited. "Maura and Sage."

Through the window, Taryn saw them walk into the diner, and her stomach started to hurt.

Her grandmother's eyes lit up. "Ask them to join us! We can make room."

Fear and guilt were twisting snakes inside her. She didn't want them to sit here. Layla's mother and sister. She couldn't look at them.

They must hate her. Layla was dead and it was her fault. Layla hadn't even wanted to go that night but Taryn had talked her into it.

And then the rest.

Everything was because of her.

She shifted in her chair, wishing so much she could get up and run out of the café without falling over.

"Are you all right?" Evie asked quietly.

"Tired," she said, a lie.

"Do you want to go home?" Evie asked, her eyes concerned.

If she moaned enough, Evie would take her back to the house. She could, but it wasn't really fair. They were here for Grandma's birthday. She couldn't be a big baby and ruin everything.

"No. Not yet."

"Okay. You just let me know if you're worn out."

Mostly she was tired in her head. It hurt to think sometimes. She was getting better. Every day, her mind seemed less cloudy and confused. Some of it was taking less medicine, she knew. Some was her healing. She worked hard when Charlie was there but maybe she should stop trying.

She didn't deserve to get better. Not when Layla was dead because of her.

"So who's watching the bookstore so you could escape for lunch together?" Evie asked as, to her surprise and delight, Maura McKnight-Parker and her daughter Sage pulled a couple of chairs over from a nearby table and squeezed in around their table.

She had been sure Maura would refuse to join them, especially after she saw Taryn there, but after a moment she seemed to collect herself and accepted the invitation. Still, Evie knew it couldn't be easy for her. Where Genevieve might see the girl as a potential embarrassment, to Maura, Evie guessed that Taryn's presence—her very survival—would be a stark reminder of all she had lost.

Great waves of pain seemed to radiate off Maura, and Evie wanted to reach across the table and squeeze her fingers, to whisper that she understood but she hadn't told any of her friends about Cassie. When she had first come to Hope's Crossing, the pain had seemed too raw to talk about with anyone else. Katherine knew and that had seemed enough. Later, the moment never seemed right. It wasn't something she could just blurt out in conversation. *Oh, by the way, I adopted a daughter with disabilities and loved her for two years before she died. So silly I never mentioned it before.*

So why, when she had held Cassie's memory so close to her, had she told Brodie? She didn't quite know the answer to that herself.

"Ruth is working for us this afternoon," Sage answered when Maura didn't respond. Maura's older daughter smiled, looking almost fey with her curly brown hair and the big, long-lashed green eyes that marked her as a McKnight. "She's been such a lifesaver this summer."

"Who ever would have guessed it?" Katherine murmured. "I think it's wonderful Ruth enjoys working at the bookstore so much."

Ruth Tatum was Claire's mother, a difficult woman who, until a few months ago, had seemed discontent with life, complaining and finding fault and basically doing her best to infect everyone around her with her own unhappiness.

That snowy April night had changed many lives in unexpected ways, Evie thought. Ruth had stepped in to help a grieving and lost Maura at Dog-Eared Books & Brew—and apparently was thriving there.

"She seems like a different person when she comes into the bead store these days," Evie said. She found it endlessly fascinating to watch people remake their lives, adapting and adjusting to new circumstances. Ruth was the perfect example.

"She hasn't changed completely." Maura's smile didn't quite reach her eyes but at least it wasn't despair. "This morning I heard her answer a customer's question by saying that since Ruth had never met his mother, she had no idea whatsoever whether she would like the thirty-dollar coffee-table book he was considering buying. I had to pull her aside and gently remind her that when a customer asked whether his mother/sister/wife would like a book, the answer was always yes."

Katherine, Sage and Evie laughed. Maura smiled that not-quite smile again, but Taryn still seemed upset and distracted.

"So when does school start, my dear?" Katherine asked Sage.

The girl gave her mother a quick look. "I'm thinking about taking another semester off."

"No, you're not," Maura said. The determined glint in her eyes crowded out the pain there for a moment. "We've talked about this. You're going back to school."

"I plan to." Sage looked just as determined. "But I think it would be better if I stick around this semester and start up again in January."

"And do what? Make lattes? I can hire people to do that. You need to go back to school."

"I will, when things are more settled here."

"Things here are fine," Maura retorted. Evie had the impression this wasn't the first time these two had had this particular argument. "Between Ruth and me, we've got Dog-Eared covered. Your place is at school."

"Wrong. If you need me here, that comes first, Mom."

"Let's take a vote," Maura said to the table at large. "All in favor of Sage going back to school, raise your hand. Taryn, you too."

Taryn raised her hand, unsmiling. Katherine lifted hers

way up and Evie did, too, though she was sympathetic to both points of view. She had been the grieving mother and she had been the dutiful daughter, wanting to take care of her mother after her sister died.

She had taken one semester off from school right after the fire and then the next after her sister died from her injuries. By the time fall semester was to start, her mother had convinced her she should return—and two weeks into the new semester, while Evie was just beginning to try to get back into the routine of her studies, her mother had overdosed on pain pills.

She knew she had done the right thing, returning to school. Her mother had insisted, much as Maura was insisting now. But Evie would always wonder what might have happened if she had taken another semester off.

If she had been home, would her mother have been so very despondent and in such grave physical and emotional pain that she would see no other choice than to take such drastic, irrevocable actions?

The circumstances were not the same, of course. Maura was surrounded by a warm, supportive family. The McKnights had rallied around her after Layla's death and they would continue to do so as long as she needed them. Mary Ella, her mother. Sisters Angie and Alex. After years of working as an undercover police officer in Northern California, even Riley lived back in Hope's Crossing and would be settling here with Claire.

"You need to go back to school," Maura insisted. "You can't afford to get off track with your undergraduate work if you want to get into architectural school."

Sage looked as if she wanted to argue the point further but she was interrupted by the server, a young man with blond dreadlocks who looked like he should be catching waves instead of slinging hash—and whom Evie was almost positive she'd seen working at the ski resort over the winter.

"Hey, ladies. I'm Logan and I'll be your server this afternoon. Sorry for the delay. Afraid we had a bit of a mix-up in station assignments. I've been given strict instructions to take good care of you all or Dermot will have my hide—and I really need my hide, you know? Want to order drinks first or have you had enough time to look at the menu?"

Evie hadn't even looked at the menu but since the turkey wrap was one of her favorites anyway, she decided to go with Dermot's suggestion. Katherine and Maura did the same, while Sage ordered the veggie burger.

"Taryn?" Evie asked. "What about you?"

"Fries," she said. "And...a cheese sandwich."

After they'd placed their beverage orders, the apologetic surfer-dude waiter hurried away. Katherine, ever the diplomat, quickly spoke up to change the subject before Maura and Sage could begin arguing about college again.

"The Angel has been hard at work again. Have you heard?"

"No. What's happened?" Evie asked.

"You know how Gretchen Kirk has been struggling since her jerk of a husband took off with that waitress from Breckenridge? Well, apparently she woke up one day this week to find boxes and boxes of brand-new school supplies from the Angel for her three boys and Hannah. Clothes, shoes, backpacks, notebooks. The whole thing. And when she went to take care of their school fees, they were already paid."

"What a great idea," Claire exclaimed. "I wish I'd thought of that."

Evie looked at Taryn and found her frowning. Hannah hadn't said anything about it during her visits, but then she didn't talk much about how things were at home, now that her father was gone.

"What's the latest rumor about the Angel's identity?" Evie asked. Between the art shows she'd been attending all summer and the last few weeks working with Taryn in virtual isolation, she felt completely out of the loop about the goings-on in town. "Is Claire still determined it's a quorum of angels rather than a solitary individual?"

"Oh, the speculation runs rampant, depending on the source," Katherine said. "I even heard one rumor that the Angel is a movie star who moved into a house up in Silver Strike Canyon."

"I got something from the Angel." Taryn had been sitting so quietly, apparently just listening to the conversation, that her unexpected contribution to the conversation seemed to take them all by surprise. Sage smiled at her but Maura looked down at her water glass, her features tight.

"What did the Angel give you?" Sage asked.

"A game system for exercising. We have…f-fun on it."

Evie gave an inward cringe, hoping the girl didn't mention that her favorite opponent was Charlie Beaumont. She didn't want to hurt Maura by bringing up what was bound to be a touchy subject, considering Charlie had been responsible for her daughter's death. To her guilty relief, Taryn subsided into silence once more and the conversation eddied around her.

The service was quick, even for the Center of Hope Café. Logan brought their meals out barely a few moments after he'd taken the order back to the grill, complete with a few garnishes Evie was sure were specially added for their table.

"Remind me to bring you here for lunch more often, if this is the kind of treatment we can expect," she teased Katherine and was amused when the older woman seemed to grow flustered. Dermot Caine had been a widower for years, just as Katherine had been a widow. Interesting that they'd never dated. Maybe they simply needed a push....

That pleasant speculation was interrupted by another person coming into their section as if he owned the place—one of Evie's least favorite people in town, Harry Lange.

"Oh. That man," Katherine exclaimed when Harry plopped down into a booth at the other end of the otherwise empty section and immediately opened a newspaper. "He thinks he owns the whole blasted town."

"It's a good thing Mary Ella's not here," Evie said. "She'd probably go dump her water glass on his head." Mary Ella, Maura's mother, had a longstanding feud of unknown origin with Harry Lange.

Lange was about the only person who had more money than the Beaumonts. Evie knew he had sold the land up in Silver Strike Canyon that had eventually been turned into the ski resort and had been on the ground floor of the project. Maybe because he was richer than anyone else, he seemed to think that gave him the right to treat people in town like dirt. He was abrasive and annoying and raised her hackles every time she was forced to interact with him, which—blessedly—was rarely.

The man seemed to bring a big rain cloud with him. Katherine glowered a few times at Harry, Sage seemed to be studying him with interest, while Maura spent the rest of lunch moving her plate around and deliberately *not* looking at him.

The only time the mood lightened was when Dermot Caine himself delivered slices of his delicious blackberry pie. Nobody could stay in a bad mood while eating Dermot's pie, with its flaky, buttery golden crust and the juicy, lemony berry filling.

"I guess we'd better get back before Ruth alienates all

our customers," Maura said when they were finished, still not looking at Harry, tucked behind his newspaper. "Happy birthday, Kat. Thanks for letting us share it. Evie, thank *you* for offering to buy lunch. I owe you next time."

"My pleasure. I'm thrilled you could join us." Evie smiled and stood up to hug her friend, vowing she would still find a moment to have a private visit. Maura turned and pressed her cheek to Katherine's for a moment and Sage did the same, then the two of them left the diner.

"I should go as well," Katherine said with regret, picking up the boxed meal they had ordered for Claire. "Claire's been alone too long at the store and she really does need to go home and pack. Thank you so much for inviting me. You've made my birthday a lovely one."

"It was all Taryn's idea," Evie insisted, winking at the girl.

Katherine squeezed her granddaughter's hand. "That makes it even more lovely."

They walked together back down Main Street toward String Fever since Brodie's minivan was parked behind the store.

Evie already thought the summer crowds were beginning to thin. Traffic seemed more manageable and the crowds on the sidewalk a little more sparse. This weekend was Labor Day and after that, Hope's Crossing would enjoy about two months of quiet before the winter ski crowds descended. Though she'd only been in town a year, Evie had learned she loved the shoulder seasons, when the year-round residents had the town to themselves, for the most part.

After saying goodbye to Katherine, Evie quickly helped Taryn into the van and began the short drive up the hill toward Brodie's house. Taryn didn't say much as they drove, she merely continued gazing out the window of the van.

Had lunch pushed her too much? She had seemed fine at the bead store but when they'd gone to the café, she had grown withdrawn and had barely spoken.

Evie tried a few more times to make conversation but Taryn didn't seem to want to talk. At the house, Evie pushed the wheelchair out of the van, trying her best to remain cheerful in the face of this brick wall. "Talking about the game system at lunch today reminded me we haven't played tennis for a while. Feel like a game?"

"I'm too tired," Taryn said, the words clipped.

"Okay." Evie worked to keep her tone agreeable. "I don't blame you. It's been a big day already and you've worked very hard. Why don't you rest for a while and we'll see how you feel a little later?"

"I don't want to play. You should go home."

Evie blinked. This was more like the Taryn of a few weeks ago. "Not yet. I still have plenty to do, writing out my treatment notes and making sure everything will be organized next week for Stephanie."

"Just go home," Taryn said. "I don't want to work more today."

"Are you sure?" She frowned. "I've only got a partial day tomorrow, remember?"

"Yes, I remember. I'm not…retarded!"

Evie straightened. "I know you're not. Which means you should remember I don't like that particular word."

"I…don't care…what you like."

Taryn's features suddenly seemed florid, unhealthy. Perhaps Evie had pushed her too hard today. A quiet afternoon wasn't necessarily a bad idea, she decided.

"I guess it's good you're only stuck with me for a few more days then, isn't it?"

"Yes!"

Taryn struggled to wheel herself through her doorway

and then she slammed the door behind her. If she hadn't glimpsed the misery in the girl's eyes or felt such sympathy for her that she couldn't stomp off in the middle of an argument like a normal teenage girl, Evie might have been upset and angry herself.

As things stood, it took a tremendous degree of effort not to follow after the girl, wrap her in her arms and whisper that everything would work out. Soon she would be herself again and this time of struggle would just be a bad dream.

To her deep regret, that was a promise she couldn't make.

Ten

Taryn's mood was even more prickly the next day. She refused to cooperate with any of the therapy activities, rolling her eyes or looking away or slumping in her chair when Evie tried to help her stand.

By early afternoon, Evie's nerves were frayed and she was praying hard for patience to endure another hour, when she would be leaving early to set up for the arts festival in Crested Butte.

"Why isn't Charlie here?" Taryn demanded as they worked with five-pound free weights to tone her weak muscles.

Evie frowned, wondering if Taryn's medications might be affecting her short-term memory or if perhaps she might be having miniseizures. They'd talked about Charlie twice already that morning. She was positive of it.

Maybe Taryn was selectively ignoring her...or maybe Evie was the one having short-term memory problems.

"He has a court appearance tomorrow, remember? He told us he wouldn't be able to come today because he would be meeting with his attorneys."

"He should be here."

"I'm sure he would agree. Even with your bad mood,

I imagine he would much rather be here than sitting with a bunch of lawyers."

"I'm not…in a bad mood." Taryn glared. "Therapy is just…boring and stupid. So are you."

She sounded as petulant as a four-year-old in need of a nap and Evie had to choke down the urge to tell her so. "Harsh," she said instead, mustering a calm smile. "And all this time I thought we were having so much fun today. That's it. Now give me three more biceps curls."

"None of this is fun. I *hate* it!" With more strength and energy than she'd shown all day, Taryn threw the free weight as hard as she could muster. Evie didn't have a chance for evasive action. The weight hit the side of her face and glanced off, landing on her shoulder before toppling to the floor.

Pain rocketed through her and she staggered backward a step or two, strangely aware as she tried to see past her graying vision that Jacques had moved protectively in front of her, even though he adored Taryn.

"Whoa!"

She heard Brodie's exclamation from the doorway but couldn't seem to make her neck muscles cooperate so she could turn toward him.

"Tell me that was an accident," he growled, moving into her field of vision, which was still hazy from the pain.

"Therapy is stupid and boring." Taryn jutted out her jaw. "I'm so…sick of it."

Evie managed to catch her breath as the pain dulled from that first rip-out-your-guts intensity to a steady *owwww*. She wasn't sure which hurt worse, her face or her shoulder. She was in for some very lovely bruises, no doubt.

She didn't worry too much about the shoulder but she was facing four days of interacting with customers at the art show in Crested Butte, and she really didn't want to show up in the String Fever booth at the festival looking as if she had just lost the battle for the women's feather-weight world title.

When she pressed a hand to her face, her fingers came away covered in blood. Though it wasn't sharp, the im-pact of the weight striking must have torn the skin on her cheekbone. She would be lucky to emerge without a bro-ken bone or two.

She had never seen Brodie so angry. His features were tight, tense, and his eyes glittered with heat. "I don't care how boring you might find it," he snapped at his daughter. "That doesn't give you any right to be hurtful to someone who's only trying to help you."

"She's mean. She makes me...work too hard. I hate her!"

The words stung even more than her physical pain. While she accepted that she could never be best friends with her clients by the very nature of their relationship, she thought things had been better between her and Taryn. Barring the last few days, anyway.

"A month ago, you couldn't stand up or put an entire sentence together," Brodie said. "Look at you now. You can thank Evie for that."

Taryn's jaw firmed with stubbornness to match her fa-ther's. "Not Evie. I'm doing...all the work."

Evie could see Brodie readying an argument and she stepped forward to head him off. "You *have* been work-ing very hard, Taryn. That's not what your dad is saying. I think we're both tired and out of sorts and in need of a break. I'll be leaving early today and then you'll have the long weekend to work a reduced therapy schedule with the home-health staff, and then Tuesday after Labor Day, Stephanie will be taking over."

"I hope she's not...a bitch, too."

"Knock it off. Right now." Brodie glowered at his daughter. "You love Evie. You told me so the other night."

"It's okay," Evie said, her voice low. She wouldn't let either of them see how the words hurt.

"No, it's not." He turned back to his daughter. "You've had a rough break, Taryn. We all know that, just like we know what a hard road you've had to walk to find your way back to where you are now. But just because you've had crap happen to you, that doesn't give you the right to take your frustration and pain out on someone else, especially someone who's only trying to help you. Apologize right now, both for throwing a temper tantrum that hurt Evie and for being rude."

She glared right back at him. "Or what? I'll have to stay here…with no friends and…do therapy all day?"

For a moment, Brodie looked as if he didn't quite know how to respond but then he frowned. "If you hate therapy so much, fine. We can stop it altogether. You want to stay where you are right now? Let's do it. Evie, don't worry about coming back next week. I'll call Stephanie and tell her to forget the whole thing. We don't need her anymore. Taryn thinks she's done with therapy. She's progressed as far as she wants to go."

Taryn looked down at her hands. "That's…not what I want."

"Then what?"

"I don't know." Her voice was small, her words more slurred and soft-edged than they'd been in a while. All the fight seemed to squeeze out of her and she slumped in her chair. "I don't hate therapy. Or Evie."

Though her face was throbbing and blood was probably dripping all over her favorite blue T-shirt, Evie stepped forward and ran her hand down Taryn's hair. "I know, honey. I know."

Taryn sniffled and turned her face into Evie's hand. Startled, Evie's gaze met Brodie's and she found him watching the two of them, his gaze arrested.

She drew a shaky breath, with an odd sense of monumental, profound shaking and settling inside her. She had seen grainy old photographs once of a dam break years ago, not far from here, and that was how she felt right now, as if every emotion she had been trying to hold back had found first one tiny break in the wall to leak through, and then another and another until she was now awash with emotions, tenderness not only for this girl who had endured far too much but for Brodie, strong and protective and concerned for his child above all else.

"I'm sorry. I'm...a brat."

"Yeah. Sometimes." She managed a smile to take the sting from her words. "I'm afraid I can be a bit of a drill sergeant. I like to see you making progress and sometimes I forget how hard-fought that progress can be."

"I shouldn't have...thrown the weight. You're still bleeding."

She could feel the hot drops sliding down her skin. Suddenly all she wanted was to escape to where she could clean up and come to terms with these emotions she didn't want.

"Don't worry. I'll be okay. I had planned to leave in an hour anyway. I'll just head out a little earlier and take care of it at home."

Brodie turned that stern, serious face on her. "Forget it. I'm not about to let you drive home with blood streaming down your face."

"Hardly streaming, I'm sure."

"Trickling, then. Either way, we need to clean it up."

She wanted to argue but she had the feeling this was one of those times when Brodie wouldn't be budged. Since she wasn't sure she had the emotional reserves to fight with him right now, she decided a wise woman would simply give in to the inevitable and let him have his way.

What was that all about?

Brodie tugged a reluctant Evie into the half bathroom off the entryway, where he kept most of the medical supplies that weren't directly associated with Taryn's care. He probably could have found everything he needed in Taryn's suite of rooms but he was grateful to have a moment to talk privately with Evie.

"Sit down. We'll get you cleaned up and check the damages."

"Really, Brodie. I can take care of this. I don't need a nurse."

"My house, my responsibility. Sit."

After a moment's hesitation, she complied and perched on the edge of the padded bench, though she looked as if she wished to be anywhere else in the world. He washed his hands before opening the cabinet for the gentle antiseptic wipes that, once upon a time, he had used to clean up Taryn's scraped knees and elbows bunged up from falling off her bike or taking a header off the swing set.

He hated the reminder that his daughter now had to suffer through things he couldn't fix with a kiss and a hug and an artfully placed Band-Aid.

With a sigh, he turned his attention back to Evie. Her cheekbone looked awful, streaked with blood, and his stomach turned all over again, as it had that moment he'd walked into Taryn's room just in time to see her throw the heavy hand weight.

"I can't believe Taryn would take out her temper on you like that. She knows better."

"She's had a couple of rough days," Evie said. "My

guess is that she's hit a bit of a plateau and is beginning to be frustrated that she's not progressing more quickly. Despite all her hard work, she's still limited in so many ways and that can't be easy for her to stomach."

"That doesn't give her an excuse to mistreat someone else."

"Keep in mind also that underneath the injuries from the car accident, she's still a teenage girl. They're not always the most emotionally steady demographic to begin with."

"There is that," he said as he slid next to Evie on the bench and cupped her chin, tugging her to face him. Her skin was soft and he had to fight the urge to spread his fingers and explore the curve of her chin, the hollow of her neck, those soft, kissable lips....

He jerked his attention back to the matter at hand and forced himself to reach for the cleansing wipes. "I'm sorry. These are pretty easy on the skin but they can still sting a little."

She winced and instinctively tried to tug away but after that first jerk, she remained motionless while he finished cleaning the cut, already beginning to discolor around the edges. With all that ethereal blond hair and those blue eyes, she looked slight and fragile. His wounded angel.

"What are the damages? Do I need stitches?" Her voice sounded a little husky in the intimate confines of the room and for some reason, color crawled across her features.

"Doesn't look like it. You are going to need a bandage, though."

"Any chance you have Spider-Man bandages in there? He's my favorite."

He had to smile. "Got a thing for guys in tights, hmm?"

"It's the 'web shooting out of his wrists' action that always gets me."

Brodie rummaged through the medicine cabinet. "Well, I'm afraid you're doomed to disappointment. I've only got plain old beige."

"That's okay." Despite everything, she gave him a winsome look. "I can always draw a smiley face on it later."

He gazed at her for a long moment, that tenderness jumbling around in his chest again. How did she do it? She had been deeply touched by sadness and grief in her life, but somehow she had still managed to climb out of it to reach out to others. He liked her, far more than he had ever expected a few weeks ago. She was sweet and funny, kind and compassionate.

She made him laugh as he hadn't in years and reminded him life was meant to be savored, not conquered and subdued.

He was crazy about her.

He stuck the bandage on her cheek with fingers that suddenly felt thick and awkward. "There you go. All better now."

On a whim, he leaned forward, intending only to brush his mouth just to the left of her injury, as he might have once done to Taryn's owies, as a sort of lighthearted joke. But once he tasted her skin, sweet and smooth and smelling of flowers and spice, he couldn't stop. He trailed a soft kiss above the bandage to the other cheekbone and then unerringly found her mouth.

Only a friendly kiss, he told himself. Casual. Easy. Comfortable. That might have been great in theory, but her mouth was silky and soft and she hitched in a ragged little breath that slid across his shoulders and down his spine as if she had just trailed her fingers there.

She tasted sweet and delicious, like berries and cream, and he couldn't seem to get enough. He kissed her again and again, savoring her lithe curves pressed against him.

Her arms circled his neck and he could feel her fingers dancing in his hair and he took that as permission to do the same. She had pulled her hair back loosely with a beaded clasp and he pulled it free, releasing all those delicious waves. He wanted to bury his face in her hair and just stay there for a few weeks, but right now her mouth was too delicious to abandon so he contented himself with letting the silky curls cascade through his fingers.

"Brodie," she murmured against his mouth and he smiled a little at the ragged note in her voice and deepened the kiss again, wanting nothing but to lose himself inside her.

Reality intruded slowly but with unfortunate insistence. They were standing in his guest bathroom, for pete's sake. Not the most romantic of places to seduce the woman he couldn't get out of his mind. With great effort, he wrenched his mouth away, his breathing harsh.

"This is completely crazy," he murmured, his forehead pressed to hers.

Her chest rose and fell as she tried to catch her breath, something he would have found incredibly sexy even if it didn't press her curves against him with every breath.

"Tell me about it," she finally murmured. "I don't even like you."

He decided not to be offended, especially since her arms were currently still wrapped tightly around his neck.

"What would a guy have to do to change your mind about him?" He very much wanted to know the answer to that, suddenly.

"Brodie…"

"I'm asking for purely academic reasons." Though the effort made him just about grit his teeth, he managed to step away—mostly to keep from backing her up against that wall and kissing her again until neither of them could think straight.

She stood frozen for an instant and then she curled her hands together. "I'm not going to change my mind about staying on. I won't be working here after Tuesday. You know that, right?"

"At this point, I'm seeing that as a good thing. When you're no longer theoretically in my employ, you can't sue me for sexual harassment if I were to ask you to dinner."

She chewed her delectable lip and he suddenly wanted to step forward and offer to take care of that for her.

"Why?" she asked.

"Rumor has it that once in a while, I like to eat. I do own five restaurants, after all."

"Why do you want to eat with *me*?"

"I enjoy your company." He debated for a moment and then decided that, given the circumstances, he owed it to her to be bluntly honest. "I care about you, Evie. More than I expected, but there it is."

She stared at him, blue eyes wide and still slightly unfocused. "This isn't real. This heat between us. You understand that, right?"

He leaned a hip against the sink and crossed his arms, wondering why she was so very determined to push him away. "Funny. It feels pretty damn real to me."

She drew a breath. "I'm sure it does. Feel real, I mean. But it's not, uh, uncommon for patients or their families to develop…inappropriate feelings for therapists and doctors and other caregivers. When someone helps you out during a…a stressful time, it can sometimes be easy to confuse gratitude and appreciation with something deeper."

She was absolutely adorable, all pink and flustered. "You're saying this is all in my head. How you wrapped your arms around me and kissed me back and murmured my name in that sexy low voice I can still hear?" he asked.

She turned even more pink. "No. I…no. But this isn't… I'm not looking for a relationship right now."

"I didn't say anything about a relationship. Only dinner."

Her mouth firmed into a tight line and she looked away. "Right now your focus should be on your daughter, don't you think?"

"Don't tell me where my focus should be, Evie. For nearly the last five months, everything I've done has been for her. You know that." He straightened from the counter, annoyed with her for throwing up roadblocks where there didn't need to be any. "My business has suffered, I've had to put several lucrative projects on the back burner for the foreseeable future and I haven't so much as looked at a woman in a physical way for months. In fact, not until you came into our lives."

"Until you *dragged* me into your lives! I didn't want to be here, remember? I can't afford to get involved. Can't you understand that?"

"Not really." His words sounded harsh but he couldn't help it. "This is not just a physical thing between us. Don't lie to me and say that's all it is. I care about you and I believe you're beginning to care about me. All this *I don't want a relationship right now*. That's bullshit. You're just scared."

"You're absolutely right." She let out a shaky breath. "You terrify me, Brodie. You and Taryn. I've spent the last two years trying to piece my life back together from losing Cassie. I was in a good place until you asked me to help you. I need to get back to that place. Can't you understand?"

He wanted to argue with her, tell her he didn't understand throwing away something between the two of them that could be incredible, but she didn't give him a chance. She left the room and headed down the hallway back to Taryn's room, leaving him no choice but to follow her.

By the time he'd walked into the room, just half a dozen steps behind her, she was already reaching for her slouchy bag and the dog's retractable leash on the hook behind the door. Taryn must have transferred herself to the bed while he and Evie were out of the room.

He still marveled at how much better Taryn was becoming at that sort of thing. She was stretched out on her bed now, flipping through channels with the remote, the dog stretched out beside her.

"I'm going to take off a little early, like we talked about," Evie said, her voice stiff. "Have a great weekend, Taryn. I'll bring you back something from Crested Butte."

It took her a few times to work the buttons on the oversize remote but Taryn managed to mute the TV. She looked at Evie's bandage, and he was happy to see the contrition in her eyes. "I...really am...sorry I hurt you."

"I'm fine. Your dad fixed me right up."

"It looks...good."

Evie smiled. "Dashing, isn't it?"

"Yes." Taryn continued petting Jacques, who appeared to be happy, curled up beside her on the bed.

"Come on, Jacques. Time to go." Evie rattled his leash but the dog didn't budge from Taryn's side, probably because she was giving him the love.

"Jacques," Evie said again.

Taryn looked down at the dog, then at Evie. "Can't he stay here...while you're gone?"

"Taryn," Brodie exclaimed. After the way Taryn had treated her that afternoon, why should Evie allow her to care for the dog she plainly adored?

"I'll take…good care of him. I promise."

To his surprise, Evie seemed to be considering the idea. "It *is* kind of boring for him, sitting around an arts festival for four days. I'm sure he would enjoy hanging out here much more than that, but are you sure you want the trouble of it? He can be a lot of work."

"Yes! We'll have so much fun together."

"I'm sure you will. Jacques loves you."

"So can he stay?"

"It's up to your father, really."

Evie finally met his gaze for the first time since she had walked away and he didn't know what to do with this wild surge of tenderness.

She didn't want to leave her dog. He could see it in her eyes, but she was considering it purely to make Taryn happy. For all her protests about letting them get close, she was sacrificing something she cared deeply about to help someone else. That was just so Evie. No wonder he couldn't get her out of his head.

"Sure. He can stay. Tomorrow if you're up to it, maybe we all go for a walk on that paved trail around the reservoir."

"That would be great! Thanks, Dad."

"You're welcome."

"I'll send his food and his water dish and a couple of his favorite toys back with your grandmother."

"Good idea," Brodie said. "Good luck with your show."

He wasn't half as noble as Evie, he thought as he watched her go. He supposed that made him a terrible person. She might be willing to give up her dog's company for a few days in order to help someone she cared about.

Not Brodie. He wasn't at all willing to give up what he was discovering he wanted most. Her. If he had to fight to keep her, he was damn well ready.

Eleven

"What can you tell me about this one? What are those gorgeous green beads?"

Evie smiled at the woman holding up one of her favorite pieces. "They're antique Bakelite. I found this tattered old necklace in a thrift store when I was living in California. It was really quite hideous, missing half the beads and in an awful setting. Since it couldn't be repaired, I repurposed the beads into this. The rest of it is from your garden variety costume jewelry, though."

"What a brilliant idea. I have got to learn to bead! I've been meaning to take a class for *ages*." The woman was round and cheerful, with short red pixie hair, designer jeans, a tailored blouse and off-the-rack jewelry that still managed to be tasteful and well coordinated.

Evie enjoyed this part of working the arts-festival circuit. What was not to like when she had the chance to talk to people about something she enjoyed so much? Most people were browsers, asking casual, basic questions, but once in a while she found someone who had genuine interest.

"You have no idea how much out-of-style costume jewelry I have lying around." The woman, who had introduced herself as Sandy, rolled her eyes. "My mother had three sisters and none of them had any daughters. Can you believe that? So somehow I ended up with all of it, along with my mother-in-law's god-awful collection of jeweled kittens. It's all in boxes at my house and I would love to, what did you call it, *repurpose* some of it. What do I need to get started?"

"A few basic knots, new findings, some rudimentary tools. I know there are a couple of bead stores around town where you could probably take a beginning class."

"That would be wonderful except I'm only here for the weekend. My husband is a photographer and has a booth on the other side of the festival. We live in Golden most of the time."

"I work at a store in Hope's Crossing, String Fever."

"Oh, I love Hope's Crossing! Such a pretty town. We took our kids skiing there this winter. Well, my husband did. I'm more of the stay-at-the-hotel-and-have-a-massage sort. A friend of ours owns a condo there and loaned it to us."

Evie smiled. "If you come again this winter, make sure you stop in. We teach beginning classes every Saturday."

"I just might do that. Thank you!" The woman beamed at her. "You know, I think I'll buy this. My husband will have a cow, but he can't expect me to hang around all this gorgeous stuff for three days and not come back with anything."

"That's wonderful. I hope you enjoy it. You might be interested to know that all the sale proceeds for this particular necklace will be donated to a scholarship fund in honor of a teenage girl killed in a car accident earlier this year."

"Oh, how sad."

"A portion of the proceeds for all our jewelry goes into the fund but a few of the pieces were made exclusively to benefit the fund. Right now we've got enough in there for an endowment to fund two scholarships. We're hoping for three, especially since the girl's father just gave a healthy donation to the fund."

He could certainly afford it. Chris Parker's latest album had gone double platinum, but Evie didn't mention that to Sandy.

"You know, my best friend's birthday is in a few weeks. She would love a piece of custom jewelry—and I don't mind spending a little more than I'd planned if I'm helping a charity."

By the time Sandy left, she'd bought three necklaces, a cocktail ring and a chunky watch and beaded band that Alex McKnight had made out of some of Evie's extra beads, and had slipped a String Fever card into her bag.

"My husband is definitely going to have a cow. He'd better be selling tons of prints," she said with a rueful laugh. "I hope I see you this winter—though I imagine he would be happy if our paths never crossed again."

After the woman left, the crowd thinned. Evie had found that the slow times at art fairs like this were generally first thing in the morning and midafternoon. She sat watching the few stragglers in the ceramics booth across the grassy pathway, wishing she could stretch out in the shade and take a little siesta.

She hated to admit it, but she missed Jacques's company. He was actually a good draw for the booth. When she had him with her, more than one shopper would dawdle at her booth to ask a question about Jacques's still relatively uncommon breed and would end up walking out with a necklace or a bracelet.

Jacques was so well-mannered that he usually would just plop on his belly and let everyone fuss over him. He loved children too and would especially put out the charm when impatient little kids would come in, dragged by mothers who often wanted to browse through the beadwork.

Taryn probably was enjoying him. The dog adored her with unconditional love and the feeling was abundantly mutual.

Thinking of Taryn inevitably led to thoughts of Brodie. Had he taken Taryn and Jacques for a walk around the Silver Strike Reservoir trail, as he'd promised? She loved that trail. The sugar maples would be turning red to go with the aspen gold at the higher elevations already and it was a lovely walk in the fall—especially good for the wheelchair, as it was paved and relatively level. Maybe Taryn would even be able to work on her walking on the wide path, as long as Brodie provided plenty of support. She should have suggested he take the girl's walker with them to give her a chance....

She pressed a hand to the deep ache in her shoulder. The cut on her cheek had been small, the bruise already beginning to heal, but her shoulder where the five-pound weight had fallen before tumbling to the floor hurt far worse. She had been icing it every night back at her hotel but it still ached constantly, probably a deep contusion from the weight striking her shoulder.

Wasn't that always the way? The worst pains were typically the ones most hidden from the rest of the world.

She leaned her head back against the comfortable lawn chair she'd picked up after the first art show. If she closed her eyes, she would once more be back in the guest bathroom of Brodie's home, feeling the warmth of his fingers as he washed away the residue of blood and applied a bandage—and then the warmth of those fingers as the moment turned into something much more.

That stunning kiss seemed burned into her memory,

sneaking out at the most inconvenient moments to trip up her thoughts.

I care about you and I believe you're beginning to care about me.

She had been able to think about little else through the long drive from Hope's Crossing to Crested Butte. He couldn't mean it. From all her mother had told Evie, Brodie didn't go for long-term arrangements. He rarely dated, and when he did it, he picked cool and reserved professional women. They probably spent all their time together comparing stock portfolios.

He couldn't seriously be interested in her. If he *had* been, he wouldn't be now.

I don't want a relationship with you.

He didn't seem to have taken that declaration very well but the truth was, she had a lousy track record with men— her fault, not theirs.

Some part of her wondered if losing her father when she was an impressionable teenager had left her somehow broken when it came to men. She tended to push away everyone who wanted to get close to her, from her first boyfriend to the fiancé she had brushed aside.

Paulo, her college boyfriend, had been a study in contrasts: brilliant scientist who would someday probably come up with the cure to all manner of diseases, and passionate Italian who loved to cook elaborate meals and engage in deep philosophical discussions with his hands flying as he expressed his impassioned views about everything from animal rights to Fellini movies.

She had loved him deeply—or thought she had. Though they had talked about moving in together when her lease ran out and she started graduate school, the wildfire that had scorched through her family home her senior year of college had changed everything.

She had rushed home to help her mother and sister and had let her and Paulo's love wither and die from inattention—phone calls she didn't take, emails she didn't return, visits she canceled at the last minute.

Eventually Paulo hadn't been content to let their relationship slip away into oblivion, as she probably would have preferred by that point. He had confronted her in his intense, passionate way. He couldn't have picked worse timing. Her sister was dying, her mother still badly injured. She didn't have time or patience for his drama and moods and had told him so in no uncertain terms.

Six years later, she had repeated the pattern, this time with an actual fiancé. On paper she and Craig Addison should have had a perfect life together. He was a rehab physician and their relationship had been forged on a mutual love of the outdoors, on hiking and mountain biking, sailing in the summer, cross-country skiing in the winter.

They had decided not to live together until after the wedding, but three months before they were scheduled to exchange vows at her favorite beach near Santa Barbara, she had had that fateful dinner party when Meredith had asked if Evie would consider adopting Cassie.

Craig hadn't wanted her to take on the responsibility. Why would she possibly want to destroy the lifestyle they both had worked so hard to earn? he had argued, quite persuasively. How could they go hiking, mountain biking, take his sailboat over to Catalina for a long weekend, if they were saddled with the burden of a wheelchair-bound girl, dependent on others for the most basic of needs?

She had listened to him carefully as he argued his case. She even agreed with some of his points. But the idea of tossing Cassie into the foster care system had been untenable. She couldn't do it. She'd seen too many children with disabilities shuffled around from placement to placement until they ended up warehoused in a facility somewhere, with only staff to care for them. She loved Cassie. She couldn't do that to the girl, not when she had the means, the skill and the opportunity to provide a comfortable home for her.

She refused to waver from her view and Craig ultimately demanded she choose: a life with him or guardianship of Cassie. Easy as that. And just as simply, she'd picked Cassie, without reservation or regrets.

Craig had ended up marrying a girl he had met mountain climbing, just six months after he and Evie had been set to exchange vows on that Santa Barbara beach.

At times, the ease with which she had moved on without a backward glance after both breakups worried Evie, made her wonder if something was wrong with her that precluded her from throwing herself wholeheartedly into a relationship.

She had friends who loved that passionately. Claire and Riley, for instance. The air around them seemed to shiver with their happiness when the two of them were together and some secret part of Evie envied that at the same time she feared it.

Her mother had loved her father like that but it had been one-sided. Her father's life had revolved around his work, not his family, and Evie had witnessed the toll it took on her mother. After her father's massive heart attack, her mother had shut herself away from both of her daughters for a long time, leaving Evie again charged with watching over her sister.

If she were truthful, she wanted to give herself wholeheartedly to someone and have them love her that way in return. So why did she persist in holding some part of her heart separate and safe?

She feared Brodie was already well on his way to

breaching that last defense, which was probably the reason she was fighting so hard to protect it. The man had only asked her to dinner, she reminded herself sternly. He wasn't asking her to move in, for heaven's sake. What was the harm in going to dinner with him?

A pair of elderly women who had to be sisters wandered into her booth and began roaming gnarled hands over the beads while they talked about the pieces. She always loved it when customers surrendered to the tactile appeal of beads, something she loved herself. No, beading wasn't all soft and comforting like knitting or quilting, but it presented its own particular pleasures.

"Oh, this is lovely," one of the women exclaimed, holding up a wire-wrapped necklace made of semiprecious stones that Claire had made earlier in the summer.

"Those are all native Colorado stones," Evie said, grateful for the distraction from her thoughts. "We work with a rock collector in Denver who finds them and prepares them for us."

"Exquisite. Simply exquisite," the woman said.

"Buy it, May," the other one said. "It can be a birthday present to yourself."

"Oh, I shouldn't," May said.

"Go ahead and try it on," Evie said, pulling out the hand mirror from below the makeshift counter.

The older women hesitated for a moment then acquiesced and Evie knew she had the sale. Once the customer tried something on, odds were great she would decide she liked the feel of it enough to buy it.

Sure enough, May turned this way and that in the mirror before pulling out her credit card. Eventually she and her sister left with two pairs of earrings each and another necklace centered around an antique cameo brooch Evie had found in a thrift store and repurposed.

Would she be like that woman when she was in her seventies, buying birthday presents for herself because she didn't have anyone else to buy them for her? Or would she ever be able to take that risk and love without holding that safe piece back?

Almost home.

The happy lift of her spirits to be returning to Hope's Crossing always took Evie a little by surprise. As the curves in the road—the shape of the mountains—became more familiar to her, she sat up a little straighter and some of the leftover tension from the hectic weekend seemed to seep away.

A storm was moving in. Lightning flashed in the mountain peaks from black-edged, roiling clouds. She adored thunderstorms in Hope's Crossing, when she could sit on the wide ledge of her windows overlooking Main Street and watch the lighting arc across the tops of the mountains.

She was sure to enjoy this one even more, knowing she wouldn't have to scramble under the awning at the festival, trying frantically to protect the wares from the elements. All the remaining inventory—what little was left of it—was safely tucked away in boxes in the back of her car now and she was done with showing beadwork except at the store for a while.

The weather had been gorgeous all weekend and the arts fair had drawn huge crowds looking to escape the heat of lower elevations. Sales had been brisk, much better than any of the other fairs she'd attended all summer. Even so, she was happy to be done with the traveling.

As she'd expected, the town was quiet. People were probably having Labor Day barbecues or driving back from camping or boating somewhere.

She felt as if she'd been out of touch for weeks instead

of only a few days. Much to her chagrin, she had been so discombobulated by that kiss she and Brodie had shared that she had somehow forgotten to pack the charger for her cell phone. Though she'd been more than a little lost without her phone and had been tempted to search Crested Butte until she could find another charger, the hours of the art fair had left her with little free time the first day, and by the second day she had decided no one needed to reach her that badly.

Woodrose Mountain loomed above town and she had a sudden wild urge to unwind with a moonlight hike after the long drive. Probably not the smartest idea, with that lightning flashing around, even if Jacques were with her to scare away any night-roaming critters.

She missed that crazy dog. She was almost tempted to drive to the Thornes' to get him, if she could figure out a way to sneak him out without encountering Brodie. Wouldn't that be embarrassing, if he caught her at it? Better to just wait until the morning, she supposed.

Thunder rumbled as she parked behind the store. A few drops of rain splattered her as she hurried for the back garden with her suitcase. She fumbled in the darkness with the garden gate latch but finally found it and pushed it open—only to be met by a familiar, well-mannered bark.

She froze. Impossible. Brodie would never have dropped Jacques off and just left him there, would he, especially not with inclement weather threatening? She must be imagining things.

After a few moments, her eyes adjusted to the darkness in time to see Jacques bounding to her, his fur gleaming as the moon briefly peeked out from behind the rain clouds.

The dog wasn't alone, she realized an instant later as Brodie uncoiled from one of the chairs around the patio table.

"Brodie! What are you doing here?"

"Waiting for you."

The low words shivered down her spine and she swallowed. "This is becoming a bad habit."

His face was a pale blur in the dim light. "Tell me about it. I was a little desperate to talk to you tonight."

Her pulse skittered. "Oh?"

"My mother told me you planned to be home this evening. I figured it would be easier to catch you tonight than in the morning."

"Has Jacques really been *that* much trouble?"

He scratched the dog behind the ears and received an adoring gaze in return. "What? No. He's been fine. Taryn had a great time with him. You were right. He's a very well-mannered dog. We quite enjoyed having the company."

As if in punctuation, lightning flashed and almost simultaneously a huge thunderclap shook the building. She jumped and Jacques instantly left Brodie's side to pad toward her. He brushed against her, his sturdy body warm and comforting, and her heart swelled with affection for this creature who gave his love with such sweet generosity.

Rain began to spatter in earnest now, stirring up the delicious scent of dirt and flowers and wet brick. Another flash of lighting arced across the sky, followed by the rumble of thunder.

"Why don't you come inside before we're all drenched? We can talk upstairs."

"Good idea." He grabbed her suitcase from her before she could protest and headed for the narrow stairway.

As she expected, her house was once more stuffy, as it had been the first time he had come to see her. She went to the windows and opened them and immediately a cool, rain-scented breeze floated in, fluttering the curtains.

"Sit down. Can I get you something to drink?"

"You just returned from a trip. You don't need to play the perfect hostess here. You sit down."

She *was* tired. Exhaustion crashed over her in waves now that she was done driving. She sank onto the couch and he sat next to her on the comfy armchair she'd bought at a furniture show in Denver and hauled home on top of her car.

Jacques wandered around the apartment, sniffing every corner as if reacquainting himself with the space. That intense awareness of Brodie seemed to curl through her and all she could think about was how wonderful it would feel to have his arms wrapped around her right now, to lean on someone else for a change.

"What's going on, Brodie?"

He sighed, looking suddenly uncomfortable. "I need advice."

And he was coming to *her*? "Of course. What's up?"

"You heard about Charlie's court appearance, right?"

"Oh, I'd forgotten that. I haven't heard anything. My phone's been dead and I forgot to take my charger."

"Ah. So that's why you didn't take my calls. I've been trying to reach you since you left town. I thought perhaps you were avoiding me."

"Why would I do that?" she asked innocently, but even *she* wasn't convinced. If her phone had been working she probably *would* have avoided his call.

"I couldn't figure it out. But I'm heading out tomorrow on business and before I left I really needed your opinion about what to do."

"I'm sorry. Start from the beginning. What happened with Charlie's court appearance?"

"You're not going to believe it."

"Then tell me, for pity's sake!" she exclaimed.

He made a rueful face. "I'm still trying to soak it in, if you want the truth. He pleaded guilty to all counts. The negligent homicide, underage drinking, driving while intoxicated. All of it. It was a total shock to everyone."

She stared, not quite sure how to respond. *Oh, Charlie,* she thought. "And his father was okay with that?"

"I don't think he had any idea what the kid was planning. I thought he and the other attorneys were going to wet themselves trying to shut the kid up."

"The judge allowed it?"

He nodded solemnly. "If you had heard Charlie, you would have understood why. He was very convincing. He said he understood what he'd done was wrong, that he deeply regretted the harm he had caused to individuals and the town as a whole, and he was prepared to pay his debt to society. He was quite persuasive. Judge Kawa couldn't help but take him at his word."

She pictured Mayor Beaumont and his wife, Laura. She imagined both of them were completely certain their son would wriggle out of the charges against him. Why wouldn't he, when he had their money and power to help him?

Maybe this was all some sort of elaborate plea agreement in exchange for leniency at sentencing.

She turned her attention back to Brodie and found him waiting for her reaction. She still didn't understand what this had to do with her and why he was here soliciting her opinion. "This is what you wanted, isn't it?"

"Yes. Of course. His actions took one life and ruined another. He needs to pay." He raked a hand through his hair, his features torn.

"But?"

"I don't know. Nothing. Just…it struck me in that courtroom that he's just a kid. Barely seventeen."

This was the first time she'd seen him be at all compassionate toward the boy. It warmed her deep inside and, foolishly, made her want to weep.

"Thank you for telling me about Charlie," she finally managed. "I'm still curious about what you need from me."

"Taryn is beside herself. She overheard me talking to my mother about it and she totally freaked. Since Friday, the only thing she wants to talk about is how she is going to speak at his sentencing hearing this week. I need you to help me convince her not to do that."

"Why?"

"She listens to you. She trusts you. You've been able to reach her in ways no one else has since the accident."

She shook her head. "*I* haven't been the one to reach her, Brodie. I don't know why you refuse to listen to me about this. Charlie is the one who helped her turn the corner."

"Maybe he's helped, but you have a bond with her. I know how hard you've worked to help her. She won't listen to me but maybe she'll pay attention if you tell her what a mistake it would be for her to appear at the hearing."

"What's so very terrible about it?"

He stood up restlessly and paced to the window, where he leaned against the sill. "She's come a long way, no doubt. Compared to where she was when she first came home from the hospital, she's like a different girl. But this. Standing in front of the whole damn town and trying to communicate her thoughts inside the pressure cooker of a crowded courtroom. She's not ready for that. It's too much, too soon."

She understood his position. He was concerned for his child and wanted to protect her as much as he could. He didn't want her to be hurt, which was perfectly understandable. Yet how could she make him understand that Taryn ought to be the judge of her own capabilities? His daughter was more than competent enough to make this decision. If she thought she could handle the stress of trying to speak in a courtroom, Brodie needed to give her the chance.

"I'm going to say something here. I don't want you to take it the wrong way."

He laughed roughly. "When somebody prefaces a sentence like that, it's usually very tough to take it any other way."

"I know you have Taryn's best interests at heart. She knows that, too. You're a good father and you want to protect your daughter from ridicule and embarrassment. That's admirable, Brodie."

"But?"

Lightning flashed behind him and the low rumble of thunder that followed left her in an odd, restless mood. She didn't want to get into this with him right now, when she was tired and feeling so strange and out of sorts—but if he was leaving town, she wouldn't have another chance to argue on Taryn's behalf.

She drew in a breath and stood as well, joining him at the window where the cooling breeze helped settle her a little. "You need to have a little more faith in Taryn. You're not doing her any favors by protecting her and wanting to keep her tucked away safe at home. She's got to rejoin the world sooner or later. I think you need to let her go back to school like she wants. And I think you should let her speak at this sentencing hearing, if that's her wish. She's tougher than you think."

He leaned against the window and closed his eyes. "Every father would like to believe he's raised his daughter to be tough and resilient. But not every father has lived through what I have these last four months. Not every father has had to hold his daughter in his arms, knowing she's a dozen machines away from dying. Not every father has had to sit by his child's bedside day after gut-wrenching day, praying she was still somewhere trapped inside this twisted, damaged, unresponsive body. While she was in a coma, I prepared myself that we were going to lose her. For nearly two freaking months, I had to brace myself whenever I walked into that damn hospital, wondering if this would be the day."

Lightning flashed behind him again and tears scorched her throat at the raw pain in his eyes. He was not a man who shared his emotions easily and she was extraordinarily touched that he would choose to do so with her.

"Yeah, I might be too overprotective. Maybe I need to let go a little. But I can't seem to help wanting to shield her from any more pain after everything she's been through. Don't you think I've earned that?"

"Yes," she murmured, helpless against the urge to comfort him, to ease a little of that pain in the only way she could. Though her brain warned her this was foolhardy in the extreme, the emotion of the moment demanded she do something.

She wrapped her arms around his waist and offered the only comfort she could. He didn't move for a long second and then he wrapped his arms tightly around her and held on as if she were the only thing between him and a raging ocean.

They stood together for a long time in her stuffy apartment while the thunder rumbled outside and the rain clicked against the window. A soft peace seemed to eddy around them like the breeze, quiet and sweet.

She was falling in love with him. The truth poured over her like that breeze and the urge to weep again burned behind her eyelids.

She pushed it away for now, quite certain she would have plenty of time to fret about that stunning truth later, after he left. For now, she needed to focus on the reason he had come to her.

"I understand you want to protect your daughter, Brodie. You absolutely *have* earned that right. You've done everything you can to give her the life she had before." She paused, choosing her words carefully. "But don't you think that after everything she's been through, Taryn has also earned the right to have a hand on the rudder of her destiny?"

He stared at her and then closed his eyes, pulling her closer. She wanted to run from these feelings inside her, from this soft and subtle binding of their hearts.

"Damn it. Why do you have to be so smart about everything?"

Oh, if he only knew. She had been so very, very foolish about so many things. She should have said no that very first night he had come to her here to ask for her help with Taryn. She had known somehow that if she agreed, everything would change. All her careful barriers would tumble down and she would become vulnerable once more to pain and heartbreak and *life*.

The world she had created here in Hope's Crossing—safe and serene, comfortable—would drift away now like fall-turned leaves caught in the current.

She was falling in love with Brodie Thorne and she knew it would not end well for her.

Despite that knowledge singing through her mind, when he lowered his head to kiss her she didn't have the requisite strength to step away. All she could do was lean into him and savor the sense of rightness that defied all sense.

The kiss began as merely a soft brush of his mouth against hers, easy and slow, like a quiet rain just before dawn. The sheer sweetness destroyed the last of her defenses and she was helpless to pull away when he leaned his hips against the edge of the deep windowsill, his long legs stretched out on either side of her, and pulled her closer so her mouth was perfectly on level with his.

Lightning flashed behind him. Would she ever view a Hope's Crossing thunderstorm in exactly the same way, or would that burst of atmospheric energy forever remind her of this moment, in her apartment with Brodie's arms around her and his mouth teasing and tasting each inch of hers until her thoughts were tangled and her knees were weak?

They kissed there for a long time while the wet breeze drifted in and the rain pattered down outside the window and the lightning slowed to only occasional flares.

Some annoying little part of her mind cautioned her they needed to stop before things went too far but as the kiss deepened and Brodie's mouth licked and teased hers, the rest of her decided to ignore the warning for now.

She didn't protest when he tugged her to the sofa and pulled her down beside him, his body male and solid and wonderful next to hers. She was too busy relishing the solid strength of him, the delicious heat.

Nor did she think to object when his mouth trailed delectable kisses across the curve of her cheekbone and down the length of her neck, his breath warm and erotic against her skin.

By the time his fingers began to play at the buttons of her shirt, that voice of warning had quieted to barely discernable whimpers. This was Brodie. She was falling in love with him and being here with him while the rain whispered against the window seemed exactly right.

Twelve

So much for his good intentions.

Brodie had assured himself in those few moments he was waiting for her outside in that little garden that he had come only to seek Evie's help. He trusted her—sometimes he was astonished at how much.

His grand plan had been only to ask her to help him convince Taryn of the foolishness of her wish to testify.

However, when she had stepped forward and wrapped her arms around him, offering that generous comfort he was beginning to depend on, he had been unable to resist her. What man could? Evie Blanchard was soft and beautiful and giving.

He wanted her so fiercely he couldn't think around it. He had never known this kind of hunger, to want everything from a woman. Always before, he would try to maintain some sort of control over himself but this reckless abandon with Evie was completely unexpected.

He wanted everything. To taste and touch and explore every part of her until he learned just what brought her the most pleasure...

Her skin was warm and tasted like wildflowers as he trailed his mouth from her lips to her cheek, then down the long, silky column of her throat. She wore a pale green shirt that made her exotically tilted eyes look vibrant and mysterious. She closed them halfway as he brushed his mouth at that sexy little spot where neck met shoulder, then moved his lips to her shoulder, all while his fingers were busy working the top button of her shirt.

Even though he was more aroused than he'd ever been in his life, he wanted to spend all night exploring these secret little places, like here, the hollow just above her collarbone.

He pressed his mouth there…then froze when she suddenly hissed in a breath and tried to move her shoulder away.

He frowned, easing up on his elbow. "Did I hurt you?"

Her eyes were huge, dazed. "Sorry?"

"You caught your breath there with a sort of whimper. And it wasn't a do-that-again sort of whimper."

"Sorry." She cleared the huskiness out of her voice. "I, uh, didn't even realize I had."

Did she have any idea how powerfully arousing he found it that she hadn't been aware of her own subconscious reaction?

"I hurt you." He drew back farther and pushed the collar of her shirt aside so he could see in the low light from the bead-covered lamp beside the sofa. He frowned at the apple-size, vivid black-and-purple bruise on her shoulder.

"What did you do?" he exclaimed. As soon as the words were out, he remembered that scene with Taryn the week before, that horrible moment when his daughter had lashed out in anger and frustration, throwing the free weight at Evie. It had struck her cheek, he remembered, then landed on her shoulder before falling to the ground.

"Taryn did that to you, didn't she?"

Evie stared at him, her eyes still aroused and unfocused.

She shifted her gaze to her shoulder and then back to him. "Yes. It looks worse than it feels."

"Liar." He had seen the way she winced when he kissed her there. She was hurt because of his daughter, and here he was pawing her like a horny teenager.

He sat up. "I completely forgot about what happened in therapy Thursday. I'm sorry, Evie. I guess Charlie's hearing thrust it completely from my mind."

With each passing second, she seemed to be gathering her composure around her until she gave a heavy sigh and eased away from him. He could do nothing but watch as she rose from the sofa and moved to the easy chair adjacent to the couch, where she perched on the edge of the cushion, her fingers intertwined as if in prayer. He could almost see each of her defenses snap back into place.

Right now, with his body still throbbing and his nerves still humming, he sincerely wished he were the sort of guy who could have ignored that wince of pain and taken what they both wanted.

"Don't worry about it," she murmured. "It's no big deal."

He wanted to grab her to go back to the wild heat between them but she was too much in control now. The moment was gone. Damn it.

"Evie," he began, not sure what he wanted to say to her, but she shook her head.

"Don't. We've got to stop doing this, Brodie."

"Why? We're both adults. Neither of us is involved with someone else right now. We've got this heat that seems to spontaneously combust whenever we're together. We can't just ignore it."

"You might not be able to but I can."

He frowned. "Why do we have to?"

Jacques padded over to her—apparently done giving

them the privacy Brodie was suddenly grateful for—and Evie dug her hands in the dog's short, wiry fur for a moment before she spoke. "You probably can't understand this because you have lived here all your life," she went on, without waiting for an answer, "but… I need Hope's Crossing. I can't explain it very well, but this has become my home. I've found peace here. I have friends here and a life I love. But what happens if we give in to that heat and what we both want and make love?"

"I don't know, other than I have no doubt it would be incredible."

She closed her eyes briefly. When she opened them, they were distant. "I know it would be. But it wouldn't last, Brodie. How could it? We're far too different. This heat is not enough. When things between us ended, as I have no doubt they would, where would I be? I wouldn't be able to stay here in this place I love. I would have to leave Hope's Crossing and I would hate that."

"You're really choosing a town over what we could have?"

She shook her head. "That's a little too simplistic, don't you think? I'm choosing to protect myself."

How could he argue with that? She was right. They *were* very different people. What had he once thought about her? *Color and chaos, passion and heat.* He already had a brain full of chaos and had struggled like hell as an adult to contain it. As drawn as he was to her, as much as his body ached for her, Evie could threaten everything he had worked so hard to overcome. Was he willing to pay the cost?

"So that's it," he said.

"I'm sorry."

"So am I," he said roughly.

"I'll still try to talk to Taryn for you in the morning," she said.

He was so messed up, it took him a minute to register what she meant and then he remembered. Right. That was the whole reason he had come here, to convince her to help him talk Taryn out of speaking at Charlie Beaumont's sentencing hearing.

"Don't," he said. "If she wants to speak, I won't stop her. Like you said, she's earned it."

Her lovely features softened and she opened her mouth to speak but he couldn't stay here any longer, not with this ache of hunger in his gut.

"Sorry I bothered you about Taryn and…everything else."

"Brodie…"

He decided it would be wiser not to look at her right now or he would waver. "And thank you for your hard work with Taryn. You've done far more than I asked. I'll have my assistant send a check tomorrow to the Layla Parker fund, doubling the amount we talked about."

"You don't have to do that," she murmured.

"But I'm going to anyway," he answered. "Good night, Evie."

He headed for the door, but not before he heard her whispered goodbye behind him.

A sleepless night following a long, arduous weekend, following an even *longer* week did not make a good combination.

Evie was gritty-eyed and exhausted the next morning when she arrived at the house for her last day with Taryn. She half feared she would see Brodie and wondered what she would possibly say after last night, but only Taryn's new therapist was in evidence.

Stephanie Kramer was young and clever and bubbled with energy. Already, she and Taryn seemed to have a rapport. A recent graduate from P.T. school, Stephanie had just finished her internship. Though she was taking a position at a clinic in Denver, they didn't need her until after Christmas, which made her perfect for the job of Taryn's full-time P.T. aide.

Everything would work out great, Evie knew, and Taryn could continue on her road to recovery.

One part of her was deeply relieved to turn over the responsibility to someone competent who would provide exactly what Taryn needed. At the same time, Evie was more than a little disconcerted by how sorry she was to put this time behind her.

She would miss Taryn. The lump that had been hovering in her throat all morning swelled a little bigger. Oh, this was exactly what she'd been afraid of when Brodie had dragged her into this. Deep in her heart, she had known she would struggle to walk away after all their hard work, to turn over both the responsibility and the satisfaction of the girl's progress to someone else.

She couldn't alter course now. For heaven's sake, her replacement had already been hired. She couldn't just suddenly announce, *Oh, excuse me, I've changed my mind. Go on about your business now.*

Anyway, she wouldn't do that even if she could, especially after last night with Brodie. She needed to make a clean break before it became not simply difficult but utterly impossible to walk away.

"I guess that's everything. We've been through it all several times. I showed you the pool exercises, what we've been doing in here on the equipment and the schedule of other therapists who come in and out. Do you have any more questions?"

Stephanie shook her dark ponytail. "I don't think so. Your notes are amazingly clear. If I do have questions, I can always call you, right?"

"Yes. Of course. My cell number is right at the top of the notes and if you can't reach me there, you can always find me at the bead store in town."

"Great. I'm superexcited about this. We're going to have so much *fun.*"

She would do a wonderful job, Evie told herself. "Make sure you bring Taryn into the store often so we can bead."

"I'd like to make something for… Hannah." Taryn spoke from the mat, where she was brushing a delighted Jacques and working her arm and shoulder muscles in the process.

"That is an excellent idea. Hannah will love it."

"Can… Jacques still come to visit me?" she asked.

"I'm sure we can work something out." Evie couldn't ignore the yearning in Taryn's eyes as she gazed at the dog. "Maybe your grandmother could bring him out to spend an afternoon with you. And of course you can always visit him at the store whenever you come in."

"I'll miss him." Taryn sighed a little and shifted on the mat.

"You'll still see him. Don't worry."

Evie grabbed the box containing some beads, a book, a sweater—the last of her own things that had slowly migrated to the Thorne home over the course of her time here.

"I guess that's it."

"Thank…you." Taryn looked almost teary-eyed and that lump in Evie's own throat expanded.

"You're welcome, honey."

Unable to leave with just a wave and goodbye, Evie set the box back down, then knelt on the mat beside Taryn. She folded the girl in her arms, thinking she already felt more sturdy and less fragile than she had nearly a month ago when she had first come home from the care center. Much to Evie's delight, Taryn returned the hug with a strength that hadn't been there even a week ago.

"You've rocked, Taryn," she murmured. "Don't ever forget you did it all yourself."

Taryn shook her head and sniffled a little. After a moment, Evie made herself rise to her feet and take Jacques's leash and walk out the door.

Mrs. Olafson met her at the door with a bag in her hand. "These are some of those oatmeal cookies you liked so well," she said rather gruffly, and Evie couldn't help hugging her as well.

"Thank you, for what you did for our girl," Mrs. O. said.

It wasn't me, she wanted to protest once more but she decided to let it rest for once. Some part of Taryn's recovery *was* because of her. Yes, the girl had done the work but Evie had guided her path and she would forever be proud of that.

Jacques whimpered a little as he climbed into the backseat of her vehicle.

"I know, bud. I'm sad about it, too," she said.

The dog continued to whine all the way down the hill, as if he understood they wouldn't be back. Hot tears burned in Evie's eyes but she blinked hard to keep them from taking over. After the short drive through town, she pulled up to her spot behind String Fever but Jacques was still whimpering.

Evie turned around and looked at her dog, who looked so morose, then she shifted her gaze to Woodrose Mountain, solid and peaceful in the afternoon sunlight.

Suddenly she knew what she had to do. It hurt like the devil but that didn't change the fact that it was the right thing to do for everyone involved.

Except her.

"Stay here," she murmured to the dog. She rolled down both windows so he had plenty of air, then hurried into her apartment before she could change her mind. She dumped the contents of the box she had just brought from Brodie's house on the sofa and filled it with what she needed, then hurried back down the stairs, her chest tight and achy.

Brodie probably wouldn't like it, she thought as she drove back up the hill, but a little healthy annoyance wasn't necessarily a bad thing. Maybe if he was upset with her, he would be less likely to come around with more of those seductive, soul-stealing kisses. Not that he would after last night, but a contingency plan was always a good thing.

Mrs. O. looked surprised to see her when she rang the doorbell, Jacques padding along beside her. "Did you forget something?"

"Sort of." She headed back to the therapy room, biting her lip hard to keep from sobbing out loud. This hurt more than she would ever have imagined but in her heart, she knew it was the right thing.

Taryn was still on the mat, her legs balanced on a small ball. She looked up, shocked, when Evie came back into the room with Jacques.

"Hi, again!"

Evie drew in a ragged breath that seemed to sear away the lining of her lungs. "Would you like to keep Jacques?"

Taryn's eyes widened and she stared at Evie and then the dog. "What? You mean...all the time?"

She nodded, clenching her hand on the leash so hard she could feel her nails digging into flesh. "Though he's been very understanding about it and I do try to walk him as often as I can, it's really not fair to a big dog like Jacques to keep him in just a small second-floor apartment and that little garden spot behind String Fever. It was never meant

to be a permanent arrangement anyway. I was only sup
posed to be fostering him until I could find a good hom
for him. I think I finally have."

She smiled while she felt her heart rip in two. What sh
said was all true. She *had* been temporarily fostering th
dog, but after only a few days with him, she had fallen i
love with the big, gentle lug and the temporary situatio
had stretched into weeks and then months.

"Here with you, he would have room to run and stretcl
plus he could continue to help with your therapy."

"Oh." Taryn still looked stunned, as if she didn't quit
know what else to say.

"If you don't want to take the responsibility, don't worr
about it. We can just forget the whole thing. But if yo
think you and your d-dad could make him part of you
family, I think he would be very happy here."

Her voice broke a little on a few words and she coul
feel the quiver of her chin but she firmed it with ruthles
resolve.

"Yes! Yes! Are you…are you sure? You love… Jacques.'

"I do. But you love him too and I can't help but thinl
the two of you need each other."

As if to illustrate her point, Jacques finally tugged th
leash away from her and padded to Taryn, licking he
cheek and nudging her face with his. The girl threw he
arms around the dog and held on tightly and Evie knew sh
had to get out of there before she broke down completely

"Thank you. Thank you so much."

"You're welcome." With great effort, Evie forced a
smile. "Your dad probably won't be thrilled about it, bu
if he says anything, you tell him for me that you've earned
this, too."

"Too?"

"He'll know what it means. I want to see you up out of

that chair and taking Jacques for walks in a few weeks,
got it? No slackers here."

Taryn glowed as she hugged the dog. Most fifteen-year-
old girls probably wouldn't get this excited about a dog, but
Taryn and Jacques had bonded over the last few weeks. Evie
had watched it happen. Perhaps some part of her had even
known somewhere deep inside that this was inevitable.

"Won't you miss him?" Taryn asked.

More than she could ever say. Her apartment would
seem deathly empty without him to greet her in the morning with a cold nose against her cheek or curling up beside
her bed at night, just a comforting stretch of her arm away.
She already dreaded it. Maybe she would have to move
away from the ghost of him in every corner.

She might have to look into buying a little house somewhere, maybe up the canyon. Somewhere big enough for
a dog, and wouldn't that be freaking ironic?

"I'll be fine," she said firmly, more to herself than
Taryn. "This is where he belongs."

She could hardly see now for the blur of tears but she
hugged Jacques hard, then Taryn. The dog looked confused
at her for about ten seconds, then plopped down at Taryn's
feet as if he, indeed, belonged exactly there.

After mumbling something that was probably incoher-
ent to Stephanie she rushed out the door, brushing without
a word past a startled Mrs. Olafson.

The Angel of Hope would approve, she thought as
she climbed into her car. She sat behind the wheel and
scrubbed at her eyes with the heels of her hands for a moment, then let out a heavy sigh and started the engine.

This was just the sort of thing the Angel would have
been all over—reaching beyond your own interests to give
somebody else exactly what he or she needed. Even when
it hurt like hell.

* * *

"Are you sure you don't want to come with us? Girls' night out at the Lodge? It's Holly's first time leaving the baby with Jeff," Claire said. "We're placing bets on how long she'll last before she gives up pretending to have fun with us and drives home in a panic, afraid he's diapered the wrong end or something."

Evie laughed and shook her head. It defied all logic to her that Claire had convinced her friends to allow her ex-husband's new wife into their social circle. Claire's theory was that—like it or not—she, Jeff and Holly, and soon Riley when they married, were co-parenting her children. Claire wanted the best possible relationship with the woman who had Owen and Macy half the time.

If it were her, Evie probably would have found a way to stab Holly a few times with an eye pin—or at least she would have wanted to. But then, she never claimed to be as good a person as Claire.

"We're going to have a great time. You don't want to miss it." Alex grinned, her green McKnight eyes alight with infectious laughter. Alex was always pretty and vibrant, though Evie sometimes thought her bright gaiety was simply a satiny bit of fondant that concealed the real person beneath.

"Oh, please, Evie," Mary Ella McKnight—Alex's mother and Claire's good friend and future mother-in-law—added her voice. "It won't be the same without you!"

She shook her head. "I'd better not. You have no idea how behind I am after the last month with Taryn. I have a half dozen commissioned pieces I promised would be done by the middle of September. I'm not going to make it if I don't put in some serious bead time."

Despite her obligations, she was tempted. Hanging out with her friends, surrounding herself with laughter and conversation and food, held undeniable appeal. A pall had descended on her life the last few days, greasy and dark, and she knew only part of that was losing Jacques. She felt…lost, somehow.

"The price of fame and talent, I guess." Mary Ella smiled warmly.

More like the price of having given in to Katherine and Brodie's appeal in the first place a month ago, and then falling hard for a certain man with blue eyes and a solemn smile.

"Something like that," she murmured. As much as she might be momentarily tempted to spend the night with her friends instead of work, she needed to be here right now. She yearned for the peace and serenity she found feeling the beads slide through her fingers, threading the wire knots that would tie them together, watching something beautiful emerge from her efforts.

"Katherine and Ruthie are going to meet us there," Alex said. "Even Maura said she might stop by after she closes the bookstore. I hope so. She's a little lonely, now that Sage has gone back to school."

"You all have a wonderful time. I'll be there next time, I promise. I'm just going to stay here since my tools are all out and the beads I need are close at hand."

Claire frowned. "Are you sure? After the robbery, I hate to think about you here in the store by yourself, especially now that you don't even have…" Her voice trailed off and she flushed a little. "Anyone else to keep you company."

Evie ignored the little spasm in her chest, the familiar twinge of pain she experienced whenever she thought about Jacques. She used to love having him here at the shop while she worked late, not for protection, necessarily, but simply the quiet calm of his presence.

"I'm fine. Don't worry about me. You all go and have a fantastic time and I promise I'll be there next time."

The women looked as if they wanted to protest but Mary Ella, bless her, seemed to sense Evie didn't have the strength to continue arguing. She tugged her daughter and Claire toward the door and finally the store was blessedly silent.

Evie locked the door after them and engaged the security system with a relieved sigh. She stood for a moment in the quiet, surrounded by the beads she loved and the scent of the soft vanilla candle Claire had been slowly heating that day. Even after the warmer was turned off, the scent lingered in the store.

Evie breathed deeply a few times to relax away the stress of the day. When she was suitably calm, she wandered into the office and found a station on the satellite radio that played the classical jazz she most enjoyed working to, then returned to the worktable.

With Miles Davis, Chet Baker and Bill Evans to keep her company, the work went quickly and she finished the first project on her to-do list in just under an hour. She was deep into the second when, over the low music, she heard a sharp, peremptory knock at the front door.

Evie rolled her eyes. The store was clearly closed. If the sign out front wasn't enough to prove it, the lights in the showroom were off. No doubt whoever it was could see her back here working and just assumed she wouldn't mind ringing up some seed beads or spacers or something.

She would just ignore it, she decided, and go on with her business.

That brilliant plan worked for all of thirty seconds, then the rude person only knocked harder. With a heavy sigh, Evie finally set down her round-nose pliers on the felt pad she liked to bead on and headed for the door, fully intent on telling her unwanted visitor in no uncertain terms they could come back in the morning. She was just in the mood to do it, too, even if it was rude.

At the door, her stomach dropped when she recognized her visitor—Laura Beaumont, Charlie's mother, stood on the other side. She wasn't quite tapping her toe with impatience but it was a close thing. Reluctantly, Evie opened the door and the woman brushed past her into the store before Evie could even form a word.

"I need to talk to you." The mayor's wife seemed flustered. Her hair was usually so shellacked with hair spray nothing short of an F4 tornado could budge it, but now it was slightly mussed and her lipstick was a bit smeared, as if she'd put it on in a hurry.

"Sure. Come in," Evie muttered under her breath, then forced a smile, a little embarrassed at her childishness.

"I was about to go around back and ring the doorbell to your apartment upstairs when I saw the lights on in the store and caught a glimpse of you working in the back room."

"I have a couple of commissions I'm trying to finish tonight." She had to hope Mrs. Beaumont would pick up the hint but instead she moved farther into the room, leaving behind the scent of the expensive, flowery perfume she favored. Even when she appeared less than perfect, Laura Beaumont seemed elegant and contained. Evie knew she purchased all her clothes from a couple of pricy boutiques in Denver. Heaven knew, she wouldn't be caught dead in anything for sale in Hope's Crossing.

Laura headed for the worktable where Evie had set up her supplies. She fingered the piece Evie had just finished, an intricate necklace and earring set recycled from a 1950s four-strand bead necklace.

"I like this. I have the perfect dress it would go with. How much?"

"It's not for sale. It's a commissioned piece."

"Can you make another one?"

"I'm afraid that's a one-of-a-kind item I was asked to make out of someone's mother's costume jewelry. I wouldn't be able to duplicate it if I tried."

Laura made a face. "You could make something similar."

"Perhaps." Or Laura could make it herself. But while the other woman claimed she loved to bead, she had a particular genius for enlisting someone else to do any work required for it. "What can I do for you tonight, Laura?"

Laura touched some leftover blue faux-pearls from the project and dribbled them through her fingers. Her usual haughty air seemed to trickle away like the pearls and she shifted, her eyes strangely vulnerable. "I must ask something of you. Not for my sake, you understand. I would never presume so much. This is for Charles."

Evie tensed. "Oh?"

"He pleaded guilty. You know that, don't you?"

"I heard."

The other woman sank into the folding chair across from Evie's workstation. "He can't go to prison. He can't! He's just a boy."

Laura paused, apparently waiting for her to respond to that dramatic declaration.

"I'm sorry," Evie finally said. "I'm not sure what this has to do with me."

"I need your help. I want you to speak at his hearing. Tell the judge all he's done to help you with the Thorne girl."

Oh, crap. She released a breath. She *so* didn't want to get tangled up in this. Yes, she felt sorry for Charlie. Despite everything he had done, she liked the boy and respected him greatly for standing up and taking responsibility for his actions over his family's obvious objections. That didn't mean she was ready to go to court and speak on his behalf. She could only imagine how *that* would play with Brodie.

"I don't..." she began, then stopped, fumbling for words.

"You *have* to." Laura was at once pleading and arrogant. "He's seventeen years old. He'll be eighteen in six months. Since he pleaded guilty in adult court, they could send him to an adult prison. He won't survive it! If you speak on his behalf, perhaps the judge will consider leniency."

Leniency. Was that really what was called for here? Layla Parker was dead and, despite all the progress Taryn had made, Evie had no doubt that the girl would be impacted in some ways by the accident for the remainder of her life.

"I'm not sure that's likely, Laura," she said, trying to be as gentle as possible. "What Charlie did was very wrong. Don't you think he deserves punishment?"

Laura's hands trembled a little and Evie was startled by the strain in her eyes. "My son has made terrible mistakes, yes. But he's trying. You see that, right? He's helping you with that girl, isn't he?"

That girl, as if Taryn were simply a nameless inconvenience. What did that make Layla? she wondered. "Yes. Charlie has been very patient with Taryn and she seems to enjoy having him come. I would have to say his visits have been helpful."

"I wasn't happy when he started to visit her. I didn't think it was good for him, being involved with her again. On some level, I still believe I was right. If he hadn't had that firsthand exposure to her, he would never have pleaded guilty to the charges against him, especially over the objections of his father and his attorneys."

Evie tended to agree with her. She hadn't brought it up with Brodie that night at her apartment, but she was certain Charlie's time with Taryn had given him a true understanding of the extent of her injuries and the long rehabilitation road she still faced. Evie remembered what she'd said to him that night when he had stood on the other side of the garden gate to ask if he could visit Taryn again.

You won't be able to hide from it, Charlie. You will know that every frustration, every single exercise she has to do, every painful muscle spasm I have to put her through, is because of you.

"I do have to say, though," Laura went on, "that Charlie has been…different these last few weeks. I can't explain it. He's not as restless, not as high-strung."

She thought of his desperation on Woodrose Mountain that early morning and her vague, unsettled fear that he had intended to harm himself that day. "Sometimes a person simply needs a purpose. Maybe helping Taryn provided that for him and showed him that reaching outside himself to help someone else can give a peace you simply can't find anywhere else."

The words seem to clog in her throat as the truth smacked into her like that weight Taryn had thrown.

She was the world's biggest hypocrite. She had retreated deep into herself, had fought ever helping anyone. She had subconsciously decided protecting herself was more important than risking pain by choosing to let others close to her.

Oh, she might have done superficial things like help paint an older lady's fence during the Giving Hope day Claire had organized earlier in the summer, or sitting at art fairs all summer to raise money for the scholarship fund in Layla's name, but she had been very careful to keep that part of herself separate.

For the last two years since Cassie died, she had turned away from the very thing she had always known was the answer to that elusive serenity—losing herself in helping other people.

She had needed a purpose, too. Oh, she loved working with beads and always would, creating something lovely out of disparate elements. But did that really compare to actually helping someone live a more fulfilling life?

Across from her, Laura fidgeted with the pliers on the table, opening and closing them at random intervals as if she were snapping at ghosts. "For the last year he's nearly flunked out of school, but now he's talking about paying his debt to society and finishing his last year of high school and then trying to go to college. He wants to go into medicine now. He told me that. He wants to be a doctor or a physical therapist like you."

She wasn't a physical therapist anymore, Evie wanted to automatically correct, but those words tasted like chalk, too. No, she might not be a practicing physical therapist but she couldn't run away from what was in her heart. Working with Taryn had only reinforced how much she loved it.

"So will you do it?" Laura asked.

She had no idea how to answer. She couldn't betray Brodie—and she knew that if she spoke to urge leniency, he would see it as nothing else but disloyalty. On the other hand, she wasn't sure a harsh punishment was the best option for the boy.

Finally she sighed. "Laura, the only thing I will do is speak to the judge about Charlie coming to work with Taryn and explain what he did while he was there. I will not take any position either way as to whether that should affect his sentencing. I can't argue for leniency, only provide information. I want you to be perfectly clear on that."

The other woman's mouth compressed into a line as

if holding back her arguments. "I suppose that will have to be enough, won't it? I'll inform our attorneys. We will need you to attend the hearing on Friday afternoon at one. I'll have your name added to the list," she said, just as if she were extending some elite invitation to a swanky society event.

What had she just agreed to do? Evie fretted as she let Laura out of the store and set the security system behind her. So much for her calm, relaxing, productive evening. Now she was going to worry all night about how she could convince Brodie that speaking out about the help Charlie had given Taryn—help Brodie hadn't sought or wanted in the first place—wasn't a complete betrayal.

Thirteen

He ought to be shot for ever thinking this idea had any semblance of sanity attached to it.

His stomach muscles were taut with tension as Brodie pushed Taryn's wheelchair out of the elevator to the courthouse floor where Charlie Beaumont's hearing was set. He wanted nothing so much as to turn right around and go back downstairs, out the door and up the hill to their house, away from what he very much worried would be a complete disaster.

The wooden floors of the old courthouse that had once played host to horse rustlers and claim jumpers seemed to echo with each step he took toward the courtroom and his head pounded in unison.

In contrast to his own apprehension, Taryn was calm and composed. She rode with her hands folded neatly in her lap and looked around with interest at the high ceilings and the old-fashioned moldings around the doorframes.

He wasn't being biased about it when he thought she looked lovely. Her hair, growing out now from where they'd had to shave it during her numerous operations, was pulled back from her face with a beaded headband his mother had fashioned. Her features looked delicate and pretty and she had even applied her own makeup, with the help of Stephanie Kramer.

If not for the ever-present wheelchair, she would look like the high school cheerleader she had once been.

Pride for her and the young woman she was becoming burned in his chest. She had more courage and grace than most women twice her age. That didn't mean he thought she was at all ready for the coming ordeal.

"You don't have to do this, kid."

"I want to." Her voice was clear and firm, with no trace of hesitation.

He still wanted to tuck her away, take her somewhere safe. How could any responsible father allow her to go through this? He stopped outside the door, fiercely wishing he could put his foot down and forbid this. She was still a minor. As her parent, he was well within his legal rights to put a stop to something he couldn't support.

But Evie was right. Taryn had earned the right to make her own choice about this. She had traveled a long, hard road these last nearly five months and had miles yet to go. If she really wanted it—and she had made it abundantly clear the last week that she did—he couldn't deny her.

That didn't mean he had to like it.

With a heavy sigh, Brodie pushed her through the open doorway. Immediately the buzz of conversation inside the room from onlookers waiting for the judge to appear seemed to cut off in midflow. Yeah. Taryn's appearance, wheelchair and all, created just the stir he'd expected.

The courtroom was packed. Since the district attorney's office had chosen to file charges in adult court because of the severity of the incident, the hearing was open and plenty of people in town seemed to feel they had a vested interest in the outcome. Many did. Several of the business owners who had been robbed in the initial crime spree had shown up. Maura McKnight-Parker and several members of her family were seated in one entire row.

Much to his surprise, he suddenly spotted Evie seated near the aisle on one of the benches near the back. She gave him a tentative smile and slid over to make room for him.

Since he knew she wasn't the voyeuristic type, as he imagined many of the onlookers to be, he assumed she must be here to provide moral support for Taryn. Just seeing her—lovely and cool and surprisingly constrained in a navy blazer and plain white-silk blouse, seemed to calm him.

He didn't understand it but he was deeply grateful anyway. He needed a little calm if he was going to make it through this without dragging Taryn back through the doors.

After he parked the wheelchair in the wide aisle, he sat down in the space she had cleared for him. The scent of her, sweet and clean and indefinably Evie, stirred softly in the air and he was fiercely happy to see her.

He knew it made no sense. The tenderness of those kisses the other night seemed a lifetime ago, though he had relived those moments over and over. He had wanted to call her a dozen times while he was in California meeting with suppliers, just to hear her calm voice of reason. He'd even dialed the number a couple of times but had ended the calls before they could go through, hating that he felt like a stupid, unsure teenager around her.

She had made it clear she didn't want to take the risk of being involved with him and he needed to respect that, as difficult as he found it. "Thank you for coming," he said, when the silence between them had stretched out far too long.

She shifted and looked down at her hands. "Don't thank me yet, Brodie."

"Why not?"

Before she could answer, the generalized buzz in the courtroom cut off again as Laura and William Beaumont entered the courtroom, along with their son and the team of attorneys Brodie had seen at every court appearance.

The Beaumonts looked like a unit, solid and unbreakable. Charlie, far from being happy to see Taryn, frowned fiercely in their direction.

Brodie did his best to analyze that reaction as the Beaumonts moved toward the front of the courtroom. Mrs. Beaumont stopped when she reached their aisle. She looked aristocratically bored by the whole proceeding, though Brodie thought he saw a shadow of nerves in her eyes.

"I wasn't sure you would come," she said. He thought for a moment she was talking to him, then realized her comments were directed toward Evie.

"I said I would," Evie answered rather stiffly.

"Thank you," Laura murmured, then moved up to sit beside her husband and son.

He frowned. "Why is she thanking you?" he asked. "Why are you here?"

She met his gaze, her fingers curled in her lap. "I've been asked to make a statement about Charlie."

For a moment he could only stare, a mix of hurt and anger and a deep sense of betrayal settling in his gut. She wasn't here to support him and Taryn. She was here to speak for Charlie *freaking* Beaumont. That warm calm that had washed over him at the sight of her was now lost in the sucking whirlpool of his anger. "And you agreed?"

She seemed to be steeling herself for his fury, as if she had fully expected it. Of course she must have. Yet she was going to do it anyway and that hurt more than anything else.

"Yes," she said simply.

"You and your damn bleeding heart. It's bad enough you've convinced me to let Taryn speak today. Now you're going to get up there and talk about how he's just some poor, misunderstood kid with a heart of gold who's filled with remorse and has suffered enough. That little punk you think is some kind of damn angel took my daughter's future."

"Wrong. She still has a future," Evie said quietly. "A very bright one, in part because that *little punk* helped her believe in it again."

He wanted to yell and curse and generally vent this hot, jumbled mess of emotions in him, but before he could, the bailiff stepped to the front of the courtroom.

"All rise for the Honorable Judge Kawa."

Everyone in the courtroom except Taryn stood up and then Ivy Kawa walked in, slight of stature but tougher than any Wild West judge who had ever sat on that bench.

He knew her socially, of course. At heart, Hope's Crossing was really a small town, despite the sometimes overwhelming tourist numbers. Theirs was only a casual relationship, though. If he remembered correctly, her husband golfed with William Beaumont. He doubted Judge Kawa would let that sway her opinion on Charlie's sentencing either way.

The judge's instructions to the courtroom were terse as she explained that the purpose of the hearing was to ascertain proper placement for Charlie after his guilty plea of the week before. "No dramatics and no hysterics. This is a legal proceeding."

Taryn fidgeted a little in her wheelchair. "If you change your mind just say the word, honey," he said in a low voice. "We don't have to be here."

"I won't."

"I'm just saying, if you do." Though he didn't look at

her, he was aware of Evie seated beside him, tense and silent and the hot ache of betrayal in his gut.

She badly wanted to touch him—a hand on his arm or
even a shoulder nudge. Anything.

He wouldn't appreciate it, she knew. With the anger
she could still feel radiating from him, she didn't want to
think how he might respond if she tried, so she kept her
hands carefully folded on her lap while she listened to several business owners read their impact statements about
the crime spree Charlie had been involved with the night
before the accident.

Mike Payson from Mike's Bikes talked about the loss
of business he had sustained and the generalized feeling
of invasion.

Claire spoke about the accident and the strain of her
injuries and how Macy and Owen still tensed every time
they had to drive up Silver Strike Canyon for any reason.

Through it all, Evie wondered how she could possibly withdraw her name from those speaking and sneak
away. She was still trying to come up with a way when,
after about forty minutes of testimony, the bailiff called
out her name.

Nerves fluttered inside her as she rose to take her place
behind the podium set up at the front of the courtroom. At
least she wouldn't have to sit in the witness box for this.

"Please state your full name and occupation for the record," Judge Kawa instructed.

Evie drew a deep breath. "My name is Evaline Marie
Blanchard. I am a…" She paused here for only an instant.
"I am a licensed physical therapist," she said firmly. "For
the last month I have been working one-on-one setting
up an intensive rehabilitation program for Taryn Thorne
in her home."

"And you have a statement on behalf of the defendant?" the judge asked.

"No," she said and was vaguely aware of the low stir of surprise in the courtroom. "When I was asked to make a statement, I clearly indicated I was only willing to provide information about my dealings with the defendant over the last month and allow the court to interpret that information, not offer my opinion as to proper sentencing."

"Proceed," the judge said, a furrow of confusion between her eyebrows.

Evie clutched the paper with the few short paragraphs she had agonized over for the last two days. "Several weeks ago I encountered Charlie Beaumont on a hiking trail in the mountains. In the course of our conversation, he discovered I had been working with Taryn Thorne and he expressed concern for her condition. Believing Taryn might find interaction with young people motivational to her therapy—and knowing Charlie and Taryn were friends prior to the accident—I invited him to visit her. This was without the knowledge or approval of her father, let me add, and was a completely unilateral decision on my part. Taryn seemed to enjoy his visit and she responded better to her regular therapy than she had done previously. When Charlie asked if he could return another day, I agreed, though I had reservations as to whether it would be beneficial."

She looked up and found Maura watching her with eyes that were solemn but dry. Brodie was looking somewhere over her shoulder, not at her, and her insides clenched with regret. Too late to get out of this now. She was stuck, like it or not.

She cleared her throat, anxious only to finish now. "Over the past three weeks, Charlie has become a regular visitor during Taryn's therapy sessions. He visits as often as four times a week, for an hour at a time. To my great surprise, he has displayed remarkable calm and patience with her and Taryn has made great progress in that time. She can stand for longer periods of time, she is taking more steps on her own and her core strength has improved. Whether that is because of Charlie, I cannot and will not say. Thank you."

Brief and to the point, without embellishment or elaboration. She had told Laura she would only relay the information about Charlie's visits to Taryn, not color it with her opinion. She had to hope she had accomplished her goal. Whether the judge would give any weight to the information was now out of her hands.

She left the podium, more than a little tempted to push through the doors and keep walking out of the courtroom. That would be cowardly, though, and she couldn't leave before she heard what Taryn wanted so strongly to say.

She would have vastly preferred finding another seat, but every spot in the courtroom seemed full except where she had been sitting before, next to Brodie.

With no small degree of reluctance, she returned to her seat and felt the heat of his disapproval like a sunlamp beating down on her.

She wanted to tell him she was sorry but the impulse itself annoyed her. She hadn't done anything so terribly egregious, only presented the basic facts about what had transpired the last three weeks in therapy. None of it was a lie. If he still couldn't accept how much Charlie had helped with Taryn's therapy, that was his problem, not hers.

After one of Charlie's Sunday-school teachers gushed on and on about what a good boy he was and his high school soccer coach spoke about how hard he worked for the team, it was Taryn's turn.

Beside Evie, Brodie seemed to brace himself. Despite

everything, she again wanted badly to touch him, to offer some sort of physical encouragement, but she didn't have the chance, even if she had been able to find the nerve. He rose and pushed his daughter's wheelchair to the front of the courtroom, then set the brake so that Taryn could laboriously pull herself to her feet.

Judge Kawa watched this with confusion at first and then surprise. "Young lady, there is no need to stand. You may certainly remain seated."

Taryn shook her head, gripping the edge of the podium. "No. I want to...stand," she said.

"If you're certain. Of course, you may be seated at any time."

Taryn nodded, then angled around to look at Brodie, behind her. "Dad. Go sit down," she said, to a nervous little titter from the courtroom.

Brodie looked as if he wanted to argue, wanted to stay there behind her through her entire statement, but after an awkward pause, he returned to sit tensely beside Evie.

"My name is Taryn Thorne." She spoke clearly and concisely and Evie glowed with pride in her at how very far she had come from those early days when no one was sure she would even survive.

"I was hurt in the accident. I still can't walk...very well and I talk a little f-funny. But I—I'm getting better. Charlie is my friend. He helps me with therapy, even when it's boring."

She was quiet for several beats, so long that Evie could feel the leashed tension in Brodie and knew he was about a heartbeat away from jumping out of his seat and returning to her side.

"Judge, I want to tell you," Taryn finally continued, "Charlie shouldn't go to jail. He shouldn't. It's wrong. None of it...was his f-fault."

"Yes it is!" Charlie suddenly jerked to his feet. "Don't listen to her."

"Young man, this is a court of law. You can't just shout things out. Please be seated," the judge said sternly.

"She doesn't know what she's talking about. She doesn't remember!"

"Yes. I do. I...remember. All of it." Taryn gripped the podium tightly. "We were so stupid. Just...messing around. It was never Charlie's f-fault. It was all...my idea. To rob those stores, I mean. I was mad at my dad. He was going to make me quit...cheerleading because I broke curfew a lot and my grades were bad. I wanted to hurt him."

Brodie's jaw tightened and he drew in a ragged-sounding breath and Evie couldn't simply sit beside him and do nothing. His hand was a tight fist on his thigh and she covered it with her own hand. After a startled moment, she could feel some of the tension seep away. He relaxed his fingers and turned his hand over to clasp hers, though he still didn't look at her.

"It was me and Layla and Charlie and Jason and Aimee. Jason Hoyt and Aimee T-Taylor. Jason knew...how to shut off the store alarms and unlock the doors. He broke into his dad's security company or something. I don't know how. But it was...too easy. After we took stuff at my dad's store, we decided to do others. Just for f-fun."

Taryn looked guilty and small standing behind the podium. Her lip trembled as she spoke but she was still holding on tightly and remaining upright. "It wasn't for the money. Not really. We...were stupid and...and bored, I guess. Jason and Aimee were high. I wasn't. Neither were Layla or Charlie. At String F-Fever, we accidentally knocked a box of beads in the... dark and Jason thought it was so f-funny. He knocked over more and then we all... took turns dumping stuff out. We made...a big mess. I felt really bad afterward and sick to my stomach. I like Claire. But then I made it worse."

She shifted her gaze to Charlie, and Evie saw something she had missed all this time. How could she not have seen it? Taryn's feelings for the boy were obvious all over her face. Though she might say she and Charlie were only friends, Taryn's emotions ran much more deeply than that.

"I grabbed…some scissors and cut up his sister's wedding dress. It was dumb. I don't know why I did it. But Charlie's parents ignored him all the time. It hurt him. All they cared about was his sister's stupid wedding. He was sick of it and I…wanted to help him."

She was beginning to look shaky up there and Evie wasn't sure Taryn would be able to stand much longer. She wanted to go and hold her up but didn't think the judge would appreciate the interruption.

"The next night, Jason said he knew an empty cabin where we could hang out and watch a movie, with lots of…beer in the f-fridge. Charlie didn't want to have any. He was driving." A slow tear dripped down the side of her face, and beside Evie, Brodie made a low growling sound in his throat she doubted anyone else could hear. "We…we made him. We teased him until he had some beer with us."

"Taryn, shut up." Charlie jerked to his feet, his fists clenched at his sides. "It doesn't matter now. None of it matters."

"Young man, if I have to ask you again, you will be removed from this courtroom. Do you understand?"

"She doesn't need to do this. It was all my fault. I was drinking. I was driving too fast. It's all my fault."

"Mr. Beaumont. Sit down! You may continue with your statement, Ms. Thorne."

Taryn swallowed and another tear followed the first.

After a pregnant pause, Charlie sank down onto the bench and buried his face in his forearms.

"Can I...sit down now?" Taryn whispered.

"Of course," the judge said. Before Brodie could jump up to do it, the bailiff pushed the wheelchair into the correct position for her to transfer into. When Taryn sat down again, the man pulled the microphone from the podium for her and she held it on her lap.

"So... Layla didn't want to be there. At the cabin. She... wanted to go home. She told us it was w-wrong and we should go. Charlie said she was right. He said we needed to stop, that we were going to...get in real trouble. Jason told him not to be a...a pussy."

She looked embarrassed at the word and Evie wanted desperately to rush up to the podium, gather the girl into her arms and tell her to stop. Beside her, Brodie was a thick column of tension, his hand gripping hers tightly.

"Ch-Charlie said he and Layla were leaving and if we wanted to walk home, we could. So we all got in his truck." Her voice was shaking and she used her most unaffected hand to swipe at the tears now dripping down her cheeks.

"Enough," Brodie growled. "She needs to stop now."

"Ms. Thorne, would you like to take a recess?" Judge Kawa asked gently.

Taryn shook her head. "No. I just...want to say it all. Is that okay?"

"Go on."

She looked miserable and lost sitting alone there in her wheelchair. Had she been carrying this burden inside her all this time? Was that the reason the girl hadn't wanted to cooperate with her therapy?

"I didn't put my seat belt on. Neither did Layla. I don't know why. We just didn't. Charlie was telling us on the way home he was going to turn himself in and tell the police what he had done. We were all f-fighting and yelling and then we…saw lights behind us. Charlie swore. He said he was going to pull over." She hitched in a little sob of a breath. "I told him to go. I screamed at him, over and over. I said, *Just go! Just go! Just go!* I knew…my dad would kill me."

"Just be quiet, Taryn!" Charlie yelled, but his white-faced father restrained him.

"No!" she shouted back. "It wasn't…your f-fault. You wanted to stop. We all made you drive f-faster. Even… Layla said to keep going. She said her uncle wouldn't chase us in the snow and we could get home. You wanted to stop. We should have let you stop. I'm so sorry. It's my f-fault. All of it…was my idea. I should have been…the one to die. Not Layla. Not Layla."

She was weeping now, great gusting sobs. Brodie jerked to his feet and rushed to his daughter's side, heedless of courtroom decorum. He leaned down and folded her into his arms and she sobbed against him and Evie's heart cracked and broke apart with love for both of them.

Through her own tears, her gaze landed on Maura. She looked stricken, lost. Beside her, Mary Ella hugged her daughter tightly.

Even the judge looked shaken. She banged her gavel as the courtroom seemed to quiver with reaction. "Order. Order! Is that all you wish to say, Ms. Thorne?"

Taryn's head brushed Brodie's shirt as she nodded.

"In that case, I believe we need a recess. We will reconvene in fifteen minutes for the remaining statements."

Evie sat for a moment, not sure what to do. Poor, poor Taryn. She genuinely believed she was responsible for the events of that night. She likely thought she deserved everything bad that had happened to her.

She had tried to tell them all, over and over, not to blame Charlie but no one would listen to her.

Brodie was trying to push Taryn out of the courtroom, she suddenly realized, but was struggling to make it through the crowd milling in the aisle. Evie—well used to the strange phenomenon that people seemed to not heed a wheelchair even when it was nearly rolling over their toes—stood up to help clear a path for him.

In the process, she ended up just ahead of them out in the hall. Almost as if they were a unit, as the Beaumonts had been, which she knew they absolutely were not.

"I'm sorry, Dad," Taryn said when they were clear of the crowd. "I'm so sorry. I know…you hate me now."

"I don't hate you. I could never hate you, sweetheart."

Evie didn't want to intrude on this private moment between them. She started to ease away but to her shock, Taryn reached for her hand. "Thanks… Evie. I had to tell the truth. Nobody…else would listen."

This was why she wanted so much to speak at the sentencing hearing, because her guilt was eating her up inside. Perhaps this experience would serve as a catalyst for change. Evie prayed that maybe now that the weight of this guilt was off her shoulders, Taryn would be able to truly turn her attention to allowing herself to heal.

"Have I ever told you that you're just about the bravest person I've ever met?" Evie said softly. She hugged the girl to her and closed her eyes, aching at how empty she would feel now that Taryn and Brodie were largely out of her life.

When she stood again, she found Brodie watching her with an unreadable look in those blue eyes. He opened his mouth to say something but before he could, Maura approached them, her features pale. Evie almost stepped protectively in front of Taryn, just as Jacques might have done, but she knew that was silly. Maura would never hurt the girl, no matter how deep her own pain might run.

"Taryn, there's enough blame to go all around. Layla—" Her voice broke. "Layla wouldn't have wanted you to carry this on your own, honey." She pressed a hand to Taryn's shoulder for just a moment before returning to the courtroom.

Taryn had a distant sort of look in her eyes as if she wasn't quite sure how to respond.

"She's right," Evie said. "Sometimes tragedies are just that. Tragic. Nobody is to blame. Yes, people could have made different choices. You could have understood that your dad was only trying to help you make better choices with your life. He loves you and wasn't being punitive. You could have chosen to take your frustration at him out in a healthier way. All along the way, one of you could have stopped what was happening."

The girl didn't say anything and Evie frowned. Something didn't feel right about Taryn's posture and her vacant facial expression. "Taryn?"

Suddenly the girl's head tilted backward as if someone had cut the strings holding it upright and her limbs began to tremble. Evie stepped forward and saw that Taryn's pupils were dilated and her eyes were jerking rapidly back and forth. Evie inhaled sharply. "Taryn!"

Brodie instantly picked up on the panic in her voice. "What is it? What's happening?"

"I think she's seizing," Evie said.

"Seizing? She hasn't had a seizure in months! I thought she was done with them."

"Apparently not." She didn't have time to tell him lingering seizures could be a common side effect of traumatic brain injuries, a sort of short circuit in the brain's complicated wiring.

"We need to take her out of the chair and place her onto her side right away. It's the best way to protect her airway."

Without hesitating, Brodie scooped his daughter out of the wheelchair in one fast motion and laid her on the wood floor of the courtroom hallway. He rolled her to her side and Evie tilted the girl's chin down to her chest to keep it free of obstruction and to help saliva to flow out instead of choking her throat.

"Should I call an ambulance?" Brodie asked, gazing at Evie with such trust she was overwhelmed by it.

"Let's give her a few minutes and see if she can come out of it on her own. You don't happen to keep Diastat in her bag?" she asked, referring to the instant medication that sometimes could stop a seizure quickly under certain circumstances.

"No." His features were tight, worried. "I don't think so. Like I said, she hasn't had a seizure since we left the hospital. We thought she was done with that part. Damn it! I should never have let her testify today. I knew it was too much for her."

Panic and memories swarmed her, harsh and biting, and it took all her strength to keep them at bay. She couldn't do this. Not again. Cassie had died after a prolonged seizure in her sleep, when her heart had stopped and couldn't be resuscitated. Evie had found her in the morning and now, with Taryn's seizure, once more she was back in her house in the canyon, waiting for the paramedics to arrive while she desperately did CPR by herself and begged her daughter to come back, even knowing it was too late.

No. That was the past. This was now and Taryn needed her.

"Call an ambulance," she finally said when the seizure didn't abate after another minute or two.

Brodie quickly dialed 9-1-1 and Evie was checking

Taryn's pulse—steady, thank the Lord—when Mary Ella, Claire and Katherine hurried over.

"We just heard," Katherine said, kneeling beside her granddaughter. "Oh, baby."

"What can we do?" Claire asked.

"Just keep people away," Evie said. "She would hate everybody staring at her like this."

Finally, what seemed a lifetime later, the EMTs arrived and rushed in with a stretcher. Again Evie fought the need to escape but made herself stay for now until she could be sure Taryn was safely on her way to a medical facility.

"Somebody said Taryn's sick. What's going on?"

She turned to find Charlie pushing through the crowd, his features tight and pale. "She's having a seizure," Evie said. "It can be common in people who've suffered traumatic brain injuries."

"Is she... Will she be okay?"

"I'm sure she will," she said, even as her mind flashed to Cassie, still and cold.

He let out a shuddering sort of breath. "She shouldn't have come today."

She glanced sideways at Brodie. Finally, something the two of them could agree upon. The paramedics began to load Taryn onto the stretcher and Brodie moved away from his daughter's side slightly to give them room to work, which brought him closer to Evie and Charlie. She wanted to touch Brodie somehow, to reassure him, but she wasn't sure whether he would welcome her presence now.

"She wanted to set the record straight, I think," Evie said to Charlie. "I know it bothered her to have people blame you when it sounds like you tried all along to stop events from exploding out of control. Why didn't you say something?"

He gazed at the paramedics bustling around the girl.

"What she said—none of that matters. I was driving. I was responsible. I could have done the right thing and stopped when Chief McKnight first flashed his lights at us. I didn't have to listen to everyone else. I should have been the leader and stood up to them, no matter how hard it was. None of it should have happened and if I had manned up, I could have stopped it."

Brodie was apparently close enough to catch that part. Though his attention remained largely focused on Taryn and the paramedics working on her, he turned slightly and after a long pause, he lifted his hand and rested it on Charlie's shoulder.

The boy lifted startled eyes to him, as if afraid Brodie would shove him to the ground, but he did nothing, other than stand beside the boy offering that small gesture of, if not quite forgiveness, at least reconciliation and peace.

The accord lasted only briefly and Brodie didn't even speak, but Charlie released a deep breath, astonishment and relief on his features, as Brodie turned his attention back to the paramedics, now readying the stretcher to head to the ambulance.

Evie fought a hot sting of tears as she watched him return to his daughter's side. Love for him was a heavy weight in her chest, painful and hot and wonderful at the same time.

She wasn't afraid anymore, she realized. Taryn was going to be okay. She didn't know how she knew but it was a quiet assurance that settled in her heart. This wasn't like Cassie. Already she could see Taryn's trembling begin to ease as the medication the EMTs had administered began to take effect.

She stood beside Charlie and watched the paramedics push the stretcher toward the elevator with Brodie holding his daughter's hand, and a sweet assurance seemed to flow through her.

She loved Brodie Thorne. If Taryn could confront her fears by coming to the courtroom and shouldering more blame than she should for the accident, and if Brodie could face his anger at Charlie and let the first seeds of forgiveness take root, surely she could show the requisite courage to let him into her heart.

Fourteen

He hated hospitals.

Brodie had never been all that crazy about them—who was, really?—but after the last four months with Taryn, if he never saw the inside of another one he wouldn't lose any sleep about it. Here he was again, though, at the Children's Hospital in Denver, sitting by his daughter's bedside while she slept.

Her seizure had lasted about twenty minutes, start to finish. By the time the EMTs had taken her to the emergency room at the small hospital in Hope's Crossing, it had begun to stop. Given her underlying condition, the E.R. docs hadn't wanted to take any chances and had opted to transfer her by ambulance here, to the hospital where he had spent so many long and miserable hours in the early days after the accident.

He knew every inch of this hospital, from floor to ceiling. Though it was a place of healing and hope to many and he had deep gratitude for the dedicated professionals who worked here trying to help children, these walls represented stress and worry and pivotal moments that had changed his daughter's world.

The uncomfortable bedside chair squeaked a little as he

shifted position with the restless energy that was so tough to deal with in the close confines of a hospital room. At the sound, Taryn opened her eyes. They were slightly unfocused at first and then she smiled at him.

"Dad?"

"Right here, honey."

"Go home. I'm…okay."

Taryn was bleary-eyed and exhausted from the medication and the aftereffects of the long seizure. She could barely keep her eyes open. Doctors had a term for it—*postictal,* when the body sort of shut down to allow the brain time to reset itself. He just called it *completely wiped.*

"I'm not going anywhere, sweetheart, except maybe to grab a bit to eat. Just rest. If you wake up and I'm not here, I just went downstairs to the cafeteria, but I'll be right back."

She was quiet for several minutes and he thought she'd fallen asleep again, but she slowly pried her eyes open again. "Are…you mad?"

Her halting words in the courtroom rang through his head, as they'd been doing through the long afternoon and evening. *My fault…my idea… I was mad at my dad….*

His chest ached and he reached for her hand and curled his fingers around it. "No, honey. I'm not angry with you. How could I be? You've more than paid for a few lousy choices. We all made mistakes last spring. I promise I'll try to listen better when you're struggling and I hope you feel like you can come to me next time when things aren't right between us."

"There won't be…a next time."

"That's good to hear." He squeezed her fingers and she closed her eyes. Just as he started to ease his hand away, she opened them halfway.

"What about Charlie?"

A peculiar combination of anger and guilt settled in his gut whenever he thought about Charlie Beaumont. Since April, he had nurtured his hatred of the kid, blaming Charlie for everything that had happened to Taryn. He still didn't quite know how to readjust his thinking. Some part of him still blamed Charlie. The kid had been driving and even the small amount of alcohol in his system had been enough to slow his reflexes and hinder his judgment. He could have stayed firm, no matter what kind of pressure his peers squeezed him with.

Brodie's anger didn't have the hard edge it might have that morning, though. Taryn's halting words in the courtroom had ameliorated much of it and left him conflicted about how he should feel.

Evie would probably tell him he needed to forgive in order to move on.

Remembering her and the quiet strength beside him in the courtroom also left him with that funny clench of his insides. He would have been lost without her, both during Taryn's time on the stand when she had reached for his hand, and later during the seizure when she had taken over with that calm confidence as he fought wild panic.

"Is he going to…jail?" Taryn asked.

He wasn't quite sure how to answer that. Judge Kawa's sentencing decision had come down about two hours earlier. Brodie's mother, at his request, had stayed in Hope's Crossing for the hearing instead of coming along to the hospital. She hadn't been happy about it but he'd asked her to wait until he knew how long the doctors would want to keep Taryn before she dropped everything and drove to Denver.

Since he'd ridden in the ambulance anyway, he and Taryn would need a ride home in the morning and Katherine could drive in then with the van to pick them up.

His mother had called to give him the news—Charlie had been sentenced to one year in a youth correctional facility, followed by three years' probation and a suspended driver's license until he was twenty-one.

Earlier in the day, he would have been furious. How was one year enough to atone for the loss of one life and the destruction of another? After Taryn's testimony, now he didn't know quite what to think.

"He'll spend a year in juvenile detention," he said, opting for honesty. "The judge left room for him to get out early for good behavior."

"One year," she whispered. "I'll miss him."

He couldn't believe he was actually saying this but the words tumbled out anyway. "We can visit him if you want. But you're going to have to promise to work hard on getting better."

"I want to…now," she said. His heart ached all over again that she had carried the weight of that guilt inside her, allowing it to hinder her efforts at rehabilitation.

"I know you will."

She gave him a half smile and closed her eyes again. When he was certain she had slipped fully back into sleep this time, he released her hand and leaned back in the chair, listening to the low whir of the IV pump and the hum of the other equipment in the room.

He supposed he must have drifted off into that half sleep that was usually all he could manage here in the hospital. Some time later, the quiet whoosh of the door opening pierced through his subconscious. Assuming it was one of the nurses or aides making their frequent trips in to check vital statistics, he didn't bother to open his eyes until the soft scent of wildflowers drifted to him over the astringent hospital scents.

He opened his eyes to find Evie standing just inside the

door. She was still dressed in that formal shirt, skirt and jacket she'd worn in court, as if she hadn't made it home to change, and she carried a couple of woven bags.

Their gazes met and Brodie straightened in his chair, stunned at the soft, healing peace seeping through him. How did just the sight of her do that, center and calm him so instantly? He probably ought to be a little freaked out by it but all he could manage was sheer happiness that she was there.

"I'm sorry I woke you." She pitched her voice low with a sideways glance to the still-sleeping Taryn. "When I came in and found you asleep, I thought I would just drop a few things off along with a quick note. Uh, your mother sent a change of clothing and I thought maybe you might be hungry so I had Dermot at the café pack a couple of sandwiches for you."

His stomach grumbled on cue and he remembered he hadn't eaten since before court that morning and it was now past seven. Yeah, he was hungry, but mostly he just wanted to wrap her in his arms and hold on.

He forced himself to focus on the food. "That sounds fantastic. I could eat about a half dozen of Dermot's sandwiches right about now."

"I'm not sure he loaded a half dozen in there," she said with a rueful smile, holding out the bag to him. "It should be enough to get you started, anyway. I believe he said something about chips and a slice of pie, so you should be set."

"Thank you." He had so many other things he wanted to say to her, words that had chased themselves around his head for the last week, and especially today in court as she had shared her steady strength when he needed it most.

"How is she?" Evie asked.

"Good. Sleepy. The docs want to be extracautious to

make sure she's not suddenly entering into a seizure cycle, so they're watching her carefully. By all indications, I think we'll be going home tomorrow."

"I hope so." She moved closer to the bed that dominated the room, gazing down at Taryn with deep tenderness in her eyes.

His heart ached all over again. She loved his daughter. It was clear on her features. Despite all the pain and loss of her own life, Evie was still willing to open her heart to a wounded girl who needed her desperately. She had given up the dog she loved because she simply wanted to help Taryn heal.

Was it any wonder he was crazy in love with this woman?

The realization just about knocked him back on the uncomfortable vinyl of the hospital chair.

He was in love with Evaline Blanchard. For the generous way she loved his daughter, yes, but for so many other reasons.

She made him laugh when life seemed deadly serious. He'd never realized how very much he needed those light and sweet moments until Evie had come along.

She had a way of seeing the good in everyone. Just look at how she had reached out to Charlie when everyone else in town was ready to stone the kid.

Most of all, she centered him. That part made no sense on the surface. Evie wasn't a calming person. All that vibrant life, the colorful beads, the passion and heat. He didn't understand why but when he was with her, the chaos in his head seemed to quiet.

He needed her in his life, like he needed the mountains and sunshine, and he damn well wasn't going to give her up without a fight.

"I could use some air," he said gruffly. Too gruffly, apparently. She gave him a concerned look.

"Would you like me to stay here with Taryn?"

"I'd like you to come with me." He was screwing this up, nervous around a woman for the first time since he was about fifteen years old. "I would enjoy the company. Would you like to take a walk with me downstairs to the meditation garden? There are a few tables there where I can eat this delicious dinner you brought me."

"Is it all right to leave her?"

"I doubt she'll wake for a while. She's pretty out of it. I told her if I wasn't here when she woke up, I'd only stepped out to grab something to eat. I'll leave the door open so the nurses can hear her."

Taryn didn't awake even after he picked up the nurses' call button and arranged it in reach of her most functional hand. After a quick stop at the nurses' station to let them know he was leaving for a while and to make sure they had his cell number if they needed to reach him, Brodie led the way to the elevator.

"I guess you heard about how things shook out with Charlie's sentencing," she said as they entered the waiting car.

He didn't want to talk about Charlie. He wanted to talk about how crazy he was about her and demand she tell him what steps he would have to tackle to keep her in their lives. "Katherine told me about it earlier when she called to check on Taryn."

"Are you angry? Only a year in youth corrections. It must seem far too little to you."

He was silent as the elevator reached the ground floor and the doors whirred open. "I think Judge Kawa made the right call," he said and was a little surprised he meant the words.

He didn't want to see Charlie go to adult prison. Justice had to be paid somehow, but along with justice could come a little mercy for a kid who had made stupid mistakes along the way and should have withstood the pressure of his friends.

Evie didn't move from the elevator, only gazed at him with an unguarded expression, soft and warm. That expression gave him hope that maybe the hurdles weren't quite as high as he'd feared. "I think so, too."

When they didn't move out of the elevator, the doors started to close again and Brodie thrust an arm through to open them again and tugged Evie out of the car to the foyer of the hospital.

"This is lovely," she said when they reached the garden, full of softly rippling waterfalls, a gurgling steam, overhanging trees and fall-blooming flowers. She inhaled deeply, no doubt breathing in the autumn air, so different from the antiseptic hospital smells.

"Okay, I have to get this out and then we can sit down and you can eat your lunch," she said, a hint of nervousness in her voice that piqued his curiosity.

He wasn't hungry anymore. Right now he only wanted to drop the lunch she'd brought him into the dirt, wrap her in his arms and hold on tight.

"Get what out?"

She shoved her hands in the pockets of her jacket. "I owe you an apology. Or at least an explanation."

"For speaking today at Charlie's hearing? I should apologize for being upset about it. I ought to have expected you to do nothing less, Evie. That's the kind of person you are."

It's one of the reasons I love you with everything inside me.

"No. Not that. Though I am sorry about that, too. It was

wrong to blindside you that way. You deserved a little advance warning, at least."

She drew in a breath and let it out on a sigh. "What I meant is that I'm sorry I freaked out during Taryn's seizure."

"Did you freak out? As I recall, you were the voice of calm and composure through the whole thing while everyone else was panicking. I don't want to think what would have happened if you hadn't been there, Evie. We would have been a mess."

"Good. I'm glad you couldn't tell. I guess I was only freaking out on the inside, then."

"Why? You certainly acted like you've had plenty experience with seizures, as terrifying as they can be."

She gazed at the stars overhead, then back at him. "I... It hit a little close to home, that's all. Cassie stopped breathing in her sleep during a seizure. I was so afraid for Taryn."

He stared at her, overwhelmed and awed and completely in love with her. Despite what must have been petrifying fear that history would repeat itself, she had stepped up to do everything necessary to care for Taryn during the seizure, to ensure his daughter was as safe as possible.

He couldn't help it. He dropped his lunch on the bench and reached for her. She settled into his arms with a sigh and an easing of her tension, as if she'd been waiting just as he had for this fragile connection between them.

"I thought I was doing so well," she murmured, her cheek against his chest. "Most of the time I am, but once in a while, it still feels as if somebody came along and swept my legs out from under me. I miss her."

"I know. I know, sweetheart." He smoothed a hand down her hair and tucked an errant strand behind her ear. She didn't weep, only shuddered out a breath or two, her arms clasped tightly around his waist.

"You didn't show your fear, Evie. That's the sign of true courage, you know. You feel the fear but you do it anyway. You don't owe me an apology at all. If there's anything in arrears here, it's all on our side. I owe you so much. Everything. Not just for today, for being that calm voice of strength and peace in the middle of the chaos. But for the last month. You gave me hope again, Evie. Do you have any idea what a precious gift that has been?"

She swallowed and gave him a tremulous smile and he gave in to the inevitable. He cupped her face in his hands and lowered his mouth to hers in a slow, easy kiss that shook him to the core.

He loved this woman. Holding her here in this quiet garden while the night air drifted around them and the stars sparkled overhead only reinforced that he loved her and he refused to let her go.

The sheer sweetness of Brodie's mouth easing across hers, the tenderness of his hands against her face, took her breath away and she could do nothing but stand there soaking up the sweetness of the moment.

"I needed this." Brodie's voice was low, rough. "From the moment you walked into Taryn's room, all I've been able to think about is that if I could only hold you again, everything would seem better."

The tears she had been fighting since walking out into this quiet garden spilled free and one slid down her cheek. It was the perfect thing to say, especially coming from this very serious, sometimes gruff man. She tightened her arms around him, her heart aching with love for him.

She loved this man. Nothing else seemed important, not the differences between them or her fear of pushing him away or the huge, terrifying risk she would have to take to open her heart completely to him and to Taryn.

This was real and right and she loved him with everything inside her. She couldn't go back to her safe and prudent existence before he and his daughter had thrust themselves into her life. She thought she had found tranquility in Hope's Crossing, a place to quiet the roar of pain after Cassie's death, but she suddenly realized with stark clarity she had been fooling herself. She had merely woven a cocoon around herself to keep out anything that might threaten her false peace.

Until that evening a month ago when Brodie had burst into her life, she had been hanging there, suspended and safe but in limbo, unable to truly move on to the next stage of her life until she burst out of her protective layers and reentered the cold, sometimes scary world.

"And I have to tell you," Brodie said with another of those soul-shattering kisses while she was still trying to deal with that stunning discovery, "you say you fell apart back in the courtroom during the seizure. From my point of view, Evie, you were a sea of calm and serenity. It's one of the things I love most about you."

Evie blinked, thinking she must have misheard him. Did he really just say the L-word? She opened her eyes and found him watching her with a tenderness that made her catch her breath at the same time it sent heat seeping into every cold place inside of her.

"I know you said you're not interested in a relationship with me." His voice sounded rough. "Consider this fair warning. I'm not a man who backs down when I find something I want, especially when that something is the one woman in the world who brings me happiness and peace, who quiets the chaos. I love you and I need your laughter and the…the *joy* that surrounds you in my life. I'm telling you right now, I'll do anything I have to in order to change your mind about giving us a chance."

His arms tightened around her as if he were bracing for her to yank away from him and start spouting arguments and objections. Instead she gave him a tremulous smile, certain tears must be trickling down her cheeks. "Okay."

He stared and eased away a hairsbreadth. "Okay, what?"

"Okay. You've convinced me."

Wary confusion clouded the blue of his eyes in the moonlight. "Just like that?"

She laughed, wondering if it sounded as shaky to him as it did to her. She loved this man. He was good and honorable, hardworking and devoted to his daughter's care. Strong and decent. How could she *not* love him?

"The truth is, I was already convinced. My heart has been for a while now, though it took the rest of me some time to catch up. I love you, Brodie. You are…everything to me. You and Taryn. I can't imagine going back to the way things were a month ago without both of you in my life. I don't *want* to go back."

He stared at her, his eyes stunned, then a fierce joy ignited in his expression.

"Evie," he said, her name a soft caress, and kissed her again. She settled into it, her heart lighter than it had been in…forever. They kissed for a long time there in the garden, where the busy sounds of a big-city hospital seemed muted and distant.

She couldn't believe the joy bubbling through her after the tumultuous day. It was surreal, almost. Things had seemed so bleak and dark after the ambulance had driven away with Taryn and now here she was, wrapped in the arms of the man she loved and looking at a future that suddenly seemed brighter and more precious than the loveliest beads at String Fever.

"I'd better go check on Taryn," he finally said, his voice threaded with regret.

"You never ate your sandwich," she said with a little laugh.

"Funny. Food doesn't seem very important right now." He smiled and kissed her forehead and everything inside her melted. She thought he had smiled more in the last half hour than she'd seen him smile all month. Because of *her*. She made him happy, and was there any more powerful gift a man could give a woman?

"I'll eat upstairs in Taryn's room."

"I can stay for a while if you'd like."

He smiled yet again. "I would love nothing more."

"Do you think Taryn will be okay with…this?" Evie asked. "Us?"

He laughed. "I think she'll be ecstatic. Stephanie is great and everything and she's doing a good job but Taryn has missed you. I also think there's a certain goofy-looking dog who will be over the moon at the chance to have you back in our lives."

"I've missed him, too."

"Speaking of which, I have to tell you, I couldn't believe it when I came home from my business trip and found Jacques happily ensconced in my house."

She could feel pink heat her cheeks. "Yeah, I probably should have talked to you first before thrusting a big decision like adding an animal companion to your family on you like that. It just seemed right at the moment."

"That's not what I meant, Evie. You love that dog. How could you give him to Taryn like that?"

She thought of the first few nights without Jacques in her apartment and how she had wanted to curl up into the fetal position and cry herself to sleep. "Her need was greater than mine," she said simply.

He gazed down at her, his eyes a warm and tender blue. "Is it any wonder I'm crazy about you?" he murmured.

She kissed him, her arms tight around his neck. "It may sound corny and clichéd or like some kind of New Age mumbo jumbo but I've learned the gifts you give away always come back to you somehow. Call it karma or kismet or whatever you want, but they do."

"So you're saying your dog brought us together?" he said with a laugh.

A dog and a courageous girl and a terrible tragedy that had changed dozens of lives in unexpected ways. Including hers.

"Stranger things have happened," she said.

"Well, I don't call it karma or kismet or fate," he said, his mouth warm and sweet on hers. "I just call it perfect."

She couldn't have agreed more.

Epilogue

The second annual Giving Hope Day dawned bright and sunny.

Evie finished loading her toolbox and the dozens of paintbrushes and paint trays she had purchased over the past few weeks into the back of the SUV and paused for a moment to gaze up at the pure blue of an early Colorado June morning. Though a few high clouds drifted across the sky, she would keep her fingers crossed that the twenty-percent chance of showers the weather forecasters were predicting would be completely overpowered by the eighty percent chance of sunshine.

After all the work she and the rest of the bead store regulars had put into making the massive town-wide volunteer service effort even more of a success than the first one, Evie didn't want to see storm clouds ruin everything. In another hour, hundreds of Hope's Crossing residents would be gathering at the town community center in town to receive their assignments for the day—everything from litter cleanup in the canyon to painting the picnic tables at the park to helping some of the town's senior citizens with early summer yard cleanup. She was going to keep her fingers crossed those clouds stayed high and dry.

They already had twice as many people sign up to participate in this year's Giving Hope Day as the previous event, and donations were still pouring in for the benefit auction and dance later that evening.

Anticipation danced through her and she smiled a little as she watched a mountain bluebird alight in the branches of the big blue spruce near the front door of the sprawling glass-and-cedar place she had called home for the past three months.

A year could make all the difference.

Her world wasn't remotely the same as the one she had inhabited the year before. She had loved her small, solitary apartment above String Fever and would always be grateful for the peace and serenity she had found there, but as she headed up the curving sidewalk toward the front door of Brodie's house, she was still a little astonished at how this house so quickly had become her favorite spot on earth. Sometimes she thought the walls could barely hold all the love and joy inside them.

Before she could reach the door, it opened and Jacques padded through, looking quite pleased with himself.

"Don't tell me you've mastered opening doors now," she said, stopping to give him a little of that love by scratching between his ears.

"Not yet." Taryn answered the doorway, dressed in jean shorts, the yellow T-shirt all the volunteers were wearing and tennis shoes. The sunny, flowery bracelet she and Charlie Beaumont had made so long ago flashed brightly at her wrist. "Give him time. I'm sure he'll figure it out eventually."

Her stepdaughter walked out of the house with the slight hip-swiveling hitch in her step that still lingered but she was steady as she moved toward the SUV. Sometimes Evie thought her heart would burst with pride at Taryn's progress the past six months, especially knowing she had played a part in it.

A stranger who didn't know the difficult road Taryn had traveled the past year might only see a pretty dark-haired girl with big blue eyes and a slightly lopsided, winsome smile that hinted at some secret amusement.

Just as Evie had told Brodie all those months ago, Taryn would probably never be exactly as she had been before the accident. Besides the slight awkwardness to her gait, she had trouble with memory sometimes, and once in a while she still struggled to find just the right word in the middle of a conversation and she could stumble over certain phrases.

But she had finished her junior year of high school just that week—and the highlight had been a month ago when she had been named junior prom queen at Hope's Crossing High School in an assembly where the announcement had been met with tears and hugs and a rousing standing ovation from her classmates.

Jacques, her devoted companion, planted his haunches in the middle of the sidewalk and looked over his shoulder as if to urge her to put some hustle into it. The two of them had a close and loving bond that only seemed to deepen with time.

"Really?" Evie said, finally noticing the leash in her hand. "You're seriously taking Jacques along to help today? Don't you think he might get in the way?"

"Why would he? He'll be good moral support. Anyway, I'm taking his service animal vest, just in case anybody says anything. I need him there to help me."

Katherine had made the little green vest for the dog as something of a joke but in reality Evie thought there was more than a grain of truth in categorizing the dog as a service animal. Throughout the long months of therapy,

Jacques had done far more to help Taryn progress than Evie as a trained physical therapist had been able to accomplish. She had even started using the dog with the few other rehab patients she had selectively taken on in Hope's Crossing.

There was another change over the past year. Thanks to her work with Taryn, Evie had accepted that some part of her heart would always be a therapist, even when her head tried to make excuses for her to avoid her chosen vocation. She still worked part-time at String Fever, but she was relishing her work with a few carefully chosen patients and the progress they were making.

"Is your dad ready?"

"I think he's right behind me."

"Coming," a distracted voice said. As if on cue, Brodie pushed through the door, his hair still damp and curling at his neck from his shower. He had a coffee travel mug in one hand and was reading something on his smartphone in the other as he walked. Though she had just been cuddled up beside him in bed forty-five minutes earlier, her insides still did that silly little jump of anticipation. It was like that whenever she saw him, even after three months of marriage.

She could only hope she would have the same reaction after they had been married fifty years.

He shoved his phone into the pocket of his jeans. "Sorry. I finally heard back from the city planner in Gunnison. Looks like they've finally decided to approve the new sporting goods store there."

"Oh, Brodie. That's wonderful news!" For weeks, he had been wrangling with the town over possible sites to expand his business.

She hugged him and he wrapped his arms around her and turned her quick, happy kiss into a long, leisurely, delicious one that made her momentarily wish this was one of those sleepy mornings when they could pull the comforter over their heads and slide together.

"Okay. Can we get on with things now?" Taryn grumbled. Evie wrenched her mouth away and looked over in time to catch her stepdaughter rolling her eyes at them.

Evie knew it was all for show. Taryn had welcomed her into their family with delight and acceptance—as had Katherine, who couldn't have been more thrilled when Brodie and Evie made their relationship public after Charlie's sentencing hearing in September. At their March wedding, a quiet affair in the small church in town, Katherine had laughed and cried, joyfully welcoming Evie into their small family.

Brodie pulled away with that secret smile that made her toes tingle. "Yeah, I guess you're right. We should probably move it. Can't have the whole town waiting on us."

He held the door open for Evie, then moved to the backseat to help Taryn—and Jacques—inside.

"This will be so great," Taryn declared when her father climbed inside and started heading out of the driveway. "All my friends are still talking about how much fun it was last year. Hannah is meeting us at the community center. We wanted to go up the canyon to clean up garbage."

"Having you there this year will be wonderful," Evie said.

She knew the rest of the townspeople of Hope's Crossing would be just as thrilled to see the girl participate in the day. Many saw Taryn's recovery as nothing short of miraculous. The teenager had become a talisman of sorts to the town, a symbol of hope and healing after the tragedy of the car accident and the scars it had left in countless lives. Though Taryn had shouldered much of the blame for the accident at Charlie's sentencing hearing, no one seemed inclined to hold her responsible.

Brodie reached across to squeeze Evie's fingers and she saw the emotion in his eyes. How could she ever have thought him cold and heartless? she wondered. Yes, he was very good at containing his deepest feelings, but that made the moments when he let go all the more priceless to her.

They had just left the gates of Aspen Ridge when Evie spotted a bicyclist heading up the hill toward the neighborhood. Odd, since everyone else in town was heading toward the community center that was serving as the hub of the day's events.

"Wait!" Taryn exclaimed. "Dad, stop!"

Brodie frowned in the rearview mirror. "T, we're already running late."

"I know. Just stop."

He had barely braked the vehicle before Taryn thrust open her door and raced toward the bicyclist with only a slight stumble in her gait, Jacques on her heels.

A second later, the person pulled off his helmet and tossed it aside then caught Taryn when she would have plowed him over with enthusiasm. Evie inhaled sharply as she recognized him.

"Beaumont," Brodie growled, and Evie cast a quick glance at him in time to see his hands tighten on the steering wheel. It was undoubtedly Charlie Beaumont, though his hair was a little longer and a little shaggier than it had been nine months ago when he had first entered the youth correctional facility in Denver.

"I guess the rumor mill had it right for once," he muttered. "I'd heard he might be released soon."

"And you didn't tell us?"

"You know how unreliable the grapevine can be. I

wanted to be sure before I mentioned it to Taryn. Didn't want to get her hopes up."

Though Taryn and Charlie had exchanged emails and letters and the occasional phone call—and even a few in-person visits when Brodie had reluctantly agreed to take his daughter to the correctional facility—Brodie still maintained a cool reserve toward the young man.

When he shut the engine off and opened his door to greet the boy, Evie decided she would be wise to follow, even if Brodie was much more calm about Charlie these days.

To her relief, he held out a hand as he approached the pair. Charlie, his left arm still around Taryn's shoulders, shook it, and Evie couldn't help noticing a new maturity about him. That air of troubled restlessness seemed to be gone.

"You should have called or something," Taryn exclaimed, glowing with a bright happiness that was almost painful to see. "Why didn't you tell me you were coming home?"

Charlie scratched Jacques between the ears and the dog looked at him with just as much joy as Taryn. "I wasn't sure myself. Everything's been crazy the last few days. I wanted to be certain they would really give me an early release before I said anything."

"You just sent me an email three days ago. You didn't even mention the possibility!"

He shrugged. "It might have fallen through. I thought it would be better to wait." He deftly changed the subject. "You look terrific, Taryn. Really terrific. And you're getting around so well. Not even the cane anymore."

Taryn cast a sidelong look toward her. "Evie's a slave driver. She told me if I wanted to be her maid of honor I had to ditch the cane."

"That's right," Evie said drily, playing along. "You

know me. Bridezilla. Everything had to be perfect for my special day."

"I'm sure it was. Congratulations on your wedding."

Evie reached for Brodie's hand. Even after three months, sometimes the happiness bubbled up inside her and she didn't know how to contain it. "Thank you. We loved the serving platter you sent us. We used it just the other day. You obviously put a great deal of time into sanding and polishing the wood."

He looked a little embarrassed. "Woodshop was one of the better ways to pass the time."

"You'll have to come to dinner some night soon and see how well it goes in the dining room."

"Maybe." He glanced at their vehicle and then back at the three of them. "I guess you're probably on your way into town for the Giving Hope Day. I won't keep you. I only wanted to say hey and let Taryn know I was back before she heard about it in town."

"Why don't you come with us?" Taryn said suddenly.

Charlie's laugh wasn't as harsh as it might have been nine months earlier. "I don't think that would go over real well in town. Think about it, Taryn. The whole reason for the day is to remember and honor Layla. It's her birthday, after all. I don't belong there."

"Of course you do," she said fiercely. "You belong there as much as I do. Why shouldn't you come and help us? Layla was your friend, too."

"Come on, Taryn. You know why."

A militant light sparked in her stepdaughter's eyes. Evie knew that stubborn look. She'd seen it often enough over her months of working with Taryn to know the girl could be relentless when she set her mind to something.

"I want you to come with us. You need to do this, Charlie. Lock your bike up at our house and you can ride with us."

"Taryn, let the kid make up his own mind." Brodie spoke for the first time since they'd exited the SUV.

Charlie pointed. "See? Your dad knows it's a mistake."

"Don't put words in my mouth," Brodie said mildly. "Actually, I think it's a great idea. I suspect word's already going to be out that you're home, and this way you're facing down the whispers and stares all at once."

"Gee, when you put it that way, why wouldn't I want to come?"

Brodie gave him a steady look at the sarcastic tone. "You're going to have to face people sooner or later. Might as well man up and do it now while you have the added benefit of being able to honor Layla's memory at the same time. People might stare but nobody's going to say anything—not if you're there with us and with Taryn."

Evie's throat felt achy, tight, and she wondered how it was possible to love this man more with every passing day.

Charlie stared at him for a long moment, myriad emotions chasing across his features, then he finally sighed. "You're probably right. Kind of like taking your medicine in one big gulp instead of spreading it out for weeks."

Evie smiled through the haze of tears she refused to shed. "We can put your bike in the garage and give you a ride into town."

"Yeah. Okay."

As Charlie headed toward the house, the three of them climbed back into the SUV then followed behind him at a safe distance.

"Are you sure you're ready for this?" Brodie asked her quietly when they reached the house and Taryn went to help Charlie find a place for his bike. "He's right. A few people won't be happy he's there. Some people can't let go, even after the truth came out about what really happened that night."

She nodded. "Charlie needs this. I think the whole town does. The healing process is usually messy and painful and rarely comfortable. I think we've all learned that these past months."

To her delight, Brodie reached for her hand and brought it to his mouth, one of those spontaneous gestures that charmed her to her core. "I love you, Evie Thorne."

"And doesn't that make me the luckiest woman in Hope's Crossing?" she murmured.

When the two young people slid into the backseat, Jacques perched happily between them, Brodie once more pulled out of the driveway and headed toward the town spread out below them.

Across the valley, warm morning sunshine glinted off the snow that still capped Woodrose Mountain. Evie wanted to bask in it—and in the certain knowledge that, storm clouds or not, her future here in Hope's Crossing would be filled with light and joy and peace. She refused to have it any other way.

* * * * *

New York Times bestselling author

RaeAnne Thayne

brings you back to Haven Point—a small town made for second chances...

Pick up your copy today!

"Thayne's beautiful, honest storytelling goes straight to the heart."
—*RT Book Reviews*

Be sure to connect with us at:

Harlequin.com/Newsletters
Facebook.com/HarlequinBooks
Twitter.com/HQNBooks

#1 New York Times Bestselling Author

DEBBIE MACOMBER

New York Times Bestselling Author

RAEANNE THAYNE

Two irresistible romances in one incredible collection!

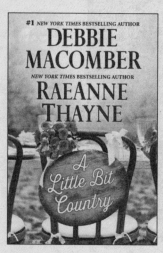

A Little Bit Country
by Debbie Macomber

When Rorie Campbell's car breaks down on an Oregon country road, rancher Clay Franklin comes to her rescue. Soon she discovers that a city girl *can* fall in love with a country man. And the other way around… But Clay is engaged to another woman! Is he willing to change that situation?

Blackberry Summer
by RaeAnne Thayne

Shop owner and single mom Claire Bradford has no time for romance—or so she tells herself. But after suffering a serious car accident, she finds she is forced to rely on other people, including the new police chief Riley McKnight. For the first time, Claire realizes that things have to change, and Riley is the man who can bring about the change she needs!

Available now, wherever books are sold!

Be sure to connect with us at:
Harlequin.com/Newsletters
Facebook.com/HarlequinBooks
Twitter.com/HarlequinBooks

www.MIRABooks.com

MDM1825R

Let #1 *New York Times* bestselling author

SUSAN WIGGS

sweep you away with a stunning tale of the
delicate ties that bind a family together...
and the secrets that can tear them apart.

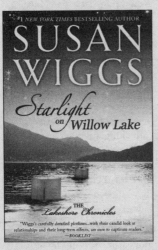

Faith McCallum is determined to rebuild her shattered life and give her two daughters a chance at a better future. Caring for her sharp-tongued new client, Alice Bellamy, is definitely a challenge, but it's Alice's charismatic son, Mason, who truly leaves Faith at a loss for words.

Mason Bellamy longs to escape the family mansion and return to his fast-paced, exciting life in Manhattan. But when Faith makes a chilling discovery about Alice's accident, Mason finds himself wondering if the supercharged life he's created for himself is what he truly wants... and whether exploring his past might lead to a new life—and lasting love—on the tranquil shores of Willow Lake.

Available now, wherever books are sold!

REQUEST YOUR FREE BOOKS!

2 FREE NOVELS
FROM THE ROMANCE COLLECTION
PLUS 2 FREE GIFTS!

YES! Please send me 2 FREE novels from the Romance Collection and my 2 FREE gifts (gifts are worth about $10). After receiving them, if I don't wish to receive any more books, I can return the shipping statement marked "cancel." If I don't cancel, I will receive 4 brand-new novels every month and be billed just $6.49 per book in the U.S. or $6.99 per book in Canada. That's a savings of at least 19% off the cover price. It's quite a bargain! Shipping and handling is just 50¢ per book in the U.S. and 75¢ per book in Canada.* I understand that accepting the 2 free books and gifts places me under no obligation to buy anything. I can always return a shipment and cancel at any time. Even if I never buy another book, the two free books and gifts are mine to keep forever.

194/394 MDN GH4D

Name	(PLEASE PRINT)	
Address		Apt. #
City	State/Prov.	Zip/Postal Code

Signature (if under 18, a parent or guardian must sign)

Mail to the **Reader Service:**
IN U.S.A.: P.O. Box 1867, Buffalo, NY 14240-1867
IN CANADA: P.O. Box 609, Fort Erie, Ontario L2A 5X3

Want to try two free books from another line?
Call 1-800-873-8635 or visit www.ReaderService.com.

* Terms and prices subject to change without notice. Prices do not include applicable taxes. Sales tax applicable in N.Y. Canadian residents will be charged applicable taxes. Offer not valid in Quebec. This offer is limited to one order per household. Not valid for current subscribers to the Romance Collection or the Romance/Suspense Collection. All orders subject to credit approval. Credit or debit balances in a customer's account(s) may be offset by any other outstanding balance owed by or to the customer. Please allow 4 to 6 weeks for delivery. Offer available while quantities last.

Your Privacy—The Reader Service is committed to protecting your privacy. Our Privacy Policy is available online at www.ReaderService.com or upon request from the Reader Service.

We make a portion of our mailing list available to reputable third parties that offer products we believe may interest you. If you prefer that we not exchange your name with third parties, or if you wish to clarify or modify your communication preferences, please visit us at www.ReaderService.com/consumerschoice or write to us at Reader Service Preference Service, P.O. Box 9062, Buffalo, NY 14240-9062. Include your complete name and address.

Turn your love of reading into
rewards you'll love with

Harlequin My Rewards

**Join for FREE today at
www.HarlequinMyRewards.com**

Earn **FREE BOOKS** of your choice.

Experience **EXCLUSIVE OFFERS** and contests.

Enjoy **BOOK RECOMMENDATIONS**
selected just for you.

PLUS! Sign up now
and get **500** points
right away!

Earn
**FREE
REWARDS**
Join
Today!
HarlequinMyRewards.com

MYR16R